COLD FIRE
'I found *Cold Fire* his most enjoyable book to date'
*The Times*

THE BAD PLACE
'He combines rich, evocative prose, some of the warmest – and also some of the most despicable – characters to be found in fiction, technical speculations that seem to come directly from today's headlines and a sense of on-the-edge-of-the-seat pacing to create thrillers that are not just convincing, but thought-provoking as well'
*Mystery Scene*

MIDNIGHT
'A triumph'                                    *New York Times*

LIGHTNING
'[It] sizzles . . . Wow! It's a mix to tingle any reader's fancy'
*New York Daily News*

WATCHERS
'His best story yet. A tightly woven plot . . . this is the sort of thoroughly frightening and

entertaining tale that has its readers listening for
noises in the night'                  *Publishers Weekly*

THE MASK
'A master of sheer fright!'         *Florida Times-Union*

THE FACE OF FEAR
'Super suspenseful with a double-take finish'
                                             *Observer*

TWILIGHT EYES
'A spine-chilling adventure . . . will keep you
turning pages to the very end!'
                                          *Rave Reviews*

STRANGERS
'The best novel he has written!'      Stephen King

PHANTOMS
'A grabber. You will read with nail-biting
compulsion!'                              *Bestsellers*

WHISPERS
'Pulls out all the stops . . . an incredible, terrifying
tale'                                 *Publishers Weekly*

NIGHT CHILLS
'Will send chills down your back!' *New York Times*

SHATTERED
'A chilling tale . . . sleek as a bullet'
*Publishers Weekly*

THE VISION
'Kept me glued to my chair . . . sinister and spine-tingling. Page-turning excitement'
*Spectator*

THE VOICE OF THE NIGHT
'A fearsome tour of an adolescent's tortured psyche. Terrifying, knee-knocking suspense'
*Chicago Sun Times*

CHASE
'This superb book is more than a novel of suspense. It is a brutally realistic portrait of the role of violence in our society'
*Saturday Review*

# THE EYES
# OF DARKNESS

Dean R Koontz

Previously published as
*The Eyes of Darkness*
by Leigh Nichols

First published in Great Britain in 1982
by Fontana Paperbacks,
a division of William Collins Sons & Co

Reprinted in hardback in 1991
by HEADLINE BOOK PUBLISHING PLC

Reprinted in paperback in 1991
by HEADLINE BOOK PUBLISHING PLC

A HEADLINE FEATURE paperback

10 9 8 7 6 5 4 3 2

ISBN 0 7472 3769 7

Typeset by St George Typesetting, Redruth, Cornwall

Printed and bound by   HarperCollins Manufacturing, Glasgow

HEADLINE BOOK PUBLISHING PLC
Headline House, 79 Great Titchfield Street, London W1P 7FN

This book is dedicated to
some folks in Bedford, Pa –
Ross and Angela Cerra,
Henry and Virginia Hillegass
– about whom I care.

# PART ONE

## TUESDAY
# DECEMBER 30

# 1

Shortly after midnight, just four minutes into Tuesday morning, on the way home from a late rehearsal of her new show, Tina Evans thought she saw her son, Danny, in a stranger's car. But of course Danny had been dead for more than a year.

Two blocks from her house, intending to buy a quart of milk and a loaf of whole wheat bread, Tina stopped at a twenty-four-hour market and parked in the eerie yellow glow of a sodium-arc outdoor light, beside a gleaming, cream-colored Chevrolet station wagon. The boy was sitting in the Chevy's front passenger seat, waiting for his mother or father to come out of the store. Tina could see only the side of his face, but she gasped in painful recognition.

*Danny.*

The boy in the station wagon was about twelve, Danny's age, and he had Danny's thick dark hair, Danny's nose, and Danny's rather delicate jawline. Unaware that she was staring at him, he put one hand to his mouth and chewed gently on his bent thumb knuckle, which was something Danny had begun to do a year or so before he died. Without success, Tina had tried to break him of that bad habit.

Now, as she watched the boy in the next car, she had the strange feeling that his resemblance to Danny was more than mere coincidence. Suddenly her mouth went dry. Her heart pounded. Because she still had not adjusted to the loss of her only child, because she never really had wanted or tried to adjust to it, she used this boy's resemblance to Danny as an excuse to fantasize that there had been no loss in the first place. She had the crazy thought that the boy she was watching actually *was* Danny, and the more she considered it, the less crazy it seemed. After all, she had never seen Danny's body. The police and the morticians had said that Danny was too badly torn up, too horribly mangled for her to look at him. Sickened, grief-stricken, she had taken their advice, and Danny's funeral had been a closed-coffin service. But perhaps they'd been mistaken in their identification of the corpse. Maybe Danny hadn't been killed in the accident. Maybe he'd only suffered a mild head injury, something just severe enough to give him . . . amnesia. Yes. Amnesia. Perhaps he had wandered away from the wrecked bus and had eventually been found miles and miles from the

4

scene of the accident, without any identification, unable to tell anyone who he was or where he came from. That was possible, wasn't it? You saw it in the movies. Sure. Amnesia. And if that were the case, then he could have ended up in a foster home, in a new life. And now here he was sitting in the cream-colored Chevrolet wagon, brought to her by fate and—

She was interrupted in the middle of her elaborate fantasy when the boy became conscious of her gaze and turned towards her. She held her breath as his face came slowly around. For a few seconds, as they stared at each other through two windows and through the strange sulphurous light, she had the feeling they were making contact across an immense gulf of space and time and destiny. But then she saw that, full face, he did not resemble Danny at all.

She pulled her gaze away from his and looked at her hands, which were gripping the steering wheel so hard and relentlessly that they ached.

'Damn,' she said.

She was angry with herself. She thought of herself as a tough, competent, level-headed woman who was able to deal with anything that life threw at her, and she was disturbed by her continuing inability to accept Danny's death.

After the initial shock, after the funeral, she *had* begun to cope with the trauma. Gradually, day by day, week by week, she had put Danny behind her, with sorrow, with guilt, with tears and bitterness, but also with firmness and determination. She had taken several steps up in her career during the past year, and she had used hard work as a sort of morphine, letting it dull her pain until the wound had healed.

But then, a couple of weeks ago, she had begun to slip back to the state she'd been in immediately after she'd received news of the accident. Again, she was possessed by the haunting feeling that her child was alive. Time should have put even more distance between her and the anguish, but instead the passing days were bringing her around full circle in her grief. This boy in the station wagon was not the first one she had imagined was Danny; in the past few weeks she seemed to see her lost son everywhere. Also, she recently began having a repeating dream in which Danny was alive, and for a few hours after she woke, she could not face reality; she convinced herself that the dream was a premonition of Danny's eventual return to her, that somehow he had survived and would be coming back into her arms one day soon. It was a warm and wonderful fantasy, but of course she could not sustain it for long. Although she always resisted the grim truth, it gradually exerted itself every time, so that she was repeatedly brought down hard and forced to accept the fact that the dream was not a premonition. Nevertheless, she knew that when she had the dream again she would find new hope in it just as she had so many times before.

And that was not good.

That was sick.

She glanced at the station wagon and saw the boy still staring at her. She looked at her hands again and found the strength to break her iron grip on the steering wheel.

Grief could drive a person crazy. She'd read that somewhere. But she wasn't going to allow such a thing to happen to her. She had to be tough on herself. She simply couldn't allow herself to hope. She had loved Danny with all her heart, but he was gone. Dammit, he was dead. Torn and crushed in a bus accident with fourteen other little boys, just one victim of a larger tragedy. Battered beyond recognition. *Dead*. In a coffin. Under the ground. Forever.

Her lower lip trembled. She wanted to cry, but she didn't.

The boy in the Chevy had lost interest in her. He was staring at the front of the grocery store again, waiting for whoever had brought him here.

Tina got out of her VW Rabbit. The night was pleasantly cool. She took a deep breath of the clean air and went into the market. Inside, it was too cold, and the fluorescent lights were too bright.

She bought a quart of skim milk and a loaf of

whole wheat bread that was sliced thin for dieters, so that each serving contained only half the calories of an ordinary slice of bread. She wasn't a dancer any more; now she worked behind the curtain, in the production end of the show, but she still felt physically and psychologically best when she weighed no more than she had when she'd been a performer.

Five minutes later she was home. She made two pieces of toast and spread peanut butter on them, poured a glass of cold milk and sat down at the kitchen table.

Peanut butter toast was always one of Danny's favorite foods, even when he was just a toddler and picky about what he would eat. When he was very young he had called it 'neenut putter'. When she closed her eyes she could still see him – three years old, peanut butter smeared all over his lips and chin – as he grinned and said, 'More neenut putter toast, please.'

She opened her eyes with a start because her mental image of him was *too* vivid, and right now she really didn't want to remember. But it was too late. Her heart seemed to knot in her chest, and her lower lip began to quiver again, and she put her head down on the table. She wept.

* * *

That night she dreamed Danny was alive.

8

Somehow. Somewhere. Alive. And he needed her.

In the dream Danny was standing at the edge of a bottomless gorge, and Tina was on the far side of it, opposite him, looking across the immense gulf. Danny was calling her name. He was lonely and afraid. She was miserable because she couldn't think of a way to reach him. Meanwhile, the sky grew darker by the second; massive, somber storm clouds squeezed the last light out of the day. Danny's cries and her responses became increasingly shrill and desperate, for both of them knew they must get together before nightfall or be lost to each other forever; there was something in the night that was waiting for Danny, something awful that would get him if he was alone after dark. Suddenly the sky was shattered by lightning, and after the flash there was infinite blackness and a hard clap of thunder.

Tina Evans sat straight up in bed, certain she had heard a noise in the house. It wasn't the thunder from the dream. The sound she had heard had come just as she was waking, a real noise, not an imagined one. She listened intently, prepared to throw off the covers and jump out of bed at the slightest sound, but there was only silence. Doubt gradually crept into her mind. She *had* been jumpy lately. This wasn't the first night she'd been sure there was an intruder. During the past two weeks, it had happened half a dozen times, but on each occasion, when she had taken the pistol from the nightstand and had searched the place, room by room, she hadn't found anyone. Recently she had been under a lot of pressure, both personally and professionally. Maybe what she'd heard tonight *had* been merely thunder from the dream. She remained on guard for a couple of minutes, but the night was so peaceful that she had to admit no one else was in the house. As her heartbeat slowed down, she eased back onto her pillow.

At times like this she wished she and Michael were still together. She closed her eyes and imagined herself beside him, reaching for him in the dark, touching, moving against him, into the shelter of his arms. He would comfort and reassure her, and in a while she would sleep again.

Of course if she and Michael were in bed right this minute, it wouldn't be like that at all. They wouldn't make love. They'd fight. He would resist her affection, turn her away by picking a fight. He would begin the argument over something trivial and goad her until the bickering escalated into a major battle. That was how it had been toward the end; he had been seething with hostility, always looking for an excuse to vent some of his anger on her. Because she had loved him to the end, she had been deeply hurt and saddened by the dissolution of their relationship, but she had also been relieved when it was finally over.

She had lost her child and her husband in the same year, the man first, and then the boy, the son to the grave and the husband to the winds of change. During the twelve years of their marriage, she had changed drastically, but Michael hadn't changed at all. They had begun as lovers, sharing everything; however, by the time the divorce was final, they had become strangers. Although Michael was still living in town, less than a mile away from her at that very moment, he was, in some respects, as far from her and as unreachable as Danny.

She sighed resignedly and opened her eyes.

She wasn't sleepy now, but she knew she had to get more rest. She would need to be fresh and alert tomorrow, for it was one of the most important days of her life. December 30. In other years that date had meant nothing special. But for better or worse, *this* December 30 was the hinge upon which her entire future would swing.

For fifteen years, ever since she turned eighteen, two years before she married Michael, Tina Evans had lived and worked in Las Vegas. She began her career as a dancer in the Lido de Paris, a gigantic stage show at the Stardust Hotel. The Lido was one of those incredibly lavish productions that could be seen nowhere in the world but Vegas, for it was only in Vegas that a multi-million-dollar show could be staged year after year with little concern for profit; such vast sums were spent on the elaborate sets and costumes, and on the enormous cast and crew, that the hotel was usually happy if the production merely broke even from ticket and drink sales. After all, as fantastic as it was, the show was only a come-on, a draw, with the sole purpose of putting a few thousand people into the hotel every night. Going to and from the showroom, the crowd had to pass all the craps tables and blackjack tables and roulette wheels and glittering ranks of slot-machines, and *that* was where the profit was made. Tina enjoyed dancing in the Lido, and she stayed there for two and a half years, until she learned that she was pregnant. She took time off to carry and give birth to Danny, then to spend uninterrupted days with him during his first few months of life. When Danny was six months old, Tina went into training to get back in shape, and after three arduous months of exercise, she won a place in the chorus line of a new spectacular. She managed to be both a good dancer and a good mother, although that was not always easy; she loved Danny, and she immensely enjoyed her work, and she didn't mind doing double duty.

Five years ago, however, on her twenty-eighth birthday, she began to realize that she didn't have more than ten years left as a show dancer, and she decided to get into the business from another angle, so that she wouldn't suddenly find herself washed up at thirty-eight. She landed a position as choreographer for a two-bit lounge revue that was only a pale imitation of the Lido, and eventually she took over the costuming job as well. From that she moved up through a series of similar jobs in larger lounges, then in small showrooms that seated four or five or six hundred, in second-rate hotels with limited show budgets. In time she directed a revue, then directed and produced another. She was rapidly becoming a respected name in the closely knit Vegas entertainment world, and she knew she was on the verge of great success.

Almost a year ago, shortly after Danny had died, she had been offered a job directing and co-producing a genuine, big-budget spectacular, a three-million-dollar extravaganza to be staged in the plush, two-thousand-seat main showroom of the Desert Mirage, one of the largest and fanciest hotels on the Strip. It seemed terribly wrong that she should get such a wonderful chance before she'd even had time to mourn her boy; it seemed almost as if fate were trying to balance the scales for her, trying to offset Danny's death with this splendid opportunity. Although she felt empty and bitter and deeply depressed because of Danny, she took the job. Indeed, she knew she *had* to accept the project and involve herself in it in order to overcome her grief. If she didn't take the challenge, if she just sat at home or worked only on smaller and easier productions, she would have too much time to dwell on the loss of her son, and she would never recover.

The new show was titled *Magyck!* because the variety acts between the big dance numbers were all magicians and because the numbers themselves were constructed around supernatural themes. The tricky spelling of the title was not Tina's idea, but most of the rest of the program was, and she was pleased with what she had wrought. Exhausted, too. The past year had gone by in a blur of twelve- and fourteen-hour days, no vacations, with hardly ever a day off.

And still, even as preoccupied with *Magyck!* as she was, she had had difficulty adjusting to Danny's death. Only a month ago she had thought that maybe, at last, she'd begun to overcome her grief. She was able then, for the first time, to think about the boy without crying, to visit his grave without getting hysterical. All things considered, she felt reasonably good, cheerful. She would never forget him, that sweet child who had been such a large part of her life, but she would no longer have to live her life around the gaping hole he had left in it. The wound was tender but healed-over. That's what she had thought a month ago. She had continued to think that way for a week, two weeks. And then the dreams had begun. And they were worse than the dreams she'd had immediately after Danny had been killed.

Perhaps her anxiety about reaction to *Magyck!* was causing her to recall the greater anxiety she had felt about Danny. In less than seventeen hours – at 8:p.m., December 30 – the Desert Mirage Hotel would present a special, invitational, VIP premiere of *Magyck!*, and the following night, New Year's Eve, the show would open to the general public. If audience reaction was as strong and as positive as Tina hoped it would be, her financial future was assured, for her contract gave her two and one-half percent of the gross receipts, minus liquor sales, after the first three million. If *Magyck!* was a hit and ran for three years, as sometimes happened with successful Vegas shows, she would be a millionaire by the end of the run. Of course, if the production was a flop, if it failed to please the audience, she might be back working the small lounges again, on her way down. It was a merciless business.

She had good reason to be suffering from anxiety attacks. Her obsessive fear of intruders in the house, her disquieting dreams about Danny, her renewed grief – all of those things might merely be outgrowths of her concern about *Magyck!* If that were the case, then all those symptoms would disappear as soon as the fate of the show was clear. She only needed to ride it out a few more days, and in the relative calm that would follow, she could straighten herself out.

But right now she absolutely *had* to get some sleep. At ten o'clock in the morning, she had a meeting with two tour booking agents who were considering reserving as many as eight thousand tickets to *Magyck!* in the next three months. At one o'clock the entire cast and crew would assemble for the final dress rehearsal.

She fluffed her pillows, rearranged the covers, tugged at the short nightgown in which she slept. She tried to relax by closing her eyes and envisioning a gentle night tide lapping at a silvery beach.

*Thump!*

She sat straight up in bed.

Something had fallen over in another part of the house. It was something fairly large and heavy because the sound was muffled by intervening walls yet was loud enough to rouse her.

But it hadn't simply fallen. No. Whatever it was – it had been knocked over. Things didn't just fall down of their own accord in deserted rooms.

She cocked her head, listened closely. There was another sound, softer than the first, stealthier, but it didn't last long enough for Tina to identify the source or the meaning of it.

This time she hadn't just been imagining a threat. Someone really was in the house.

She switched on the lamp and pulled open the nightstand drawer. The pistol was loaded. She flicked off the two safety catches.

She listened.

Nothing now. Just the brittle silence of the dry desert night.

She got out of bed, stepped into her slippers. Holding the gun in her right hand, she went to the bedroom door.

Nothing. Silence.

She considered calling the police, but she was afraid of making a fool of herself. What if they came, lights flashing and sirens screaming, and found no one? If she had summoned the police every time she imagined hearing a prowler in the house during the past two weeks, they would have decided long ago that she was a bit scramble-brained. Of course she was sure it wasn't her imagination now. Pretty sure. Not positive. There was no way she could be absolutely positive about a thing like this. She was a proud woman who couldn't bear the thought of looking hysterical to a couple of macho cops who would grin at her and, later, make jokes about her over donuts and coffee. She would search the house herself, alone.

She pointed the pistol at the ceiling and jacked a bullet into the chamber.

Taking a deep breath, she unlocked the bedroom door and stepped into the hall.

# 2

Tina searched the entire house, except for Danny's old room, and she did not find the intruder. She almost would have preferred to discover someone lurking in the kitchen or crouching in a closet, rather than be forced to look in Danny's room. But now she had no choice.

Danny's bedroom was at the opposite end of the small house from the master bedroom, in what had once been the den. Not long after his tenth birthday, a little more than a year before he had been killed in the accident, the boy had voiced a desire for more space and privacy than he could get in his original, tiny bedroom. Michael and Tina had helped him move his things to the den, then had shifted the couch, armchair, coffee table, and television set from the den into the quarters the boy had previously occupied.

At the time Tina was certain that Danny was aware of the nightly arguments she and Michael were having in their own bedroom, which was next to his, and that he wanted to move into the den so he wouldn't be able to hear them bickering. She and Michael hadn't yet begun to raise their voices to each other; their disagreements had been conducted in normal tones, sometimes even in whispers, yet Danny had heard enough to know they were having problems. She had felt sorry about that, sorry he'd had to know, but she hadn't said a word to him; she'd offered no explanations, no reassurances. For one thing, she hadn't known what she *could* say. She certainly couldn't share with him her own appraisal of the situation: *'Danny, sweetheart don't worry about anything you might have heard through the wall. Your father is only suffering an identity crisis. He's been acting like an ass lately, but he'll get over it.'* And that was another reason she didn't attempt to explain her and Michael's problems to Danny – she thought it was only a temporary thing. She had loved her husband, and she had been sure that her love would smooth out all the wrinkles. Six months later, she and Michael separated, and less than five months after the separation, they were divorced.

Now, anxious to complete her search for the burglar – who was rapidly beginning to look as imaginary as all the other burglars she had looked for on other nights – she opened the door to Danny's bedroom. She switched on the lights and stepped inside.

No one.

Holding the pistol in front of her, she went to the closet, hesitated, then slid the door back. No one was hiding in there either. In spite of what she had heard, she was alone in the house.

As she stared at the contents of the musty closet – the boy's shoes, his jeans, dress slacks, shirts, sweaters, his blue Dodgers' baseball cap, the small gray suit he had worn on special occasions – a lump rose in her throat. She quickly pulled the door shut and put her back against it.

Although the funeral had been more than a year ago, she had not yet been able to dispose of Danny's belongings. Somehow, the act of giving away his clothes seemed even sadder and more final than watching his casket being lowered into the ground.

And it wasn't just his clothes that she had kept. His room was exactly as he had left it. The bed was properly made, several Star Wars toys lined up on the wide headboard. More than a hundred paperbacks were ranked alphabetically on a five-shelf bookcase. His desk occupied one corner; tubes of glue, miniature bottles of enamel in every color, and a variety of model-crafting tools stood in soldierly ranks on one half of the desk, and the other half was bare, waiting for him to begin work. Nine model airplanes filled a display case, and three others hung on wires from the ceiling. The walls were decorated with evenly spaced posters – three baseball stars,

21

five monsters from horror movies – that Danny had carefully arranged. Unlike many boys his age, he had been concerned about orderliness and cleanliness, and, respecting his preference for neatness, Tina had instructed Mrs. Neddler, the cleaning lady who came in twice a week, to vacuum and dust his unused bedroom as if nothing had happened to him.

She looked around at the dead boy's hobbies and toys and pathetic treasures, and (not for the first time) she realized that it wasn't healthy for her to maintain this place as if it were a museum. Or a shrine. So long as she left his things undisturbed, she could continue to entertain the hope that Danny was not dead, that he was just away somewhere for a while, and that he would shortly pick up his life where he had left off. Her inability to clean out his room suddenly frightened her; for the first time it seemed like more than just a weakness of spirit; it seemed like an indication of serious mental illness. She *had* to let the dead rest in peace. If she were ever to stop dreaming about the boy, if she were ever to get control of her grief, she must begin her recovery here, in this room, by conquering her irrational need to preserve his small possessions perfectly.

She made up her mind to clean this place out on Thursday, New Year's Day. Both the VIP premiere and the opening night of *Magyck!* would be behind her then. She would be able to relax a bit, take a little time off. She would start by spending a few hours here, Thursday afternoon, boxing up the clothes and toys and posters.

As soon as she made that decision, most of her nervous energy was dissipated. She sagged, limp and tired and ready to return to bed.

She started toward the door, but she caught sight of the easel and stopped, turned. Danny had liked to draw, and the easel, complete with a box of pencils and pens and paints, had been a birthday gift when he was nine. It was an easel on one side and a chalkboard on the other. Danny had left it at the far end of the room, beyond the bed, against the wall, and that was where it had stood the last time Tina had been in the room. But now it lay at an angle, the base of it against the wall, the easel itself slanted, chalkboard-down, across a game table. An Electronic Battleship game had stood on that table, as Danny had left it, ready for play, but the easel had toppled into it and had knocked it to the floor.

Apparently, that was the noise she had heard. But what had knocked the easel over? How could it have fallen all by itself?

She walked around the foot of the bed and set up the easel, where it belonged. She stooped and retrieved the pieces of the Electronic Battleship game and returned them to the table.

When she picked up the scattered sticks of

chalk and the felt eraser and turned again to the chalkboard, she realized that two words were crudely printed on the black surface.

## NOT DEAD

She stared at the message, scowling. She was virtually positive there had been nothing on the chalkboard when Danny had gone away on that scouting trip. She was sure it had been blank the last time she'd been in the room.

Belatedly, the possible meaning of the words struck her, and she went cold. *Not dead*. It was a denial of Danny's death. An angry refusal to accept the awful truth. A challenge to reality.

Had she written those two words herself?

She didn't remember doing it.

In one of her terrible seizures of grief, in a moment of crazy dark despair, had she come into this room and unknowingly printed those words on Danny's chalkboard?

If she had left this message, she must be having blackouts, temporary amnesia of which she was totally unaware. That was unacceptable. My God. Unthinkable.

Therefore the words must have been there all along. Danny must have left them. His printing was neat, like everything else about him, not sloppy like this, but, nevertheless, he must have done it. Must have.

And the obvious reference that those two words made to the bus accident?

Coincidence. Just coincidence. That was all. That was all it could be.

She refused to consider any other possibility because the alternatives were too frightening.

She hugged herself. Her hands were icy; they chilled her sides even through her nightgown.

Shivering, she erased the words on the chalkboard and left the room.

She was wide awake.

She had to get some sleep. There was so much to do in the morning. Big day.

In the kitchen she took a bottle of Wild Turkey from the cupboard by the sink. It was Michael's favorite bourbon. She poured two ounces of it into a water glass. She was not much of a drinker, keeping mostly to wine, and she had no capacity at all for hard liquor; but she finished the bourbon in two swallows, grimacing at its bitterness and wondering why Michael had always extolled this brand's smoothness. She hesitated, then poured two more ounces, finished that, quickly, like a child taking medicine, and put the bottle away.

In bed again, she snuggled down in the covers and closed her eyes and tried not to think about the chalkboard. But an image of it appeared behind her eyes. When she found she could not banish that image, she attempted to alter it, wiping the words away. But they came back again. And again. She kept erasing them, and they kept coming back as she grew dizzy from the bourbon and finally slipped into welcome oblivion.

# 3

Tuesday afternoon Tina watched the final dress rehearsal of *Magyck!* from a seat in the middle of the Desert Mirage showroom. The theater was shaped like an enormous fan, spreading under a high, domed ceiling. The room stepped down toward the stage in alternating wide and narrow galleries. On the wide levels, long dinner tables, covered with white linen, were set at right angles to the stage. Each narrow gallery consisted of a yard-wide aisle with a low railing on one side and a curving row of raised, plushly padded booths on the other side. The focus of all the seats was, of course, the stage, which was a marvel of the size required for a Las Vegas spectacular, more than half again as large as the largest stage on Broadway. It was so huge that a DC-9 airliner could be rolled onto it without using more than half the space available (a feat that had been accomplished as part of a production number on a similar stage at the MGM Grand Hotel in Reno). In spite of its size, a lavish use of blue velvet, dark leather, crystal chandeliers, and thick blue carpet, plus an excellent sense of dramatic lighting, gave the mammoth chamber some of the feeling of a cozy cabaret. Tina sat in one of the third-tier booths, nervously sipping ice water as she watched her show.

The dress rehearsal went without a single hitch. With seven massive production numbers, five major variety acts, forty-two girl dancers, forty-two boy dancers, fifteen showgirls, two boy singers, two girl singers (one of them temperamental), forty-seven crewmen and technicians, a twenty-piece orchestra, one elephant, one lion, two black panthers, and twelve white doves, the logistics were mind-numbingly complicated, but a year of arduous labor was evident in the slick and faultless unfolding of the program. At the end, the cast and crew gathered on stage and applauded themselves, hugged and kissed one another. There was electricity in the air, a feeling of triumph, a quaverous expectation of huge success.

Joel Bandiri, Tina's co-producer, had watched the show from a booth in the first tier, the VIP row, where high rollers and other friends of the hotel would be seated every night of the run. As soon as the rehearsal ended, Joel got up, raced to the aisle, climbed the steps to the third tier, and hurried toward Tina.

'We did it!' Joel shouted as he came toward her. 'We made the damn thing work!'

Tina slid out of the booth to meet him.

'We got a hit, kid!' Joel said, and he hugged her fiercely, planted a wet kiss on her cheek.

She hugged him back. 'You think so, Joel?'

'Think? I know! A giant. That's what we've got. A real giant! A gargantua!'

'Thank you, Joel. Thank you, thank you, thank you.'

'Me? What are you thanking me for?'

'For giving me a chance to prove myself.'

'Hey, I did you no favors, kid. You worked your butt off. You earned every penny you're going to make out of this baby, just like I knew you would. We're a great team. Anybody else tried to handle all this, they'd just end up with one goddamn big *mishkadenze* on their hands. But you and me, we made it into a hit.'

Joel was an odd little man, five-feet-four, slightly chubby but not fat, with curly brown hair and a broad clown's face that he could stretch into an endless series of rubbery expressions. He wore plain blue jeans, a cheap blue workshirt – and about eighty thousand dollars' worth of rings. He had six rings, three on each hand, some with diamonds, some with emeralds, one with a large ruby, one with an even larger opal. As always, he seemed to be high on something, bursting with energy. When he finally stopped hugging Tina, he could not stand still. He shifted from foot to foot as he talked about *Magyck!*, turned this way and that, gestured expansively with his quick, gem-speckled hands, almost doing a little jig.

At forty-six, he was the most successful producer in Las Vegas, with twenty years of hit shows behind him. The words 'Joel Bandiri Presents' on a marquee were a guarantee of first-rate entertainment. He had plowed some of his substantial earnings into Las Vegas real estate, parts of two hotels, an automobile dealership, and a slot machine casino downtown. He was so rich that he could retire tomorrow and live the rest of his life in the high style and splendor for which he had a taste. But Joel would never stop willingly. He loved his work. He would most likely die on the stage, in the middle of puzzling out a big production problem.

He had seen Tina's work in some lounges around town, and he had surprised her when he'd offered her the chance to co-produce *Magyck!* At first she hadn't been sure if she should take the job. She knew he had a reputation as a perfectionist, a producer who demanded almost super-human efforts from his people. She was also worried about being responsible for a three-million-dollar budget. Working with that kind of money wasn't just a step up for her; it was a giant leap. Joel convinced her that she would have no difficulty matching his pace or meeting his standards, and he assured her that she was equal to the challenge. He helped her discover new reserves of energy, new areas of competence in herself. He had become not just a valued business associate, but a good friend as well, a big brother. Now it looked as if they had shaped a hit show together.

As Tina stood in that beautiful theater, glancing down at the colorfully costumed people milling about on the stage, then looking at Joel's rubbery face, listening as her co-producer unblushingly raved about their handiwork, she was happier than she had been in a long, long time. If the audience at tonight's VIP premiere reacted enthusiastically to *Magyck!*, she might have to buy lead weights to keep herself from floating off the floor when she walked.

Twenty minutes later, at 3:45, she stepped onto the smooth cobblestones in front of the hotel's main entrance and handed her claim check to the valet parking attendant. While he went to fetch her VW Rabbit, she stood in the warm late-afternoon sunshine, unable to stop grinning.

She turned and looked back at the Desert Mirage Hotel-Casino. Her future was inextricably linked to that gaudy but undeniably impressive pile of concrete, steel, and glass. The heavy bronze and glass revolving doors glittered as they spun with a steady flow of people. Ramparts of pale pink stone stretched hundreds of feet on both sides of the entrance; those walls were windowless and garishly decorated with giant stone coins, a torrent of coins flooding from a stone cornucopia. Directly overhead, the ceiling of the immense porte-cochere was lined with hundreds of lights; none of the bulbs were burning now, but after nightfall they would rain dazzling, golden luminosity upon the glossy cobblestones below. The Desert Mirage had been built at a cost in excess of one hundred and forty million dollars, and the owners had made certain that every dime showed. Tina supposed that some people would say the hotel was gross, crass, tasteless, ugly, but she loved the place because it was here that she had been given her big chance.

Thus far, the thirtieth of December had been a busy, noisy, exciting day at the Desert Mirage. After the relative quiet of Christmas week, an uninterrupted stream of guests was pouring through the front doors. Advance bookings indicated a record New Year's holiday crowd for Las Vegas. The Desert Mirage, with almost twenty-one hundred rooms, was booked to capacity, as was every other hotel in the city. At a few minutes past eleven o'clock, a secretary from San Diego put five silver dollars in a slot machine and hit a jackpot worth $195,000; word of that even reached backstage in the showroom. Shortly before noon, two high rollers from Dallas sat down at a blackjack table and, in three hours, lost almost a quarter of a million dollars; they were laughing and joking when they left to try another game. Carol Hirson, a cocktail waitress who was a friend of Tina's had told her about the Texans a few minutes ago. Carol had been shiny-eyed and breathless because the high rollers had tipped her with green chips, as if they'd been winning instead of losing, and for bringing them half a dozen drinks, she had collected four hundred dollars. Sinatra was in town, at Caesar's Palace, and in Vegas he generated more excitement than any other famous names; perhaps because a lot of high rollers had been kids when Frankie's career first blossomed, they flocked to town each time he appeared, thousands of them, far more than could possibly get seats for one of his nightly performances. All along the Strip and in the less posh but nonetheless jammed casinos downtown, things were jumping, sparking. And in just four hours *Magyck!* would premiere.

The valet brought Tina's car, and she tipped him.

He said, 'Break a leg tonight, Tina.'

'God, I hope so,' she said.

She was home by 4:15, with two and a half hours to fill before she had to leave for the hotel again. She didn't need that much time to shower, apply her makeup, and dress, so she decided to pack some of Danny's belongings. Now was the right time to begin the unpleasant chore, for she was in an excellent mood, and she didn't think the sight of his room would be able to bring her down, as it usually did; she felt *that* good. No use putting it off until Thursday, as she had planned. She had at least enough time to box up the boy's clothes, if nothing else.

When she went into Danny's bedroom, she saw at once that the easel-chalkboard had been knocked over again. She put it right.

Two words were printed on it.

## NOT DEAD

A chill swept down her back.

Last night, after drinking the bourbon, had she come back here and—?

*No!*

She hadn't blacked out. She had not printed those words. She wasn't going crazy. She wasn't the sort of person who would snap over a thing like this. Not even a thing like this. She was tough. She always prided herself on her toughness and her resiliency.

She snatched up the felt eraser and wiped the slate clean.

Someone was playing a very sick and nasty trick on her. Someone had come into the house while she was out and had printed those two words on the chalkboard again. Someone wanted to rub her face in the tragedy she was trying so hard to forget.

The only person who'd had a right to be in the house was the cleaning woman, Vivian Neddler. Vivian had been scheduled to work this afternoon, but she had canceled. Instead, she was coming in for a few hours this evening, while Tina was at the premiere. But even if Vivian had kept her scheduled appointment, she wouldn't have written those words on the chalkboard. Vivian was a sweet old woman, somewhat feisty and very independent-minded, but she was not the type to play cruel pranks.

For a moment Tina wondered who could be responsible, and then she came up with a name. It was the only possible suspect. Michael. There was no sign that anyone had broken into the house, no obvious evidence of forced entry, and Michael was the only other person with a key. She hadn't changed the locks after the divorce.

Michael had blamed her for Danny's death. He had been so shattered by the loss of his son that he had been irrationally vicious with her for months after the funeral. Because she was the one who had given Danny permission to go on the field trip, Michael blamed her for the accident. But Danny had wanted to go more than anything else in the world. Besides, Mr. Jaborski, the scoutmaster, had taken other groups of scouts on winter survival hikes every year for fourteen years, and no one had been even slightly injured. They didn't go into the true wilderness, just a bit off the beaten path, and they planned for every contingency. The experience was supposed to be good for a boy. And safe. Carefully managed. Everyone had assured her there was no chance of trouble. She had no way of knowing that Mr. Jaborski's fifteenth trip would end in disaster, yet Michael blamed her. She thought he had regained his perspective during the last few months, but evidently not.

She stared at the chalkboard and thought of the two words that had been printed there, and she started to get angry. Michael was behaving like a spiteful child. Didn't he realize that her grief was as difficult to bear as his? What was he trying to prove?

Furious, she went into the kitchen, picked up the telephone, and dialed Michael's number. After five rings she realized that he was at work, and she hung up.

In her mind the two words burned, white on black: NOT DEAD.

She would call Michael tonight, when she got home from the premiere and the party afterward. She was bound to be quite late, but she wasn't going to worry about waking him up.

For a moment she stood indecisively in the center of the small kitchen, trying to work up the will power to go to Danny's room and box up his clothes, as she had planned. But she had lost her nerve. She couldn't go in there again. Not today. Maybe not for a few days.

*Damn* Michael!

In the refrigerator there was a half-empty bottle of white wine. She poured a glassful and carried it into the master bathroom.

She took a long shower. She let the hot water beat down on her neck for several minutes, driving out the stiffness in her muscles.

After the shower the chilled wine further relaxed her body, although it did little to calm her mind and allay her anxiety. She kept thinking of the chalkboard.

*NOT DEAD.*

# 4

At 6:50, Tina was again backstage in the showroom. The place was relatively quiet, except for the muffled oceanic roar of the VIP crowd that waited in the main showroom, beyond the velvet curtains.

Eighteen hundred guests had been invited – Las Vegas movers and shakers, plus high rollers from out of town – and more than fifteen hundred had returned their RSVP cards. Already, white-coated waiters, waitresses in crisp blue uniforms, and scurrying bus boys had begun serving the *filet mignon* dinners.

By seven-thirty the backstage area was bustling. Technicians were double-checking the motorized sets, the electrical connections, and the hydraulic pumps that raised and lowered portions of the stage. Stagehands counted and arranged props. Wardrobe women mended tears and sewed up unraveled hems that had been discovered at the last minute. Hairdressers and lighting technicians rushed about on last-minute tasks. Male dancers, wearing black tuxedos for the opening number, stood tensely, an eye-pleasing collection of lean, handsome types.

Dozens of beautiful showgirls were backstage, too. Some wore satin and lace. Others wore velvet and rhinestones – or feathers or sequins or furs. Many were still in the communal dressing rooms, while other girls, already costumed, waited in the halls or at the edge of the stage, talking about children and husbands and boyfriends and recipes, as if they were secretaries on a coffee break and not some of the most beautiful, glamorous women in the world.

Tina wanted to stay in the wings throughout the performance, but she knew there was nothing more she could do. *Magyck!* was now in the hands of the performers and technicians.

Twenty-five minutes before show time, Tina left the stage and went into the noisy showroom. She headed toward the center booth in the VIP row, where Charles Mainway, general manager and principal stockholder of the Desert Mirage Hotel, waited for her.

She stopped first at the booth next to Mainway's. Joel Bandiri was there with Eva, his wife of eight years, and a couple of their friends. Eva was twenty-nine, seventeen years younger than Joel, and, at five foot eight, she was also four inches taller than he was. She was an ex-showgirl, blonde, willowy, delicately beautiful. She gently squeezed Tina's hand. 'Don't worry. You're too good to fail.'

'We got a hit, kid,' Joel assured Tina once more.

In the next semicircular booth, Charles Mainway greeted Tina with a huge warm smile. Mainway carried and held himself as if he were an aristocrat. His mane of silver hair and his clear blue eyes contributed to the image he wanted to project. However, his face belied the facade of aristocracy. His features were large, square, and utterly without evidence of patrician blood. He greeted Tina enthusiastically, but even after the mellowing influence of elocution teachers, his naturally low, gravelly voice made her think of hard times and street life.

As Tina slid into the booth beside Mainway, a tuxedoed captain appeared and poured a glass of Dom Pérignon for her.

Helen Mainway, Charlie's wife, sat at his left side. Helen was, almost by nature, everything Charlie struggled to be: impeccably well-mannered, sophisticated, graceful, at ease and confident in absolutely any situation. She was a tall, slender, striking woman, fifty-five years old, who would have passed for a well-preserved forty.

'Tina, my dear, I want you to meet a friend of ours,' Helen said, indicating the last person in the booth. 'This is Elliot Stryker. Elliot, this lovely

41

young lady is Christina Evans, the guiding hand behind *Magyck!*'

'One of *two* guiding hands,' Tina said. 'Joel Bandiri is more responsible for the show than I am – especially if it's a flop.'

Stryker laughed. 'I'm pleased to meet you, Mrs. Evans.'

'Just plain Tina,' she said.

'And I'm just plain Elliot.'

He was a lean, good-looking man, neither big nor small, about forty. His dark eyes were quick, marked by intelligence, amused.

'Elliot is my attorney,' Charlie Mainway said.

'Oh,' Tina said, 'I thought Harry Simpson was—'

'Harry's a hotel attorney. Elliot handles my private affairs.'

'And handles them very well,' Helen said. 'Tina, if you need an attorney, you're looking at the best in Las Vegas.'

To Tina, Stryker said, 'But if it's flattery you need – and I'm sure you already get a lot of it, lovely as you are – no one in Vegas can flatter with more charm and style than Helen does.'

'You see what he just did?' Helen asked Tina. 'In just one sentence he managed to flatter you, flatter me, and impress all of us with his modesty. You see what a wonderful attorney he is?'

'Imagine him arguing a point in court,' Charlie said.

'A very smooth character indeed,' Helen said.

Stryker grinned at Tina. 'As you can see, smooth as I might be, I'm no match for these two.'

They made pleasant small talk for the next fifteen minutes, and none of it had to do with *Magyck!* Tina was aware that they were trying to take her mind off the show, and she appreciated their effort.

Of course no amount of amusing talk, no quantity of icy Dom Pérignon could render her unaware of the excitement that was building in the showroom as curtain time drew near. Minute by minute the cloud of cigarette smoke overhead thickened. Waitresses, waiters, and captains rushed back and forth, attempting to fill the drink orders before the show began. The roar of conversation grew louder as the seconds ticked away, and the quality of the roar became more frenetic, gayer, and more often punctuated with laughter.

Somehow, even though her attention was partly on the mood of the crowd, partly on Helen and Charlie, Tina was nevertheless aware of Elliot Stryker's reaction to her. He made no great show of being more than ordinarily interested in her, but the attraction she held for him was evident in his eyes. Beneath his cordial, witty, slightly cool exterior, his secret response was that of a healthy male animal, and her awareness of it was more instinctual than intellectual, like a mare's response to the stallion's first faint stirrings of desire.

It had been at least a year and a half, maybe two years, since a man had looked at her in quite that fashion. Or perhaps it was just that this was the first time in all those months that she had been aware of being stared at. Fighting with Michael, coping with the shock of separation and divorce, grieving for Danny, putting together the show with Joel Bandiri – all of those things had filled her days and nights to overflowing, so that she'd had no chance to think of romance.

She felt herself responding to the unspoken need in Elliot's smoky eyes, and she was suddenly warm, and she thought: My God, I've been letting myself dry up! How could I have forgotten *this*?

Now that she had spent more than a year grieving for her broken marriage and her lost son, now that *Magyck!* was almost behind her, she would have time to be a woman again. She would *make* time. Time for Elliot Stryker? She wasn't sure about that. She didn't have to be in a rush to make up for lost pleasures. She didn't have to jump at the first man who wanted her. Surely that wasn't the smart thing to do. On the other hand, he *was* rather handsome. And there was an appealing gentleness in his face. She had to admit that he sparked the same feelings in her that she apparently fired up in him.

The evening was turning out to be even more interesting than she had expected.

# 5

Vivian Neddler parked her vintage 1955 Nash Rambler against the curb, careful not to scrape the whitewall. The car was immaculate, in better shape than most new cars were these days. In a world of planned obsolescence, Vivian took pleasure in getting long, full use of everything she bought, from a toaster to an automobile. She enjoyed making things last. She had lasted quite a while herself: she was seventy, still in good health, a short sturdy woman with the sweet face of a Botticelli madonna and the no-nonsense walk of an army sergeant. She got out of the car and headed up the walk toward Tina Evans's house.

The yellowish light from the street lamps failed to reach all the way across the lawn to the front door. Beside the walk, low oleander bushes rustled in the breeze. Behind the house there was an imitation–antique carriage lamp, and the dark water in the swimming pool shimmered with splintered reflections of the crescent moon that rode high in the cloudless sky.

Vivian let herself in through the kitchen door. She had been cleaning house for Tina Evans for almost two years, and she had been entrusted with a key nearly that long.

The place was silent except for the softly humming refrigerator.

Vivian began work in the kitchen. She wiped off the counters and the appliances, sponged off the slats of the Levelor blinds, and mopped the Mexican-tile floor. She did a good job. She believed in the moral value of hard work, and she always gave her employers their money's worth.

Ordinarily she worked during the day, not at night. This afternoon, however, she had been playing a pair of lucky slot machines at the Hilton Hotel, and she hadn't wanted to walk away from them while they were paying off so generously. Some of the people for whom she cleaned house insisted that she keep regularly scheduled appointments, once or twice a week, and they did a slow burn if she showed up more than a few minutes late. But Tina Evans was sympathetic; she knew how important the slot machines were to Vivian, and she wasn't upset if Vivian occasionally had to reschedule her visit.

Vivian was a nickel duchess. That was the term by which casino employees referred to local, elderly women whose social lives revolved around an obsessive interest in one-armed bandits. Nickel duchesses always played the cheap machines, nickels and dimes, never quarters or dollars. They pulled the handles for hours at a time, often making a five-dollar bill last a long afternoon. Their gaming philosophy was simple: *It doesn't matter if you win or lose, so long as you stay in the game.* With that attitude plus a few money management skills, they were able to hang on longer than most slot players who plunged at the dollar machines after getting nowhere with nickels, and because of their patience and perseverance the duchesses won more jackpots than did the tide of tourists that ebbed and flowed around them. Nickel duchesses wore black gloves to keep their hands from turning black after half an hour of handling coins, and they always sat on stools when they played, and they remembered to alternate hands when pulling the levers of the machines in order not to strain the muscles of one arm, and they carried bottles of liniment just in case. The duchesses, who for the most part were widows and spinsters, often ate lunch and dinner together; they cheered one another on those rare occasions when one of them hit a really large jackpot; and when one of them died, the others went to the funeral en masse. Together they formed an odd but solid community, and they had a satisfying sense of belonging. In a country that seemed to worship youth, most elderly Americans devoutly desired to discover a place where they belonged, but many of them never found it.

Vivian had a daughter, a son-in-law, and three grandchildren in Sacramento. For five years, ever since her sixty-fifth birthday, they had been pressuring her to come live with them. She loved them very much, and she knew they actually wanted her with them; they were not inviting her out of a misguided sense of guilt and obligation. Nevertheless, she didn't want to live in Sacramento. After several visits there, she had decided that it must be one of the dullest cities in the world. Vivian liked the action, noise, lights, and excitement of Las Vegas. Besides, living in Sacramento, she wouldn't be a nickel duchess any longer; she wouldn't be anyone special; she would be just another old lady, living with her daughter's family, playing grandma, marking time, waiting to die.

A life like that would be intolerable.

Vivian valued her independence more than anything else. She prayed that she would remain healthy enough to continue working and living on her own until, at last, her time came.

As she was mopping the last corner of the kitchen floor, as she was thinking about how dreary life would be without her friends and her slot machines, she heard a sound in another part of the house. Toward the front. The living room.

She stood very still, listening.

The refrigerator motor stopped running. A clock ticked softly.

After a long silence there was another noise, a chattering sound that startled Vivian.

Then silence again.

She went to the drawer next to the sink and selected a long, sharp knife from an assortment of knives. She didn't even consider calling the police. If she phoned for them and then ran out of the house, they might not find an intruder when they came, and they would think she was just a foolish old woman. Vivian Neddler refused to give anyone reason to think her a fool. Besides, for the past twenty-one years, ever since her Harry died, she had always taken care of herself, and she had done a pretty damned good job of it, too.

She stepped out of the kitchen, found the light switch to the right of the doorway, and saw that the dining room was deserted.

In the living room she clicked on a Stifel lamp. No one was there.

She was about to head for the den when she noticed something odd about four glossy, eight-by-ten photographs that were grouped above the sofa. That display had always contained six pictures, not just four. But the fact that two of them were missing wasn't what drew Vivian's eye. All four of the photos were swinging back and forth on the hooks that held them. No one was near them, yet suddenly two of the pictures began to rattle violently against the wall, and then both

51

of them flew off their mountings and clattered to the floor behind the beige, brushed-corduroy sofa.

'What the hell?' Vivian said, surprised.

A second later the remaining two photographs abruptly flung themselves away from the wall. One of them dropped behind the sofa, and the other fell onto it.

Vivian blinked in amazement, unable to understand what she had just seen. An earthquake? But she hadn't felt the house move; the windows hadn't rattled. Any tremor that was too mild to be felt would also be too mild to tear the photographs from the wall.

She went to the sofa and picked up the photo that had fallen onto the cushions. She knew it well. She had dusted it many times. It was a portrait of Danny Evans, as were the other five that usually hung around it. In this one he was ten or eleven years old, a brown-haired boy with dark eyes and a lovely smile.

Vivian wondered if there had been a nuclear test; maybe *that* was what had shaken things up. The Nevada Nuclear Test Site, where underground detonations were conducted several times a year, was less than a hundred miles north of Las Vegas. Whenever the military exploded a high-yield weapon, the tall hotels swayed in Vegas, and every house in town shuddered at least a little bit.

But the house hadn't shuddered just a minute

ago, which meant the photographs hadn't been jolted off the wall by an atomic test. Anyway, the tests never took place at night.

Puzzled, frowning thoughtfully, Vivian put down the knife she was carrying, pulled one end of the sofa away from the wall, and collected the framed eight-by-tens that were on the floor behind it. There were five photographs in addition to the one that had dropped onto the sofa; two of them were responsible for the noises that had drawn her into the living room, and the other three were those she had seen popping off the picture hooks. She put them back where they belonged, then slid the sofa into place.

A burst of high-pitched electronic noise suddenly filled the house: *Aiii-eee, aiii-eee, aiii-eee* . . .

Vivian gasped, whirled, looked behind her. She was still alone.

Her first thought was: *Burglar alarm!* But the Evans house didn't have an alarm system.

Vivian winced as the electronic squeal grew louder. The window began to vibrate, as did the glass top of the coffee table, and she felt a sympathetic resonance in her teeth and bones.

She couldn't identify the source of the painfully sharp sound. It seemed to be coming from every corner of the house.

'What in the blue devil is going on here?' she said aloud.

She didn't bother picking up the knife, for she

was sure the problem wasn't an intruder. It was something else; something weird.

She crossed the room to the hallway that served the bedrooms, bathrooms, and the den. She snapped on the light. The noise was louder in the corridor than it had been in the living room. The nerve-fraying sound bounded off the walls of the narrow passageway, echoing and re-echoing. Vivian looked both ways, then moved to the right, toward the closed door at the end of the hall, toward Danny's old room.

The air was cooler in the hallway than it was in the rest of the house. At first Vivian thought she was imagining the change in temperature. But the closer she drew to the end of the corridor, the colder it got. By the time she reached the closed door, her skin was goose-pimply, and her teeth were chattering.

Her curiosity now began to give way to fear. Something was very wrong. An ominous pressure seemed to compress the air around her.

*Aiii-eee, aiii-eee . . .*

She thought the wisest thing she could do would be to turn back, walk away from the door and out of the house. But she wasn't completely in control of herself; she felt a bit like a sleepwalker; a power she could sense, but which she could not define, drew her inexorably to Danny's room.

*Aiii-eee, aiii-eee, aiii-eee . . .*

Vivian reached for the doorknob but stopped

before touching it, unable to believe what she was seeing. She blinked rapidly, then closed her eyes for a moment, opened them again, but *still* the doorknob appeared to be sheathed in a thin, irregular jacket of ice. She finally touched it. Yes: *ice.* Her hand almost stuck to the knob; she pulled it away and looked at her damp fingers. Moisture had condensed on the metal and then had frozen.

But how is that possible? she wondered. How in the name of God could there be ice here, in a warm house?

The electronic squeal began to warble faster, but it was no quieter, no less piercing than it had been.

Stop, Vivian told herself. Get away from here. Get out as fast as you can.

But she ignored her own advice. She pulled her blouse out of her slacks and used the tail of it to protect her hand from the icy metal doorknob. The knob turned, but the door wouldn't open. The intense cold had caused the wood to contract and warp. She put her shoulder against it, pushed gently, then harder, and finally the door swung inward.

# 6

*Magyck!* was by far the best stage show Elliot Stryker had ever seen. The program opened with an electrifying rendition of 'That Old Black Magic'. The singers and dancers, brilliantly costumed, performed in a stunning set constructed of mirrored steps and mirrored panels and revolving crystal ballroom chandeliers that, when the stage lights were periodically dimmed, cast swirling splinters of color over all of them. The choreography was complex, and the two lead singers had strong, crisp voices. That number was followed by a first-rate magic act in front of the drawn curtains. Less than ten minutes later, when the curtains opened again, the mirrors had been taken away, and the stage had been transformed into an ice rink; the second production number was done on skates against a winter backdrop so real that it made you feel cold.

Although *Magyck!* excited the imagination and commanded the eye, Elliot wasn't able to give his undivided attention to it. He kept looking at

Christina Evans, who was every bit as dazzling as the show she had created. She watched the performers intently, unaware of his gaze. A flickering, nervous scowl played across her face, alternating with a tentative smile that appeared whenever the audience laughed, applauded, or gasped in surprise.

She was a singularly beautiful woman. She was trim, lean, yet ripe, with long legs, slim but womanly hips, and an impossibly narrow waist. The V-neck of her dress revealed the warm curves of full, well-shaped breasts. But it was not her body, lovely as it was, that contributed most to her beauty. The face. That was it. Her thick, glossy hair was deep brown, almost black, shoulder-length, swept across her brow, feathered back at the sides, framing her face as if it were a painting by a great master. And her face *was* a masterpiece. My God, that face! The bone structure was so delicate, so clearly defined, so quintessentially feminine that the very sight of it made his heart beat faster. Her flawless complexion was a dusky, olive shade, not so dark that her features were lost in it, but dark enough to give her an exotic, intriguing aspect. Her mouth was full, sensuous. And her eyes . . . She would have been extraordinarily lovely if her eyes had been dark, in harmony with the shade of her hair and skin, as one expected them to be. But her eyes were blue, a crystalline blue, not a flat ice-blue, but bright and hot, the blue of a gas flame. The contrast between her Italian good looks and her Nordic eyes was devastating. Elliot supposed that other people might find flaws in her face. Perhaps some would say that her brow was too wide. Her nose was so straight that some might say it gave her a severe look. Others might think her mouth was too wide, her chin just a bit too pointed. But to Elliot, her face was perfect. Perfect.

Although it was her face that first stirred desire in him, and although her sensuous body stoked his desire, it was not even her physical beauty that most excited him. He was interested primarily in learning more about the mind that could create a work like *Magyck!* He had seen less than one-fourth of the program, but already he knew it was a hit; it was far superior to anything else of its kind. A Vegas show of this nature could easily go off the rails. If the gigantic sets and the lavish costumes and the intricate choreography were overdone, or if any element was improperly executed, the show would quickly stumble across the thin line between marvelous show-biz flash and just plain vulgarity. A glittery fantasy could metamorphose into a crude, tasteless, and stupid bore, if the wrong hand guided it. Elliot wanted to know more about Christina Evans. And on a more fundamental level, he just plain wanted her.

No woman had affected him so strongly since Nancy, his wife, had died three years ago.

Sitting there in the dark theater, he grinned, not at the comic magician who was now performing in front of the closed stage curtains, but at his own sudden, youthful exuberance.

# 7

The warped door protested with a groan and a creak as Vivian forced it open.

*Aiii-eee, aiii-eee . . .*

A wave of frigid air washed out of the dark room, into the hallway.

Vivian reached inside, fumbled for the light switch, found it, and entered warily. The room was deserted.

*Aiii-eee, aii-eee . . .*

It was like the bedrooms of thousands of other young boys. The walls were covered with posters of baseball stars and horror-movie monsters. Three model airplanes were suspended from the ceiling. Those things were as they always had been, since Vivian had first come to work here, before Danny had died.

*Aiii-eee, aiii-eee, aiii-eee . . .*

The electronic squeal issued from a pair of small stereo speakers that were hung on the wall behind the bed. The turntable and an accompanying AM-FM tuner were on one of the nightstands.

Although Vivian could see where the noise was coming from, she couldn't locate any source for the bitterly cold air that filled the room.

She started toward the stereo equipment. She could see there was no record on the turntable, so the sound had to be coming from the radio.

But what radio station played electronic noise instead of music?

Just as she reached the AM-FM tuner, the banshee wail stopped. Silence fell over her like collapsing walls of cotton, and for a few seconds, as her ears adjusted to the abrupt cessation of the torture they had been enduring, she was too stunned to hear anything at all. Gradually she began to perceive the soft empty hiss of the stereo speakers, which were still turned on. Then she heard the thumping of her own heart.

The metal parts of the stereo's casing gleamed with a brittle crust of ice. She touched it wonderingly. A sliver of ice broke loose under her finger and fell onto the nightstand. It didn't begin to melt; the room was *cold*.

The dresser mirror was frosted. So was the window.

It's cool outside, Vivian thought. But not *that* cool. Maybe fifty degrees. Maybe even fifty-five.

The radio's tuning knob began to turn by itself, and the frequency indicator moved rapidly across the lighted dial, sweeping through one station after another. Scraps of music, split-second flashes of disc jockeys' chatter, single words from several different somber-voiced newscasters, and bits of commercial jingles blended in a cacophonous jumble of meaningless sound. The indicator reached the end of the dial and started back the other way.

Trembling, Vivian switched off the radio.

As soon as she let go of the knob, the radio switched itself on again.

She stared at it, frightened and bewildered.

The indicator moved rapidly across the dial.

She snapped off the radio a second time.

It immediately turned itself on.

'This is crazy,' she said shakily.

When she shut it off the third time, she held the knob tightly in place. For several seconds she was sure she could feel it straining under her fingers as it tried to move back to the 'on' position.

Overhead, the three model airplanes began to move. Each of them was hung from the ceiling on a length of fishing line, and the upper end of each line was knotted to its own eye-hook that had been screwed firmly into the plaster. The planes jiggled and jerked and twisted and trembled.

'It's just a draft,' Vivian said.

Then she said, 'But I don't feel a draft.'

The model planes began to bounce violently up and down on the ends of their lines.

'God help me,' Vivian said.

One of the planes began to swing in tight circles, faster and faster, then in wider circles, steadily decreasing the angle between the line on which it was suspended and the bedroom ceiling. After a moment the other two models ceased their erratic dancing and began to spin around and around, like the first plane, as if they were actually flying, and there was no mistaking this deliberate movement for the random effects of a draft.

Ghosts? Vivian thought. A poltergeist? But I don't *believe* in ghosts. There are no such things.

The sliding closet doors began to move on their runners, and for one horrible instant Vivian Neddler had the feeling that some awful *thing* was going to come out of that dark space. But there wasn't a monster in the closet. There wasn't anything in the closet but clothes. Nevertheless, untouched, the doors glided open and then shut . . . and then open . . .

The model planes went around, around.

The air seemed to grow even colder.

The bed started to shake. The legs at the foot of the bed rose as high as three or four inches before crashing back into the casters that had been put under them to protect the carpet. Then they rose up again. The springs began to sing as if metal fingers were strumming them.

Vivian backed into the wall and stood there, rigid, eyes wide, hands fisted at her sides.

As abruptly as the bed had started bouncing up and down, it now stopped. The closet doors closed with a jarring crash – but they didn't open again. The model airplanes slowed down, swinging in smaller and smaller circles, until they were finally just hanging there, as before, motionless.

The room was silent.

Nothing moved.

The air was getting warmer.

Vivian was aware of her heartbeat subsiding from the hard, frantic rhythm that it had been keeping for the past couple of minutes. She hugged herself and shivered.

'A logical explanation,' she said. 'There's got to be a logical explanation.'

But she wasn't able to imagine what it could be.

As the room grew warm again, the doorknobs and the stereo casing and a few other metal objects quickly shed their fragile skins of ice, leaving damp spots in the carpet. The frosted window cleared.

The room held no indication that something unusual had just transpired. Now it was only a young boy's bedroom, a room like countless thousands of others.

Except, of course, that the boy who had once slept here had been dead now for a year. And maybe he was coming back, haunting the place.

But I don't believe in ghosts, Vivian reminded herself. There are no such things as ghosts.

Nevertheless, it might be a good idea for Tina Evans to finally get rid of the boy's belongings. That was a step she should have taken a long time ago.

Vivian didn't have a logical explanation for what had happened, but she did know one thing for sure: She wasn't going to tell anyone what she had seen here tonight. Regardless of how convincingly and earnestly she described these bizarre events, no one would believe her. They would nod and smile woodenly and agree that it was a strange and frightening experience, but all the while they would be thinking that poor old Vivian was finally getting senile. Sooner or later, word of her rantings about poltergeists might even get back to her daughter in Sacramento, and then the pressure to move to California would become unbearable. Vivian wasn't going to jeopardize her precious independence.

She left the bedroom, returned to the kitchen, and drank two shots of Tina Evans's best bourbon. Then, with characteristic stoicism, she continued with her house cleaning.

She refused to let a poltergeist scare her off.

It might be wise, however, to go to church on Sunday. She hadn't been to church in a long time. Maybe it would be good for her every once in a while. Not every week, of course. Just one or two Masses a month. And confession now and then. She hadn't seen the inside of a confessional in ages. Better safe than sorry.

# 8

Everyone in show business knew that non-paying preview crowds were among the toughest to please. The fact that they had gotten in free usually didn't guarantee their appreciation or even their amicability. The person who paid a fair price for something was likely to place far more value on it than the man who got the same thing for nothing. That old saw applied in spades to stage shows and to on-the-cuff invited audiences.

But not tonight. *This* crowd wasn't able to sit on its hands and keep its cool.

The final curtain came down at eleven minutes till ten, and the ovation continued until after Tina's wristwatch had marked the hour. The cast of *Magyck!* took several bows, then the crew, then the orchestra, all of them flushed with the excitement of being part of an unqualified hit. At the insistence of the happy, boisterous VIP audience, both Joel Bandiri and Tina were spotlighted in their booths and were rewarded with their own thunderous round of applause.

Tina was on an adrenaline high, grinning, breathless, barely able to absorb the over-whelming response to her work. Helen Main-way chattered excitedly about the spectacular special effects, and Elliot Stryker had an endless supply of compliments as well as some astute observations about the technical aspects of the production, and Charlie Mainway poured a third bottle of Dom Pérignon, and the house lights came up, and the audience reluctantly began to leave, and Tina hardly had a chance to sip her champagne because of all the people who stopped by the table to congratulate her.

By ten-thirty most of the audience had left, and those who hadn't gone yet were in line, moving up the steps toward the rear doors of the showroom. Although there wasn't a second show tonight, as there would be every night henceforth, bus boys and waitresses were busily clearing tables, resetting them with fresh linen and silverware for tomorrow evening's eight o'clock performance.

When the aisle in front of the booth was finally empty of well-wishers, Tina got up and met Joel as he started to come to her. She threw her arms around him and, much to her surprise, began to cry with happiness. She hugged him very hard, and Joel proclaimed the show to be 'a gargantua if I ever saw one'.

By the time they got backstage, the opening-night party was in full swing. The sets and props had been moved from the main floor of the stage, and eight folding tables had been set up. The tables were draped with white cloths and burdened with food. There were five kinds of hot *hors d'oeuvres*, macaroni salad, potato salad, three-bean salad, cold roast beef, cold ham, hot breast of chicken in wine sauce, four cheeses, buttery noodles in a steaming cheddary casserole, garnishes, rolls, three cakes, three pies, *petits fours*, nut pudding, and fresh fruit. Hotel management personnel, showgirls, dancers, magicians, crewmen, and musicians crowded around the tables, sampling this and that while Phillippe Chevalier, the hotel's head chef, personally watched over the affair. Knowing this feast had been laid on for the party, few of those present had eaten dinner; and of course the dancers had eaten little or, in most cases, nothing at all since a light breakfast. They exclaimed over the food and clustered around the portable bar; and with the memory of the applause still fresh in everyone's mind, the party was soon jumping.

Tina mingled, moving back and forth, upstage and downstage, through the crowd, thanking everyone for his contribution to the show's success, complimenting each member of the cast and crew on his dedication and professionalism. Several times she encountered Elliot Stryker, and he seemed genuinely interested in learning how the splashy stage effects had been achieved. Each time that Tina had to move on to talk to someone else, she regretted leaving Elliot, and each time she found him again, she stayed with him longer than she had before. After their fourth encounter she lost track of how long they were together. Finally she forgot all about circulating.

They stood near the left proscenium pillar, out of the main flow of the party. They nibbled at pieces of cake and talked about *Magyck!* some more, then about other things – the law, Charlie and Helen Mainway, Las Vegas real estate, favorite old movies – and she found him increasingly appealing. He was intelligent and articulate; he had a wry sense of humor; and his dark good looks reminded her of Al Pacino.

He said, 'I guess you'll have to be here most nights for a long time to come.'

'No,' she said. 'There's really no need for me to be.'

'I thought a director—'

'Most of the director's job is finished. I just have to check on the show once every couple of weeks to make sure the tone of it isn't drifting away from my original intention.'

'But you're also the co-producer,' Elliot said.

'Well, now that the show has opened success-fully, most of my share of the producer's chores will be in the area of public relations and promotion. And a little logistical stuff to keep the production rolling along smoothly. But nearly all of that can be handled out of my office. I won't have to hang around the stage. In fact, Joel says it isn't healthy for a producer to be backstage every night . . . or even most nights. He says I'd just make the performers nervous and cause the technicians to look over their shoulders for the boss when they should have their eyes on their work.'

'But will you be able to resist?'

She grinned. 'It isn't going to be easy staying away. But there's a lot of sense in what Joel says, so I'm going to try to play it cool.'

'Still, I guess you'll be here every night for the first week or so.'

'No,' she said. 'If Joel's right – and I'm sure he is – then it's best to get in the habit of staying away right from the start.'

'Tomorrow night?' he asked.

'Oh, I'll probably pop in and out a few times.'

'I guess you'll be going to a New Year's Eve party.'

'Wrong again,' she said, smiling. 'I hate New Year's Eve parties. Everyone's drunk and boring.'

'Well, then . . . in between all that popping in

and out of *Magyck!*, do you think you'd have time
for dinner?'

'Are you asking me for a date?'

'I'll try not to slurp my soup.'

'You *are* asking me for a date,' she said, pleased.

'Yes,' Elliot said. 'And it's been a long time
since I've been this awkward about it.'

'Why is that?'

'You, I guess.'

'I make you feel awkward?'

'You make me feel young. And when I was
young, I was very awkward.'

'That's sweet.'

'I'm trying to charm you.'

'And you're succeeding.'

He had such a warm smile. 'Suddenly I don't
feel so awkward any more.'

'You want to start over?'

'Will you have dinner with me tomorrow
night?'

'Sure. How about seven-thirty?'

'Fine. Dressy or casual?' he asked.

'Blue jeans.'

He fingered his starched collar and the satin
lapel of his dinner jacket. 'I'm so glad you said
that.'

'I'll give you my address,' she said, looking in
her purse for a pen.

'We can stop in here and watch the first few
numbers in *Magyck!* and then go to the restaurant.'

'Why don't we just go straight to the restaurant?'

'You don't want to pop in here?'

'I've decided to go cold turkey.'

'Joel will be proud of you.'

'If I can actually do it, *I'll* be proud of me.'

'You'll do it. You strike me as a woman with true grit.'

She grinned. 'In the middle of dinner, I might be seized by a desperate need to dash over here and act like a producer.'

'I'll park the car in front of the restaurant door, and I'll leave the engine running just in case.'

Tina gave him her address, and then somehow they were talking about jazz and Benny Goodman, and then about the miserable service provided by the Las Vegas phone company, just chatting away as if they were old friends. He had a variety of interests; among other things he was a skier and a pilot, and he was full of funny stories about learning to ski and fly. He made her feel comfortable, yet at the same time he intrigued her. He projected an interesting image, a blend of male power and gentleness, aggressive sexuality and kindness.

A hit show . . . lots of royalty checks to look forward to . . . an infinity of new opportunities made available to her because of this first smashing success . . . the prospect of a new and very exciting lover . . . As she listed her blessings,

Tina was astonished at how much difference one year could make in a life. From bitterness, pain, tragedy, and unrelenting sorrow, she had turned around to face a horizon lit by rising promise. At last the future looked worth living. Indeed, she couldn't see how anything could go wrong.

# 9

The skirts of the night were gathered around the Evans house, and a dry desert wind rustled them. A neighbor's white cat crept across the lawn, stalking a wind-tossed scrap of paper; the cat pounced, missed its prey, stumbled, scared itself, and streaked like lightning into another yard.

Inside, the house was mostly silent. Now and then the refrigerator switched on, purring to itself. A loose windowpane in the living room rattled slightly whenever a strong gust of wind struck it. The heating system rumbled to life, and for a couple of minutes at a time the blower whispered wordlessly as hot air pushed through the vents.

Shortly before midnight, Danny's room began to grow cold. On the doorknob, on the stereo casing, and on a couple of other metal objects, moisture began to condense out of the humidified air. The temperature plunged rapidly now, and the beads of water froze. Frost formed on the window.

The stereo came on all by itself.

For a few seconds the silence was split wide open by an electronic squeal as sharp as an ax blade. Then the shrill noise abruptly stopped, and the station selector began to move rapidly back and forth across the lighted radio dial. Snippets of music and shards of voices crackled in an eerie audio-montage that filled the cold room.

But there was no one in the house to hear it.

The closet door opened, closed, opened . . .

Inside the closet, shirts and jeans began to swing wildly on the pole from which they hung, and some clothes fell to the floor.

The bed began to shake.

The display case that held nine model airplanes began to rock, banging repeatedly against the wall. One of the models was flung from its shelf, then two more, then three more, then another, until eventually all nine lay in a pile on the floor.

On the wall to the left of the bed, a poster of Willie Stargell tore down the middle.

The radio dial ceased scanning, its movement arrested on an open frequency that hissed and popped with distant static. After a few seconds of silence, a voice blared from the speakers. It was a child's voice. A boy. There were no words. Just a long, agonized scream.

The voice faded after a minute, but the bed began to bang up and down harder than it had before.

And the closet door slammed open and shut with substantially more force.

Other things began to move, too. For almost five minutes the room seemed to have come alive.

And then it died.

Silence returned.

The air grew warm again.

The frost left the window, and outside the white cat still chased the scrap of paper.

# PART TWO

**WEDNESDAY**
## DECEMBER 31

# 10

Tina didn't get home from the opening-night party until shortly before two o'clock Wednesday morning. She went straight to bed, exhausted and slightly tipsy, and fell immediately into a sound sleep.

Later, after only a couple of dreamless hours, she had another nightmare about Danny. He was trapped at the bottom of a very deep hole. She heard his scared little voice calling to her, and she looked over the edge of the pit, and he was so far down in there that his face was just a tiny, pale smudge. He desperately wanted out, and she wanted to bring him out more than she had ever wanted anything else; but he was chained down there, unable to climb, and she had no way to get to him. And then a man dressed entirely in black from head to foot, his face hidden by shadows, stepped up to the far side of the pit and began to shovel dirt into it. Danny's cry became a scream of terror; he was being buried alive. Tina shouted at the man in black, but he ignored her and kept shoveling dirt on top of Danny. She started around the edge of the pit, determined to make him stop what he was doing, but he took a step away from her for every step she took toward him, and he always stayed directly across the hole from her. She couldn't reach him, and she couldn't reach Danny, and the dirt was up to the boy's knees, and now up to his hips, and now over his shoulders. Danny wailed and shrieked, and now the earth was even with his chin, but the man in black wouldn't stop. She wanted to kill the bastard, club him to death with his own shovel; and when she thought of doing that, he looked at her, and she saw his face, and it was little more than a skull with skin stretched over it and burning red eyes and a yellow-toothed grin. And a cluster of maggots clung to the man's left cheek and to the corner of his left eye, feeding off him. Her terror over Danny's impending entombment was now mixed with fear for her own life. Then Danny's screams became muffled, but even more urgent than before, as the dirt began to cover his face and pour into his mouth, and she knew she had to get down there and push the earth from his face before he suffocated, so in blind panic she threw herself into the pit, and she was falling, falling—

She wrenched herself out of sleep. Gasping. Shuddering. She had the creepy feeling that the man in black was in her bedroom right this minute, standing silently in the darkness, grinning. Heart pounding, she fumbled with the bedside lamp, afraid that a cold, damp hand was going to close over hers just as she located the switch. She blinked in the sudden light and – thank *God*! – saw that she was alone.

'Jesus,' she said weakly.

She wiped one hand across her face and found that she was sloughing off a film of perspiration. She dried her hand on the sheets.

She did some deep-breathing exercises, trying to calm herself.

She couldn't stop shaking.

She went into the bathroom and washed her face. In the mirror she looked drawn and bloodless.

Her mouth was dry and sour. She drank two glasses of cold water.

Back in bed, she didn't want to turn off the light. Her fear made her angry with herself, and at last she twisted the switch.

The returning darkness seemed threatening.

She wasn't sure she would be able to get any more sleep, but she had to try. It wasn't even five o'clock. She'd been asleep less than three hours. She needed a lot more rest than she'd gotten, and that was not just true of tonight, but of the entire past month as well.

In the morning she would clean out Danny's

room. Then, the dreams would stop. She was pretty much convinced of that.

She remembered the two words that she had twice erased from Danny's chalkboard – NOT DEAD – and she realized she'd forgotten to call Michael. She had to confront him with her suspicions. She had to know if he'd been in the house, in Danny's room, without her knowledge or permission.

It *had* to be Michael.

She could turn on the light and call him now. He would be sleeping, but she wouldn't feel guilty if she woke him, not after all the sleepless nights he had given her. But right now she just didn't feel up to the battle. Her wits were dulled by wine and exhaustion. And if Michael *had* slipped into the house like a little boy playing a cruel prank, if he *had* written that message on the chalkboard, then his hatred of her was far greater than she had thought. He might even be a very sick man. If he became verbally violent and abusive, if he were irrational, she would need to have a clear head to deal with him. She would call him tomorrow, when she had regained some of her strength.

She yawned and turned over and drifted off to sleep. She didn't dream any more, and when she woke at ten o'clock, she was refreshed and newly excited by last night's success.

She called Michael, but he wasn't home. Unless he'd changed shifts in the past six months, he didn't go to work until noon, and she decided to try his number again in half an hour.

After retrieving the morning newspaper from the front stoop, she read the rave review of *Magyck!* written by the *Review-Journal*'s entertainment critic. He couldn't find anything wrong with the show. His praise was so effusive that, even reading it by herself, in her own kitchen, she was slightly embarrassed by it.

She ate a light breakfast of grapefruit juice and one English muffin, then went to Danny's room to box up his belongings. When she opened the door, she stopped, stunned by what she saw.

The room was a mess. The airplane models were no longer in the display case; they were strewn across the floor, and a few of them were broken. Danny's collection of paperbacks had been pulled from the bookcase and tossed into every corner. The tubes of glue, miniature bottles of enamel, and model-crafting tools that had stood on his desk were now on the floor, with everything else. A poster of one of the boy's baseball idols had been ripped apart; it hung from the wall in several pieces. The Star Wars toys had been knocked off the headboard. The closet doors were open, and all the clothes inside appeared to have been thrown on the floor. The game table had been overturned. The easel lay on the carpet, the chalkboard facing down.

Shaking with rage, Tina slowly crossed the

room, carefully stepping through the debris. She stopped at the easel, set it up as it belonged, hesitated, then turned the chalkboard side of it toward her.

**NOT DEAD**

'Damn!' she said, furious.

Vivian Meddler had been in to clean last evening, but this simply wasn't the kind of thing that Vivian would be capable of doing. If the mess had been here when Vivian arrived, the old woman would have cleaned it up and would have left a note about what she'd found. Clearly, the intruder had come in after Mrs. Neddler had left.

Fuming, Tina went through the house, meticulously checking every window and door. There was no sign of forced entry.

In the kitchen again, she called Michael. He still didn't answer. She slammed down the phone.

She pulled the yellow pages from a drawer and leafed through them until she found the advertisements for locksmiths. She chose the company with the largest ad and dialed their number.

'Anderlingen Lock and Security,' said the woman who answered the phone.

'Your ad in the yellow pages says you can have a man here to change my locks in one hour.'

'That's our emergency service. It costs more.'

'I don't care what it costs,' Tina said.

'But if you just put your name on our work list, we'll most likely have a team there by four o'clock this afternoon, tomorrow morning at the latest. And the regular service is forty percent cheaper than an emergency job.'

'Vandals were in my house last night,' Tina said.

'What a world we live in,' said the woman at Anderlingen.

'They wrecked a lot of stuff—'

'Oh, I'm sorry to hear that.'

'—so I want the locks changed immediately.'

'Of course.'

'And I want good locks installed. The best you've got.'

'Just give me your name and address, and I'll send a team out right away.'

A couple of minutes later, having completed the call, Tina went back to Danny's room to survey the damage again. As she looked over the wreckage, she said aloud, 'What the hell do you want from me, Mike?'

She doubted that he would be able to answer that question even if he were there to hear it. What possible excuse could he have? What twisted logic could justify this sort of sick behavior? It was crazy, hateful.

She shivered.

# 11

Tina got to the MGM Grand Hotel at ten minutes till two, Wednesday afternoon, and she left her VW Rabbit with a valet parking attendant.

The Grand was one of the most popular hotels in town, and on this last day of the year it was packed. At least two or three thousand people were in the casino, which was larger than a football field. Hundreds of gamblers – pretty young women, sweet-faced grandmothers, young dudes in jeans and body-shirts, older men in expensive but nonetheless tacky leisure outfits, a few guys in three-piece suits, salesmen, doctors, mechanics, secretaries, attorneys, Americans from all of the Western states, junketeers from many of the Eastern cities, Japanese tourists, some Frenchmen, a sprinkling of Arab men – sat at the semi-elliptical blackjack tables, pushing money and chips forward, sometimes taking back their winnings, eagerly grabbing the cards that were dealt from the five-deck shoes, each of them reacting in one of several predictable ways: some players squealed with delight; some grumbled; others smiled ruefully and shook their heads; some of them teased the dealers, pleading for better cards; and still others were silent, polite, attentive, and businesslike, as if they thought they were engaged in some reasonable form of investment planning. Hundreds of other people stood behind the players, watching, waiting for a seat to open. At the craps tables the crowds, composed primarily of men, were more boisterous than the blackjack aficionados; they screamed, howled, cheered, groaned, encouraged the shooter, and prayed loudly to the dice. On the left, slot machines ran the entire length of the casino, bank after bank of them, brightly and colorfully lighted, attended by gamblers who were more vocal than the card players but not as loud as the craps shooters. On the right, beyond the craps tables, halfway down the long room, elevated from the main floor, the white-marble and brass baccarat pit catered to a more affluent and sedate group of gamblers; at baccarat the pit boss and the floormen and the dealers all wore tuxedos. And everywhere in the gigantic casino, there were cocktail waitresses in brief costumes, revealing long legs and lots of cleavage; they bustled here and there, back and forth, as if they were the threads that bound the crowd together.

Tina pressed through the milling onlookers who filled the wide center aisle, and she located

Michael almost at once. He was dealing blackjack at one of the first tables. It was a five-dollar-minimum game, and all seven seats were taken. Michael was grinning, chatting with the players. Some dealers were cold and uncommunicative, but Michael always said that the day went faster if you were friendly with people. Not unexpectedly, he had always received more tips than most dealers did.

Michael was lean and blond, with eyes nearly as blue as Tina's. He looked a bit like Robert Redford, almost too pretty. It was no surprise that women players tipped him more often and more generously than did men.

When Tina squeezed into the narrow gap between the tables and caught Michael's attention, his reaction to her was far different from what she had expected. She'd thought the very sight of her would wipe the smile off his face. Instead, his smile broadened, and there seemed to be genuine delight in his eyes.

He was shuffling cards when he saw her, and he continued to shuffle while he spoke. 'Hey, hello there. You look terrific, Tina. A sight for sore eyes.'

She wasn't prepared for him to be pleasant, and she was put off her stride by the warmth of his greeting. 'Uh . . . thank you.'

'That's a nice sweater. I like it. You always looked good in blue.'

She smiled uneasily and tried to remember that she had come here to accuse him of playing a cruel prank on her. 'Look, Michael, I have to talk to you.'

He glanced at his watch. 'I have a break coming up in five minutes.'

'Where should I meet you?'

'Why don't you wait right where you are? You can watch these nice people beat me out of a lot of money.'

Everyone playing at the table groaned, and they all had comments to make about the unlikely possibility that they might win anything from this dealer.

Michael grinned and winked at Tina.

She smiled woodenly.

She waited impatiently as the five minutes crawled by; she was never comfortable in a casino when it was busy. The frantic activity and the unrelenting excitement, which bordered on hysteria at times, abraded her nerves.

The huge room was so noisy that the blend of sounds seemed to become a visible substance, like a humid, yellow haze that hung in the air. Slot machines rang and beeped and whistled and buzzed; coins clanged into the high-resonance, metal jackpot trays that had been designed to draw fortune-seekers from all over the casino. Balls clattered around spinning roulette wheels. A five-piece band hammered out wildly amplified

94

pop music from the small stage in the open cocktail lounge beyond and slightly above the slot machines. The paging system blared names. Ice rattled in glasses as gamblers drank while they played. And everyone seemed to be talking at once.

When the time arrived for Michael to take his break, a replacement dealer took over the table, and Michael stepped out of the blackjack pit, into the center aisle. 'You want to talk?'

'Not here,' she said, half shouting. 'I can't hear myself think.'

'Let's go down to the arcade.'

'All right.'

To reach the escalators that would carry them down to the shopping arcade on the lower level, it was necessary for them to cross the entire casino. Michael led the way, gently pushing and elbowing through the holiday crowd, and Tina followed quickly in his wake, before the path he made could close up again.

Halfway across the long room, they stopped at a clearing where a middle-aged man lay on his back, unconscious, in front of a blackjack table. He was wearing a beige suit, a dark brown shirt, a beige-patterned tie. An overturned stool was behind his head, and several hundred dollars' worth of green chips were scattered on the carpet around him. Two uniformed security men were performing first aid on the man, loosening his tie and collar, taking his pulse; and a third guard was keeping curious customers out of the way.

Michael said, 'Heart attack, Pete?'

The third guard looked around. 'Hi, Mike. Nah, I don't think it's his heart. Looks like a combination of blackjack blackout and bingo bladder. He was sitting at that table for eight hours straight.'

On the floor, the man in the beige suit groaned; his eyes fluttered.

Shaking his head, obviously amused, Michael moved around the clearing and through the crowd on the other side.

When at last they reached the end of the casino and were on the escalators, heading down toward the shopping arcade, Tina said, 'What is blackjack blackout?'

'It's stupid is what it is,' Michael said, still amused. 'The guy sits down to play cards and gets so involved that he loses track of time, which is exactly what the management wants him to do, of course; that's why there aren't any windows or clocks in a casino. But once in a while, a guy *really* loses track, doesn't get up for hours and hours and hours, just keeps on playing like a zombie. Meanwhile, he's drinking too much. When he *does* finally stand up, he does it too fast. The blood drains from his head – *bang!* – and he faints dead away. Blackjack blackout.'

'Ah.'

'We see it all the time.'

'Bingo bladder?'

'Sometimes a player will get so interested in the game that he's virtually hypnotized by it. He's been drinking pretty regularly, but he's so deep in a trance that he can completely ignore the call of nature – until he has a bladder spasm. If it's really a bad one, he finds out his pipes have blocked up on him; he can't relieve himself, and he has to be taken to the hospital and catheterized.'

'My God, are you serious?'

'Yep.'

They stepped off the escalator, into the shopping arcade. Crowds of people surged past the souvenir shop, art galleries, jewelry stores, clothing stores, and other retail businesses, but they were not shoulder-to-shoulder as they were upstairs in the casino.

'I still don't see any place where we can talk privately,' Tina said.

'Let's walk down to the ice cream parlor and get a couple of pistachio cones. What do you say? You always liked pistachio.'

'I don't want any ice cream, Michael.'

She had lost the momentum occasioned by her anger, and now she was afraid of losing all sense of her purpose in coming to see him. He was trying so hard to be nice. That wasn't what she had expected. And it wasn't like Michael to be this way with her. At least it wasn't like the

Michael she had known for the past few years. He had been fun, charming, easy-going when they'd first been married, but he had not been that way with her in a long, long time. She was nonplussed.

'No ice cream,' she repeated. 'Just some talk.'

'Well, if you don't want some pistachio, *I* certainly do. I'll get a cone, and then we can go outside, take a walk around the parking lot. It's a fairly warm day.'

'How long is your break?'

'Twenty minutes. But I'm tight with the pit boss. He'll cover for me if I don't get back in time.'

The ice cream parlor was at the far end of the arcade, near the movie theater that played only old MGM films. As they walked, Michael continued to try to amuse her by telling her about other unusual maladies to which gamblers were prone.

'There's what we call ''Jackpot attack'',' Michael said. 'For years and years, people go home from Vegas and tell all their friends that they came out ahead of the game. Everyone pretends to be a winner. And when all of a sudden someone *does* hit it big, especially on a slot machine where it can happen in a flash, they're so surprised that they pass out. Heart attacks are more frequent around the slot machines than anywhere else in the casino, and a lot of the victims are people who've just lined up three bars and won a bundle.

'Then there's "Vegas syndrome". That's when someone gets so carried away with gambling and running from show to show that he forgets to eat for a whole day or longer. He or she; it happens to women as often as it does to men. Anyway, when he finally gets hungry and realizes he hasn't eaten, he gulps down a huge meal, and the blood rushes from his head to his stomach, and he passes out in the middle of the restaurant. It's not usually dangerous, except if he has a mouthful of food when he faints, because then he might choke to death.

'But my favorite is what we call the "time warp syndrome". People come here from a lot of dull places, and Vegas is like an adult Disneyland to them. There's so much going on, so much to see and do, constant excitement, that people get out of their normal rhythms. They go to bed at dawn, get up in the afternoon, and they lose track of what day it is. When the excitement wears off a little, they go to check out of the hotel, and they discover their three-day weekend has somehow turned into five days. They can't believe it. They think they're being overcharged somehow, and they argue with the desk clerks. When someone shows them a calendar and a daily newspaper, they're really shocked. They've been through a time warp and lost a couple of days. Isn't that weird?'

Michael kept up the friendly chatter while he got his ice cream. Then, as they stepped out of the rear entrance of the hotel and walked along the edge of the non-valet parking area in the sixty-five-degree winter sunshine, he said, 'So what did you want to talk about?'

Tina wasn't sure how to begin. Her original intention had been to accuse him of ripping apart Danny's room; she had been prepared to come on strong and hard with him, so that, even if he didn't want her to know he'd done it, he might be rattled enough to unwittingly reveal his guilt. But now, if she started making nasty accusations after he had been so pleasant to her, she would look like a hysterical harpy; and if she still had any advantage left at all, she would quickly lose it. At last she said, 'Some strange things have been happening at the house.'

'Strange? Like what?'

'I think someone broke in.'

'You *think*?'

'Well . . . I'm sure of it.'

'When did this happen?'

Thinking of the two words on the chalkboard, she said, 'Three times in the past week.'

He stopped walking and stared at her. 'Three times?'

'Yes. Last evening was the latest.'

100

'What do the police say?'

'I haven't called them.'

He frowned. 'Why not?'

'For one thing, nothing was taken.'

'You mean to tell me that somebody broke in three times but didn't steal anything?'

If he was faking innocence, he was a much better actor than she thought he was, and she thought she knew him very well indeed. After all, she had lived with him for a long time, through years of happiness and years of misery, and she had come to know the limits of his talent for deception and duplicity. She always had been able to tell when he was lying. She didn't think he was lying now. There was something peculiar in what had happened at the house. Perhaps he'd had nothing to do with it.

But if Michael hadn't torn up Danny's room, if Michael hadn't written those words on the chalkboard, then who had?

'Why would someone break in and leave without taking anything?'

'I think they were just trying to upset and frighten me.'

'Who would want to frighten you?' he asked, genuinely concerned.

She didn't know what to say.

'You've never been the kind of person who makes a lot of enemies,' he said. 'You're a damned hard woman to hate.'

'You managed,' she said, and that was as close as she could come to accusing him of anything.

He blinked in surprise. 'Oh, no. No, no, Tina. I never hated you. I was disappointed by the changes in you. I was angry with you. Angry and hurt. I'll admit that. There was a lot of bitterness on my part. Definitely. But it was never as bad as hatred.'

She sighed.

Michael hadn't wrecked Danny's room. She was absolutely sure of that now.

'Tina?'

'I'm sorry. I shouldn't have bothered you with this. I'm not really sure why I did,' she lied. 'I ought to have called the police right away.'

He licked his ice-cream cone and studied her for a moment. Then he smiled and said, 'I understand. It's hard for you to get around to it. You don't know how to begin. So you come to me with this story.'

'Story? Michael, it's not just a story.'

'Relax. It's okay, Tina,' he said gently.

'Someone *has* been breaking into the house.'

'I understand how you feel.' His smile changed; it was smug now. 'I really do understand, Tina,' he said softly, in a reassuring and somewhat condescending tone of voice. 'You don't need an excuse to ask me what you've come here to ask. You don't need a story about someone breaking into the house. I understand, and I'm with you.

So go ahead. Don't feel awkward about it. Just get right down to it. Go ahead and say it.'

She was perplexed. 'Say what?'

'We let the marriage go off the rails. But there at first, for a good many years, we had a great thing going. We can have it again if we really want to try for it.'

She was stunned. 'Are you serious?'

'I've been thinking about it the last few days. When I saw you walk into the casino a while ago, I knew I was right. As soon as I saw you, I knew everything was going to turn out exactly like I had it figured.'

'You *are* serious.'

'Sure,' he said, mistakenly seeing happiness in her astonishment. 'Now that you've had your fling as a producer, you're ready to settle down. That makes a lot of sense, Tina.'

*Fling!* she thought angrily. He still persisted in regarding her as a flighty woman who wanted to take a fling at being a big Vegas producer. The insufferable bastard! She was furious, but she said nothing; she didn't trust herself to speak, for she was afraid she would start screaming at him the instant she opened her mouth.

'There's more to life than just having a flashy career,' Michael said pontifically. 'Home life counts for something. Home and family. That has to be a part of life, too. Maybe it's the most important part. These last few days, as your show's been getting ready to open, I've had the feeling that you might finally realize you need something more in life, something a lot more emotionally satisfying than whatever it is you can get out of just producing stage shows.'

Tina's ambition was, in part, what led to the dissolution of their marriage; the problem wasn't so much the fact that she had a yearning to succeed; the problem lay primarily in Michael's childish attitude toward her. He was happy being a blackjack dealer; his salary and his good tips were enough for him, and he was content to coast through the years. But merely drifting along in the currents of life wasn't enough for her. As Tina had struggled to move up from dancer to costumer to choreographer to lounge-revue coordinator to producer, Michael had been displeased with her commitment to work. She had never neglected him and Danny. She had been determined that neither of them would have reason to feel that his importance in her life had diminished. Danny had been wonderful; Danny had understood. Michael couldn't or wouldn't. Gradually Michael's displeasure over her ambition was complicated by a darker emotion; he grew jealous of even her smallest successes. She had tried to encourage him to seek advances in his own line of work – from dealer to floorman to pit boss to something even higher in casino management – but he had had no interest in climbing that ladder. He became waspish, petulant. Eventually he started seeing other women. She was shocked by his reaction, then confused, and at last deeply saddened. The only way she could have held on to her husband was to abandon her new career, and she had refused to do that.

In time Michael had made it clear to her that he hadn't actually ever loved the real Christina. He didn't tell her that directly, but his behavior said as much. He had adored only the showgirl, the dancer, the cute little thing that other men coveted, the pretty woman whose very presence at his side had inflated his ego. As long as she remained just a dancer, as long as she devoted most of her life to him, as long as she hung on his arm and simpered and looked delicious, he approved of her. But the moment she wanted to be something more than a sex object, he rebelled. Badly hurt by that discovery, she had given him the freedom that he had wanted.

And now he actually thought she was going to come crawling back to him. That was why he'd smiled when he'd seen her standing at his blackjack table. That was why he had been so charming. The size of his ego astounded her.

He stood in front of her, in the sunshine, his white shirt decorated with shimmering bands of reflected light that bounced off the chrome bumpers of the parked cars, and he favored her with that self-satisfied, superior smile that made her feel as cold as this winter day was meant to be.

Once, long ago, she had loved him very much. But now she couldn't imagine how or why she'd cared.

'Michael, in case you haven't heard, *Magyck!* is a hit. A big hit.'

'Sure,' he said. 'I know that, baby. And I'm happy for you. I'm happy for you *and* me. Now that you've proved whatever you needed to prove, you can relax.'

'Michael, I intend to continue working as a producer. I'm not going to—'

'Oh, I don't expect you to give it up,' he said magnanimously. 'No, no. Of course not. It's good for you to have something to dabble in. I see that now. But with *Magyck!* running successfully, you won't have all that much to do; it won't be like before.'

'Michael—' she began, intending to tell him that she was going to stage another show within the next year, that she didn't want to be represented by only one production at a time, and that she even had distant designs on New York and Broadway, where the return of Busby Berkeley-style musicals might be greeted with cheers.

But he was so involved with his fantasy that he wasn't aware that she had no wish to be part of it. He interrupted her before she'd said more than his name. 'We can do it, Tina. It was good for us once, those early years. It can be good again. We're still young. We have time to start another family. Maybe even two boys and two girls. That's what I've always wanted.'

When he paused to lick his ice-cream cone, she said, 'Michael, that's not the way it's going to be.'

'Well, maybe you're right. Maybe a large family isn't such a wise idea these days, what with inflation and all the turmoil in the world. But we can take care of two easily enough, and maybe we'll get lucky and have one boy and one girl. Of course we'll wait a year or so. I'm sure there's a lot of work to do on a show like *Magyck!* even after it opens. We'll wait until you're sure it's running smoothly, until it doesn't need much of your time. Then we can—'

'Michael, stop it!' she said harshly.

He blinked.

'I'm not feeling unfulfilled these days,' she said. 'I'm not pining for the domestic life. You don't understand me one bit better now than you did when we divorced'.

His expression of surprise turned slowly to a frown.

She said, 'I didn't make up that story about someone breaking into the house just so you could play the strong, reliable man to my imitation of a weak, frightened female. Someone really *did* break in. I came to you because I thought . . . Well, that doesn't matter any more.' She turned away from him and started toward the rear entrance of the hotel, out of which they'd come just a few minutes ago.

'Wait!' Michael said, 'Tina, wait!'

She stopped, looked back at him.

He hurried to her. 'I'm sorry. It's my fault, Tina. I botched it. Jesus, I was babbling like an idiot. I didn't let you do it your way. I knew what you wanted to say, but I should have let you say it at your own speed. I was wrong. But it's just that I was excited, Tina. That's all. I should have shut up and let *you* get around to it first. I'm sorry. I really am sorry, baby.' His ingratiating, boyish grin was back. 'Don't get mad at me. We both want the same thing: a home life, a good family life. Let's not throw away this chance.'

She glared at him. 'Yes, I want a home life, a satisfying family life. You're right about that. But you're wrong about everything else. I don't want to be a producer merely because I need a sideline to dabble in. *Dabble!* Michael, that's stupid. No one gets a show like *Magyck!* off the ground by dabbling. I can't believe you said that! It wasn't a fling. It was a hard, mentally and physically debilitating experience, and I loved every minute of it! God willing, I'm going to do it again. And again and again and again. I'm going to produce shows that'll make *Magyck!* look amateurish by comparison. Some day I may also be a mother

108

again. And I'll be a damned good mother, too. A good mother and a good producer. I have the intelligence and the talent to be more than just one thing. And I certainly can be more than just your trinket and your housekeeper.'

'Now wait a minute,' he said, beginning to get angry. 'Wait just a damned minute. You don't—'

She interrupted him. For years she had been filled with hurt and bitterness. She had never vented any of her black anger because, initially, she'd wanted to hide it from Danny; she hadn't wanted to turn him against his father. Later, after Danny was dead, she'd repressed her feelings because she'd known that Michael truly had been suffering from the loss of his child, and she hadn't desired to add to his misery. But now some of the acid came out of her as she cut him off in mid-sentence and said, 'You were wrong to think I'd come crawling back. Why on earth would I? What do you have to give me that I can't get elsewhere? You've never been much of a giver, anyway. You only give when you're sure of getting back twice as much. You're basically a taker, Michael. And before you give me any more of that treacly talk about your great love of the family lifestyle, let me remind you that it wasn't *me* who tore our family apart. It wasn't me who jumped from bed to bed. You were the one who started fucking anything that breathed, and then you flaunted each cheap little affair in order to hurt me. It was *you* who didn't come home at night. It was you who went away for weekends with your girlfriends. And let me tell you something, Michael. Those bed-hopping weekends broke my heart, and that was what you hoped to do; so that was all right with you. But did you ever stop to realize what effect your absences had on Danny? If you loved family life so much, why didn't you spend all those weekends with your son?'

'So I'm not a giver, huh? Who gave you the house you're living in? Who was it had to move into an apartment when we separated, and who was it kept the house?'

He was trying desperately to deflect her and change the course of the argument. She could see what he was up to, and she was not going to be distracted from her main intention.

She said, 'Don't be pathetic, Michael. You know damned well that the down payment for the house came out of my earnings. You always spent your money on fast cars and good clothes. I paid every loan installment. You know that. And I never asked for alimony. Anyway, all of that's beside the point. We were talking about family life, about Danny.'

'Now you listen to me,' Michael said angrily.

'No. It's your turn to listen. After all these years, it's finally your turn to listen. If you know how. You could have taken Danny away for the

110

weekend if you didn't want to be near me. You could have gone camping with him. You could have taken him down to Disneyland for a couple of days. Or down to the Colorado River to do some fishing. But you were too busy using all those women to hurt me and to prove to yourself what a great stud you were. You could have enjoyed that time with your son. He missed you, Michael. He didn't understand why you weren't there, and he missed you. You could have had that precious time with him. But you didn't want it. And as it turned out, Danny didn't have much time left.'

Michael was milk-white, trembling. His eyes were dark with rage. 'You're the same god-damned bitch you always were.'

She sighed and sagged a bit. She was exhausted. When she finished telling him off, she felt pleasantly wrung out, as if some evil, nervous energy had been drained from her.

'You're the same ball-breaking bitch,' Michael said.

'I don't want to fight with you, Michael. I'm even sorry if some of what I said about Danny hurt you, although, God knows, you deserve to hear it. I don't really want to hurt you. Oddly enough, I don't really hate you any more. I don't feel anything for you. Not anything at all.'

She walked away, leaving him in the sunshine,

111

the ice cream melting down the cone onto his hand.

She walked back through the shopping arcade, rode the escalator up to the casino, and made her way through the noisy crowd to the front doors. One of the valet parking attendants brought her car, and she drove down the MGM Grand's steeply slanted exit drive. She headed toward the Desert Mirage Hotel, where she had an office, and where there was work waiting to be done.

She had driven only a block when she was forced to pull to the side of the road. She couldn't see where she was going because hot tears were streaming down her face. She put the car in park, and, surprising herself, she began to sob loudly.

At first she wasn't sure what she was crying about; she just surrendered to the wracking grief that swept through her and did not question it. After a while she decided that she was crying for Danny. Poor, sweet Danny. He'd hardly begun to live. It wasn't fair. And she was crying for herself, too, and for Michael. She was crying for all the things that might have been, and for what could never ever be again.

In a few minutes she got control of herself. She dried her eyes and blew her nose.

Chiding herself, she said aloud, 'Stop being so gloomy, for God's sake! You've had enough gloom in your life. A whole hell of a lot of gloom. Try for some *happiness*, why don't you? Think positive. Maybe the past wasn't so great, but the future looks pretty damned good.'

She inspected her face in the rear-view mirror to see how much damage the crying jag had done. She looked better than she had thought she would. Her eyes were red at the corners, but she wouldn't pass for Dracula. She opened her purse, found her makeup and powder, and touched up the tear stains as best she could.

She pulled the VW back into traffic and headed for the Desert Mirage again.

A block farther, as she waited at a red light, she realized that she had a mystery on her hands. She was positive that Michael had not done the damage in Danny's bedroom. But then, who *had* done it? No one else had a key. It would take a skilled burglar to break in without leaving a trace. And why would a first-rate burglar leave without taking something? Why would he break in only to write on Danny's chalkboard and to wreck the dead boy's things?

It was weird. When she had suspected Michael of doing the dirty work, she had been disturbed and distressed; but she really had not been scared by it. However, if there were a *stranger* out there who wanted her to feel more pain over the loss of her child, that was definitely unsettling. That was scary because it didn't make sense. A stranger? It must be. Michael was the only person she knew who had blamed her for Danny's death. Not one other relative or acquaintance had ever suggested that she was even indirectly responsible. Yet the taunting words on the chalkboard and the destruction in the bedroom seemed to be the work of someone who felt that she should be accountable for the accident. Which meant it had to be someone she didn't even know. Why would a stranger harbor such passionate feelings about Danny's death?

The red light changed.

A horn tooted behind her.

As she drove across the intersection and into the entrance drive that led to the Desert Mirage Hotel, Tina couldn't shake the creepy feeling that she was being watched by someone who meant to harm her. She looked in the rear-view mirror to see if she was being followed. As far as she could tell, no one was tailing her.

# 12

The third floor of the Desert Mirage Hotel was given over entirely to management and clerical personnel. Here, there was no flash, no Vegas glamour. This was where the work got done. This was the place that housed the machinery that supported the walls of fantasy, beyond which the tourists gamboled.

Tina had a moderately large office, paneled in dark wood, with comfortable furniture and low, amber lighting. One wall was covered by heavy, wine-colored drapes that blocked out the fierce desert sun. The windows behind the drapes faced the Las Vegas Strip.

At night the Strip was a dazzling sight, a surging river of light, red and blue and green and yellow and purple and pink and every color within the visual range of the human eye, incandescent and neon, flashing, rippling, hundred-foot-long signs, five-hundred-foot-long signs, signs towering four and five stories above the street, glittering, winking, thousands of miles of bright glass tubing filled with glowing gas, blinking, swirling, hundreds of thousands of bulbs, spelling out hotel names, forming pictures with light, computer-controlled designs ebbing and flowing, an insane but furiously beautiful excess of energy consumption.

During the day, however, the merciless sun was unkind to the Strip. In the hard, sharp light, the enormous architectural confections were not always appealing; at times, in spite of the billions of dollars of value it represented, the Strip looked slightly grubby.

The view of the fabled boulevard was wasted on Tina; she didn't often make use of it. Because she was seldom in her office at night, the drapes were rarely open. This afternoon, as usual, the drapes were shut, the office was shadowy, and she was at her desk in a pool of soft light.

Tina was poring over a final bill for carpentry work on some of the *Magyck!* sets when Angela, her secretary, stepped in from the outer office and said, 'Is there anything more you need before I leave?'

Tina glanced at her watch. 'It's only a quarter of four.'

'I know,' Angela said. 'But we get off at four today because it's New Year's Eve.'

'Oh, of course,' Tina said. 'I completely forgot about the holiday.'

'If you want me to, I could stay a little longer.'

'No, no, no,' Tina said. 'You go home at four with the others.'

'So is there anything more you need?'

Leaning back in her chair, Tina said, 'Yes. In fact, there is something . . . A lot of our regular junketeers and high rollers couldn't make it to the VIP opening of *Magyck!* I'd like you to get their names from the computer, plus a list of the wedding anniversaries of those who're married.'

'Can do,' Angela said. 'What've you got in mind?'

'During the year I'm going to send special invitations to the married ones, asking them to spend their anniversaries at the Desert Mirage, with room and board on the house for two or three days, of course. We'll sell it this way: ''Spend the magic night of your anniversary with the magic world of *Magyck!*'' Something like that. We'll make it very romantic. We'll serve them champagne at the show. It'll be a great promotion, don't you think?' She raised her hands, as if framing her next words, ' ''The Desert Mirage – a *Magyck!* place for lovers''.'

'The hotel ought to be happy,' Angela said. 'That'll get us a lot of favorable media coverage.'

'The casino bosses will be happy because a lot of our high rollers will probably make an extra trip this year. The average gambler won't cancel other planned trips to Vegas; he'll just add on an extra trip for his anniversary. And I'll be happy because the whole stunt will generate more talk about the show.'

'It's a great idea,' Angela said. 'I'll go coax the computer right away.'

Tina returned to her inspection of the carpenter's bill, and after a minute, the high-speed clatter of the computer-run typewriter drifted in from the outer office.

Angela was back at five minutes past four with the requested information. It was all contained on a five-yard-long sheet of print-out paper that she had folded into a compact, accordion-like bundle.

'Thank you,' Tina said.

'No trouble.'

'Are you shivering?'

'Yeah,' Angela said. 'Must be some problem with the air conditioning or something. While I was getting feedback from the computer, my office got chilly.'

'It's warm enough in here,' Tina said.

'Maybe it's just me. Well, I'll be going now.'

'Out to a party?'

'Yeah, later. Over on Rancho Circle.'

'Millionaire's Row?'

'Yeah. It's going to be a big bash. My boyfriend's boss lives over there.' She turned to leave, looked back, 'Happy New Year, Tina.'

'Happy New Year.'

'See you Monday.'

'Oh? Oh yeah, that's right. It's a four-day weekend. Well, just watch out for that hangover.'

Angela grinned. 'There's at least one out there with my name on it; that's for sure.'

Tina finished checking the carpenter's bill and approved it for payment.

Alone now on the third floor, she sat in the pool of amber light at her desk, surrounded by shadows, and she yawned. Another hour. She'd work until five o'clock, and then go home. She'd need two hours to get ready for her date with Elliot Stryker. She smiled when she thought of him, then picked up the print-out, anxious to finish her work.

It was amazing how much information the hotel had on its favored customers. If she needed to know how much money each of these people earned in a year, the computer could tell her. It could tell her each man's preferred brand of liquor, each wife's favorite flower and perfume, the make of car they drove, the names and ages of their children, the nature of any illness or other medical conditions they might have, their favorite foods, their favorite colors, their tastes in music, their political affiliations, and dozens, perhaps hundreds, of other things – both important and trivial – about them. These were customers to whom the hotel wished to cater, and the more the Desert Mirage knew about them, the better it could serve them. Though the hotel collected this data with, for the most part, the customers' happiness in mind, Tina wondered how pleased these people would be to learn that the Desert Mirage kept fat dossiers on them.

She scanned the list of VIP customers who hadn't attended the opening of *Magyck!* Using a red pencil, she circled those names that were followed by anniversary dates, trying to get some idea of how large a promotion she was letting herself in for. She had counted only twenty-two names when she came to an incredible message that the computer had inserted in the list.

Her heart seemed to stop for a moment.

Her chest felt tight. She couldn't breathe.

She stared at what the computer had printed, and fear welled up in her – dark, cold, oily fear.

Between the names of two high rollers, there were five lines of type that had nothing to do with the information she had requested.

**NOT DEAD**
**NOT DEAD**
**NOT DEAD**
**NOT DEAD**
**NOT DEAD**

The paper rattled as her hands began to shake.

First at home. In Danny's bedroom. Now here. Who was doing this to her?

Angela?

No. Absurd.

Angela was a sweet kid. She wasn't capable of anything as vicious as this. Angela hadn't noticed this interruption in the print-out because she hadn't watched the machine typing, and later she had folded up the long paper without really looking at it.

Besides, even though Angela could have programmed this bit of nastiness into the computer, she couldn't have broken into the house. Angela wasn't a master burglar, for God's sake!

Tina quickly unfolded the print-out, looking for more of the sick prankster's work. She found it after just another twenty-six names.

**DANNY ALIVE**
**DANNY ALIVE**
**HELP**
**HELP**
**HELP ME**

Her heart was no longer frozen. It was beating now. It was hammering like an automated industrial sledge: *wham, wham, wham, wham!*

She was suddenly aware of how very alone she was. More likely than not, she was the only person on the entire third floor.

She thought of the man in her nightmare, the man in black whose face had been lumpy with maggots, and the shadows in the corner of her office seemed darker and deeper than they had been only a moment ago.

She stood up, letting the long print-out unravel onto the floor, so that she could pull it through her hands faster. She scanned another forty names, and she cringed when she saw what else the computer had printed.

**I'M AFRAID**
**I'M AFRAID**
**GET ME OUT**
**GET ME OUT OF HERE**
**PLEASE . . . PLEASE**
**HELPHELPHELPHELP**

That was the last insertion. The remainder of the list was as it should be.

Tina threw the print-out on the floor and went into the outer office.

Angela had turned the light off. Tina switched it on.

She went to Angela's desk, sat in the typist's chair, swung away from the typewriter to the computer terminal. She switched it on, and the read-out screen glowed green.

In the center drawer of the desk, there was a book that listed the code numbers with which a programmer could withdraw information from the computer's memory banks, which were housed in another room at the far end of the building.

Tina paged through the book until she found the code she needed to call up the list of the hotel's best customers. The code number was 1001012, and it was identified as the access for 'Comps', which meant 'complimentary guests', which was a euphemism for 'big losers', who were never asked to pay their room and board after they dropped a small fortune in the casino.

Tina typed her own personal access number into the terminal – EO13331555. Because a lot of the material in the hotel's files was confidential information about high rollers, and because the Desert Mirage's list of favored customers would be of great value to competitors, only approved people could obtain data. After a moment's hesitation, the computer asked for her name, and she typed that out, and it matched her number to her name. Then:

## CLEARED

She typed in the code number for the list of complimentary guests, and the machine responded at once.

## PROCEED

Her fingers were damp. She wiped them on her slacks and then quickly tapped out her request. She asked the computer for the same information that Angela had requested of it a while ago. The names and addresses of VIP customers who had missed the opening of *Magyck!* – along with the wedding anniversaries of those who were married – began to flash on the screen. At the same time, the computer printed the names and addresses on the roll of paper that fed the printer.

It clattered rapidly through twenty names, forty, sixty, seventy, without typing the lines about Danny that had been on the first print-out. Tina waited until at least a hundred names had been listed before she decided that the system had been programmed to print the lines about Danny only one time, only on her office's first data request of the afternoon, and on no later call-up. She tapped the key that was marked CANCEL. The machine stopped; the words on the cathode-ray tube vanished, leaving only the glowing green background.

Just a couple of hours ago, she had concluded that the person behind this cruel prank had to be a stranger. But how could any stranger so easily gain entrance to both her house and the hotel computer? Didn't he, after all, have to be someone she knew?

But who?

And *why*?

What stranger could possibly hate her so much?

Fear, like an uncoiling snake, twisted and slithered inside of her, and she shivered.

Then she realized it wasn't only fear that made her quiver. The air was chilly.

She remembered the complaint that Angela had made earlier. It hadn't seemed important at the time.

But the room had been warm when Tina had first come in to use the computer terminal, and now it was quite cool. How could the temperature have dropped so far in such a short time? She listened for the sound of the air conditioner, but the telltale whisper wasn't issuing from the wall vents. Nevertheless, the room definitely was much colder than it had been only a couple of minutes ago.

With a sharp, loud, electronic snap that startled Tina, the computer abruptly began to churn out additional data, although she hadn't requested any. She glanced at the banging automatic typewriter, then at the words that were flickering on the screen.

**NOT DEAD NOT DEAD
NOT DEAD NOT DEAD
NOT IN THE GROUND
NOT DEAD
GET ME OUT OF HERE
GET ME OUT OUT OUT**

The message stopped. The typewriter fell silent. The room was getting colder by the second.

125

Or was it just her imagination?

She had the crazy feeling that she wasn't alone. The man in black. Even though he was only a creature from a nightmare, and even though it was utterly impossible for him to be here in the flesh, she couldn't shake the heart-stopping feeling that he was in the room. She tried to laugh at herself. She couldn't. The man in black. The man with the evil, fiery eyes. The yellow-toothed grin. Behind her. Reaching toward her with a hand that would be cold and damp. She looked wildly around, but no one had come into the room.

Of course.

He was only a nightmare monster.

How stupid of her.

Yet she felt that she was not alone.

She didn't want to look back at the screen, but she did; she had to.

The words were still burning there.

Then they disappeared.

She managed to break the grip of fear just a little, the iron grip that had paralyzed her, and she put her fingers on the programmer's keyboard. She tried to tap in a question. She wanted to know who had generated this unrequested data feedback. She intended to ask if the words about Danny had merely come off a tape or whether, perhaps, those hateful lines had been typed into the computer just seconds ago, by someone at another terminal in another office.

If the lines had not come off pre-recorded magnetic tape – and she had an almost psychic feeling that the perpetrator of this vicious prank was in the building *now* – then the sonofabitch might be on the third floor. She might be able to get up, search for him, and catch him before he left. She pictured herself moving down the long, long hallway, opening doors, looking into silent, deserted offices, until at last she found a man sitting at another programmer's console. He would turn toward her, astonished that she had caught him, and she would see his face and finally know who he was.

And then what?

Would he kill her?

That was a new thought: the possibility that his ultimate goal was to do something much worse than just scare her.

She hesitated, fingers on the keyboard, not certain if she should ask questions of the computer. She probably wouldn't get the answers she needed, and she would only be acknowledging her presence to whomever might be out there at another console. Then she realized that, if he really was nearby, he already knew she was in her office, alone. She had nothing to lose by querying the computer. But when she tried to type in her first question, the machine wouldn't let her. It started printing out another message of its own. If there was a man at another keyboard, he either didn't want to engage her in a dialogue or wasn't capable of manipulating the computer well enough to do that.

The room grew colder, colder.

On the cathode-ray tube:

> **I'M COLD AND I HURT**
> **MOM? CAN YOU HEAR?**
> **I'M SO COLD**
> **I HURT BAD**
> **GET ME OUT OF HERE**
>
> **PLEASE PLEASE PLEASE**
> **NOT DEAD NOT DEAD**

The screen glowed with those words for a second, then went blank.

Again, she tried to feed in her questions. But the keyboard seemed to be frozen.

She still felt another presence in the room. Indeed, the feeling was growing stronger as the room got colder.

How could he make the room get colder without using the air conditioner? Whoever he was, he could use a programmer's console; she could accept that. But how could he possibly make the air grow so cold so fast?

Suddenly, as the screen began to fill with the

same seven-line message that had just been wiped
from it, Tina had had enough. She switched the
console off, and the green glow faded from the
screen.

As she was getting up from the low chair, the
terminal switched itself on.

**I'M COLD AND I HURT**
**GET ME OUT OF HERE**
**PLEASE PLEASE PLEASE**

'Get you out of where?' she screamed. 'The
*grave*?'

**GET ME OUT OUT OUT**

She had to get a grip on herself. She had
just spoken to the machine as if she actually
thought she was talking to Danny. It wasn't
Danny tapping out those words on the cathode-
ray tube. Danny didn't know how to use a
programmer's keyboard. And goddamn it, *Danny
was dead!*

She snapped the machine off.

It turned itself on.

She started to cry. She had to be losing her
mind. The damned thing *couldn't* be switching
itself on.

She hurried around the desk, banging her hip
against one corner of it, heading for the wall

socket as the automatic typewriter slammed out its message in a demonic frenzy.

**GET ME OUT OF HERE**
**GET ME OUT OUT**
**OUT**
**OUT**

Tina stooped beside the wall outlet from which the terminal received its electrical power and its data feed. She took hold of the two lines – one heavy cable and one ordinary insulated wire – and they seemed to come alive in her hands, like a pair of snakes, resisting her. She jerked on them and pulled both plugs.

The console went dark.

It remained dark.

Immediately, rapidly, the room began to warm up.

'Thank God,' she said shakily.

She started around Angela's desk, wanting nothing more at the moment than to get off her rubbery legs and onto a chair, and suddenly the door to the hall opened, and she cried out in alarm.

*The man in black?*

Elliot Stryker looked in, surprised by her scream, and for an instant she was relieved to see him.

'Tina? What's wrong? Are you all right?'

She took a step toward him, but then she realized he might have come here straight from a computer terminal in one of the other third-floor offices. Could he be the man who'd been harassing her?

'Tina? My God, you're white as a ghost.'

He moved toward her.

She said, 'Stop! Wait!'

He stopped, perplexed.

Voice quavering, she said, 'What are you doing here?'

He blinked. 'I was in the hotel on business. I wondered if you might still be at your desk. I stopped in to see. I just wanted to say hello.'

'Were you playing around with one of the other computers . . . one of the other terminals?'

'What?' he asked, obviously baffled by her question.

'What were you doing on the third floor?' she demanded. 'Who could you possibly have been seeing? They've all gone home. I'm the only one here.'

Still puzzled but beginning to get a bit impatient with her, Elliot said, 'My business wasn't on the third floor. I had a meeting with Charlie Mainway over coffee, downstairs, in the restaurant. We finished our work a couple of minutes ago, and I came up to see if you were here. What's wrong with you?'

She stared at him intently.

131

'Tina? What's happened?'

She searched his face for any sign that he was lying, but his bewilderment seemed genuine. And if he were lying, he wouldn't have told her the story about Charlie and coffee, for that could be substantiated or disproven with only a minimum of effort; he would have come up with a better alibi if he really needed one. He was telling the truth.

She said, 'I'm sorry. I just . . . I had . . . an . . . an experience here . . . a weird . . .'

He went to her. 'What was it?'

As he drew near to her, he opened his arms, as if it was the most natural thing in the world for him to hold and comfort her, as if he had held her many times before, and she leaned against him in the same spirit of familiarity and comfort. She was no longer alone.

# 13

Tina kept a well-stocked bar in one corner of her office for those infrequent occasions when a business associate needed a drink after a long work session. This was the first time she'd ever had the need to tap those stores for herself. At her request, Elliot poured Rémy-Martin into two snifters and gave one glass to her; she couldn't pour for them because her hands were shaking too badly.

They sat on the beige sofa, more in the shadows than in the orange glow from the lamps. She was forced to hold her brandy snifter in both hands to keep it steady.

'I don't know where to begin,' Tina said. 'I guess I ought to start with Danny. Do you know about Danny?'

'Your son?'

'Yes.'

'Helen Mainway told me he died a little over a year ago.'

'Did she tell you how it happened?'

'No.'

'He was one of the Jaborski group.'

'Jaborski group?'

'I'm sure you've heard about it,' she said. 'It was on the front page of the *Review-Journal* for at least four or five days. Bill Jaborski was a wilderness expert, a scoutmaster, too. Every year he took a group of scouts up north, beyond Reno, into the High Sierras. They went on a seven-day wilderness survival excursion.'

'Yes,' Elliot said quietly, sadly. 'I remember now.'

'It was supposed to build character. And all the boys competed hard all year long for the chance to be selected to go on the trip. It was supposed to be perfectly safe. Bill Jaborski was supposed to be one of the ten best winter-survival experts in the world. That's what everyone said. And the other adult who went along, Tom Lincoln, was supposed to be almost as good as Bill. Supposed to be,' she said bitterly.

'If I remember correctly, they'd been taking kids into the mountains for years and years, and nobody had even been scratched,' Elliot said.

Tina swallowed some cognac; it tasted good, but it didn't burn away the chill at the center of her.

'Last year,' she said, 'Jaborski took fourteen boys between the ages of twelve and eighteen. All of them were top-notch scouts. All of them

134

died along with Jaborski and Tom Lincoln.'

'Have the authorities ever figured out exactly why it happened?'

'They know *how*,' she said. 'The group went into the mountains in a four-wheel-drive minibus that had been built for use on back roads in the winter. Huge tires. Chains. Even a snowplow on the front. They weren't supposed to go into the heart of the wilderness. Just into the fringes of it. No one in his right mind would take boys as young as twelve into the deepest parts of the Sierras, no matter how well prepared, supplied, and trained they were, no matter how strong they might be, no matter how many big brothers were available to look out for them. Jaborski planned to drive the minibus off the main highway, onto an old logging trail, if conditions permitted. From there they were going to hike for three days with snowshoes and backpacks, making a big circle around the bus, coming back to it at the end of the week. They had the best wilderness clothing, the best down-lined sleeping bags, the best winter tents, a lot of charcoal and other heat sources, plenty of food, and two wilderness experts to guide them. Perfectly safe, everyone said. Absolutely, perfectly safe. So what went wrong?'

She could no longer sit still. She got up and began to pace, taking another swallow of cognac.

Elliot said nothing. He seemed to know that

she had to go through the whole story to get it off her mind, even if, by now, he had remembered all of it and didn't need to be told.

'Something sure as hell went wrong,' she said. 'Because somehow, for some reason, they drove the bus more than *four* miles off the main highway, four miles off and a hell of a long way *up*, right up in the goddamned clouds. They drove up a steep, abandoned logging trail, a deteriorated dirt road so treacherous, so choked with snow, so heavily coated with ice that only a fool would have attempted to negotiate it any way but on foot. The bus . . . went over the edge.' She took a deep breath; it wasn't easy. 'The bus dropped a hundred feet . . . onto jagged rocks. The fuel tank exploded. The bus opened up like a tin can. Rolled another hundred feet into the trees. The kids . . . everyone . . . killed.' She looked hard at Elliot Stryker. 'Why? Why did a man like Bill Jaborski do something so incredibly stupid as that?'

Elliot, still sitting on the couch, shook his head and stared down at his cognac.

She didn't really expect him to answer her question. She wasn't actually asking it of him; if she was asking it of anyone, she was asking it of God. 'Why? Jaborski was the best. The very best. He was so good that he could safely take young boys into the Sierras for fourteen years, a challenge a lot of other winter survival experts wouldn't touch. Bill Jaborski was smart, tough, clever, and filled with respect for the dangers involved in what he did. He wasn't foolhardy. Why would he do something so dumb, so reckless, as to drive that far up that road in those conditions?'

Elliot looked up at her. There was kindness in his eyes, a deep sympathy. 'You'll probably never know the answer,' he said. 'I understand how hard it must be for you to live with the knowledge that you'll never have a satisfactory explanation.'

'Hard,' she said. 'Very hard.'

She returned to the couch and sat down.

He took her glass out of her hand. It was empty. She didn't remember finishing her cognac. He got up and headed toward the bar.

'No more for me,' she said. 'I don't want to get drunk.'

'Nonsense,' he said. 'In your condition, throwing off all that nervous energy the way you are, two brandies won't affect you in the slightest.'

He came back from the bar with more Rémy-Martin. This time she was able to hold the glass in one hand.

'Thank you, Elliot.'

'Just don't ask for a mixed drink,' he said. 'I'm the world's worst bartender. I can pour anything straight or over ice, but I can't even mix vodka and orange juice properly.'

'I wasn't thanking you for the drink. I was

thanking you for listening to all of that. You're a damned good listener, Elliot.'

'Most attorneys talk too much,' he said. 'I noticed that before I was even out of law school. Maybe they're always practicing, staying in form for courtroom debate. Anyway, I decided early on to be a lawyer who listened. As the years have gone by, I've found that I do a much better job for my clients because I listen to them and learn to know them so well.'

For a moment they sat in silence, sipping cognac.

Tina was still tense, but she no longer felt cold inside.

Elliot said, 'Losing your child like that would be just devastating. Even though it's been more than a year, I'm sure you've hardly begun to learn to live with the loss. Even so, it wasn't any recollection of your son that had you so upset when I walked in a little while ago.'

'In a way it was.'

'Want to talk about it?'

She did. She told him about the bizarre things that had been happening to her lately: the messages on Danny's chalkboard; the wreckage she'd found in the boy's room; the hateful, taunting words that had shown up on the computer lists.

Elliot looked at the print-outs with her, and together they examined the computer terminal in Angela's office. They plugged it in and tried to get it to repeat what it had done earlier, but they had no luck; the machine behaved exactly as it was meant to behave.

'Someone could have programmed it to spew out this stuff about Danny,' Elliot said. 'But I don't see how he could make the terminal switch itself on.'

'It happened,' she said.

'I don't doubt you. I just don't understand.'

'Someone could have come in at night; he could have done some special wiring on this programmer's board.'

'Seems far-fetched.'

'Not any more far-fetched than the rest of it.'

'What about the temperature change you mentioned?'

'What about it?'

'How could he have managed that?'

'I don't know.'

'And why would he bother?'

She shrugged.

'I mean,' Elliot said, 'even if he found some way to rig the air conditioner – and you said it *wasn't* the air conditioner – why would he go to all of that trouble? What would be the point?'

'I don't know,' she said again.

'Could the temperature change have been subjective?'

Tina frowned. 'Are you asking me if I imagined it?'

'You were frightened and—'

'But I'm sure I didn't imagine it. Angela felt the chill first, when she got the initial print-out with those lines in it about Danny. It isn't very likely that Angela and I *both* just imagined it.'

'True,' he said. He stared thoughtfully at the computer terminal for a few seconds, his dark eyes appearing to stare through it, and then he said, 'Come on.'

'Where?'

'Back in your office. I left my drink there. I need it to lubricate my thoughts.'

She followed him into the wood-paneled inner sanctum.

He picked up his brandy snifter from the low table in front of the sofa, and he sat on the edge of her desk. 'Who?' he asked. 'Who's doing it to you?'

'I haven't a clue.'

'You must have somebody in mind,' Elliot said.

'I wish I did.'

'Well, obviously, it's somebody who, at the very least, dislikes you, if he doesn't actually hate you. An ordinary prankster wouldn't go to all this trouble. It must be someone who has a burning desire to see you suffer. I'd venture to say this person, whoever he is – whoever he or *she* is – blames you for Danny's death. And he feels the boy's death as a deep, personal loss. So it can hardly be a stranger.'

Tina was disturbed by his analysis because it seemed so sensible, yet it led her right back into the same blind alley she'd traveled before. She paced back and forth between the desk and the drapery-covered windows. 'This afternoon I decided it *has* to be a stranger. I can't think of anyone I know who'd be capable of this sort of thing even if they did hate me enough to contemplate it. And I don't know of anyone but Michael who places any part of the blame for Danny's death on me.'

Elliot raised his eyebrows. 'Michael is your ex-husband?'

'Yes.'

'And he blames you for Danny's death?'

'He says I never should have let him go with Jaborski. But this isn't Michael's dirty work.'

'He sounds like an excellent candidate to me.'

'No.'

'Are you certain?'

'Absolutely. It's someone else.'

Elliot tasted his cognac. 'Well, it looks like maybe you'll need professional help to catch him in the middle of one of his tricks.'

'You mean the police?'

'I don't think the police would be much help in a thing like this. First of all, they probably wouldn't think it was serious enough for them to waste their time on it; after all, you haven't been threatened with harm or anything of that nature.'

'There's an implicit threat in all of this.'

'Oh, certainly. I agree. It's scary. But the cops are a very literal sort. They aren't much impressed by implied threats. Besides, to properly watch your house . . . well, that alone would require much more manpower than the police have to spare for anything except a murder case, a hot kidnapping, or a narcotics investigation.'

She stopped pacing in front of him. 'Then what did you mean when you said I'd probably need professional help to catch this creep?'

'Private detectives.'

'Isn't that a bit melodramatic?'

He smiled sourly. 'The person who's harassing you has a melodramatic streak a mile wide. It's never unwise to match like for like.'

She sighed and drank some cognac and sat down on the edge of the couch. 'I don't know . . . Maybe I'd hire private detectives, and they wouldn't catch anyone but me.'

'Send that one by me again.'

She had to take another small sip of cognac before she was able to say what was on her mind, and she realized that he had been right about the liquor having little effect on her; she felt more relaxed than she'd been ten minutes ago, but she wasn't even slightly tipsy. 'It's occurred to me,' she said, 'that maybe I wrote those words on Danny's chalkboard. Maybe I wrecked his room.'

'You've lost me.'

'I could have done all of it in my sleep.'

'That's ridiculous, Tina.'

'Is it? I thought I'd begun to get over Danny's death back in September. I started sleeping well then. I didn't dwell on it when I was alone, like I did for a long time. I thought I'd put the worst of the pain behind me. But a month ago I started dreaming about Danny again. The first week, it happened twice. The second week, four nights. And the past two weeks, I've dreamed about him every night without fail. And the dreams are getting worse all the time. They're full-fledged nightmares now.'

Elliot slid off the desk, returned to the couch, and sat beside her. 'What are they like?'

'I dream he's alive, trapped somewhere, usually in a deep pit or a gorge or a well, someplace underground. He's calling to me, begging me to save him. But I can't. I'm never able to reach him. And then the earth starts closing in around him, and I wake up screaming, soaked with sweat. And I . . . I always have this powerful feeling . . . this almost psychic feeling that Danny isn't really dead. It never lasts for long, but when I first wake up I'm sure he's alive somewhere. You see, I've convinced my conscious mind that my boy is dead, but when I'm asleep it's my subconscious mind that is in charge; and my subconscious just isn't convinced that Danny's gone.'

'So you think your subconscious could be making you sleepwalk. You think your subconscious is making you write out its rejection of Danny's death on his chalkboard.'

'Don't you believe that's possible?'

'I guess it is,' Elliot said. 'I'm no psychologist; however, it sounds like a viable theory to me. But I don't buy it. I'll admit I don't know you all that well yet, but I think I know you well enough to say that you wouldn't react that way. You're a person who meets problems head-on. If your inability to accept Danny's death was a serious problem, you wouldn't push it down into your subconscious; you'd learn to deal with it.'

She smiled. 'You have a pretty high opinion of me.'

'Yes,' he said. 'I do. Besides, if it was you who wrote on the chalkboard and smashed things in the boy's room, then it was also you who came in here during the night and programmed the hotel computer to spew out that stuff about Danny. Do you really think you're so far gone that you could do something like that and not remember it? Do you think you're schizophrenic?'

She sank back in the sofa, slouched down. 'No.'

'All right.'

'So where does that leave us?'

'Don't despair. We're making real progress.'

'We are?'

'Sure,' he said. 'We're eliminating possibilities. We've just crossed you off the list of suspects. And Michael. And I'm positive it can't be a stranger, which rules out most of the world.'

'And I'm just as positive it isn't a friend or a relative. So you know what that leaves?'

'What?'

She leaned forward, put her brandy snifter on the table, and for a moment she sat with her face in her hands.

'Tina?'

She lifted her head. 'I'm just trying to think how best to phrase what's on my mind. It's a wild idea. Ludicrous. Probably even sick. Now that you've convinced me that I'm not about to start frothing at the mouth, I don't want to say something that'll change both our minds about my sanity or lack of it.'

'I'm not going to think you're out of your head,' Elliot assured her. 'What is it? Tell me.'

She hesitated, trying to hear how it was going to sound before she said it, wondering if she really believed it enough even to give voice to it. The possibility of what she was going to suggest was so remote . . . yet . . . At last she just plunged into it: 'What I'm thinking is that maybe Danny *is* alive.'

Elliot cocked his head, studied her with those probing, dark eyes. 'Alive?'

'I never saw his body.'

'You didn't? Why not?'

'The coroner and the undertaker said it was in terrible condition, horribly mutilated, damaged by the cold and the accident. They didn't think it was a good idea for either me or Michael to see it. Neither of us would have been anxious to see the body even if it had been in perfect shape, so naturally we accepted the mortician's recommendations. It was a closed-coffin funeral.'

'How did the authorities identify the body?'

'They asked for pictures of Danny. But mainly I think they used dental records.'

'Dental records are almost as good as finger-prints.'

'Almost,' she said. 'But maybe Danny didn't die in that accident. Maybe he survived. Maybe someone out there knows where he is. Maybe that someone is trying to tell me that Danny's alive. Maybe there isn't any threat in all these strange things that have happened to me. Maybe someone's just dropping a series of hints, trying to wake me up to the fact that Danny isn't dead.'

'Too many maybes,' he said.

'Maybe not.'

Elliot put his hand on her shoulder, squeezed gently. 'Tina, you know that this theory doesn't make sense. Danny is dead.'

'See? You *do* think I'm crazy.'

'No. I think you're distraught, and that's understandable; you've certainly got reason enough to be distraught.'

'Won't you even consider the possibility that he's alive?'

'How could he be?'

'I don't know.'

'How could he have survived the accident you described?' Elliot asked.

'I don't know.'

'And where would he have been all this time if not . . . in the grave?'

'I don't know that either.'

'If he were alive,' Elliot said patiently, 'someone would simply come and tell you. They wouldn't be this mysterious about it, would they?'

'Maybe.'

Aware that her answer had disappointed him, she looked down at her hands, which were laced together so tightly that her knuckles were white.

Elliot touched her face, turning it gently toward him.

His beautiful, expressive eyes were filled with concern for her.

'Tina, you know there isn't any ''maybe'' about it. You know better than that. If Danny were alive, and if someone were trying to get that news to you, it wouldn't be done like this, not with these dramatic hints. Am I right?'

'Probably.'

'Danny is gone.'

She said nothing.

'If you convince yourself he's alive,' Elliot said, 'you're only setting yourself up for another fall.'

She stared deeply into his eyes for a moment, then sighed, nodded. 'You're right.'

'Danny's gone.'

'Yes,' she said thinly.

'You're really convinced of that?'

'Yes.'

'Good.'

Tina got up from the couch, went to the window, and pulled open the drapes. She had a sudden urge to see the Strip. After so much talk about death, she needed to get a glimpse of movement, action, life; and although the Strip sometimes looked grubby in the flat glare of the desert sun, the boulevard was always, day or night, bustling and filled with life. As she opened the heavy, wine-colored drapes, the early winter dusk was just settling over the city, and millions of lights were winking on in the enormous signs. Hundreds of cars progressed sluggishly through the busy street; taxicabs darted in and out, recklessly seeking the smallest advantages; and crowds of people streamed along the sidewalks, on their way from this casino to that casino, from one lounge to another, from one show to another.

After a moment Tina turned to Elliot again. 'You know what I want to do?'

'What?'

'Reopen the grave.'

'Have Danny's body exhumed?'

'Yes. I never saw him. That's why I'm having such a hard time accepting the fact that he's gone. That's why I'm having nightmares. If I'd seen the body, I'd have known for sure; my subconscious wouldn't have had a chance to fantasize about Danny still being alive.'

'But the condition of the corpse . . .'

'I don't care,' she said.

Elliot frowned. Clearly, he wasn't convinced of the wisdom of exhumation. 'Even though the body's in an airtight casket, it's bound to look even worse now than it did a year ago when they recommended you not look at it.'

'I've got to *see*.'

'You'd be letting yourself in for a horrible—'

'That's the idea,' she said quickly. 'Shock. A powerful shock treatment. The shock of it will finally blow away all of my lingering doubts. If I see Danny's . . . remains, I won't be able to entertain any more doubts, not consciously or subconsciously. The nightmares will stop.'

'Perhaps. Or perhaps you'll wind up with even worse dreams.'

She shook her head. 'Nothing could be worse than the ones I'm having now.'

'Of course,' he said, 'exhumation of the body won't answer the main question. It won't help you discover who has been harassing you.'

'It might,' Tina said. 'Whoever the creep is, whatever his motivations are, he's not well-balanced mentally. He's one sort of sickie or another. Who knows what it might take to make a person like that reveal himself? If he finds out there's going to be an exhumation, maybe he'll react strongly to that and give himself away. Anything's possible.'

Elliot thought about that for a moment, then said, 'Yeah. I suppose you could be right.'

'Anyway,' she said, 'even if reopening the grave doesn't help me find out who's responsible for these sick jokes, at least it'll settle my mind about Danny. That'll improve my psychological condition for sure, which will make me better able to deal with the creep. So it'll work out for the best either way.' She walked away from the window, sat on the couch again, beside Elliot. 'I'll need an attorney to handle this, won't I?'

'The exhumation? Yes, an attorney would make it easier for you.'

'Will you represent me?'

He didn't hesitate. 'Yes.'

'How difficult will it be?'

'Well, there's no urgent legal reason to have the body exhumed. I mean, there isn't any doubt about the cause of death, no court trial hinging on a new coroner's report. If that were the situation, we'd have the grave opened very quickly. But even so, this shouldn't be terribly difficult. I'll play up the mother-suffering-distress angle, and the court ought to be sympathetic.'

'Have you ever handled anything like this before?'

'In fact, I have,' Elliot said. 'Five years ago. An eight-year-old girl died suddenly and unexpectedly of a congenital kidney disease. Both of her kidneys failed virtually overnight. One day she was a happy, normal child; the next day she seemed to have a touch of flu; and the third day she was dead. Her mother was so shattered that she couldn't bear to view the body in the casket, even though the daughter hadn't suffered any substantial, exterior physical damage, as Danny did. The mother wasn't even able to attend the services. A couple of weeks after the little girl was buried, her mother started feeling guilty about not paying her last respects.'

Remembering her own ordeal, Tina said, 'I know. I know how it is.'

'The guilt eventually developed into more serious emotional problems. Because the mother hadn't seen the body in the funeral home, she couldn't bring herself to believe that her daughter was actually dead. Her inability to accept the truth was much worse than yours. She was hysterical most of the time, on the edge of a nervous breakdown. I arranged to have the grave reopened. In the course of preparing the exhumation request for the authorities, I discovered that my client's reaction was typical in a situation like that. Apparently, when a child dies, one of the worst things a parent can do is refuse to look at the body while it's lying in a casket. You need to spend time with the deceased, enough to accept the fact that the body is never going to be animated again.'

'Was your client helped by the exhumation?'

'Oh, yes. Her emotional problems abated immediately. Eventually, they disappeared altogether.'

'You see?'

'But don't forget,' Elliot said, 'her daughter's body wasn't mutilated. And we reopened the grave only two months after the funeral, not a whole year later. The body was still in pretty good shape. But with Danny . . . it won't be that way.'

'I'm aware of that,' she said. 'God knows, I'm not looking forward to it, but I'm absolutely convinced it's something I must do.'

'Okay, I'll take care of it.'

'How long will you need?' she asked.

'Will your husband contest it?'

She recalled the hatred in Michael's face when she'd left him a few hours ago. 'Yes,' she said. 'He probably will.'

Elliot carried their empty brandy glasses to the bar in the corner. He switched on the light there. 'If your husband's likely to cause trouble, then we'll move fast and without fanfare. If we're clever he won't know what we're doing until the exhumation is a *fait accompli*. Tomorrow's a holiday, so we can't get anything done officially until Friday.'

'Probably not even then, what with the four-day weekend.'

Elliot found the bottle of liquid soap and the dishcloth that were stored under the sink. 'Ordinarily I'd say we'd have to wait until Monday. But it happens I know a very reasonable judge. Harold Kennebeck. We served in Army Intelligence together. He was my senior officer. If I—'

'Army Intelligence? You were a spy?'

'Nothing as grand at that,' he said, smiling. 'No trench coats. No skulking about in dark alleys.'

'Karate, cyanide capsules, that sort of stuff?' she asked.

'Well, I've had a lot of martial arts training. I still work at that a couple of days a week because it's a good way to keep in shape. Really, though, it wasn't like what you see in the movies. No James Bond cars with machine guns hidden behind the headlights. It was quite prosaic.'

'Somehow,' she said, 'I get the feeling it was

considerably more . . . interesting than you make it out to be.'

'Nope,' he said. 'Document analysis, interpretation of satellite reconnaissance photographs, that sort of thing. Boring as hell most of the time. Anyway, Judge Kennebeck and I go back a long way. We respect each other, and I'm sure he'll do something for me if he can. I'll be seeing him tomorrow afternoon at a New Year's Day party. I'll discuss the situation with him. Maybe he'll be willing to slip into the courthouse long enough on Friday to accept my exhumation request and rule on it. He'd only need a few minutes. Then we could open the grave early Saturday.'

Tina went to the bar and sat on one of the three stools, across the counter from Elliot. 'The sooner the better,' she said. 'Now that I've made up my mind to do it, I'm anxious to get it over with.'

'That's understandable,' he said. 'And there's another advantage in doing it this weekend. If we move fast, it isn't likely Michael will find out what we're up to. And if he does somehow get a whiff of it, he'll have to locate another judge who'll be willing to stay or vacate the exhumation order.'

'You think he'll be able to do that?'

'No. That's my point. There won't be many judges around over the holiday. Those who are doing duty will be swamped with arraignments and bail hearings for drunken drivers and for people involved in drunken assaults. Most likely, Michael won't be able to get hold of a judge until Monday morning, by which time it'll be too late.'

'Sneaky.'

'That's my middle name,' he said as he finished washing the first brandy snifter, rinsed it in hot water, and put it in the drainage rack to dry.

'Elliot Sneaky Stryker,' she said.

He smiled. 'At your service.'

'I'm glad you're my attorney.'

'Don't congratulate yourself on the wisdom of your selection. Not yet, anyway. Better wait till we see if I can actually pull it off.'

'You can,' she said. 'You're the kind of person who meets every problem head-on.'

'You have a pretty high opinion of me,' he said.

'Yes, I do,' she said, repeating what he'd said earlier when she'd responded to the identical compliment.

They laughed. It was a mild laugh, but it was the first deeply felt laugh they'd had since he walked into the office, and it changed the quality of the conversation. All of the talk about death and fear and madness and pain seemed to have taken place further back in the past than just a few seconds ago. They wanted to have a little fun during the evening that lay ahead, and they began putting themselves in the mood for it.

As Elliot rinsed the second snifter and put it in the rack, Tina said, 'You do that very well.'

'But I don't wash windows.'

'I like to see a man being domestic.'

'Then you should see me cook.'

'You cook?'

'Like a dream.'

'What's your best dish?'

'Everything I make.'

'Obviously, you don't make humble pie.'

'Every great chef must be an egomaniac when it comes to his culinary art. He must be totally secure in his estimation of his talents if he is to function well in the kitchen.'

'What if you cooked something for me, and I didn't like it?'

'Then I'd eat your serving as well as mine.'

'What would I eat?'

'Your heart out.'

She laughed. It felt good to laugh after so many months of sorrow. It felt even better to be sharing an evening with an attractive man again.

Elliot put away the dishwashing liquid and the wet dishcloth. As he dried his hands on the towel, he said, 'Why don't we forget about going out to dinner? Let me cook for you instead.'

'On such short notice?'

'I don't need a lot of time to plan a meal. I'm a whiz. Besides, you can help by doing the drudgery, like cleaning the vegetables and chopping the onions.'

Teasing him, she said, 'Well . . . I don't know. What restaurant would we go to if we went out?'

'I was thinking of Battista's Hole in the Wall. I know Rio and Battista very well. We'd probably get some extra service, a special dish or two.'

'Mmmmmm,' Tina said, still teasing. 'The Hole in the Wall has the best food in town. Could you possibly make anything even half as good?'

'I can whip up some pretty terrific fettuccine Alfredo.'

Grinning, she said, 'But maybe it'll be one of those nights when Battista sings for the customers. I'd hate to miss that. He's got such a beautiful voice.'

'I whistle,' Elliot said.

'Battista sings opera. I love opera.'

'I whistle opera.'

'Oh? What opera do you whistle?'

Elliot licked his lips, puckered up, and forcefully whistled the familiar melody of 'Vesti la guibba' from *Pagliacci*.

She burst out laughing. 'That's dreadful!'

'My cooking's better than my whistling.'

'It would have to be.'

'Say you'll come to my place and let me cook for you tonight, or I'll whistle some more. Something from *Turandot*.'

'No, no! Please don't. *Turandot* is one of my favorites.'

He gave her a mock-sinister look. 'Well, then, will you let me cook for you?'

'Yes, yes. Anything. Just so long as you don't whistle any more opera.'

'Okay.' He came out from behind the bar and held out a hand to her. 'Then let's be off to the kitchen.'

'I should go home and freshen up,' she said.

'You're already too fresh for me.'

'My car—'

'You can drive it. Follow me to my place.'

They turned out the lights and left the room, closing the door after them.

As they crossed Angela's office on their way toward the hall, Tina glanced nervously at the computer terminal. She was afraid it was going to start clattering again, all by itself, and ruin the whole evening.

But she and Elliot left the outer office, flicking off the lights as they went, and they walked down the long hall to the elevators without hearing the sound of an automatic typewriter.

# 14

Elliot Stryker lived in a big, pleasant house, overlooking the golf course of the Las Vegas Country Club. The rooms were warm, inviting, decorated primarily in earth tones, with Henredon furniture complemented by carefully selected antique pieces, and richly textured Edward Fields carpets. He owned a fine collection of paintings by Eyvind Earle, Jason Williamson, Larry W. Dyke, Charlotte Armstrong, Carl J. Smith, and other artists who made their homes in the western United States and who usually took their subject matter from either the old or the new West.

As he showed her through the house, he was eager to hear her reaction to it, and she didn't make him wait long.

'It's beautiful,' she said. 'Stunning. Who was your interior decorator?'

'You're looking at him.'

'Really?'

'When I was poor, I looked forward to the

day when I would have a lovely home, full of beautiful things, all arranged by the very best interior decorator. Then, when I had the money, I didn't want some stranger furnishing it for me. I wanted to have all the fun myself. Nancy, my late wife, and I decorated our first home. The project became a vocation for her, and I spent nearly as much time on it as I did on my legal practice. The two of us haunted furniture stores from Vegas to Los Angeles to San Francisco, antique shops, galleries, everything from flea markets to the most expensive stores we could find. We had a damned good time. And when she died . . . I discovered that I couldn't learn to cope with the loss if I stayed in a place that was so crowded with memories of her. For five or six months, I was an emotional wreck because every object in the house reminded me of Nancy. Finally, I took a few mementos, a dozen pieces by which I'll always remember her, and I moved out, sold the house, bought this one, and started decorating all over again.'

'I didn't realize you'd lost your wife,' Tina said. 'I mean, I thought it must have been a divorce or something.

'She passed away three years ago,' he said.

'What happened?'

'Cancer.'

'I'm so sorry, Elliot.'

'At least it was fast,' he said. 'A very virulent

cancer. She was gone a month after they diagnosed it.'

'Were you married long?'

'Twelve years,' he said.

She put a hand on his arm. 'Yes. I know what the pain was like.'

She had spoken with such conviction that he looked more closely at her, and then he realized they had even more in common than he had thought. 'That's right. You had Danny for nearly twelve years, too, didn't you?'

'Yes. With me, of course, it's only been little more than a year since . . . since I've been alone. With you, it's three years. Maybe you can tell me . . .'

'What?'

'Does it ever stop?' she asked.

'The hurting?'

'Yes.'

'So far it hasn't,' he said. 'Maybe it will after four years. Or five. Or ten. It doesn't hurt as bad now as it once did. And the ache isn't constant any more. But still there are moments when . . .'

He didn't finish, and she didn't say anything more about it, and during the long evening, that was the only occasion when the conversation was somber.

He showed her through the rest of the house, which she wanted to see. Her ability to create a stylish stage show was not a fluke; she had taste and a sharp eye that instantly knew the difference between prettiness and genuine beauty, between cleverness and art. He enjoyed discussing antiques and paintings with her; an hour passed in what seemed to be only ten minutes.

The tour ended in the huge kitchen, with its copper ceiling, Mexican-tile floor, and restaurant-quality equipment. She looked into the walk-in freezer, inspected the yard-square grill, the two stoves, the microwave, and the array of labor-saving appliances, and she said, 'You've spent a small fortune here. Obviously, your law practice isn't just another Vegas divorce mill.'

Elliot grinned. 'I'm one of the founding partners of Stryker, Cohen, Dwyer, Coffey, and Napotino. We're one of the largest law firms in town. I can't take a whole lot of credit for that. We were lucky. We were in the right place at the right time. Orrie Cohen and I opened for business in a cheap storefront office eleven and a half years ago, right at the start of the biggest boom this town has ever seen. We represented some people no one else would touch, entrepreneurs who had a lot of good ideas but not much money for start-up legal fees. Some of our clients made smart moves and were carried right to the top by the explosive growth of the gaming industry and the Vegas real estate market; and we just sort of shot up there along with them, hanging on to their coattails.

'Interesting,' Tina said.

'It is?'

'You are.'

'I am?'

'You're so modest about having built a splendid law practice, yet you're an egomaniac when it comes to your cooking.'

He laughed. 'That's because I'm a far, far better cook than I am an attorney. Look, why don't you mix us a couple of drinks while I go change out of this suit. I'll be back in five minutes, and then you'll see how a true culinary genius operates.'

'If it doesn't work out,' she teased, 'we can always jump in the car and go to McDonald's for a hamburger.'

'*Philistine!*'

'Their hamburgers are hard to beat.'

'I'll make you eat crow.'

'How do you cook it?' she asked.

'Very funny.'

'Well, if you cook it very funny, I don't know if I want to eat it.'

'If I *did* cook crow,' he said, 'it would be delicious. You would eat every scrap of it, lick your fingers, and beg for more.'

Her smile was so lovely that he could have stood there all evening, just staring at the sweet curve of her lips.

\* \* \*

Elliot was amused by the effect that Tina had on him. He could not remember ever having been half so clumsy in the kitchen as he was tonight. He dropped spoons. He knocked over cans and bottles of spices. He forgot to watch a pot; it boiled over. He made a mistake blending the salad dressing and had to begin again from scratch. She flustered him, and he loved it.

'Elliot, are you sure you aren't feeling those cognacs we had at my office?'

'Absolutely not.'

'Then the drink you've been sipping on here.'

'No. This is just my kitchen style.'

'Spilling things is your style?'

'It gives the kitchen a pleasant, *used* look.'

'Are you sure you don't want to go to McDonald's?'

'Do *they* bother to give their kitchen a pleasant, *used* look?'

'They not only have good hamburgers—'

'Their hamburgers have a pleasant, *used* look.'

'—their French fries are terrific.'

'So I spill things,' he said. 'A cook doesn't have to be graceful to be a good cook.'

'Does he have to have a good memory?'

'Huh?'

'That mustard powder you're just about to put into the salad dressing.'

'What about it?'

'You already put it in a minute ago.'

'I did? Oh, Jesus. Thanks. I wouldn't want to have to mix this damn stuff *three* times.'

She laughed – and accidentally bumped a large, round loaf of Italian bread that was on the counter, knocking it to the floor; it landed on the Mexican tiles with a soft *flump!*

'Hey, you must be feeling your drinks,' he said.

'No.'

'Then what is it? I'll bet you're excited just being here with a handsome, successful rogue like me.'

'Nope,' she said. 'I just like my bread a little dirty.'

'You like dirty bread?'

'Haven't you ever heard that old saying – eating a little dirt every day is good for you?'

'I sprinkle mine on my breakfast eggs.'

She laughed. She had a throaty laugh that was not unlike Nancy's had been.

She was different from Nancy in many ways, but being with her was like being with Nancy. It felt good. She was easy to talk to, as Nancy had been; bright, funny, sensitive.

Perhaps it was too soon to tell for sure, but he had the feeling that fate had given him a second chance at happiness.

\*   \*   \*

When he and Tina had finished dessert, Elliot poured second cups of coffee for both of them. 'Still want to go to McDonald's for a hamburger?'

'The mushroom salad, the fettuccine Alfredo, the zabaglione – it was all superb, every last bite of it,' Tina said. 'You really *can* cook.'

'Would I lie to you?'

'I guess I'll have to eat that crow now.'

'I believe you just did.'

'And I didn't even notice the feathers.'

While Tina and Elliot had been joking around in the kitchen, even before dinner had been completely prepared, she had begun to think they might go to bed together, tonight. By the time they finished eating dinner, she *knew* they would. Elliot wasn't pushing her. For that matter, she wasn't pushing him either. They were simply both being driven by natural forces. Like the rush of water downstream. Like the relentless building of a storm wind and then the lightning. On an instinctual level, they both realized that they were in need of each other, physically and mentally and emotionally, and that whatever happened between them would be right and good.

It was inevitable.

At first, the undercurrent of sexual tension made her nervous. She hadn't been to bed with any man but Michael in the past fourteen years, since she was nineteen! She hadn't been to bed with *anyone at all* for almost two years now.

Suddenly, it seemed to her that she had done a mad, stupid thing when she'd hidden away like a nun for two years. Of course, during the first of those two years, she still had been married to Michael, and she had felt compelled to remain faithful to him, even though a separation and then a divorce had been in the works, and even though he had not felt constrained by any similar moral sense; and later, with the stage show to produce and with poor Danny's death weighing heavily on her, she hadn't been in the mood for romance. But, good God, now she felt like an inexperienced girl! She wondered if she would know what to *do*. She was afraid she would be inept, clumsy, ridiculous, foolish in bed. She told herself that sex was just like riding a bicycle, impossible to *un*learn, and the silliness of that analogy made her laugh inwardly, but it didn't increase her self-confidence.

Gradually, however, as she and Elliot went through all the standard rites of courtship, all the indirectly sexual thrusts and parries of a budding relationship, the familiarity of the games reassured her. Amazing that it should be so familiar! Although fourteen years had passed since she'd played the game, it seemed like only yesterday. It really was a little bit like riding a bicycle.

After dinner they adjourned to the den, where Elliot built a fire in the used-brick fireplace.

167

Although winter days in the desert often could be as warm as springtime (as today had been), winter nights were always cool, sometimes downright bitter. With a chilly night wind moaning at the windows and howling incessantly under the eaves, the blazing fire was not out of place.

Elliot put a stack of Sinatra albums on the stereo.

Tina kicked off her shoes.

They sat side by side on the sofa in front of the fireplace, watching the flames and the occasional bursts of orange sparks, listening to music, sipping crème de menthe, and talking, talking, talking. It seemed to Tina that they had talked without pause all evening, speaking with quiet urgency, as if each of them had a vast quantity of terribly important information that he must pass on to the other before they parted. The more they talked, the more they found in common. As an hour drifted by in front of the fire, and then another hour, Tina discovered that she liked Elliot Stryker more with each new thing she learned about him.

She never was sure who initiated the first kiss. He may have leaned toward her, or perhaps she tilted toward him. But before she realized what was happening, their lips met softly, briefly. Then again. And a third time. And then he began planting small kisses all over her face: on her forehead, on her eyes, on her cheeks, her nose, the corners of her mouth, her chin. He kissed her ears, her eyes again, and left a chain of kisses along her neck, and when at last he returned to her mouth, he kissed her more deeply than before, and she responded at once, opening her mouth to him, nibbling, licking, pushing her tongue between his lips, taking his tongue into her mouth.

His hands moved slowly over her, testing the firmness and resilience of her, and she touched him, too, gently squeezing his shoulders, his arms, the hard muscles of his back. Nothing had ever felt better to her than he felt at that moment.

As if drifting in a dream, they left the den, went into the bedroom. He turned on a small, dim lamp that stood upon the dresser, and he turned down the sheets.

During the minute that he was away from her, she was afraid that the spell had broken. But when he returned, she kissed him tentatively, found that nothing had changed, and pressed against him once more.

She hugged him fiercely as they kissed, and he cupped her buttocks in his hands. She felt as if the two of them had been here, like this, locked in an embrace, many times before.

'We hardly know each other,' she said.

'Is that the way you feel?'

'No.'

'Me neither.'

'I know you so well.'

'For ages.'

'Yet it's only been two days.'

'Too fast?' he asked.

'What do you think?'

'Not too fast for me.'

'Not too fast at all,' she agreed.

'Sure?'

'Positive.'

'You're lovely.'

'Love me.'

He was not a particularly large man, but he picked her up in his arms as if she were a child.

She clung to him. She saw a longing and a need in his dark eyes, a powerful wanting that was only partly sex, and she knew the same need to be loved and valued must be in her eyes for him to see.

He carried her to the bed, put her down, and urged her to lie back. Without haste, with a breathless anticipation that lit up his face, he undressed her.

He quickly stripped off his own clothes and joined her on the bed, took her in his arms.

He explored her body slowly, deliberately, first with his eyes, then with his loving hands, then with his lips and tongue.

Tina realized that she had been wrong to think that celibacy should be a part of her period of mourning. Just the opposite was true. Good, healthy sex with a man who cared for her would have helped her recover much faster than she had done, for sex was the antithesis of death, a joyous celebration of life, a denial of the tomb's existence.

The amber light molded to his muscles.

He lowered his face to hers. They kissed.

She slid a hand between them, squeezed and stroked him.

She felt wanton, shameless, insatiable.

As he entered her, she let her hands travel over his body, along his lean flanks.

'You're so sweet,' he said.

He began the age-old rhythm of love. For a long, long time, they forgot that death even existed, and they explored the delicious, silken surfaces of love, and it seemed to them, in those shining hours, that they would both live forever.

# PART THREE

## THURSDAY
# JANUARY 1

# 15

Tina stayed the night with Elliot, and he realized that he had forgotten how pleasant it could be to share a bed with someone you truly, deeply cared for. He'd had other women in this bed during the past two years, and a few of them had stayed the night, but not one of those other lovers had made him feel warm and profoundly content, just by the sheer fact of her presence, as Tina did. With Tina, sex was a delightful bonus, but it wasn't the main reason he wanted her there beside him. She was an excellent lover – silken, smooth, long-legged, full-breasted, eager to please, and uninhibited in the pursuit of her own pleasure – but she was also a *person*, a person worth knowing, not stamped out of any mold, *different*, and it was her unique personality, heart, and soul that made sharing the bed with her a very special privilege. It was nice knowing someone like her was there, a woman with whom he could share more than just good times. For a while he just lay there, listening to her breathing. The vague, shadowy shape of her under the covers, in the darkness, was a talisman to ward off loneliness.

Eventually, he fell asleep, but at four o'clock in the morning, he was awakened by her screams.

She sat straight up, fighting with the sheets, catapulted out of a nightmare. She was gasping for breath, quaking, babbling about a man who was dressed all in black, a monstrous figure from her dream.

Elliot had to switch on the bedside lamp in order to prove to her that they were alone in the room.

She had told him about the dreams, but he hadn't realized, until now, just how awful they were for her. He began to think the exhumation of Danny's body would be good for her, regardless of the horror that she might have to look upon when the coffin lid was raised. If seeing the remains would put an end to these bloodcurdling nightmares, she would come out ahead.

He shut off the light and persuaded her to lie down again. He held her until she stopped shuddering.

To his surprise, her fear rapidly changed to desire; and to his even greater surprise, he was ready for her, even though he had been completely exhausted, earlier, by their marathon session of love-making.

They already had tried every position and had sampled every thrill together. Now they didn't experiment; they fell easily into the pace and rhythm that best pleased them both. Afterwards, they slipped into sleep again.

In the morning he astonished himself by making love to her in the shower, with both of them wet and soapy. It was fast and passionate, and when he came he felt as if it were his bone marrow that was spurting out of him.

Over breakfast he asked her to go with him to the afternoon party to which he'd been invited; it was there that he was going to corner Judge Kennebeck and ask about the exhumation. But Tina wanted to go back to her place and clean out Danny's room. She felt up to the challenge now, and she wanted to do it before she lost her nerve again.

'We'll see each other tonight, won't we?' he asked.

'Yes.'

'I'll cook for you again.'

She smiled lasciviously. 'In what sense do you mean that?'

'In the culinary sense. After last night, I won't be cooking in the bedroom any more until my batteries are recharged, and that's going to take a couple of days.'

She rose out of her chair, leaned across the table, kissed him. 'I'll bet you'll be all charged up in a couple of hours.'

The smell of her, the vibrant blue of her eyes,

the feel of her supple skin as he put a hand to her face – those things generated waves of affection and longing within him. He said, 'By God, I think you might be right. It's incredible. I feel like I've reverted to the age of sixteen. I'm just a horny kid again.'

'Isn't it terrific?'

'I'll burn myself out. I'll wind up just a shell, a charred husk of a man.'

He walked her to the VW Rabbit in the driveway, then leaned in the window after she was behind the wheel, delaying her for another fifteen minutes while he planned, to her satisfaction, every dish of that night's dinner.

When at last she drove away, he watched her car until it turned the corner and disappeared, and when she was gone he knew why he hadn't wanted to let her go. He also knew why he had compulsively made love to her in the shower, even though he had barely had enough stamina to finish what he'd started. By each of his acts, he had been trying to postpone her departure because he was afraid he would never see her again after she drove off.

He had no rational reason to entertain that fear. Certainly, the unknown person who had been harassing Tina might have violent intentions. But for various reasons Tina really didn't think there was any danger, and Elliot tended to agree with her. The malicious prankster wanted her to suffer a great deal of mental anguish and spiritual pain; but he didn't want her to die, for that would spoil his fun.

Her leaving frightened Elliot because he was just plain superstitious. He was convinced that, with her arrival on the scene, he had been granted too much happiness, too fast, too soon, too easily. He had an awful suspicion that fate was setting him up for another hard fall. He was afraid Tina Evans would be taken away from him just as Nancy had been.

Unsuccessfully trying to shrug off the grim premonition, he went into the house.

He spent an hour and a half in the library. He paged through legal casebooks, boning up on precedents for the exhumation of a body that, as the court had put it, 'was to be disinterred in the absence of a pressing legal need, solely for humane reasons, in consideration of certain survivors of the deceased.' Elliot didn't think Harold Kennebeck would give him any trouble, and he certainly didn't expect him to request a list of precedents for something as relatively simple and harmless as reopening Danny's grave, but he intended to be well prepared. In Army Intelligence, Kennebeck had been a fair but always demanding superior officer.

At one o'clock Elliot drove his silver Mercedes 450-SL to the New Year's Day party on Sunrise Mountain. The sky was blue and clear, and he wished he had time to take the Cessna up for a couple of hours. It was perfect weather for flying, one of those crystalline days when being above the earth made you feel especially clean and free. On Sunday, when the exhumation was out of the way, maybe he would fly Tina to Arizona or to Los Angeles for the day.

On Sunrise Mountain most of the big, expensive houses had 'natural landscaping' – which meant rocks and colored stones and artfully arranged cacti instead of grass, shrubs, and trees – acknowledgment of the fact that man's grip on this part of the desert was new and perhaps tenuous. At night the view of Las Vegas from the mountain was undeniably spectacular, but Elliot couldn't understand what other reasons anyone could possibly have for choosing to live here rather than in the older, much greener parts of the city. These barren, godforsaken, sand-blasted slopes would not be made lush and green for another ten years at least – more like twenty years. On the brown hills the huge houses thrust up like the bleak monuments of an ancient, dead religion. The residents of Sunrise Mountain could expect to share their patios and sun decks and pool aprons with occasional visiting scorpions, tarantulas, and rattlesnakes. On windy days the dust was as thick as fog, and it pushed its dirty little cat feet under doors, around windows, and through attic vents. As far as Elliot could tell, Sunrise

Mountain had become a prestigious address only because the first couple of homes had been built by millionaires. Other people, certain that millionaires could not be wrong, soon followed, without realizing that the original residents had opted for life on the mountain only because they had been too senile to know better.

The party was at a large neo-Spanish house, halfway up the slopes. A three-sided, fan-shaped tent had been erected on the back 'lawn', to one side of the forty-foot pool, with the open side facing the house. An eighteen-piece orchestra performed at the rear of the gaily striped canvas structure. Approximately two hundred guests danced or milled about behind the house, and another hundred partied within its fifteen rooms.

A great many of the faces were familiar to Elliot. Half of the guests were attorneys and their wives. Although a judicial purist might have disapproved, prosecutors and public defenders and tax attorneys and criminal lawyers and corporate counsel all were mingling and getting pleasantly drunk with the judges before whom they argued cases most every week.

After twenty minutes of diligent mixing, Elliot found Harold Kennebeck. The judge was a tall, dour-looking man with curly white hair. He greeted Elliot warmly, and they talked about their mutual interests, mainly cooking, flying, and river-rafting.

Elliot didn't want to ask Kennebeck for a favor within the hearing of a dozen lawyers, and today there was nowhere in the house where they could find real privacy. They went outside and strolled down the street, past the party-goers' cars, which ran the gamut from Rolls-Royces to Hondas.

Kennebeck listened with interest to Elliot's unofficial feeler about the chances of getting Danny's grave reopened. Elliot didn't tell the judge about the malicious prankster, for that seemed like an unnecessary complication; he still believed, once the fact of Danny's death was established by the exhumation, that the quickest and surest way of dealing with the harassment was to hire a good firm of private investigators to track down the perpetrator. Now, for the judge's benefit, and to explain why an exhumation had suddenly become such a vital matter, Elliot exaggerated the anguish and confusion that Tina had undergone as a direct consequence of never having seen the body of her child.

Harry Kennebeck had a poker face that also *looked* like a poker, and it was difficult to tell if he had any sympathy whatsoever for Tina's plight. As he and Elliot ambled along the sun-splashed street, Kennebeck mulled over the problem in silence for almost a minute. At last he said, 'What about the father?'

'I was hoping you wouldn't ask.'

'Ah,' Kennebeck said.

'The father will protest.'

'You're positive?'

'Yes.'

'On religious grounds?'

'No. There was a bitter divorce shortly before the boy died. Michael Evans hates his ex-wife.'

'Ah. So he'd contest the exhumation for no other reason but to cause her grief?'

'That's right,' Elliot said.

'Still, I've got to consider the father's wishes.'

'As long as there aren't any religious objections, the law requires the permission of only one parent in a case like this,' Elliot said.

'Nevertheless, I have a duty to protect everyone's interests in the matter.'

'If the father has a chance to protest,' Elliot said, 'we'll probably get involved in a knock-down-drag-out legal battle. It'll tie up a hell of a lot of the court's time.'

'Ah. I wouldn't like that,' Kennebeck said thoughtfully. 'The court's calendar is overloaded now. We simply don't have enough judges or enough money. The system's creaking and groaning.'

'And when the dust finally settled,' Elliot said, 'my client would win the right to exhume the body anyway.'

'Probably.'

'Definitely,' Elliot said. 'Her husband would be engaged in nothing more than spiteful obstructionism. In the process of trying to hurt his ex-wife, he'd waste several days of the court's time, and the end result would be exactly the same as if he'd never been given a chance to protest.'

'Ah,' Kennebeck said, frowning slightly.

They stopped at the end of the next block. For a minute Kennebeck stood with his eyes closed and his face turned up to the warm sun.

At last the judge said, 'You're asking me to cut corners.'

'Not really. Simply issue an exhumation order on the mother's request. The law allows it.'

'You want the order right away, I assume.'

'Tomorrow morning if possible.'

'And you'll have the grave reopened by tomorrow afternoon.'

'Saturday at the latest.'

'Before the father can get a restraining order from another judge,' Kennebeck said.

'If there's no hitch, maybe the father won't ever find out about the exhumation.'

'Ah.'

'Everyone benefits. The court saves a lot of time and effort. My client is saved from a great deal of unnecessary anguish. And her husband saves a bundle in attorney's fees that he'd just be throwing away in a hopeless attempt to stop us.'

'Ah,' Kennebeck said.

In silence they walked back to the house where the party was getting louder by the minute.

In the middle of the block Kennebeck finally said, 'I'll have to chew on it for a while, Elliot.'

'How long?'

'Ah. Will you be here all afternoon?'

'I doubt it. With all these attorneys it's sort of a busman's holiday, don't you think?'

'Going home from here?' Kennebeck asked.

'Yes.'

'Ah.' He pushed a curly strand of white hair back from his forehead. 'Then I'll call you at home this evening.'

'Can you at least tell me how you're leaning?'

'In your favor, I suppose.'

'You know I'm right, Harry.'

Kennebeck smiled. 'I've heard your argument, counselor. Let's leave it at that for now. I'll call you this evening, after I've had a chance to think about it.'

At least Kennebeck hadn't refused the request; nevertheless, Elliot had expected a quicker and more satisfying response. He wasn't asking the judge for much of a favor. Besides, the two of them went back a long way indeed. He knew that Kennebeck was a cautious man, but he usually wasn't excessively cautious. The judge's hesitation in this relatively simple matter struck Elliot as being somewhat odd, but he said nothing more; he just had to wait for Kennebeck's call tonight.

As they approached the house they began to

talk about the delights of pasta served with a thin, light sauce of olive oil, garlic, and sweet basil.

* * *

Elliot stayed at the party only two hours. There were too many attorneys there and not enough civilians to make an interesting bash. Everywhere he went he heard talk about torts, writs, briefs, suits, countersuits, motions for continuation, appeals, plea bargaining, and the latest tax shelters. The conversations were like those in which he had to involve himself at work, eight or ten hours a day, five days a week, and he didn't intend to spend a holiday nattering about the same damned things.

By four o'clock he was home again, working in the kitchen. Tina was supposed to arrive at six. He had a few chores to finish before she came, so that they wouldn't have to spend so much time doing galley labor tonight as they had done last night. Standing beside the sink, he peeled and chopped a small onion, cleaned some celery, and peeled several slender carrots. He had just opened a bottle of wine vinegar and had poured four ounces of it into a measuring cup when he heard movements behind him.

He turned and saw two strange men entering the kitchen from the dining room. One of them was about five feet eight, with a narrow face and a neatly trimmed blond beard. He was wearing a dark brown suit, a beige shirt, a dark brown tie, and he was carrying what appeared to be a physicians's bag. He looked nervous. The second man was considerably more formidable than the first. He was tall, hard-looking, with large, big-knuckled, leathery hands. In freshly pressed slacks, a crisp blue shirt, a patterned tie, and a gray sports jacket, he looked like a professional football player uncomfortably gotten up for an awards dinner. But he didn't look nervous at all. Both men stopped near the refrigerator, twelve or fourteen feet from Elliot; the small man fidgeted, and the tall man smiled.

'How'd you get in here?' Elliot demanded, too surprised to think of asking who they were or what they wanted.

'A master key,' the tall man said, smiling, nodding. 'Bob here' – he indicated the smaller man – 'has master keys for every sort of lock. Makes things easier.'

'What the hell is this all about?'

'Relax,' said the tall man.

'Robbery?'

'No, no,' the tall man said.

Bob shook his head in agreement, frowning, as if he was dismayed to think that he could be mistaken for a common thief.

'If you're kidnapping me—'

'We aren't,' the tall man said.

'Then what the hell *is* this?'

'Just relax.'

'You've got the wrong man.'

'You're the one, all right,' the tall man said.

'Yes,' Bob said. 'You're the one. There's no mistake.'

'I can't think of anyone who has a serious grudge against me,' Elliot said. 'You've got to be mistaken. Look, if you—'

'Calm down, Mr. Stryker,' the tall one said.

'Yes,' Bob said. 'Please calm down.'

Elliot took a step toward them.

The tall man pulled a silencer-equipped pistol out of a shoulder holster that was concealed under his gray sports jacket. 'Easy. Just you take it real nice and easy.'

Elliot backed up against the sink.

'That's better,' the tall man said.

'Much better,' Bob said.

'Who are you guys?'

'As long as you cooperate, you won't get hurt,' the tall man assured him.

Bob said, 'Let's get on with it.'

The tall man said, 'We'll use the breakfast area over there in the corner.'

Bob went to the oak table. He put down the black, physician's bag, opened it, and took out a compact cassette tape recorder. He removed other things from the bag, too: a length of flexible rubber tubing, a sphygmomanometer for monitoring blood pressure, two small bottles of amber-coloured fluid, and a packet of disposable hypodermic syringes.

Elliot's mind raced through a list of cases that his law firm was currently handling, searching for some connection with these two intruders; he couldn't think of one.

The tall man waved the gun at Elliot. 'Go over to the table and sit down.'

'Not until you tell me what this is all about,' Elliot said.

'I'm giving the orders here.'

'But I'm not taking them.'

'I'll put a hole in you if you don't move.'

'No. You won't do that,' Elliot said, wishing he felt as confident as he sounded. 'You've got something else in mind, and shooting me would ruin it.'

'Move your ass over to the table,' the tall man said sharply, angrily.

'Not until you explain yourself.'

The tall man glared at him.

Elliot met the stranger's eyes and didn't look away.

At last the tall man said, 'Look, we've just got to ask you some questions.'

Determined not to let them see that he was frightened, aware that any sign of fear would be taken as a sign of weakness, Elliot said,

'Well, you've got one hell of a weird approach for someone who's just taking a public-opinion survey.'

'Very funny,' the tall man said, but he wasn't smiling. 'Now move.'

'What are the hypodermic needles for?'

'Move.'

'What are they for?'

The tall man sighed. 'We've got to be sure you answer truthfully.'

'Drugs?'

'They're very effective and reliable.'

'Yeah. And when you're finished I'll have a brain the consistency of grape jelly.'

'No, no,' Bob said. 'These drugs won't do any lasting physical or mental damage.'

'What sort of questions?' Elliot asked.

'I'm losing my patience with you,' the tall man said.

'It's mutual,' Elliot said.

'Move.'

Elliot didn't move an inch. He refused to look at the muzzle of the gun; he wanted them to think that guns didn't scare him at all. Inside, he was vibrating like a tuning fork.

'You sonofabitch, *move*!'

'What sort of questions do you want to ask me?'

The big man scowled furiously.

Bob said, 'For Christ's sake, Vince, tell him.

He's going to hear the questions anyway when he finally sits down. Let's get this over with and split.'

Vince, the tall man, scratched his chin and then reached inside his jacket. He pulled a few sheets of folded typing paper from an inner pocket.

The gun wavered, but it didn't move off target far enough to give Elliot a chance.

'I'm supposed to ask you every question on this list,' Vince said, shaking the folded papers at Elliot. 'It's a lot, thirty or forty questions altogether, but it won't take long if you just sit down over there and cooperate.'

'Questions about what?' Elliot insisted.

'Christina Evans.'

That was the last thing Elliot had expected. He was dumbfounded for a moment. *Christina?* Then he shook his head as if that action would loosen his tongue, and he said, 'Tina Evans? What about her?'

'We've got to know why she wants to have her little boy's grave reopened.'

Elliot stared at him, amazed. 'How do you even know about that?'

'Never mind,' Vince said.

'Yeah,' Bob said. 'Never mind *how* we know. The important thing is we *do* know.'

'Are you the bastards who've been harassing Tina?' Elliot asked.

'Huh?'

191

'Are you the ones who keep sending her messages?'

'What messages?' Bob asked.

'Are you the ones who wrecked the boy's room?'

'What are you talking about?' Vince asked. 'We haven't heard anything about this.'

'Someone's sending her messages about the kid?' Bob asked.

They appeared to be genuinely surprised by that bit of news, and Elliot was pretty sure they weren't the people who had been trying to frighten Tina. Besides, they didn't seem to be hoaxers or borderline psychopaths who got their kicks by scaring defenseless women. They looked and acted like a couple of organization men, even though the big one was almost rough enough at the edges to pass for a common hoodlum. A silencer-equipped pistol, master keys to fit any lock, truth serums – those things indicated that these men were part of a highly sophisticated outfit with substantial resources.

'What about the messages she's been getting?' the big man asked, still watching Elliot closely.

'I guess that's just one more question you're not going to get an answer for,' Elliot said.

'We'll get the answer,' Vince said coldly.

'We'll get all the answers,' Bob said.

'Now,' Vince said, 'are you going to walk over to the table and sit down, or am I going to have to motivate you with this?' He waved his pistol again.

'Kennebeck!' Elliot said, startled by a sudden insight. 'The only way you could have found out about the exhumation so quickly is if Kennebeck told you.'

The two men glanced at each other. They were obviously unhappy to hear the judge's name.

'That's why he stalled me,' Elliot said. 'He wanted to give you time to get to me. Why in the hell should Kennebeck care whether or not Danny's grave is reopened? Why should *you* care? Who the hell are you people? Why does the prospect of an exhumation frighten you?'

'We're not frightened,' Vince said, beginning to turn red in the face.

'Someone's obviously pretty damned concerned about it,' Elliot said. 'Your presence here, your entire approach, the gun, the drugs – all of that doesn't indicate just idle curiosity. Why? What's behind all of this?'

The tall man was no longer merely impatient; he was angry. 'Listen, you stupid fuck, I'm not going to humor you any longer. I'm not going to answer any more of your questions, but I *am* going to put a bullet in your crotch if you don't move over to the table and sit down.'

Elliot pretended not to have heard the threat. The pistol still frightened him, but he was now thinking of something else that scared him more than any gun could. A chill spread from the base of his spine, up his back, on hundreds of imaginary spider feet as he began to realize what the presence of these men implied about the accident that had killed Danny. 'There's something about Danny's death . . . something strange about the way all those scouts died . . . The truth isn't anything like the version everyone's been told. The bus accident is a lie, isn't it?'

Neither man answered him.

'The truth is a lot worse,' Elliot said. 'Yes. Of course. It's something awful . . . something so terrible that some powerful people are spending a lot of time and energy to hush it up. In fact, it's probably the government that's trying to keep the lid on this. Sure. Who else would Kennebeck be squealing to? He's been a good government employee all his life. All those years in Army Intelligence, then the domestic agencies . . . he's probably still got contacts in all the intelligence services . . . Once an agent, always an agent. Which set of letters do you guys work for? Not the FBI. They're all Ivy Leaguers these days, polished, educated. You're both too crude to be FBI. Same for the CIA; neither of you has enough style to be working for The Company. So who is it? Not the CID, for sure; there's no aura of military discipline about you. Let me guess. You work for some set of letters the public hasn't even heard about yet. Something secret and dirty. Am I right?'

The tall man's face was very dark now, painted with rage. He was breathing hard. 'Goddamn it, I said *you* were going to answer the questions from now on.'

'Relax,' Elliot said. 'I've played your game. I was in Army Intelligence back when. I'm not exactly an outsider. I know how it works. I know the rules and the moves. You don't have to be so hard-assed with me. Open up. Give me a break, and I'll give you a break.'

Sensing Vince's onrushing blowup, aware that it wouldn't help them accomplish their mission, Bob quickly said, 'Listen, Stryker, we can't answer most of your questions because we simply don't know. Yes, we work for a government agency. Yes, it's one you've never heard of and probably never will hear of. But we don't know exactly why this Danny Evans kid is so important. We know he *is* important, but not *why*. You understand? Of course you do. We haven't been told the details, not even half of them. And we don't *want* to know all of it, either. You understand what I'm saying; the less a guy knows, the less he can be nailed for later. Christ, we're not big shots in this outfit. We're strictly hired help. They only tell us as much as we need to know. So will you cool it? Just come over here, sit down, let me inject you, give us a few answers, and then we can all get on with our lives. We can't just stand here forever.'

'If you're working for a government intelligence agency, then go away and come back with all the legal papers,' Elliot said. 'Show me search warrants and subpoenas.'

'You know better than that,' Vince said harshly.

'The agency we work for doesn't officially exist,' Bob said. 'That's why you've never heard our letters. So how can an agency that doesn't exist go to court for a subpoena? Get serious, Mr. Stryker.'

'If I do submit to the drug, what happens to me after you've got your answers?' Elliot asked.

'Nothing,' Vince said.

'Nothing at all,' Bob said.

'How can I be sure?'

At this sign of surrender, the tall man relaxed a bit, but his face was still flushed with anger. 'I told you. When we've got what we want, we'll leave. We just have to find out exactly why the Evans woman wants the grave reopened. We have to know if someone's ratted to her, you know. If someone has, we have to spike his ass to a barn door. But we don't have anything against you. After we find out what we want to know, we'll just leave.'

'And let me go to the police?' Elliot asked.

'The damned cops don't scare us,' Vince said arrogantly. 'Hell, you won't be able to tell them who we were or where they can start looking

196

for us. They won't get anywhere. Nowhere. Zip. And if they *do* pick up our trail somehow, we can put pressure on them to drop it fast. Like you figured, this is government business, national security, the real big time. The government is allowed to bend the rules if it wants; after all, it makes them.'

'That's not quite the way they explained the system in law school,' Elliot said.

'That's ivory tower,' Bob said, nervously straightening his brown tie.

'Right,' Vince said. 'And this is real life. So will you face facts and just sit down at the table like a good boy?'

'Please, Mr. Stryker,' Bob said.

'No,' Elliot said. His intuitive sense of danger, which had been well honed by his years in Army Intelligence, was no longer dormant; it was awake, a presence within him that, having analyzed the situation, was ringing all the alarm bells. When these two men got their answers, they would kill him. He was sure of that. If they intended to let him live, they wouldn't use their real names in front of him. And if they intended to let him live, they wouldn't be wasting all this time coaxing him to cooperate; they would use force without hesitation. They were trying to gain his cooperation without violence because they didn't want to mark him, and the only reason they didn't want to mark him was because they wanted his death to look like an accident or a suicide. The scenario was obvious. Probably a suicide. While he was still under the influence of the drug, they would most likely be able to make him write a suicide note and sign it in a legible, identifiable script. Then they would carry him out to the garage, prop him up in his little Mercedes, put the seat belt snugly around him, and start the engine without opening the garage door. He would be too drugged to move, and the carbon monoxide would do the rest. In a day or two, someone would find him out there, his face blue-green-gray, his tongue dark and lolling, his eyes bulging in their sockets as he stared through the windshield as if on a drive to death. If there were no unusual marks on his body, no injuries incompatible with the coroner's determination of suicide, the police would be quickly satisfied. He was convinced that was how it would be; he knew the rules and the moves of the game.

'No,' he said again, louder this time. 'If you bastards want me to sit down at that table, you're going to have to drag me there.'

# 16

Tina had cleaned up the mess in Danny's room and had nearly finished packing his belongings, which she intended to donate to Goodwill Industries. Several times she had felt on the verge of tears as the sight of one object or another released a flood of memories, but she had gritted her teeth and had resisted the urge to leave the room with the job uncompleted.

Now there was not much left, just a few cartons of stuff in the back of the deep closet. She tried to lift one of those boxes, but it was too heavy for her. She dragged it into the room, across the carpet, into the the shafts of reddish-gold afternoon sunlight that filtered through the sheltering trees outside and then through the dust-filmed window.

When she opened the carton, she saw that it contained part of Danny's collection of comic books. Horror comics. She'd never been able to understand that morbid streak in him. Monster movies. Horror comics. Vampire novels. Scary stories of every kind, in every medium. His fascination with the macabre had not seemed entirely healthy to her, but she had never denied him the freedom to pursue it. Most of his friends had seemed to share his avid interest in ghosts and ghouls, and that sort of thing hadn't been his *only* interest, so she had decided that it wasn't anything to worry about.

The carton held two stacks of comic books, and the two issues on top sported gruesome, full-color covers. On the one, a black carriage, drawn by four black horses with evil glaring eyes, rushed along a night highway, beneath a pale moon, and a headless man held the reins, urging the horses on. Bright blood streamed from the ragged stump of the man's neck, and gelatinous clots of blood clung to his white, ruffled shirt. His head stood on the driver's seat beside him, and it was grinning fiendishly, obviously alive in spite of the fact that it had been brutally detached from its body.

Tina grimaced. If this was what Danny had read before going to bed at night, how had he been able to sleep so well? He'd always been a deep, unmoving sleeper, never troubled by bad dreams. It was amazing.

She dragged another carton out of the closet. It was as heavy as the first, and she figured it contained more comic books, but she opened it to be sure.

She screamed.

*He* was looking up at her from inside the box. From the cover of another horror comic. *Him*. The man. The man who was dressed all in black. That same face. Mostly skull and withered flesh. Prominent sockets of bone, and the menacing, inhuman red eyes staring out with intense hatred. The cluster of maggots on his cheek, at the corner of one eye. The rotten, yellow-toothed grin. He was precisely like the hideous creature that had stalked her dreams for the past two nights, alike in absolutely every disgusting detail.

How? How could she dream about this awful thing just last night and then find it waiting for her here, today, only hours later?

She stepped back from the cardboard box.

The burning, scarlet eyes of the monstrous figure in the drawing seemed to follow her.

I must have seen it a long time ago, she told herself. I must have seen that lurid cover when Danny first brought the magazine into the house. The memory of it was firmly fixed in my subconscious, festering down there, until I finally incorporated it into one of my nightmares.

That seemed logical. It seemed to be the only possible explanation.

But she knew it wasn't true.

She had never seen this drawing before. When Danny had first begun buying horror comics with his allowance, she had looked closely at the books, trying to decide whether or not they were harmful to him. But after she had made up her mind to let him read such stuff, if that was what he wanted, she never thereafter even glanced at his purchases.

Yet she had dreamed about the man in black.

And here he was. Grinning at her.

Curious about the story from which the illustration had been taken, Tina stepped up to the box again and reached in for the comic book, and as her fingers touched the glossy cover, the doorbell rang.

She jumped and gasped.

The bell rang again, and she realized what it was.

Heart thumping, she went to the front door.

Through the fish-eye lens, she saw a young, clean-cut man wearing a blue cap with an unidentifiable emblem on it. He was smiling at the lens, waiting to be acknowledged.

She didn't open the door. She called through it: 'What do you want?'

'Gas company. We need to check our lines where they come into your house.'

Tina frowned. 'On New Year's Day?'

'Emergency crew,' the man said through the closed door. 'We're investigating a possible gas leak in the neighborhood.'

She hesitated, then opened the door without removing the heavy-duty security chain. She studied him through the narrow gap. 'Gas leak?'

He smiled reassuringly. 'There probably isn't any danger. We've lost a bit of pressure in our lines, and we're trying to find the cause of it. No reason to evacuate people or panic or anything. But we're trying to check every house. Do you have a gas stove in the kitchen?'

'No.'

'What about the heating system?'

'Yes. There's a gas furnace.'

'Yeah. I believe all the houses in this area have gas furnaces. I'd like to have a look at it, check the fittings, the incoming feed, all that.'

She looked him over carefully. He was wearing a gas company uniform, and he was carrying a large tool kit with the gas company emblem on it.

She said, 'Can I see some identification?'

'Sure.' He reached into his shirt pocket and withdrew a laminated ID card with the gas company seal, his picture, his name, and his physical statistics.

Feeling slightly foolish, like an easily spooked old woman, Tina said, 'I'm sorry. It's not that you look like a dangerous person or anything. I just—'

'Hey, it's okay,' he said. 'Don't apologize. You did the right thing, asking for an ID. These days, you're crazy if you open your door without knowing exactly who's on the other side of it.'

She closed the door long enough to slip off the security chain, then she opened up again and stepped back. 'Come in.'

'Where's the furnace?' he asked. 'In the garage?'

'Yes.'

'If you want, I could just go in through the garage door.'

'Well,' she said, 'it's an automatic door, and the gizmo that opens it is in the car, and the car's in the garage, so you might as well go in through the house.'

He stepped across the threshold.

She closed and locked the door.

'Nice place you've got here.'

'Thank you.'

'Cozy. Good sense of color. All these earth tones. I like that. It's a little bit like our house. My wife has a very good sense of color.'

'It's relaxing,' Tina said.

'Isn't it? So nice and natural.'

'The garage is this way,' she said.

He followed her past the kitchen, into the short hall, into the laundry room, and from there into the garage.

Tina switched on the light. The darkness was dispelled, but shadows remained along the walls and in the corners.

The garage was slightly musty. But there was no odor of escaping gas.

'Doesn't smell like there's trouble here,' she said.

'You're probably right,' he said. 'But you never can tell. It could be an underground break on your property. The gas might be leaking under the foundation and building up down there, in which case it's possible you wouldn't detect it right away, but you'd still be sitting on top of a bomb.'

'What a lovely thought.'

'Makes life interesting.'

'It's a good thing you're not working in the gas company's public relations department.'

He grinned. 'Don't worry. If I really believed there was even the tiniest chance of anything like that, would I be standing here so cheerful?'

'I guess not.'

'You can bet on it. Really. Don't worry. This is just going to be a routine check.'

He went to the furnace, put his heavy tool kit on the floor, and hunkered down. He opened a hinged metal plate, exposing the furnace's workings. A ring of brilliant, pulsing flame was visible in there, and it bathed his face in an eerie light.

'Well?' she said.

He looked up at her and said, 'This will take me maybe fifteen or twenty minutes.'

'Oh. I thought it was just a simple thing.'

'It's best to be thorough in a situation like this.'

'By all means, be thorough.'

'Look, if you've got something to do, feel free to go ahead with it. I won't be needing anything.'

Tina thought of the comic book with the man in black on its cover. She was very curious about the story out of which that creature had stepped, for she had the peculiar feeling that, in some way, it would be similar to the story of Danny's death. That was a bizarre notion, and she didn't know where it had come from, but she couldn't dispel it.

'Well,' she said, 'I *was* cleaning up a bit in the back room. If you're sure—'

'Oh, certainly,' he said. 'Go ahead. Don't let me interrupt your housework.'

She left him there in the shadowy garage, his face painted by shimmering blue light, his eyes gleaming with twin reflections of fire.

# 17

When Elliot refused to move from in front of the sink to the breakfast table in the far corner of the big kitchen, Bob, the smaller man in the brown suit, hesitated, then reluctantly took a step toward him.

'Wait,' Vince said.

Bob stopped, obviously relieved that the big man was going to deal with Elliot.

'Don't get in my way,' Vince said. He tucked the sheaf of typewritten questions back into his coat pocket, so that his left hand would be free. 'Let me handle the bastard.'

Bob retreated to the table, and Elliot turned his attention to the other intruder.

Vince held the pistol in his right hand, and he made a fist with his left hand. He smiled, and when he spoke to Elliot there was mockery in his voice. 'You really think you want to tangle with me, little man? I used to do a lot of street fighting when I was younger. Never once lost. Never once. I've got big arms. Big and strong.

I've been lifting weights every day for most of my life. And you see that hand, little man?' He brandished his enormous fist at Elliot. 'My hands were always what gave me the advantage. One of my hands is as big as both of yours. Basketball player's hands. Great hands for a street fighter, don't you think? Hell, my fist is just about as big as your head! You know what this fist is going to feel like when it hits, little man?'

Elliot had a pretty good idea of what it would feel like, and he was sweating under his arms and in the small of his back, but he didn't move, and he didn't respond to the stranger's taunting.

'It's going to feel like a freight train ramming straight through you. That's what it's going to feel like,' Vince said. 'You want to stop being so damned stubborn?'

They were going to great lengths to avoid using violence, and that only confirmed Elliot's suspicion that they wanted to leave him unmarked, so that later his body would bear no cuts or bruises incompatible with suicide.

The tall man took a step toward him. 'You want to change your mind and be cooperative?'

Elliot held his ground.

Another step closer.

Elliot waited.

The big man's smile was now a nasty grin.

He's enjoying this, Elliot thought. He likes to intimidate people. He likes to threaten. And he probably likes to deliver on a threat, too.

'One good, hard punch in the gut,' Vince said, 'and you'll be throwing up all over your shoes.'

Another step.

'And when you're done puking your guts out,' Vince said, 'I'm going to grab you by your balls and drag you over to the table.'

One more step.

Then the big man stopped.

They were only an arm's length apart.

Elliot glanced at Bob, who was still standing at the breakfast table, the packet of syringes in his hand.

'Last chance to do it the easy way,' Vince said.

In one lightning-fast, smooth movement, Elliot seized the measuring cup into which he had poured four ounces of vinegar a few minutes ago, and he threw the contents in Vince's face. The big man cried out in surprise and pain, temporarily blinded. Elliot dropped the measuring cup and seized the gun, but Vince reflexively squeezed off a shot that breezed past Elliot's face and smashed the window behind the sink. Elliot ducked a wild punch, stepped in close, still holding on to the pistol that the other man wouldn't surrender. He swung one arm around, slamming his bent elbow into Vince's throat. The big man's head snapped back, and Elliot chopped the exposed Adam's apple with the flat blade of one hand. He quickly rammed his knee into his adversary's crotch, then tore the gun out of the big hand as those clutching fingers suddenly lost all their strength. Vince bent forward, gagging, and Elliot brought the butt of the gun around hard against the side of his head. Elliot stepped back. Vince dropped to his knees, then onto his face, hard, noisily, all the way to the floor, and stayed there.

The entire battle took less than ten seconds.

The big man had been overconfident. He had been certain that his six-inch advantage in height and his extra fifty pounds of muscle made him unbeatable. He had been wrong.

As Elliot had told Tina just yesterday, he had continued his martial arts training after getting out of the service. He used it as a way to keep in shape. He worked out three days a week with the best teacher in Las Vegas, and he was proficient in aikido, karate, judo, and a couple of other exotic disciplines.

As soon as Vince dropped and made no effort to get up, Elliot swung toward the other intruder, pointing the confiscated pistol.

Bob was already out of the kitchen, in the dining room, running toward the front of the house. Evidently he wasn't carrying a gun, and he was impressed by the speed and ease with which his partner – who *had* been armed – had been taken out of action.

Elliot went after him but was slowed down by the dining-room chairs, which the fleeing man had overturned in his wake. In the living room other furniture was knocked over, and books were strewn on the floor, and the route to the entrance foyer was an obstacle course.

By the time Elliot reached the front door and rushed out of the house, Bob had run the length of the driveway and had crossed the street. He was climbing into a dark green, unmarked Chevy sedan. Elliot got to the street in time to watch the Chevy pull away with tires screeching and engine roaring; he couldn't get the license number, for the plates were smeared with mud.

He hurried back to the house.

The man in the kitchen was still unconscious and would probably remain that way for at least another ten or fifteen minutes. Elliot checked his pulse and pulled back one of his eyelids. Vince would survive, although he might need hospitalization, and he wouldn't be able to swallow without pain for quite a few days to come.

Elliot went through the man's pockets. He found some small change, a comb, a wallet, and the sheaf of papers on which were typed the questions that Elliot had been expected to answer.

He folded the pages one more time and stuffed them into his hip pocket.

He opened Vince's wallet. It contained ninety-two dollars, no credit cards, no driver's license, no identification of any kind. Definitely not FBI.

Bureau men always carried the proper credentials. Not CIA, either. CIA operatives were usually loaded down with ID, even if all of it was in a phony name. As far as Elliot was concerned, the complete absence of any identification was far more sinister than a collection of patently false papers would have been, for such absolute anonymity as this smacked of a totally secret police organization.

*Secret police.* That thought scared the hell out of Elliot. Not in the good old USA. Surely not. In the Soviet Union, yes. In a South American banana republic, yes. In half the countries in the world, there were secret police, modern Gestapos, and the people learned to live in fear of a late-night knock on the door. But not in America, damn it!

But even if the government has formed a secret police force, Elliot thought, why has it targeted me? Why is it so anxious to cover up the true facts of Danny's death? What in the name of God are they trying to hide about the Sierra tragedy? What *really* happened up there in the mountains?

*Tina!*

Suddenly he realized that she was in as much danger as he was. If these people were determined to kill him in order to stop the exhumation, they would *have* to kill Tina. In fact she must be their primary target.

*Jesus.*

He was shaking.

He ran to the kitchen phone, snatched up the receiver, and realized he didn't know her number. He put the receiver down and quickly leafed through the phone book. But there was no listing for Christina Evans.

*Shit!*

There was no way he would be able to con an unlisted number out of the directory-assistance operator. And by the time he called the police and managed to explain the situation, they might be too late to help Tina.

For a moment he stood in terrible indecision, temporarily incapacitated by the prospect of losing Tina. He thought of her slightly crooked smile, her dark hair flowing in the wind, her eyes as quick and deep and cool and blue as a pure mountain stream . . . The pressure in his chest grew so great that he couldn't get his breath.

Then he remembered her address. She had given it to him two nights ago, at the opening-night party after the premiere of *Magyck!* She didn't live far from him. He could be there in less than five minutes.

He still had the silencer-equipped pistol in his hands, and he decided to keep it. The gun might come in handy. In fact he was sure it would.

He ran to the car in the driveway.

# 18

Tina left the man from the gas company in the garage and returned to Danny's room. She took the comic book out of the carton and sat on the edge of the bed in the path of the tarnished copper sunlight that fell like a shower of pennies through the window.

The magazine contained half a dozen illustrated horror stories. The one from which the cover painting had been drawn was sixteen pages long. In letters that were supposed to look as if they had been formed from rotting shroud cloth, the artist had emblazoned the title across the top of the first page, above a somber, well-detailed scene of a rain-swept graveyard. Tina stared at those words in shocked disbelief.

## THE BOY WHO WAS NOT DEAD

She thought of the words on the chalkboard and on the computer print-out: *Not dead, not dead, not dead . . .*

Her hands shook. She had trouble holding the magazine steady enough to read it.

The story was set in the mid-nineteenth century, when a physician's perception of the thin line between life and death was often cloudy. It was the tale of a boy, Kevin, who fell off a roof and took a bad knock on the head, thereafter slipping into a deep coma. The boy's life signs were undetectable to the medical technology, such as it was, of that era. The doctor pronounced him dead, and his grieving parents committed Kevin to the grave. That was a time when the corpse was not embalmed, when nothing was done (or could be done) to preserve it even for a little while; therefore, it was possible for the boy to be buried while still alive. Kevin's parents went away from the city immediately after the funeral, intending to spend a month at their summer house, where they could be free from the press of business and social duties, the better to mourn their lost child. But the first night at the summer house, the mother had a vision in which Kevin was seen to be buried alive and calling for her. The vision was so vivid, so disturbing, that she and her husband decided to race back to the city that very night and have the grave reopened at dawn. But Death decided that Kevin belonged to him because the funeral had been held already, and because the grave had been closed. Death was determined that the parents would not reach the grave in time to save their son. Most of the story dealt with Death's attempts to stop the mother and father on their night journey; they were assaulted by every form of the walking dead, every manner of living corpse and vampire and ghoul and zombie and ghost, but they triumphed. They arrived at the grave by dawn, had it opened, and found their son alive, released from his coma. The last panel of the comic-book story showed the parents and the boy walking out of the graveyard, with Death watching them leave, and Death saying, 'Only a temporary victory. You'll all be mine sooner or later. You'll be back some day. I'll be waiting for you.'

Tina was dry-mouthed, weak.

She didn't know what to make of the damned thing.

It was just a silly comic book, an absurd horror story. Yet . . . there seemed to be certain parallels between this gruesome tale and the recent ugliness in her own life.

She put the magazine aside, cover-down, so she wouldn't have to look into Death's wormy, red-eyed gaze.

*The Boy Who Was Not Dead.*

It was weird.

She had dreamed that Danny had been buried alive. Into her dream she had incorporated a grisly character from an issue of a horror-comics magazine that was in Danny's collection. The lead story in that issue was about a boy, approximately Danny's age, who was mistakenly pronounced dead, then buried alive, and then exhumed.

Coincidence?

No. It was simply too much to pass for coincidence.

Tina felt strange; she felt as if her nightmare had not come from within her, but from without, as if some person or force had projected the dream into her mind in an effort to—

To what?

To tell her that Danny had been buried alive?

That was impossible. He could not have been buried alive. The boy had been battered, burned, frozen, horribly mutilated, dead beyond any shadow of doubt. That's what both the authorities and the mortician had told her. Furthermore, this was not the mid-nineteenth century; these days, doctors could detect even the vaguest heartbeat, the shallowest respiration, the dimmest traces of brain-wave activity.

Danny was dead. And he certainly had been dead when they had buried him.

And if, by some million-to-one-chance, the boy *had* been alive when he'd been buried, why would it take an entire year for her to finally get a vision from the spirit world, or from wherever clairvoyant experiences were sent?

The last thought shocked her. Spirit world? Visions? Clairvoyant experiences? She didn't believe in any of that psychic and supernatural stuff. At least she always had thought that she didn't believe in it. Yet now she was seriously considering the possibility that her dreams had some tremendous, otherworldly significance. That was sheer claptrap. Utter nonsense. The roots of all dreams were to be found in the store of experiences in the psyche; dreams were not sent like ethereal telegrams from spirits or gods or demons. Her sudden gullibility dismayed and alarmed her, for it indicated that the decision to have Danny's body exhumed was not having the stabilizing effect on her emotions that she had hoped it would.

Tina got up from the bed, went to the window, looked out at the quiet street, the palms, the olive trees.

I've got to concentrate on just the cold, hard facts, she told herself sternly. I've got to rule out all of this crazy stuff about the dream having been sent to me by some outside force. It was *my* dream, entirely of *my* making. So with that in mind, I've got to consider the possible explanations for the similarities between my nightmare and the story in Danny's horror-comics magazine.

There was, as far as she could see, only one rational explanation. She *must* have seen the grotesque figure of Death on the cover of the magazine when Danny first brought the issue home from the newsstand.

Except that she knew she hadn't.

And even if she had seen the color illustration before, she knew damned well she hadn't read the story – *The Boy Who Was Not Dead*. She had looked through only two of the magazines that Danny had bought, the first two, when she had been trying to make up her mind whether such unusual reading material could have any harmful effects on him. From the date on its cover, she knew that the issue containing *The Boy Who Was Not Dead* could not be one of the first two pieces in Danny's collection. It had been published only a little over two years ago, long after she had decided that horror comics were harmless.

She was back where she'd started.

Her dream had been patterned after the images in the illustrated horror story. That seemed indisputable.

But she hadn't read the story until a few minutes ago. That was a fact.

*Damn!*

Angry at herself for her inability to solve the puzzle, frustrated, she turned away from the window. She started back to the bed to have another look at the magazine, which she'd left there.

The gas company workman called from the front of the house, startling Tina.

He was waiting by the front door. 'I'm finished,' he said. 'I just wanted to let you know I was going, so you could lock the door behind me.'

'Everything all right?'

'Oh yeah. Sure,' he said. 'Everything here is in great shape. If there's a gas leak in this neighborhood, it's not anywhere on your property.'

She thanked him, and he said he was only doing his job, and they told each other to have a nice day, and she locked the door after he left.

She went back to Danny's room and picked up the lurid magazine. Death glared hungrily at her from the cover. She sat on the edge of the bed and began to read the story again, hoping she might see something important in it that she had overlooked in the first reading.

Three or four minutes later, the doorbell rang – one, two, three, four times, one right after the other.

Carrying the magazine, she went out to see who was there. The bell rang three more times during the ten seconds it took her to reach the front door.

'Don't be so damned impatient,' she muttered.

She looked through the fish-eye lens and saw Elliot on the stoop.

When she opened the door, he came in fast, almost in a crouch, looking past her, looking left and right, toward the living room, then toward

the dining area, speaking rapidly, urgently. 'Are
you okay? Are you all right?'

'I'm fine. What's wrong with you?'

'Are you alone?'

'Not now that you're here.'

He closed the door, locked it.

'Pack a suitcase.'

'What?'

'I don't think it's safe for you to stay here.'

'Elliot, is that a gun?'

'Yes. I was—'

'A real gun?'

'Yes. I took it off the man who tried to kill me.'

'Oh? Why was he so mad at you? Did he hear
you whistling opera?'

'Tina, I'm serious.'

She didn't know what he was up to, and
he wasn't acting like himself; but she couldn't
believe he was serious about someone trying to
kill him. 'What man? When?'

'A few minutes ago. At my place.'

'But—'

'Listen, Tina, they wanted to kill me just
because I was going to help you get Danny's
body exhumed.'

She gaped at him. 'What are you talking about?'

'Murder. Conspiracy. Something damned
strange. They probably intend to kill you, too.'

'But that's—'

'Crazy,' he said. 'I know. But it's true.'

'Elliot—'

'Can you pack a suitcase fast?'

At first she was certain he was trying to be funny, playing a game of some sort just to amuse her, and she was going to tell him that none of this struck her as funny. But she stared into his dark, expressive eyes, and she knew he'd meant every word he'd said.

'My God, Elliot, did someone really try to kill you?'

'I'll tell you about it later.'

'Are you hurt?'

'No, no. But I think we both ought to lay low until we can figure this thing out.'

'Did you call the police?'

'I'm not sure that's a good idea.'

'Why not?'

'Maybe they're part of it somehow. Where do you keep your suitcases?'

She felt dizzy. 'Where are we going?'

'I don't know yet.'

'But—'

'Come on. Hurry. Let's get you packed and the hell out of here before any more of these guys show up.'

'I have suitcases in my bedroom closet.'

He put a hand against her back, gently but firmly urging her out of the foyer.

She headed for the master bedroom, confused, beginning to be frightened.

He followed close behind. 'Has anyone been around here this afternoon?'

'Just me.'

'I mean, anyone snooping around? Anyone at the door?'

'No.'

'I can't figure why they'd come for me first.'

'Well, there was the gas man,' Tina said as she hurried down the short hall toward the master bedroom.

'The what?'

'The man from the gas company.'

Elliot put a hand on her shoulder, stopped her, turned her around just as they entered the bedroom. 'A gas company workman?'

'Yes. Don't worry. I asked to see his credentials.'

Elliot frowned. 'But it's a holiday.'

'He was an emergency crewman.

'What emergency?'

'They've lost some pressure in the gas lines. They think there might be a leak in this neighborhood.'

The furrows in Elliot's brow grew deeper. 'What did this workman need to see you for?'

'He wanted to check my furnace and make sure there wasn't any gas escaping.'

'You didn't let him in?'

'Sure. He had a photo ID card from the gas

company. He checked the furnace, and it was okay.'

'When was this?'

'He left just a couple of minutes before you came in.'

'How long was he here?'

'Fifteen or twenty minutes.'

'It took him that long to check out the furnace?'

'Yes.'

'Were you with him the whole time?'

'No. I was cleaning out Danny's room and—'

'Where's your furnace?'

'In the garage.'

'Show me.'

'What about the suitcase?'

'There may not be time,' he said.

He was pale. Fine beads of sweat had popped out along his hairline.

She felt the blood drain from her face.

She said, 'My God, you don't think—'

'The furnace!'

'This way.'

She rushed through the house, past the kitchen, into the laundry room. There was a door at the far end of the narrow, rectangular work area. As she reached for the knob, she smelled the gas building up out there in the garage.

'*Don't open that door!*' Elliot shouted.

She snatched her hand back as if she had almost picked up a tarantula.

'The latch might cause a spark,' Elliot said. 'Let's get the hell out. The front door. Come on. *Fast!*'

They hurried back the way they had come.

Tina passed a leafy green plant, a four-foot-high schefflera that she had owned since it was only one-fourth that tall, and she had the insane urge to stop, risking getting caught in the coming explosion, just long enough to pick up the plant and take it with her. But an image of red eyes, yellow skin – the leering face of death – flashed through her mind, and she kept moving.

She still held the horror-comics magazine in her left hand. She tightened her grip on it. For some reason it seemed important that she not lose it.

In the foyer, Elliot jerked open the front door, pushed her through it ahead of him, and they both plunged into the golden late-afternoon sunshine.

'Into the street!' Elliot shouted.

Tina saw a blood-freezing picture at the back of her mind: the house being torn apart by the blast, pieces of wood and glass and metal flying toward her, sharp fragments piercing her in a hundred places . . .

The flagstone walk that stretched across her front lawn seemed to be a mile long, but at last she reached the end of it and dashed into the street. She saw Elliot's 450-SL parked at the far curb, and she was six or eight feet from the car when the sudden outward-sweeping shock of the explosion shoved her forward. She stumbled and fell into the side of the Mercedes, banging her knee painfully.

She twisted around in terror, calling Elliot's name, and she saw that he was safe. He was close behind her, knocked off balance by the force of the shock wave, staggering forward, but unhurt.

The garage had gone up first, the big door ripping from its hinges and splintering into the driveway, the roof dissolving in a confetti-shower of shake shingles and flaming debris. But even as Tina looked from Elliot to the fire, before all of the shingles had fallen back to earth, a second explosion slammed through the house, and a billowing cloud of flame roared from one end of the structure to the other, bursting those few windows that had miraculously survived the first blast.

Tina watched, stunned, as flames leaped from a window of the house and ignited some dry palm fronds on a nearby tree.

Elliot pushed her away from the Mercedes, so that he could open the door on the passenger's side. 'Get in. *Quick!*'

'But my house is on fire!'

'You can't do anything to save it now.'

'We have to wait for the fire company.'

'The longer we stand around, the better targets we make,' he said.

'But—'

He grabbed her arm, swung her away from the burning house, the sight of which affected her as much as if it had been a hypnotist's slowly swinging pocket watch.

'For God's sake,' Elliot said, 'get in the car, and let's get away from here before the shooting starts.'

Frightened, dazed by the incredible speed at which her world had begun to disintegrate, she did as he said.

When she was in the car, he shut her door, ran to the driver's side, and climbed in behind the wheel.

'Are you all right?' he asked.

She nodded dumbly.

'At least we're still alive,' he said.

He put the pistol on his lap, the muzzle facing toward his door, away from Tina. He fished in his pocket for the keys, found them, and started the car. His hands were shaking.

She looked out the side window, and she watched in disbelief as the flames spread from the shattered garage roof to the main roof of the house, long tongues of lambent fire, licking, licking, hungry, blood-red in the last orange light of the afternoon.

# 19

As Elliot drove away from the burning house, his instinctual sense of danger was as sensitive as it had been in his military days. He was on the thin line that separated animal alertness from nervous frenzy.

He glanced at the rearview mirror and saw a black van pull out from the curb, half a block behind them.

'We're being followed,' he said.

Tina had been looking back at her house. Now she turned all the way around and stared through the rear window of the sports car. 'I'll bet the one who rigged my furnace is in that truck,' she said.

'I wouldn't doubt it.'

'I'd like to get my hands on the sonofabitch,' she said vehemently. 'I'd gouge the bastard's eyes out.'

Her fury surprised and pleased Elliot. Stupefied by the unexpected violence, by the loss of her house, and by her close brush with death, she had seemed to be in a trance; now she had snapped out of it. He was impressed and encouraged by her resilience.

'Put on your seatbelt,' he said. 'We'll be moving fast and loose.'

She faced front and buckled up. 'Are you going to try to lose them?'

'I'm not just going to *try*.'

The street was in a residential neighborhood, and the speed limit was twenty-five miles per hour. Elliot stomped on the accelerator, and the low, sleek, two-seat Mercedes jumped forward.

Behind them the van dwindled rapidly, until it was a block and a half away, and then it finally stopped dwindling as it, too, accelerated.

'He can't catch up,' Elliot said. 'The best he can hope to do is avoid losing more ground.'

Along the street people were coming out of their houses to see what the explosion had been about. Heads turned as the Mercedes whizzed past.

When Elliot rounded the corner two blocks later, he had to brake down from sixty miles an hour. The tires squealed, and the car slid sideways a bit, but the superb suspension and the sensitive steering held the Mercedes firmly on four wheels all the way through the turn.

'You don't think they'll actually start shooting at us?' Tina asked.

'I don't know. They wanted it to look as if you'd died in an accidental gas explosion. And

I think they had a fake suicide planned for me. But now that they know we're on to them, they might panic. They might start shooting right out in the open. They might do anything. I don't know. The only thing I *do* know is that they can't let us just walk away.'

'But who—'

'I'll tell you what I know, but later.'

'What do they have to do with Danny?'

'Later,' he said impatiently.

'But it's all so crazy.'

'You're telling me?'

He wheeled around another corner, then another, trying to disappear from the men in the van long enough to leave them with so many choices of streets to follow that they would have to give up the chase in confusion. Too late, he saw the sign at the fourth corner – NOT A THROUGH STREET – but they were already around the bend and headed down the narrow dead end, with nothing but a row of ten modest stucco houses on each side.

'Damn it!'

'Better back out,' she said.

'And run right into them.'

'You've got the gun.'

'There's probably more than one of them, and they'll be armed.'

At the fifth house on the left, the garage door was open, and there wasn't a car inside.

'We've got to get off the street and out of sight,' Elliot said.

He drove into the open garage as boldly as if it were his own. He switched off the engine, scrambled out of the car, and ran to the big door. It wouldn't come down. He struggled with it for a moment, and then he realized that it was equipped with an automatic system.

Behind him, Tina said, 'Stand back.'

He turned, looked at her.

She had gotten out of the car and had located the control button on the garage wall.

He glanced outside, up the street. He couldn't see the van.

The door rumbled down, concealing them from anyone who might drive past.

Elliot went to her. 'That was close.'

She took his hand in hers, squeezed it. Her hand was cold, but her grip was firm.

She said, 'Let's hope the people who live here don't come home while we're hiding out in their garage.'

'We won't be here long. We'll only have to stay until the men in that van decide we've skipped out of the neighborhood. They'll stop looking for us around here if they don't spot us in the next five minutes.'

'Okay. So who the hell are they?'

'Well, first of all, I saw Harold Kennebeck, the judge I mentioned yesterday. He—'

The door that connected the garage to the house opened without warning, but with a sharp, dry squeak of unoiled hinges. Both Elliot and Tina jumped.

An imposing, barrel-chested man in rumpled slacks and a white T-shirt snapped on the garage light and peered curiously at them. He had meaty arms; the circumference of one of them almost equaled the circumference of Elliot's thigh. And there wasn't a shirt made that could be buttoned easily around his thick, muscular neck. He appeared to be in good shape, even with his beer belly, which bulged slightly over the waistband of his trousers.

'Who're you?' he asked in a soft, gentle voice that did not fit his appearance.

Elliot had the awful feeling that the man would reach for the button Tina had pushed less than a minute ago, and that the garage door would lift up just as the black van was rolling slowly by in the street.

Stalling for time, he said, 'Oh, hi. My name's Elliot, and this is Tina.'

'Tom,' the big man said. 'Tom Polumby.'

Tom Polumby didn't appear to be worried by their presence in his garage; he was just perplexed. A man of his size probably wasn't often frightened of anyone.

'Nice car,' Tom said with an unmistakable trace

of reverence in his voice. He looked covetously at the 450-SL.

Elliot almost laughed out loud. *Nice car!* They pulled into the man's garage, parked, closed the door, and all he had to say was, *Nice car!*

'Very nice little number,' Tom said, nodding, licking his lips as he studied the 450-SL.

Apparently it had never occurred to Tom that burglars, psychopathic killers, and other low-life types were permitted to purchase a Mercedes-Benz if they had the money for it. To him, evidently, anyone who drove a Mercedes had to be the right kind of people.

Elliot wondered how good old Tom would have reacted if they had zoomed into his garage in a Pinto.

Tom pulled his gaze away from the car. 'What're you doing here?' he asked, not belligerently.

'We're expected,' Elliot said.

'Huh? I wasn't expecting you.'

'We're here . . . about the boat,' Elliot said, not even knowing where he was going to go with that line, willing to say anything at all just to keep Tom from putting up the garage door and throwing them out.

Tom blinked. 'What boat?'

'The twenty-footer.'

'I don't own a twenty-footer.'

'The one with the Evinrude motors.'

'Nothing like that here.'

'You must be mistaken,' Elliot said.

'I figure you've got the wrong place,' Tom said, stepping out of the doorway, into the garage, reaching for the button that would raise the door.

Tina said, 'Mr. Polumby, wait. There must be some mistake, really. This is definitely the right place.'

Tom's hand stopped short of the button.

Tina continued: 'You're just not the man we were supposed to see, that's all. He probably forgot to tell you about the boat. That must be it.'

Elliot looked at her, amazed.

'Who's this guy you're supposed to see?' Tom asked, frowning.

Tina said, 'Sol Fitzpatrick.'

'Nobody here by that name.'

'But this is the address he gave us,' Tina said. 'He told us the garage door would be open and that we were to pull right inside.'

Elliot wanted to hug her. 'Yeah. Sol said we were to pull in, out of the driveway, so that he'd have a place to put the boat when he got here with it.'

Tom scratched his head, pulled on one ear. 'Fitzpatrick?'

'Yeah.'

'Never heard of him,' Tom said. 'What's he bringing a boat here for anyway?'

'We're buying it from him,' Tina said.

Tom shook his head. 'No. I mean, why *here*?'

'Well,' Elliot said, 'the way we understood it, this was where he lived.'

'But he doesn't,' Tom said. 'I live here. Me and my wife and our little girl. They're out right now, and there's nobody ever been here named Fitzpatrick.'

'Well, why would he tell us this was his address?' Tina asked, scowling.

'Lady,' Tom said, 'I don't have the foggiest. Unless maybe . . . Did you already pay him for the boat?'

'Well . . .'

'Maybe just a down payment?' Tom asked.

'We did give him a couple of hundred on deposit,' Elliot said. 'It was a refundable deposit. Just to hold the boat until we could see it and make up our minds.'

Smiling, Tom said, 'I think the deposit might not turn out to be as refundable as you thought.'

Pretending surprise, Tina said, 'You don't mean that this Mr. Fitzpatrick would cheat us?'

Obviously it pleased Tom to think that people who could afford a Mercedes were not really so smart after all. 'If you gave him a deposit, and if he gave you this address and said he lived here, then *I'd* say it's sure not very likely that Sol Fitzpatrick even owns any boat in the first place.'

'Damn,' Elliot said.

'We were swindled?' Tina said, feigning shock.

Grinning broadly now, Tom said, 'Well, you can look at it that way if you want. Or you can think of it as an important lesson that this Fitzpatrick fellow taught you.'

'Swindled,' Tina said, shaking her head.

'Sure as the sun will come up tomorrow,' Tom said.

Tina turned to Elliot. 'What do you think?'

Elliot glanced at the garage door, then at his watch. He said, 'I think it's safe to leave.'

'Safe?' Tom asked.

Tina stepped lightly past Tom Polumby and pressed the button that raised the garage door. She smiled at her bewildered host and went to the passenger's side of the car, while Elliot opened the driver's door.

Polumby looked from Elliot to Tina to Elliot, puzzled. 'Safe?' he asked again.

Elliot said, 'I sure hope it is, Tom. Thanks a lot for your help.' Then he got in the car and backed it out of the garage.

Any amusement he felt at the way they had handled Polumby evaporated instantly as he moved warily out of sanctuary. He sat stiffly behind the wheel, clenching his teeth, listening to his pounding heart, wondering if a bullet would crack through the windshield and shatter his face.

He wasn't used to this kind of tension.

Physically, he was hard, tough, but mentally and emotionally he was perhaps softer than he had been in his prime. Definitely out of shape in that regard. A long time had passed since the war, since his years in military intelligence, since the muggy nights of fear in Saigon and in other cities scattered around Southeast Asia. Then, he'd had the resiliency of youth, and he had been less burdened with respect for death than he was now. In those days it had been easy to play the hunter. He had taken pleasure in stalking human prey; there had even been a measure of joy in *being* stalked, for it gave him the opportunity to prove himself by outwitting the hunter on his trail. Much had changed. He was soft. Too damned soft. A successful, very civilized attorney. Living the good life. He had never expected to play that game again. But once more, incredibly, he was being hunted, and he wondered how long he could last.

Tina looked up and down the street as Elliot swung the car out of the driveway. 'No black van,' she said.

'So far.'

Several blocks away an ugly column of smoke rose into the twilight sky, roiling, night-black, the upper reaches of it tinted around the edges by the last pinkish rays of the setting sun. The smoke was coming from Tina's house, of course. Or rather, more accurately, it was rising from what little was left of her house.

As he drove from one residential street to another, steadily heading away from the smoke, working toward a major thoroughfare, Elliot expected to encounter the black van at every intersection.

Tina appeared to be no less pessimistic about their hope of escape than he was. Each time he glanced at her, she was either crouched forward, squinting at every new street they entered, or she was twisted halfway around in her seat, looking out the rear window. Her face was drawn, and she was constantly biting her lower lip.

However, by the time they reached Charleston Boulevard – via Maryland Parkway, Sahara Avenue, and Las Vegas Boulevard – they both began to relax. They were far away from Tina's neighborhood now. No matter who was looking for them, no matter how large the organization that was pitted against them, this city was just too big to harbor danger for them in every nook and crevice. With almost 350,000 full-time residents, with twelve million tourists a year, and with a vast desert on which to sprawl, Vegas offered thousands of dark, quiet corners in which two people on the run could safely stop to catch their breath and choose a course of action.

At least that was what Elliot wanted to believe.

'Where to?' Tina asked as he turned west on Charleston Boulevard.

'Let's ride out this way for a few miles and

239

talk. We've got a lot to discuss. We have plans to make.'

'What have we got to plan?'

'How to stay alive.'

# 20

While he drove he told her what had happened at his house a short time ago: the two men, their interest in the possibility of Danny's grave being reopened, their admission that they worked for some government agency, the hypodermic syringes . . .

Tina interrupted him with several questions (the same ones he had been asking himself and for which he had no answers), and then she said, 'Maybe we should go back to your place. If this Vince is still there, maybe we should use those drugs on him. Even if he really doesn't know why his organization is interested in the exhumation, he'll at least know who his bosses are. We'll get some names. There's bound to be a lot we can learn from him.'

They stopped at a red light. Elliot took hold of her hand, pressed it tenderly. The contact gave him strength.

He said, 'I'd sure like to interrogate Vince, but we can't.'

'Why not?'

'Two main reasons. First of all, he probably isn't at my place any more. He'll have come to his senses and scrammed by now. And even if he was deeper under than I thought, some of his people probably went in there and pulled him out while I was rushing off to you. But most important of all, if we go back to my house, we'll just be walking into the dragon's jaws.'

'I suppose they'll be watching your place.'

'Absolutely.'

The traffic light changed to green, and Elliot reluctantly let go of her hand.

'The only way these people are going to get their hands on us,' he said, 'is if we just give ourselves over to them. No matter who they are, they're definitely not omniscient; we can hide from them for quite a long time if we have to. If they can't find us, they can't kill us.'

As they continued west on Charleston Boulevard, Tina said, 'Earlier you told me we couldn't go to the police with this.'

'Right.'

'Why can't we?'

'The police might be a part of it, at least to the extent that Vince's bosses can put pressure on them. Besides, we're dealing with a government agency, and governmental agencies tend to cooperate with one another.'

'It's all so paranoid.'

'I'm aware of that.'

'Eyes everywhere.'

'If they have a judge in their pocket, why not a few cops?'

'You told me you respected Kennebeck. You said he was a good judge.'

'He is. He's well versed in the law, and he's fair.'

'Why would he cooperate with these killers? Why would he violate his oath of office?'

'Once an agent, always an agent,' Elliot said. 'That's the wisdom of the service, not mine, but in many cases it's true. For some of them, it's the only loyalty they'll ever be capable of. Kennebeck held several jobs in a number of different intelligence organizations. He was deeply involved in that world for thirty years. After he retired . . . oh, about ten years ago, he was still a young man, fifty-three, and he looked around for something else to occupy his time. He had his law degree, but he didn't want the hassle of a day-to-day practice. So he ran for an elective position on the court, and he won. I think he takes his job pretty seriously; nevertheless, he was an intelligence agent a hell of a lot longer than he's been a judge, and I guess breeding tells. Or maybe he never actually retired at all. Maybe he's still on the payroll of some spook shop, and maybe the whole plan was for him to pretend to retire and then get elected as a judge here in Vegas, so that his bosses would have a friendly courtroom in town.'

'Is that very likely? I mean, how could they be sure he'd win the race?'

'Maybe they fixed the election.'

'You're serious, aren't you?'

'Yes. Hell, it's only been a couple of years since that Texas elections official came out with the story about how Lyndon Johnson's first local election was fixed. The man said he was just trying to clear his conscience after all these years. He might as well have saved his breath. Hardly anyone raised an eyebrow. It happens now and then. And in a small, local election like the one Kennebeck won, stacking the deck would be easy if you had enough money and government muscle behind you.'

'But why would they want Kennebeck on a Vegas court instead of in Washington or New York or someplace more important?'

'Oh, Vegas is a *very* important town,' Elliot said. 'If you want to launder dirty money, this is by far the easiest place to do it. If you want to purchase a false passport, a counterfeit driver's license, or anything of that nature, you can pick and choose from several of the best document forgery artists in the world; this is where a lot of them live. If you're looking for a freelance hit man, or someone who deals in carload lots of illegal weapons, or a mercenary who can put together a small expeditionary force for an overseas operation, you can find all of them here. Nevada has fewer state laws on the books than any state in the nation. Its tax rates are low. There is no state income tax at all. Regulations on banks and real estate agents and on everyone else – except casino owners – are less troublesome here than in other states, which takes a burden off everybody, but which is especially attractive to people trying to spend and invest dirty cash. Nevada offers more personal freedom than anyplace in the country, and that's good, by my way of thinking. But wherever there's a great deal of personal freedom, there's also bound to be an element that takes more than fair advantage of the liberal legal structure. Vegas is an important field office for any American spook shop.'

'So there really are eyes everywhere.'

'In a sense, yes.'

'But even if Kennebeck's bosses have a lot of influence with the Vegas police, would the cops let us be killed? Would they really let it go that far?'

'They probably couldn't provide enough protection to keep it from happening,' Elliot said.

'What kind of government agency would have the authority to circumvent the law like this? What kind of agency would be empowered to kill innocent civilians who got in its way?'

'I'm still trying to figure that one,' he said somberly. 'It scares the hell out of me.'

They stopped at another red light.

'So what are you saying?' Tina asked. 'That we'll have to handle this all by ourselves?'

'At least for the time being.'

'But that's hopeless! How can we?'

'It isn't hopeless.'

'Just two ordinary people against *them*?'

Elliot glanced in the rear-view mirror, which he had been doing every minute or two since they'd turned onto Charleston Boulevard. No one was following them, but he couldn't stop checking.

'It isn't hopeless,' he said again. 'We just need time to think about it, time to work out a plan. Maybe we'll come up with someone who can help us.'

'Like who?'

The light turned green.

'Like the newspapers, for one,' Elliot said, accelerating across the intersection, glancing in the rear-view mirror. 'We've got proof that something unusual is happening here: the silencer-equipped pistol I took off Vince, the fact that your house was blown up . . . I'm pretty sure we can find a reporter who'll go with that much and write a story about how a bunch of nameless, faceless people are trying to keep us from reopening Danny's grave. If they publish my theory that the story of the Sierra accident is false, that something darker lies at the bottom of it, then a lot of people are going to be pushing for an exhumation of *all* those boys. There'll be a demand for new autopsies, investigations. Kennebeck's bosses want to stop us before we sow any seeds of doubt about the official explanation of the accident. But once those seeds are sown, once the parents of the other scouts and the entire city are clamoring for an investigation, Kennebeck's buddies won't have anything to gain by eliminating us. It isn't hopeless, and it's not like you to give up so easily.'

She sighed. 'I'm not giving up.'

'Good.'

'I won't stop until I know what really happened to Danny.'

'That's better,' he said. 'That sounds more like the Christina Evans I know.'

Dusk was sliding into night, and Elliot turned on the headlights.

Tina said, 'It's just that . . . well, for the past year I've been struggling to adjust to the fact that Danny died in that stupid, pointless accident. And now, just when I'm beginning to think I can face up to it and put it behind me, I discover he might not have died accidentally after all. Suddenly . . . everything is up in the air again.'

'It'll come down.'

'Will it?'

'Yes. We'll get to the bottom of this.'

He glanced in the rear-view mirror.

Nothing suspicious.

He was aware of her watching him, and after a while she said, 'You know what?'

'What?'

'I think . . . in a way . . . you're actually enjoying this.'

'Enjoying what?'

'The chase.'

'Oh, no. I don't enjoy taking guns away from men half again as big as I am.'

'I'm sure you don't. That isn't what I said.'

'And I certainly wouldn't *choose* to have my nice, peaceful, quiet life turned upside down. I'd rather be a comfortable, upstanding, *boring* citizen than a fugitive.'

'I didn't say anything about what you'd choose if it were up to you,' Tina told him. 'But now that it's happened, now that it's been thrust upon you, you're not entirely unhappy. There's a part of you, a deep-down part, that's responding to the challenge with a degree of pleasure. I can see it. It's evident in the way you move, the way you handle yourself, the way you talk. It's a quality that wasn't there this morning.'

'Baloney,' he said.

'No. It's true. I can't describe it very well . . . but it's sort of an . . . animal awareness . . . a new kind of energy . . . a cunning that you didn't seem to have before.'

'The only thing new about me is that I wasn't scared stiff this morning, and now I am.'

'Being scared – that's part of it,' she said. 'The danger has struck a chord in you, hasn't it? I suppose it takes you back, makes you feel younger, in a way.'

He smiled. 'The good old days of spies and counterspies? Sorry, but no, I don't long for that at all. I'm afraid you're fantasizing, romanticizing, melodramatizing. I'm not a natural-born man of action. I'm just me, the same old me I always was.'

'Anyway,' Tina said, 'I'm very damned glad that I've got you on my side.'

'I like it better when you're on top,' he said.

'Have you always had such a dirty mind?'

'No. I've had to cultivate it.'

'It's grown well.'

'Thank you.'

'My God, just listen to us,' she said.

'What?'

'We're laughing.'

'So?'

'Joking in the midst of disaster,' she said.

' "Laughter is a balm for the afflicted, the best defense against despair, the only medicine for melancholy." '

'Who said that?' she asked. 'Shakespeare?'

'Groucho Marx, I think.'

'Just as good,' she said. She sighed, leaned forward, and picked something up from the floor between her feet. 'And then there's this damned thing.'

'What'd you find?'

'I brought it from my place,' she said.

In the rush to get out of her house before the gas explosion leveled it, he had not noticed that she'd been carrying anything. He risked a quick look, taking his eyes off the road for only a moment, but there wasn't enough light in the car for him to see what she held. 'I can't make it out.'

'It's a horror-comics magazine,' she said. 'I found it when I was cleaning out Danny's room. It was in a box with a lot of other horror magazines.'

'So?'

'Remember the nightmares I told you about?'

'Yes.'

'The monster that's been featured in my dreams the last couple of nights appears on the cover of this magazine. It's him. Detail for detail. There's not one iota of difference.'

'Then you must have seen the magazine before, and you just—'

'No. That's what I tried to tell myself. But I never saw it until today. I know I didn't. I never looked at Danny's collection. When he came home from the newsstand, I never looked at what he'd bought. I never snooped.'

'Maybe you—'

'Wait,' she said. 'I haven't told you the worst part.'

The traffic thinned out as they drove farther from the heart of town, closer to the looming black mountains that thrust into the last purple light in the western sky.

Tina told Elliot about *The Boy Who Was Not Dead*.

The similarities between the horror story and their attempt to exhume Danny's body chilled Elliot.

'And now,' Tina said, 'just like Death tried to stop the parents in the story, someone is trying to stop me from opening *my* son's grave.'

They were getting too far out of town. Darkness lay on both sides of the road. The land began to rise toward Mount Charleston, where, less than an hour away, there were pine forests and snow. Elliot swung the car around and started back toward the lights of the city, which were spread out like a vast, glowing fungus on the black desert plain.

'There *are* similarities,' he said.

'You're damned right there are. Too many.'

'There's also one big difference. In the story the boy was buried alive. But Danny *is* dead. The only thing in doubt is the manner in which he died.'

'But that's the only difference between the basic plot of that story and what we're going through. And the words ''Not Dead'' in the title. And the boy in the story being Danny's age. It's just too much,' she said.

They rode in silence for a minute.

251

Finally Elliot said, 'You're right. It can't be coincidence. Your dreams, the horror comics . . . I hate to say it, but it's just too much to be coincidental.'

'Then how do you explain it?'

'I don't know,' he said uneasily.

'Welcome to the club.'

A roadside diner stood on the right, and Elliot pulled into the parking lot. There was only one mercury-vapor pole lamp at the entrance, and it shed its fuzzy purple light over just the first third of the parking lot. Elliot drove around behind the restaurant and tucked the Mercedes into a slot in the deepest shadows, between a Toyota Celica and a small motor home, where it could not be seen from the street.

'Hungry?' he asked.

'I can't believe it, after what we've been through in the past couple of hours, but I'm starving.'

'So am I. And I'm not surprised. We just burned up at *least* ten thousand calories in fear and nervous tension.'

'Maybe there's a diet book in this,' she said.

'*The Terror Diet.*'

She smiled faintly. 'Before we go in, let's have a look at that list of questions they were going to make you answer. We might learn something from it.'

'Let's look at it in the café,' Elliot said. 'The light will be better. It doesn't seem to be busy in there; we should be able to talk without being overheard. Bring the magazine, too. I want to see that story.'

He got out of the car, and his attention was drawn to an uncurtained window on the side of the motor home next to which he had parked. He looked through the glass into the perfectly black interior of the camper, and he had the disconcerting feeling that someone was hiding in there, staring out at him.

Don't succumb to paranoia, he warned himself.

When he turned away from the motor home, his gaze fell on a particularly dense pool of shadows around the garbage bin at the back of the restaurant, and again he had the feeling that someone was watching him from concealment.

He had told Tina that Kennebeck's bosses were not omniscient. He must remember that. He and Tina apparently were confronted with a powerful, lawless, dangerous organization hell-bent on keeping the secret of the Sierra tragedy. But any organization was composed of men, and no man had the all-seeing gaze of God.

*Nevertheless* . . .

As he and Tina walked across the parking lot toward the diner, Elliot couldn't shake the feeling that someone or something was watching them. Not necessarily a person. Just . . . something . . . weird . . . strange. Something both more and less than human. That was a bizarre thought, not at all the sort of notion he'd ordinarily get in his head, and he didn't like it at all.

Tina stopped when they reached the purple light under the mercury-vapor lamp. She looked back toward the car, a curious expression on her face.

'What is it?' Elliot asked.

'I don't know . . .'

'See something?'

'No,' she said.

They stared at the shadows.

At length she said, 'Do you feel it?'

'Feel what?'

'I've got this . . . prickly feeling.'

He didn't say anything.

'You *do* feel it, don't you?' she asked.

'Yes.'

'As if we aren't alone.'

'It's crazy,' he said, 'but I feel eyes on me.'

She shivered. 'But there's really not anyone there.'

'No. I don't think there is.'

They continued to squint at the blackness, searching for movement.

She said, 'Are we both cracking under the strain?'

'Just jumpy,' he said, but he wasn't really convinced that they were imagining it.

A soft cool wind sprang up. It carried with it

the odor of dry, desert weeds. It hissed through the branches of a nearby date palm.

'It's such a *strong* feeling,' she said. 'And you know what it reminds me of?'

'What?'

'It's the same damned feeling I had in Angela's office, when that computer terminal started operating on its own. I don't feel just like I'm being watched. I mean, it's something more than that. It's more like . . . a *presence*.'

He knew exactly what she meant, but he didn't want to think about it because there was no way he could make sense of it, no matter how hard he tried. He was a man who liked to deal with hard facts, realities; that was why he was such a good attorney, so adept at taking a mountain of evidence and building a case out of it. 'We're both overwrought,' he said.

'That doesn't change what I feel.'

'Let's get something to eat.'

But she stayed a moment longer, staring back into the gloom, where the purple light did not reach.

'Tina . . .?'

A breath of wind stirred a ball of dry weeds and blew it across the macadam. A bird swooped through the darkness overhead; they couldn't see it, but they could hear the beating of its wings.

Tina cleared her throat and said, 'It's as if . . .

the night itself is watching us . . . the night, the shadows, the eyes of darkness.'

The wind ruffled Elliot's hair. It rattled a loose metal fixture on a garbage bin. The restaurant's big sign creaked back and forth between its two standards.

At last he and Tina went into the diner, trying not to look over their shoulders.

# 21

The diner was long, L-shaped, with lots of chrome, glass, plastic, Formica, and red vinyl. The jukebox was playing a country-and-western tune by Kenny Rogers and the music shared the air with the delicious aromas of fried eggs, bacon, and sausages. True to the rhythm of Vegas life, someone was just now beginning his day with a hearty breakfast. Tina's mouth began to water as soon as she stepped through the door.

Eleven customers were clustered at the end of the long arm of the L, near the entrance, five sitting on stools at the counter, six in the red booths. Elliot and Tina sat as far from everyone as possible, in the last booth in the short wing of the restaurant.

Their waitress was a henna-haired woman named Elvira. She had a round face with dimples, eyes that actually twinkled, and a Texas drawl. She took their orders for cheeseburgers, French fries, coleslaw, and Coors.

257

When Elvira left the table and they were alone, Tina said, 'Let's have a look at the papers you took off that guy who called himself Vince.'

Elliot fished the pages out of his hip pocket, unfolded them, and put them on the table. There were three sheets of paper, each containing ten or twelve typewritten questions.

They leaned in from opposite sides of the booth and read the material silently for a minute.

1. How long have you known Christina Evans?
2. Why did Christina Evans ask you, rather than another attorney, to handle the exhumation of her son's body?
3. What reason does she have to doubt the official story of her son's death?
4. Does she have any proof that the official story of her son's death is false?
5. If she has such proof, what is it?
6. Where did she obtain this evidence?
7. Have you ever heard of 'Project Pandora'?
8. Have you been given, or has Mrs. Evans been given, any material relating to top-secret military research installations in the Sierra Mountains?

Elliot looked up from the page. 'Have you ever heard of Project Pandora?'

'No.'

'Secret labs in the High Sierras?'

'Oh, sure. Mrs. Neddler told me all about them.'

'Mrs. Neddler?'

'My cleaning woman.'

'Jokes again.'

'At a time like this.'

'Balm for the afflicted, medicine for melancholy.'

'Groucho Marx,' she said.

'You win the sixty-four thousand dollars.'

'Evidently they think someone from Project Pandora has decided to rat on them.'

'It looks that way.'

'Is that who has been in Danny's room? Did someone from Project Pandora write on the chalkboard . . . and then fiddle with the computer at work?'

'Maybe,' Elliot said.

'But you don't think so.'

'Well, if someone had a guilty conscience, why wouldn't he approach you directly?'

'He could be afraid. Looks like he'd have damned good reason to be.'

'Maybe,' Elliot said again. 'But for some reason I think it's more complicated than that. Don't ask me why. Just a hunch.'

They read quickly through the remaining material, but none of it was enlightening. Most of the questions were concerned with how much Tina knew about the true nature of the Sierra accident, how much she had told Elliot, how much she had told Michael, and how many other people she had discussed it with. There were no more intriguing tidbits like Project Pandora, no more clues or leads, nothing of any value to them.

Elvira brought two frosted glasses and two icy bottles of Coors.

The jukebox began to play a mournful Barbara Mandrell song.

Elliot sipped his beer and looked through the horror-comics magazine that had belonged to Danny. 'Amazing,' he said when he finished skimming *The Boy Who Was Not Dead*.

'You'd think it was even more amazing if you'd suffered through those nightmares,' she said. 'So now what do we do?'

Elliot thought for a moment, then said, 'Danny's was a closed-coffin funeral. Was it the same with the other thirteen scouts?'

'About half of the others were buried without viewings,' Tina said.

'Their parents never saw the bodies?'

'Oh, yes. All the other parents were asked to identify their children, even though some of the corpses were in such a horrible state that they couldn't be cosmetically restored for viewing at a funeral. Michael and I were the only ones who were strongly advised not to look at the remains. Danny was the only one who was too badly . . . mangled.' Even after all this time, when she thought of Danny's last moments on earth – the terror he must have known, the excruciating pain he must have endured, even if it was of brief duration – she began to choke up with sorrow for him. She blinked back tears and took a big swallow of beer and said, 'Why do you ask?'

'I thought we might make some quick allies out of those other parents,' Elliot said. 'If they hadn't seen their kids' bodies, they might have just gone through a year of doubt like you did. I thought they might be easily persuaded to join us in a call for the reopening of *all* graves. If that many voices were raised, Vince's bosses couldn't risk silencing all of them, and we'd be safe. But I guess I can forget that scheme. If the other people had a chance to view the bodies, if none of them has had any reason to entertain doubts like yours, then they're finally feeling good about life again. If we go to them now with a wild story about a mysterious conspiracy, they aren't going to be anxious to listen.'

'So we're still alone.'

'Yes.'

'You said we could go to a reporter, try to get some media interest brewing. Do you have anyone in mind?'

'I know a couple of local guys,' Elliot said. 'But maybe it's not wise to go to the local press. That might be just what Vince's bosses are expecting us to do; they might be waiting, watching. We might be dead before we can tell a reporter more than a sentence or two. I think we'll have to take the story out of town, and before we do that, I'd like to have a few more facts.'

'I thought you said we had enough to interest a good newsman. The pistol you took off that man . . . my house being blown up . . .'

'That might be enough,' he said. 'Certainly, for the Las Vegas paper, it ought to be sufficient. This city still remembers the Sierra accident; it was a local tragedy. But if we have to go to the press in Los Angeles or New York or some other city, the reporters there aren't going to have a whole lot of interest in it unless they see an aspect of the story that lifts it out of the local-interest category. Maybe we've already got enough to convince them it's big news. I'm not sure. And I want to be damned sure before we try to go public with it. Ideally, I'd even like to be able to hand the reporter a neat theory about what really happened to those scouts, something sensational that he can hook his story onto.'

'Such as?'

He shook his head. 'I don't have anything completely worked out yet. But it seems to me that the most obvious thing we have to consider is that the scouts and their leaders saw something they weren't supposed to see.'

'Project Pandora?'

He drank some beer and used one finger to

wipe a trace of foam from his upper lip. 'Yes. A military secret. I can't see what else would have brought an organization like Vince's so deeply into this; an intelligence outfit of that size and sophistication doesn't waste its time on Mickey Mouse stuff.'

'But it's so bizarre. Military secrets . . . that seems so far out,' Tina said.

'In case you didn't know it, Nevada has more defense-related government installations than any state in the union. And I'm not just talking about the obvious ones like Nellis Air Force Base and the Nuclear Test Site. This state's ideally suited for secret or quasi-secret, high-security weapons research centers and other things of that sort. Nevada has thousands of square miles of remote and unpopulated land. The deserts. The deeper reaches of the mountains. And most of those remote areas are owned by the federal government. If you put a secret installation in the middle of all that lonely land, you have a pretty easy job of maintaining security.'

Arms on the table, both hands clasped around her glass of beer, she leaned toward Elliot. 'You're saying that Mr. Jaborski, Mr. Lincoln, and the boys stumbled across a place like that in the High Sierras?'

'It's possible.'

'And saw something they weren't supposed to see, some big military secret?'

'Maybe.'

'And then what? You mean . . . because of what they saw, they were *killed*?'

'It's a theory that ought to intrigue a good reporter,' Elliot said.

'But the government wouldn't murder a group of children just because they accidentally got a glimpse of a new weapon or something.'

'Wouldn't it?'

The rising night wind thrummed against the large pane of glass beside their booth. Beyond the window, on Charleston Boulevard, traffic moved through a sudden whirling cloud of dust and paper scraps.

Chilled, Tina said, 'But how much could the kids have seen? You're the one who said security was easy to maintain when one of these installations was located in the wilderness. The boys couldn't have gotten very close to a place that was well-guarded. Surely they couldn't have managed to get more than a glimpse.'

'Maybe a glimpse was enough to condemn them.'

'Kids aren't the best observers,' she argued. 'They're impressionable, emotional, excitable, given to exaggeration. If they *had* seen something, they'd have come back with a dozen different stories about it, none of them accurate. A group of young boys wouldn't have been a threat to the security of a secret installation.'

'You're probably right,' Elliot said.

'Of course I am.'

'But a bunch of hard-nosed security men might not have seen it that way.'

'Well, they'd have had to be pretty stupid to think that murder was the safest way to handle it. Killing all those people and trying to fake an accident – that was a lot riskier than letting the kids come back with their half-baked stories about seeing something peculiar in the mountains.'

'Remember, there were two adults with those kids. People might have discounted most of what the boys said about it, but they'd have believed Jaborski and Lincoln. Maybe there was so much at stake that the security men at the installation decided Jaborski and Lincoln had to die. Then it became necessary to kill the kids, too, in order to eliminate witnesses to the first two murders.'

'But that's . . . diabolical.'

'Yes. But not unlikely.'

Tina looked down at the wet circle her glass had left on the table. While she thought about what Elliot had said, she dipped one finger in the water and drew a grim mouth, a nose, and a pair of eyes in the circle; she added two horns, transforming the blot of moisture into a little, evil, demonic face. Then she wiped it away with the palm of her hand and said, 'I don't know . . . hidden installations . . . military secrets . . . it all seems just too incredible.'

'Not to me,' Elliot said. 'To me, it sounds plausible if not probable. Anyway, I'm not saying that's what really happened. It's only a theory. But it's the kind of theory that almost any smart, ambitious reporter will go for in a big, big way – if we can come up with enough facts that appear to support it.'

'What about Judge Kennebeck?'

'What about him?'

'He could tell us what we want to know.'

'We'd be committing suicide if we went to Kennebeck's place,' Elliot said. 'Vince's friends are sure to be waiting for us there.'

'Well, isn't there any way that we could slip past them and get at Kennebeck?'

He shook his head. 'Impossible.'

She sighed, slumped back in the booth.

'Besides,' Elliot said, 'Kennebeck probably doesn't know the whole story. He's just like the two men who came to see me: He's probably been told only what he needs to know.'

Elvira arrived with their food. The cheese-burgers were made of juicy ground sirloin. The French fries were crisp, and the coleslaw was tart but not sour.

By unspoken agreement, Tina and Elliot didn't talk about their problems while they ate. In fact they didn't talk much at all. They listened to the jukebox as it played more country-and-western music. They watched Charleston Boulevard

266

through the window; the desert dust storm clouded the oncoming headlights and forced the traffic to move slowly. And they thought about those things that neither of them wanted to speak of: primarily, murder past and murder present.

When they finished eating, Tina spoke first. 'You said we ought to come up with more evidence before we go to the newspapers.'

'We have to.'

'But how are we supposed to get it?' she asked. 'From where? From whom?'

'I've been pondering that,' Elliot said. 'The best thing we could do is get the grave reopened. If the body were exhumed and re-examined by a topnotch pathologist, we'd almost certainly find proof that the cause of death was not what the authorities originally said it was.'

'But we can't reopen the grave ourselves,' Tina said. 'We can't sneak out to the graveyard in the middle of the night and move a couple of tons of earth with picks and shovels. Besides, it's a private cemetery; it's surrounded by a high wall, and I'm sure there's a security system to deal with vandals.'

'And Kennebeck's cronies have almost certainly put a watch on the place,' Elliot said. 'So if we can't examine the body, we'll have to do the next best thing. We'll have to talk to the man who saw it last.'

'Who?'

'Well, I guess . . . the coroner.'

'You mean the man in Reno?'

'Was that where the death certificate was issued?'

'Yes. The bodies were brought out of the mountains, down to Reno.'

'On second thought . . . maybe we'll skip the coroner,' Elliot said. 'He's the one who had to officially designate it as an accidental death. There's a better than even chance he's been co-opted by Kennebeck's crowd. One thing for sure, he's definitely not on our side. Approaching him would be dangerous. We might eventually have to talk to him, of course, but first we should pay a visit to the mortician who handled the body. There might be a lot he can tell us. Is he here in Vegas?'

'No,' Tina said. 'An undertaker in Reno prepared the body and shipped it here for the funeral. The coffin was sealed when it arrived, and we didn't open it.'

Elvira stopped by the table and asked if they wanted anything more. They didn't. She left the check and took away some of the dirty dishes.

To Tina, Elliot said, 'Do you remember the name of the mortician in Reno?'

'Yes. Bellicosti. Luciano Bellicosti.'

Elliot finished the last swallow of beer in his glass and said, 'All right. Then we'll go to Reno.'

'Can't we just call Bellicosti?'

'These days, everyone's phone seems to be tapped. Besides, if we're face to face with him, we'll have a better idea of whether or not he's telling the truth. No, it can't be done long-distance. We have to go up there.'

Her hand shook when she raised her glass to drink the last of her own Coors.

Elliot said, 'What's wrong?'

She wasn't exactly sure. She was filled with a new dread, a fear greater than the one that had burned within her during the past few hours. Haltingly, she said, 'I . . . I guess I'm just . . . afraid to go to Reno.'

He reached across the table, put his hand over hers. 'It's okay. There's less to be frightened of up there than here. It's *here* that killers are looking for us.'

'I know that,' she said. 'Sure, I'm scared of those creeps. But more than that, what I'm afraid of . . . is finding out the truth about Danny's death. And I have a very strong feeling we'll find it in Reno.'

'I thought that was exactly what you wanted to know.'

'Oh, I do. But at the same time, I'm afraid of knowing. Because it's going to be bad. The truth is going to be something really terrible.'

'Maybe not.'

'Yes.'

'The only alternative is to give up, to back off and never know what really happened.'

'And that's worse,' she admitted.

'Anyway, we have to learn the real story behind the Sierra accident. If we know the truth, we can use it to save ourselves. It's our only hope of survival.'

'So when do we leave for Reno?' she asked.

'Tonight. Right now. We'll take my Cessna Skyline. Nice little piece of work. It'll have us in Reno in a few hours. I think it would be wise for us to stay up there for a couple of days, even after we've talked to Bellicosti, until we can figure a way out of this mess. Everyone'll still be looking for us in Vegas, and we'll be able to breathe a little easier if we aren't in town.'

'But I didn't get a chance to pack that suitcase,' Tina said. 'I need a change of clothes, at least a toothbrush and a few other things. Neither one of us has a coat, and it's damned cold in Reno at this time of year.'

'We'll buy whatever we need before we leave.'

'I don't have any money with me. Not a penny.'

'I've got some,' Elliot said. 'A couple of hundred bucks. Plus a wallet filled with credit cards. We could go around the world on the cards alone.'

'But it's a holiday and—'

'And this is Las Vegas,' Elliot said. 'There's always a store open somewhere. And the shops in the hotels won't be closed; this is one of their busiest times of the year. We'll be able to find coats and whatever else we need, and we'll find it all in a hurry.'

'I'll pay you back when—'

'Don't worry about it,' he said. 'We're in this together.' He left a generous tip for the waitress and stood up. 'Come on. The sooner we're out of this town, the safer I'll feel.'

She went with him to the cash register, which was at the entrance. The cashier was a white-haired man who looked owlish behind a pair of extremely thick spectacles. He smiled and asked Elliot if the meal had been satisfactory, and Elliot said it had been fine, and the old man began to make change with slow, arthritic fingers.

The rich odor of chilli sauce drifted out of the kitchen. Green peppers. Onions. Jalapeno peppers. The distinct aromas of Cheddar and Monterey Jack cheese melting over the top of an order of chilli.

The long wing of the diner was nearly full now; there were about forty people eating dinner or waiting to be served. Some of them were laughing. A young couple was plotting conspiratorially, leaning toward each other from opposite sides of a booth, their heads almost touching, both of them smiling. Nearly everyone was engaged in animated conversations, couples and cozy groups of friends, enjoying themselves, looking forward to the three days of the four-day holiday that still lay ahead of them.

Suddenly Tina felt a pang of envy. More than anything else in the world, she wanted to be one of these fortunate people. She wanted to be having an ordinary meal, on an ordinary evening, in the middle of an ordinary life, with every reason to anticipate a long and comfortably ordinary future. None of these people had to worry about professional killers, weird conspiracies, gas company men who were not really gas company men, silencer-equipped pistols, exhumations . . . They didn't realize how lucky they were. She felt as if a vast unbridgeable gap separated her from people like these, and she wondered if she ever again would be even half as relaxed and free from care as they appeared to be at this moment.

A sharp, cold draft prickled the back of her neck.

She turned to see who had come through the door.

The door was closed. No one had come in.

Yet the air remained cool – *changed*.

On the jukebox, which stood to the left of the door, a currently popular, country ballad was playing:

> *'Baby, baby, baby, I love you still.*
> *Our love will live; I know it will.*
> *And one thing on which you can bet*

*Is that our love is not dead yet.*
*No, our love is not dead*
*not dead—*
*not dead—*
*not dead—'*

The record stuck. It labored again and again through that same tiny length of the groove.

Tina stared at the jukebox in horror.

*'not dead—*
*not dead—*
*not dead—'*

Elliot turned away from the cashier and put a hand on Tina's shoulder. 'What the hell . . .?'

Tina couldn't speak. She couldn't move.

The air was getting colder.

She shuddered.

The other customers stopped talking and turned to stare at the stuttering machine.

*'not dead—*
*not dead—*
*not dead—*
*not dead—'*

The image of Death's rotting face flashed into Tina's mind.

'Stop it,' she said.

273

Someone said, 'Shoot the piano player.'

Someone else said, 'Kick the damned thing.'

Elliot stepped up to the jukebox and shook it gently. The needle popped out of the scratch, and the song continued smoothly for one more line. But as Elliot turned away from it, the needle stuck again on the same two words.

> *'not dead—*
> *not dead—*
> *not dead—'*

Tina wanted to walk through the diner and grab each of the customers by the throat, shake and threaten each of them, until she discovered who had rigged the jukebox. At the same time, she knew that wasn't a rational thought; the explanation, whatever it might be, was not that simple. No one here had rigged the machine. Only a moment ago, she had envied these people for the very ordinariness of their lives. It was simply ludicrous to suspect any of them of being employed by the secret organization that had blown up her house. Ludicrous and paranoid. They were just ordinary people in a roadside restaurant, having dinner.

> *'not dead—*
> *not dead—*
> *not dead—'*

Elliot shook the jukebox again, but this time the needle refused to pop out of the scratch.

The air grew colder still. Tina heard some of the customers commenting on it.

Elliot shook the machine harder than he had done the last time, then harder still, but it continued to repeat that two-word message in the voice of the country singer, as if an invisible hand were holding the phonograph arm firmly in place.

The white-haired cashier came out from behind the counter. 'I'll take care of it, folks. Just a second.' He called to one of the waitresses. 'Jenny, check the thermostat. We're supposed to have heat in here tonight, not air conditioning.'

Elliot stepped out of the way as the old man approached.

Although no one was touching the jukebox at that moment, the volume increased, and the two words boomed through the diner, thundered, vibrated in the windows and rattled silverware on the tables.

'NOT DEAD—
NOT DEAD—
NOT DEAD—'

Some people winced and put their hands over their ears.

The old man had to shout to be heard above

275

the explosive voice on the jukebox. 'There's a button on the back that'll reject the record.'

Tina wasn't able to cover her ears; her arms hung straight down at her sides frozen, rigid, hands fisted, and she couldn't find the will or the strength to lift them. She wanted to scream, but she couldn't make a sound.

Colder, colder.

She became aware of the familiar, spiritlike presence that had been in Angela's office when the computer terminal had begun to operate by itself. She had the same feeling of being watched that she'd had in the parking lot a short while ago.

The old man crouched beside the machine, reached behind it, found the button. He pushed it several times.

'NOT DEAD—
NOT DEAD—
NOT DEAD—'

'Have to unplug it!' the old man said.

The volume increased again. The two words blasted out of the speakers in all corners of the diner with such incredible, bone-jarring force that it was difficult to believe that the machine had been built with the capability of pouring out sound with this excessive, unnerving power.

Elliot pulled the jukebox from the wall so that the old man could reach the cord.

In that instant Tina realized she had nothing to fear from the presence that lay behind this eerie manifestation. It meant her no harm. Quite the opposite. In a flash of understanding, she saw through to the heart of the mystery. Her hands, which had been curled into tight fists, came open once more. The tension went out of her neck and shoulder muscles. Her heartbeat became less like the pounding of a jackhammer, but it still did not settle into a normal rhythm; now it was affected by excitement rather than terror. If she tried to scream now, she would be able to do so, but she no longer wanted to scream.

As the white-haired cashier grasped the plug in his gnarled hands and wiggled it back and forth in the wall socket, trying to free it, Tina almost told him to stop. She wanted to see what would happen next if no one interfered with the presence that had taken control of the jukebox. But before Tina could think of a way to phrase her odd request, the old man succeeded in unplugging the machine.

Following the monotonous, ear-splitting repetition of that two-word message, the silence was stunning.

After a second of surprised relief, everyone in the diner applauded the old man.

Jenny, the waitress, called to him from behind

277

the counter. 'Hey, Al, I didn't touch the thermostat. It says the heat's on and set at seventy. You better take a look at it.'

'You must have done something to it,' Al said. 'It's getting warm in here again.'

'I didn't touch it,' Jenny insisted.

Al didn't believe her, but Tina did.

Elliot turned away from the jukebox and looked at Tina with concern. 'Are you all right?'

'Yes. God, yes! Better than I've been in a long time.'

He frowned, baffled by her smile. 'But what just happened here is—'

'I know what it is,' she said. 'Elliot, I know exactly what it is!'

'You do?'

'Come on,' she said excitedly. 'Let's go.'

He was confused by the change in her demeanor, but she didn't want to explain things to him there in the diner. She opened the door and went outside.

# 22

The windstorm was still in progress, but it was not raging as fiercely as it had been when Elliot and Tina had watched it through the restaurant window. A brisk wind pushed across the city from the east; the air had a tangible quality and an unpleasant taste, laden as it was with dust and with powdery white sand that had been swept in from the desert.

They put their heads down and scurried past the front of the diner, around the side of it, through the purple light under the single mercury-vapor lamp, then into the deep shadows behind the building.

In the Mercedes, in the darkness, with the doors locked, she said, 'No wonder we haven't been able to figure it out!'

'Tina, why on earth are you so bubbly?'

'We've been looking at this thing all wrong,' she said. 'We've approached it ass-backwards. No wonder we haven't been able to find a solution.'

'What are you talking about? Did you see what

279

I saw in there? Did you hear the jukebox? I don't see how that could have cheered you up. It made my blood run cold. It was *weird*.'

'Look,' she said excitedly, 'we thought someone was sending me messages about Danny being alive just to rub my face in the fact that he was actually dead – or to let me know, in a roundabout fashion, that the *way* he died wasn't anything like what I'd been told. But those messages haven't been coming from a sadist. And they haven't been coming from someone who wants to expose the true story of the Sierra accident. They aren't being sent by a total stranger or by Michael or by an acquaintance. They are *exactly* what they appear to be!'

Confused, he said, 'And to your way of thinking, what do they appear to be?'

'They're cries for help.'

'What?'

'They're coming from *Danny*!'

Elliot gaped at her, his dark eyes reflecting a distant light. 'Are you trying to say that Danny . . . reached out from the grave to cause that excitement in the restaurant? You really think his ghost was haunting a jukebox?'

'No, no, no. I'm saying Danny isn't dead.'

'Wait a minute. Wait a minute,' he said gently.

'My Danny is alive! I'm sure of it.'

'We've already been through that argument, and we rejected it,' he reminded her.

'We were wrong,' Tina said. 'Jaborski, Lincoln, and all the other boys might have died in the High Sierras, but Danny didn't. I know it. I *sense* it. It's like . . . a revelation . . . almost a vision. Maybe there was an accident, but it wasn't like anything we were told. It was something very different, something exceedingly strange.'

'That's already obvious. But—'

'The government had to hide it, and this organization that Judge Kennebeck works for was apparently given responsibility for the cover-up.'

'I'm with you that far,' Elliot said. 'That's a logical series of deductions, considering what's happened in the past few hours. But how do you deduce that Danny's alive? That doesn't necessarily follow.'

'I'm only telling you what I *know*, what I feel,' she said. 'A tremendous sense of peace, of reassurance came over me in the diner, just before you finally managed to shut off the jukebox. It wasn't just an inner feeling of peace. It came from outside of me. Like a wave. Oh, hell, I can't really explain it. I only know what I felt. Danny was trying to reassure me, trying to tell me that he's still alive. I *know* it. Danny survived the accident, but they couldn't let him come home because he'd tell everyone that the government was responsible for the deaths of the others, and that would blow their secret military installation wide open.'

'You're reaching, grasping for straws,' he said.

'I'm not, I'm not,' she insisted.

'So where *is* Danny?'

'They're keeping him somewhere. I don't know why they didn't kill him. I don't know how long they think they can keep him bottled up like this. But that's what they're doing. That's what's going on. Those might not be the precise circumstances, but they're pretty damned close to the truth.'

'Tina—'

She wouldn't let him interrupt. 'This secret police force, these people behind Kennebeck . . . they think someone involved with Project Pandora has turned on them and has told me what really happened to Danny. They're wrong, of course. It wasn't one of them. It's Danny. Somehow . . . I don't know how . . . but he's reaching out to me.' She struggled to explain the understanding that had come to her in the diner. 'Somehow . . . some way . . . he's reaching out . . . with his mind, I guess. Danny was the one who wrote those words on the chalkboard. *With his mind.*'

'The only proof you have of this is what you say you feel . . . this revelation, this vision that you've had. And that's no proof at all.'

'It's proof enough for me,' she said. 'And it would be proof enough for you, too, if you'd had the same experience back there in the diner, if you'd felt what I felt. It was Danny who reached out for me when I was at work . . . found me in the office . . . tried to use the hotel computer to send his message to me. And now the jukebox. He must be . . . psychic. That's it! That's what he is. He's psychic. He has psychic power, and he's reaching out, trying to tell me he's alive, asking me to find him and save him. And the people who're holding him *don't know he's doing it*! They're blaming the leak on one of their own or someone from Project Pandora.'

'Tina, this is a very imaginative theory, but—'

'It might be imaginative, but it's not a theory. It's the truth. It's fact. I *feel* it deep in my bones. Can you shoot holes through it? Can you prove I'm wrong?'

'First of all,' Elliot said, 'before he went into the mountains with Jaborski, in all the years you knew him and lived in the same house with him, did Danny ever show any signs of being psychic?'

'Well . . . no.'

'Then how come he suddenly has all these amazing powers?'

She said, 'I *do* remember some little things he did that were sort of odd.'

'Like what?'

'Like the time he wanted to know exactly what his daddy did for a living. He was eight or nine years old, and he was very curious about the details of a dealer's job. Michael sat at the kitchen table with him and dealt some blackjack. Danny was just about old enough to understand the rules. But he'd never played before. And he certainly wasn't old enough or enough of a math genius to remember all the cards that were played and calculate his chances from that, like some of the very best players can do. Yet he won steadily. Michael used a jar full of peanuts to represent casino chips, and Danny won every nut in the jar.'

'The game must have been rigged,' Elliot said. 'Michael was letting him win.'

'That's what I thought at first. But Michael swore he wasn't doing that. And he seemed genuinely astonished by Danny's streak of luck. Besides, Michael isn't a card mechanic. He can't handle a deck well enough to stack it while he's shuffling. And then there was Elmer.'

'Who's Elmer?'

'He was our dog. A cute little mutt. One day, about two years ago, I was in the kitchen, making an apple pie, and Danny came in to tell me that Elmer wasn't anywhere to be found in the yard. Apparently, the pooch slipped out of the gate when the serviceman came around to put chemicals in the swimming pool. Danny said Elmer wasn't going to come back because he'd been hit and killed by a truck. I told him not to worry. I said we'd find Elmer safe and sound. But we never did. We never found him at all.'

'Just because you never found him – that's not proof he was killed by a truck.'

'It was proof enough for Danny. He mourned for weeks.'

Elliot sighed. 'Winning a few hands at blackjack – that's luck, just like you said. And predicting that a runaway dog will be killed in traffic – that's just a reasonable assumption to make under the circumstances. And even if those were examples of psychic ability, little tricks of that sort are light years away from the stuff you're attributing to Danny now.'

'I know that,' she said. 'Somehow, his abilities have grown a lot stronger. Maybe because of the situation he's in. The fear. The stress.'

'If fear and stress could increase the power of his psychic gifts, why didn't he start trying to get in touch with you months ago?' Elliot asked.

'Maybe it took a year of stress and fear to develop the ability. I don't know. Christ, how could I know the answer to that?'

'Calm down,' he said. 'You dared me to shoot holes in your theory. That's what I'm doing.'

'No,' she said. 'As far as I can see, you haven't shot one hole in it yet. Danny's alive. He's being held somewhere, and he's trying to reach me with his mind. He's able to move objects just by thinking about them. What do you call that? Isn't there a name for that ability?'

'Telekinesis,' Elliott said.

'Yes! That's it. He's telekinetic. Do you have

a better explanation for what happened in the diner?'

'Well . . . no.'

'Are you going to tell me it was coincidence that the record stuck on those two words?'

'No,' Elliot said. 'It wasn't a coincidence. That would be even more unlikely than the possibility that Danny did it.'

'You admit I'm right.'

'No,' he said. 'I can't think of a better explanation, but I'm not ready to accept yours. I've never believed in that psychic crap.'

For a minute or two, neither of them spoke. They stared out at the dark parking lot and at the fenced storage yard full of fifty-gallon drums that lay beyond the lot. Sheets, puffs, and spinning funnels of vaguely phosphorescent dust moved like specters through the night.

At last Tina said, 'I'm *right*, Elliot. I know I am. My theory explains everything. Even the nightmares. That's another way Danny's been trying to reach me. He's been sending me nightmares for the past few weeks. That's why they've been so much different from any dreams I've had before, so much stronger and more vivid.'

He seemed to find this new statement more outrageous than what she'd said before it. 'Wait, wait, wait. Now you're talking about another power besides telekinesis.'

'If he has one ability, why not the other?'

'Because pretty soon you'll be saying he's God.'

'Just telekinesis and the power to influence my dreams. That explains why I dreamed about the hideous figure of Death in this comic book. If Danny's sending me messages in dreams, it's only natural he'd use images he was familiar with – like a monster out of a favorite horror story.'

'But if he can send dreams to you,' Elliot said, 'why wouldn't he simply transmit a neat, clear message telling you what's happened to him and where he is? Wouldn't that get him the help he wants a lot faster? Why would he be so unclear and indirect? He should send a concise mental telegram. That would be a lot easier for you to understand.'

'Don't get sarcastic,' she said.

'I'm not. I'm merely asking a tough question. It's another hole in your theory.'

She would not be deterred. 'It's not a hole. There's an explanation. Obviously, Danny isn't telepathic. He's telekinetic, able to move objects with his mind. And he can influence dreams. But he's not telepathic. He can't transmit detailed thoughts. He can't send "concise mental telegrams" because he doesn't have that much power or control. So he has to try to reach me as best he can.'

'Will you listen to us?'

'I've been listening,' she said.

'We sound like a couple of prime candidates for a padded cell.'

'No. I don't think we do.'

'This talk of psychic power . . . it's not exactly levelheaded stuff,' Elliot said.

'Then explain what happened in the diner.'

'I can't. Damn it, I can't explain that,' he said, sounding like a priest whose faith had been deeply shaken. However, the faith that Elliot was beginning to question was not religious but scientific.

'Stop thinking like an attorney,' she said. 'Stop trying to herd the facts into neat corrals of logic.'

'That's exactly what I've been trained to do for most of my life.'

'I know,' she said sympathetically. 'But the world is full of illogical things that are nonetheless true. And this is one of them.'

The wind buffeted the sports car, moaned along the windows, seeking a way in to them.

Elliot said, 'If Danny has this incredible power, why is he sending messages just to you? Why doesn't he at least contact Michael, too?'

'Maybe he doesn't feel close enough to Michael to try reaching him,' Tina said. 'After all, the last couple of years we were married, Michael was running around with a lot of other women, spending most of his time away from home, and Danny felt even more abandoned than I did. I never talked against Michael. I even tried to justify some of his actions because I didn't want Danny to hate him. But Danny was hurt just the same. I suppose it's natural for him to reach out to me rather than to his father.'

Elliot thought about that a moment.

A wall of dust fell softly over the car.

'Still think you can shoot my theory full of holes?' she asked.

'No. You argued your case pretty well.'

'Thank you, Judge.'

'I still can't believe you're right. Oh, I know a lot of intelligent people believe in ESP. But I don't. I can't bring myself to accept this psychic idea of yours. Not just yet, anyway. I'm going to keep looking for some less exotic explanation of what's been happening.'

'And if you come up with one,' Tina said, 'I'll give it very serious consideration.'

He put a hand on her shoulder. 'The reason I've argued with you about this thing is because . . . well . . . I'm worried about you, Tina.'

'About my sanity?'

'No, no. Of course not. This psychic explanation bothers me mainly because it gives you hope that Danny's still alive. And that seems dangerous. It seems to me like you're just setting yourself up for a bad fall, a lot of pain.'

'No,' she said. 'I'm not. Not at all. Because Danny really is alive.'

'But what if he isn't?'

'He is.'

'If you discover he's dead, it'll be like losing him all over again.'

'But he's not dead,' she insisted. 'I feel it. I sense it. I *know* it, Elliot.'

'And if he *is* dead?' Elliot asked, every bit as insistent as she was.

She thought about it for a moment, and then she said, 'I'll be able to handle it.'

'You're sure?'

'Positive.'

In the dim light, where the brightest thing was mauve shadow, he found her eyes, held her with his intent gaze. She felt as if he were not merely looking at her but into her, through her. Finally he leaned over and kissed the corner of her mouth, then her cheek, her eyes.

He said, 'I don't want to see your heart broken.'

'It won't be.'

'I'll do what I can to see it isn't.'

'I know.'

'But there isn't much I *can* do. It's pretty much out of my hands; we just have to flow with events.'

She returned his kisses. She put a hand against the back of his neck, holding his face close. The taste of his lips and the warmth of him made her inexpressibly happy.

'Know what I'd like to do right now?' he asked.

'I can imagine.'

'I'd like to go to a hotel, check in as Mr. and Mrs. Smith, and indulge in a wild, abandoned night of forbidden passion.'

'Unchained lust,' she said.

'Sexual depravity.'

'Sounds like we've been reading the same cheap, dirty books,' she said.

'Wouldn't it be wonderful if life could occasionally be as clear and straightforward as it is in cheap, dirty books?'

In spite of the console between their seats, he leaned closer and put an arm around her and held her close, his face buried against her neck.

Although they were bantering about sex, Tina realized it wasn't really sex he needed from her now. What he needed was merely to be close, to hold her, to touch her, to obtain comfort from her. That was something she needed, too: a deep, soothing display of affection; reassurance; a quiet denial of the loneliness of existence; the soul-satisfying, asexual nuzzling that you somehow expected moles to engage in when they were wintering in their burrows. But she had always been under the impression that such innocent affection, utterly unassociated with sex, was exclusively a woman's need. She was somewhat surprised to find Elliot seeking that sort of compassion and tenderness from her. Michael hadn't been like that. With Michael, it always led inexorably to bed; tenderness was, to him, most often just a cocksman's clever technique for seduction. Now, as she held Elliot and was held by him, she realized, more profoundly than before, that she had been missing a great deal in life.

'Someday we'll have to check into one of those honeymoon suites at a Strip hotel,' Elliot said, continuing the light sexual banter that was intended only to amuse, not seduce her. 'You know, one of those places with mirrors on the ceiling, a king-size bed—'

'A vibrator in the mattress.'

'Scented oils.'

'Someday,' she said, aware that they were indirectly trying to assure each other that eventually there would be time for such foolishness and that they would survive to enjoy it.

He sighed and leaned back from her. 'Right now, though, we have some shopping to do. Winter coats. A couple of toothbrushes.'

'Hardly as exciting as a honeymoon suite.'

'Hardly,' he agreed. He started the car. 'Well, let's get moving. Once we're in Reno, we'll have to stay *somewhere*. Maybe they have hotel rooms with mirrored ceilings up there, too. After all, Las Vegas doesn't have a monopoly on wickedness and wanton degeneracy.'

In spite of their attempts to amuse each other, and in spite of the fact that she was buoyed by the unshakable feeling that Danny was alive, Tina felt fear creeping back into her as they drove onto Charleston Boulevard again. She was no longer afraid of facing the awful truth that might be waiting in Reno. What had happened to Danny might still prove to be terrible, painful, shattering, but she didn't think it would be as hard to accept as his 'death' had been. The only thing that scared her now was the possibility of finding Danny alive – and then being unable to rescue him. In the process of locating the boy, she and Elliot might be killed. If they found Danny and then perished trying to save him, that would be a nasty trick of fate, for sure. She knew from experience that fate had countless nasty tricks up its sleeve, and that was why she was frightened.

# 23

Willis Bruckster studied his keno ticket, comparing it to the series of winning numbers that were beginning to flash onto the electronic board that was suspended from the casino ceiling. He tried to appear intently interested in the outcome of this game, but he really didn't care. The marked ticket in his hand was worthless; he hadn't taken it to the betting window, hadn't wagered any money on it. He was using keno as a cover. He didn't want to attract the attention of the omnipresent casino security men, and the easiest way to escape their notice was to look like the least threatening hick in the huge room. With that in mind, Bruckster was wearing a cheap leisure suit, dark-green loafers, and white socks; he was carrying a couple of books of the discount coupons that casinos use to pull slot machine players into the house; he wore a camera on a strap around his neck; and he was playing keno, which was a game that didn't have any appeal for either smart gamblers or cheaters, the two kinds of customers who most interested the security men. Bruckster was so sure he looked dull and ordinary that he wouldn't have been surprised if a security guard had looked at him and yawned.

He was determined not to fail on this assignment. It was a career maker – or breaker. The Network wanted to eliminate everyone who might conceivably press for the exhumation of Danny Evans's body. The Network's Nevada bureau chief was sweating bullets because all eyes at the Washington HQ were on him. The Network agents targeted against Elliot Stryker and Christina Evans had thus far failed to carry out their kill orders, and their ineptitude gave Willis Bruckster a chance to shine. If he made a clean hit here, in the crowded casino, he would be assured of a promotion.

Bruckster stood at the head of the escalator that led from the lower shopping arcade to the casino level of the MGM Grand Hotel. During their periodic breaks from the gaming tables, nursing stiff necks and sore shoulders and leaden arms, the dealers retired to a combination lounge and locker room at the bottom and to the right of the moving stairs. A group of them had gone down a while ago and would be coming back up for their last stand at the tables before a whole new staff came on with the shift change. Bruckster was waiting for one of those dealers: Michael Evans.

He hadn't expected to find the man at work.

He had thought Evans might be keeping a vigil at the demolished house, while the firemen sifted through the still-smouldering debris, searching for the remains of the woman they thought might be buried there. But when Bruckster had come into the Grand thirty minutes ago, Evans had been chatting with the players and cracking jokes and grinning as if nothing of any importance had happened in his life lately. Perhaps he didn't know about the explosion at his former house. Or maybe he *did* know and just didn't give a damn about his ex-wife. It might have been a bitter divorce.

Bruckster hadn't been able to get close to Evans when the dealer left the blackjack pit at the beginning of the break. He had stationed himself here, at the head of the escalator, and had pretended to be interested in the keno board. He was confident that he would nail Evans when the man returned from the dealer's lounge in the next couple of minutes.

The last of the numbers flashed onto the board. Willis Bruckster stared at them, then crumpled his game card with an obvious display of disappointment and disgust, as if he had lost a few hard-earned dollars.

He glanced down the escalator. Dealers in black trousers, white shirts, and maroon string ties were coming up.

Bruckster stepped away from the escalator and

unfolded his keno card. He began to compare it once more with the numbers on the electronic board, as if he were praying that he had made a mistake the first time.

Michael Evans was the seventh dealer off the escalator. He was a handsome, easy-going guy who didn't walk so much as he ambled. He stopped to have a word with a pretty cocktail waitress, and she smiled at him. The other dealers streamed by, and when Michael Evans finally turned away from the girl, he was the last in the procession as it moved toward the blackjack pits.

Bruckster fell in beside and slightly behind his target as they pressed through the teeming mob that jammed the big casino. He reached into a pocket of his leisure suit and took out a tiny aerosol can. The can measured only a little larger than one of those spray-style breath fresheners, small enough to be concealed in Bruckster's hand.

They came to a standstill at a knot of laughing people. No one in the jolly group seemed to realize he was obstructing the main aisle. Bruckster took advantage of the pause to tap his quarry on the shoulder.

Evans turned around.

Bruckster smiled and said, 'I think maybe you dropped this back there.'

He held his hand eighteen inches below Michael Evans's eyes, so that the dealer was forced to look down to see what was there.

The fine spray caught him squarely in the face, across the nose and lips, penetrating swiftly and deeply into the nostrils. Perfect.

Evans reacted as anyone would. He gasped in surprise as he realized he was being squirted.

The gasp drew the deadly mist up his nose, where the active poison was absorbed through the sinus membranes with incredible speed. In two seconds it was in his bloodstream, and his heart was seizing up.

Evans's look of surprise turned to shock, then to a wild, twisted expression of agony as brutal pain slammed through him. He gagged, and a ribbon of foamy saliva unraveled from the corner of his mouth, down his chin. His eyes rolled back in his head, and he fell.

As Bruckster pocketed the miniature aerosol device, he said, 'We have a sick man here.'

Heads turned toward him.

'Give the man room,' Bruckster said. 'For God's sake, someone get a doctor!'

No one had seen the murder. It had been committed in a sheltered space within the crowd, hidden by the killer's and the victim's bodies. Even if someone had been looking, there would not have been much for him to see.

Bruckster quickly knelt at Michael Evans's side and took his pulse. There was no heartbeat, none at all, not even a faint lub-dub.

A thin film of moisture covered the victim's

nose and lips and chin, but that was only the harmless medium in which the poison had been suspended. The active poison itself had already evaporated. The medium would evaporate, too, in a few more seconds, so there would be nothing unusual to arouse the doctor's suspicion.

A uniformed security guard shouldered through the mob of curious onlookers and stooped down next to Bruckster. 'What happened?'

'Looks like a heart attack to me,' Bruckster said.

'You know him?'

'Never saw him before.'

The guard tried to find a pulse; he couldn't. He began CPR treatment, but after a couple of minutes he stopped and said, 'I think it's hopeless.'

'Looks that way,' Bruckster said, forcing a note of sadness into his voice.

'Heart attack, like you said.'

'I imagine so,' Bruckster said.

The poison was untraceable. The hotel doctor would call it a heart attack when he got a look at the body. So would the coroner. So would the death certificate.

A perfect murder.

Willis Bruckster had to suppress a smile.

# 24

Judge Harold Kennebeck built ships in bottles. The walls of his den were lined with examples of his hobby. A tiny model of a seventeenth-century Dutch pinnace was perpetually under sail in a small, pale-blue bottle. A large, exquisitely detailed four-masted topsail schooner completely filled a five-gallon jug. There were sailing ships of every description: a four-masted barkentine, a mid-sixteenth-century Swedish kravel, a fifteenth-century Spanish caravel, a British merchantman, a Baltimore clipper, and dozens of others, all created with remarkable care and craftsmanship, many of them in uniquely shaped bottles that made their construction all the more laborious and amazing.

Kennebeck stood before one of the display cases, studying the minutely detailed rigging of a late-eighteenth-century French frigate. As he stared at the model, he wasn't thinking of it so much as he was mulling over the recent developments in the Evans case. His ships, sealed in their glass worlds, relaxed him; he liked to look at them when he had a problem to work out or when he was particularly on edge, for they made him feel serene, and that serenity allowed his mind to function at its peak.

The longer he thought about it, the less Kennebeck was able to believe that the Evans woman knew the truth about her son. Surely, if someone from Project Pandora had told her what had happened to that busload of scouts, she wouldn't have reacted to the news with equanimity. She would have been frightened, terrified . . . and damned angry. She would have gone straight to the police, to the newspapers, or both.

Instead, she had gone to Elliot Stryker.

And that was where the paradox jumped up like a jack-in-the-box. On the one hand, she behaved as if she did not know the truth. But on the other hand, she was working through Stryker to have her son's grave reopened, and that seemed to indicate that she knew *something*.

If Stryker could be believed, the woman's motivations were innocent enough. According to the attorney, Mrs. Evans felt guilty about not having had the courage to view the boy's mutilated body prior to the burial. She felt as if she had failed to pay her last respects to the deceased in a proper manner. Her guilt had grown gradually into a serious psychological problem. She was in great distress, and she suffered from horrible dreams that plagued her every night. That was Stryker's story.

Kennebeck tended to believe Stryker. There was an element of coincidence involved, but not all coincidence was meaningful. That was something you tended to forget when you spent your life in the intelligence game. Christina Evans probably hadn't entertained a single doubt about the official explanation of the Sierra accident; she probably hadn't known a damned thing about Pandora when she had requested an exhumation, but her timing couldn't have been worse.

If the woman actually hadn't known anything of the cover-up, then the Network could have used her ex-husband and the legal system to delay the reopening of the grave. In the meantime, Network agents could have located a boy's body in the same state of decay as Danny's body would have been if it had been locked in that coffin for the past year. They could have opened the grave secretly, at night, when the cemetery was closed; they could have switched the remains of the fake Danny for the rocks that were in the casket. Then the guilt-stricken mother could have been permitted one last, late, ghastly look at the remains of her son. That would have been a complex operation, fraught with the danger of discovery, risking the ultimate exposure of the Network's existence, but the risks would have been quite acceptable; and there wouldn't have been any need to kill anyone.

Unfortunately, George Alexander, the chief of the Nevada bureau of the Network, hadn't possessed the patience or the skill to determine the woman's true motives. He had assumed the worst and had acted on that assumption. When Kennebeck informed Alexander of Elliot Stryker's request for an exhumation, the bureau chief responded immediately with extreme force. He planned a suicide for Stryker, an accidental death for the woman, and a heart attack for the woman's husband. Two of those assassination attempts had failed. Stryker and the woman had disappeared. Now the entire Network was in the soup, *deep* in it.

As Kennebeck turned away from the French frigate, beginning to wonder if he ought to get out from under the Network before it collapsed on him, he saw George Alexander enter the study through the door that opened off the downstairs hallway. The bureau chief was a slim, elegant, distinguished-looking man. He was wearing Gucci loafers, an expensive suit, a handmade silk shirt, and a Cartier watch. His stylishly cut brown hair shaded to iron-gray at the temples. His eyes were green, clear, and alert – and just a bit menacing. He had a well-formed face, with high cheekbones, a narrow straight nose, and thin lips. When he smiled, his mouth turned up slightly at the left corner, giving him a rather haughty expression, but at the moment he wasn't smiling.

Kennebeck had known Alexander for five years and had disliked him from the day they'd met. He suspected the feeling was mutual.

Part of the antagonism between them was a result of the fact that they had been born into very different worlds and were both proud of their origins, as well as disdainful of all others. Harry Kennebeck had come from a dirt-poor family and had, by his own estimation at least, made quite a lot of himself. Alexander, on the other hand, was the scion of a Pennsylvania family that had been wealthy and powerful for almost a hundred and fifty years. Kennebeck had lifted himself out of poverty through hard work and steely determination. Alexander knew nothing of hard work; he ascended to the top of his field as if he were a prince with a divine right to rule.

Kennebeck was also irritated by Alexander's hypocrisy. The whole damned family was a bunch of hypocrites. The Alexanders were proud of their history of public service. Many of them had been presidential appointees, occupying high-level posts in the federal government; a few had even served on the President's cabinet, though none had ever deigned to run for an elective position. The famous Pennsylvania Alexanders had always been prominently associated with the struggle for minority civil rights, the Equal Rights Amendment, the crusade against capital punishment, liberal politics, and social idealism of every sort. Yet many members of the family had rendered service (secretly, of course) to the FBI, the CIA, and various other intelligence and police agencies, often the very same organizations that they publicly criticized and reviled. Now George Alexander was the Nevada bureau chief of the nation's first truly secret police force, and that fact apparently did not weigh heavily on his liberal conscience.

Kennebeck's politics were of the extreme right-wing variety. He was an unreconstructed fascist and not the least bit ashamed of it. When, as a young man, he had first embarked upon a career in the intelligence services, Harry had been surprised to discover that not all of the people in the espionage business shared his ultraconservative political views. He had expected his co-workers to be super-patriotic right-wingers. But the snoop shops were staffed by quite a few liberals, too. Eventually Harry realized that the extreme left and extreme right shared the same two, basic goals: They wanted to make society more orderly than it naturally was, and they wanted to centralize control of the population in a strong government. Left-wingers and right-wingers differed about certain details, but their only major point of contention centered around the identity of those who would be permitted to be a part of the privileged ruling class, once the power had been sufficiently centralized.

At least I'm honest about my motives, Kennebeck thought as he watched Alexander cross the study. My public opinions are the same as those I express privately, and that's a virtue he doesn't possess. I'm not a hypocrite. I'm not at all like Alexander. Jesus, he's such a smug, Janus-faced bastard!

'I just spoke with the men who're watching Stryker's house,' Alexander said. 'He hasn't shown up yet.'

'I told you he wouldn't go back there,' Kennebeck said.

'Sooner or later he will.'

'No. Not until he's absolutely certain the heat is off. Until then he'll hide out.'

'He's bound to go to the police at some point, and then we'll have him.'

'If he thought he could get any help from the cops, he'd have been there already,' Kennebeck said. 'But he hasn't shown up. And he won't.'

Alexander glanced at his watch. 'Well, he still might pop up here. I'm sure he wants to ask you a lot of questions.'

'Oh, I'm damned sure he does. He wants my hide,' Kennebeck said. 'But he won't come. Not tonight. Not for a long time. He knows we're waiting for him. He knows how the game is played. Don't forget that he used to play it himself.'

'That was a long time ago,' Alexander said impatiently. 'He's been a civilian for fifteen years. He's out of practice. Even if he was a natural then, there's no way he could still be as sharp as he once was.'

'But that's what I've been trying to tell you,' Kennebeck said, pushing a lock of snow-white hair back from his forehead. 'Elliot isn't stupid. He was the best and brightest young officer who ever served under me. He *was* a natural. And that was when he was young and relatively inexperienced. If he's aged as well as he seems to have done, then he might even be sharper these days.'

Alexander didn't want to hear it. In spite of the fact that two of the three planned killings had gone awry, Alexander was self-assured; he was positive that he would eventually triumph.

He's always so damned self-confident, Harry Kennebeck thought. And usually there's no good reason why he should be; if he was aware of his own shortcomings, he'd probably be crushed to death under his collapsing ego.

Alexander went to the huge maple desk and sat behind it, in Kennebeck's wing-backed chair.

The judge glared at him.

Alexander pretended not to notice Kennebeck's displeasure. 'We'll find Stryker and the woman before morning. I've no doubt about that. We're covering all the bases. We've got men checking every hotel and motel—'

'Christ, that's a waste of time,' Kennebeck said. 'Elliot is too smart to waltz into a hotel and leave his name on the register. Besides, there are more hotels and motels in Vegas than in any other city in the world.'

'I'm fully aware of the complexity of the task,' Alexander said. 'But we might get lucky. Meanwhile, we're checking out Stryker's associates in his law firm, his friends, the woman's friends, anyone with whom they might have taken refuge.'

'You don't have enough manpower to follow up on all those possibilities,' the judge said. 'Can't you see that? You should use your people more judiciously. You're spreading yourself too thin. What you should be doing—'

'I'll make those decisions,' Alexander said icily.

'What about the airport?'

'That's taken care of,' Alexander said. 'We've got men going over the passenger lists of every outbound flight.' He picked up an ivory-handled letter opener, turned it over and over in his hands. 'Anyway, even if we are spread a bit thin in all those areas, it doesn't matter much. I already know where we're going to nail Stryker. Here. Right here in this house. That's why I'm still hanging around. Oh, I know, I know, you don't think he'll show up. But a long time ago you were Stryker's mentor, the man he looked up to, the man he learned from, and now you have betrayed him. He'll come here to confront you, even if he knows it's risky. I'm sure he will. I *know* it.'

'Christ,' Kennebeck said sourly. 'Our relationship was never like that. He—'

'I know human nature,' Alexander said, putting an end to the discussion.

Angry, frustrated, Kennebeck turned again to the bottle that contained the French frigate. Suddenly he remembered something important about Elliot Stryker. 'Ah,' he said.

Alexander looked up from the enameled cigarette box that he had been studying. 'What is it?'

'Elliot is a pilot. He owns his own plane.'

Alexander frowned.

'Have you been checking small craft leaving the airport?' Kennebeck said.

'No. Just airliners.'

'Ah.'

'He'd have had to take off in the dark,' Alexander said. 'You think he's licensed for instrument flying? Most businessmen-pilots and hobby pilots aren't certified for anything but daylight.'

'Better get hold of your men at the airport,' Kennebeck said. 'I already know what they're going to find. I'll bet a hundred bucks to a dime that Elliot has slipped out of town under your nose.'

\* \* \*

The Cessna Turbo Skylane RG knifed through the darkness, two miles above the Nevada desert.

'Elliot?'

'Hummm?'

'I'm sorry I got you mixed up in this.'

'You don't like my company?'

'You know what I mean. I'm really sorry.'

'Hey, you didn't get me mixed up in it. You didn't twist my arm. I practically volunteered to help you with the exhumation, and it all just fell apart from there. It's not your fault.'

'Still . . . here you are . . . running for your life, and all because of me.'

'Nonsense. You couldn't have known what would happen after I talked to Kennebeck.'

'I can't help feeling guilty about involving you.'

'If it wasn't me, it would have been some other attorney. And maybe he wouldn't have known how to handle Vince. In which case, both he and you might be dead. So if you look at it that way, it worked out as well as it possibly could.'

'You're really something else,' she said.

'What else am I?'

'Lots of things.'

'Such as?'

'Terrific.'

'Not me. What else?'

'Brave.'

'Bravery is a virtue of fools.'

'Smart.'

'Not as smart as I think I am.'

'Tough.'

'I cry at sad movies. See, I'm not as great as you think I am.'

'You can cook.'

'Now *that's* true!'

The Cessna hit an air pocket, dropped three hundred feet with a sickening lurch, then swept back up to its correct altitude.

'A great cook but a lousy pilot,' she said.

'That was God's turbulence. Complain to Him.'

'How long till we land in Reno?'

'Eighty minutes.'

\* \* \*

George Alexander hung up the phone. He was still sitting in Kennebeck's wing-backed chair. 'Stryker and the woman took off from McCarran International more than two hours ago. They left in his Cessna. He filed a flight plan for Flagstaff.'

The judge stopped pacing. 'Arizona?'

'That's the only Flagstaff I know. But why would they go to Arizona, of all places?'

'They probably didn't,' Kennebeck said. 'I

312

imagine Elliot filed a false flight plan to throw you off his trail.' He was perversely proud of Stryker's cleverness.

'If they actually headed for Flagstaff,' Alexander said, 'they ought to have landed by now. I'll call the night manager at the airport down there, pretend I'm with the FBI, and see what he can tell me.'

Because the Network did not officially exist, it couldn't openly use its authority to gather information. As a result, Network agents routinely posed as FBI men, with counterfeit credentials in the names of actual FBI agents.

While he waited for Alexander to finish with the night manager at the Flagstaff airport, Kennebeck moved from one model ship to another. Tonight, the sight of them didn't calm him at all.

Fifteen minutes later Alexander put down the receiver. 'Stryker isn't on the Flagstaff field. And he hasn't yet been identified in their air space.'

'Ah. So his flight plan *was* a red herring.'

'Unless he crashed between here and there,' Alexander said hopefully.

Kennebeck grimaced. 'He didn't crash. But where the hell *did* he go?'

'Probably in the opposite direction,' Alexander said. 'Southern California.'

'Ah . . . Los Angeles?'

'Or Santa Barbara. Burbank. Long Beach. Ontario. Orange County. There are quite a few airports within the range of that little Cessna.'

They were both silent for a moment, thinking. Then Kennebeck said, 'Reno. That's where they went: Reno.'

'You were so sure they didn't know a thing about the Sierra labs,' Alexander said. 'Have you changed your mind?'

'No. I still think you could have avoided issuing all those kill orders,' Kennebeck said. 'Look, I don't think they're going to the mountains. They don't know where the laboratories are. They don't know anything more about Project Pandora than what they picked up from that list of questions they took off Vince Immelman.'

'Then why Reno?'

Pacing, Kennebeck said, 'Consider this. Now that we've tried to kill them, they *know* the story of the Sierra accident was entirely contrived. They figure there's something wrong with the little boy's body, something odd that we can't afford to let them see. So of course they're *twice* as anxious to see it. They'd exhume it illegally if they could, but they can't get near the cemetery with us watching it. And Stryker knows for sure that we're watching it. So if they can't open the grave and see for themselves what we've done to Danny Evans, what are they going to do? I'll tell you. They're going to do the next best thing; they are going to talk to the person who was supposedly the last one to see the boy's corpse before it was sealed in the coffin. They're going to ask him to describe the condition of the body in minute detail.'

'Richard Pannafin is the coroner in Reno. He issued the death certificate,' Alexander said.

'No. They won't go to Pannafin. They'll figure he's involved in the cover-up.'

'Which he is. Reluctantly.'

'So they'll go to see the mortician who supposedly prepared the boy's body for burial.'

'Bellicosti.'

'Was that his name?'

'Luciano Bellicosti,' Alexander said. 'But if that's where they went, then they're not just hiding out, licking their wounds. Good God, they've actually gone on the offensive!'

'That's Stryker's military intelligence training taking hold,' Kennebeck said. 'That's what I've been trying to tell you. He's not going to be an easy target. He could destroy the Network, given half a chance. And the woman's evidently not one to hide or run away from a problem, either. We have to go after these two with more care than usual. What about this Bellicosti? Will he keep his mouth shut?'

'I don't know,' Alexander said uneasily. 'We have a pretty good hold on him. He's an Italian immigrant. He lived here for eight or nine years before he decided to apply for citizenship. He hadn't gotten his papers yet when we found ourselves needing a cooperative mortician. We put a freeze on his application with the Bureau of Immigration, and we threatened to have him deported if he didn't do what we wanted. He didn't like it. But citizenship was a big enough carrot to keep him motivated. However . . . I don't think we'd better rely on that carrot any longer.'

'This is a hell of an important matter,' Kennebeck said. 'And it sounds to me as if Bellicosti knows too much about it.'

'Exactly,' Alexander said. 'He'll have to be eliminated. And the coroner, too, I think.' He reached for the phone.

'You don't want to take drastic action until you're positive that Stryker actually is headed for Reno. And you won't know for sure until he lands up there.'

Alexander hesitated with his hand on the phone. 'If I wait, I'm just giving him a chance to keep one step ahead.' He chewed his lip for a moment, then said, 'There might be a way of finding out if it's really Reno he's headed for. When he gets there, he'll need a car. Maybe he's already arranged for one to be waiting. I'll call downtown and ask the communications office to check all the rental agencies at the Reno airport that provide late-night pickup service. Most of them probably don't, so it ought to be an easy thing to track down.'

'Good idea,' Kennebeck said, even though he hated to admit it.

Ten minutes later, communications called back with its report. Elliot Stryker had a car reserved for late-night pickup from Avis, at the Reno airport; he was scheduled to take possession of it shortly before midnight.

'That's a bit sloppy of him,' Kennebeck said, 'considering how clever he's been so far.'

'He figures we're looking in Arizona, not Reno.'

'It's still sloppy,' Kennebeck said, disappointed. 'He should have built a double blind to protect himself.'

'So it's like I said.' Alexander smiled. 'He *isn't* as sharp as he used to be.'

'Let's not start crowing too soon,' Kennebeck said. 'We haven't caught him yet.'

'We will,' Alexander said, his composure restored. 'Our people in Reno will have to move fast, but they'll manage. I don't think it's a good idea to hit Stryker and the woman in a public place like an airport. I don't even think we should put a tail on them as soon as they get there. Stryker will be looking for a tail; maybe he'll elude it, and then he'll be spooked.'

'Get to the car Avis is holding for him. Slap a beeper on it. Then they can follow him without being seen.'

'We'll try it,' Alexander said. 'We've got less than an hour, so there might not be time. But even if we don't get a beeper on the car, we're okay. We know exactly where they're going. We'll just eliminate Bellicosti and set up a trap at the funeral home.' He picked up the phone and dialed the Network office in Reno.

# 25

In Reno, which billed itself as 'The Biggest Little City in the World', the temperature hovered only twenty-one degrees above zero as midnight approached. Above the lights that cast a frosty glow on the airport parking lot, the night sky was moonless, starless, perfectly black. Snow flurries were dancing on an erratic, sometimes gentle, sometimes fierce wind.

Elliot was glad they had taken time to buy a couple of heavy coats before leaving Las Vegas. He wished they'd thought of gloves; his hands were freezing.

He threw their single suitcase into the trunk of the rented Chevrolet, which Avis had held for them on a special, late-hour pickup arrangement. In the cold air, white clouds of exhaust vapor swirled around Elliot's legs. He slammed the trunk lid and looked around at the snow-dusted cars in the lot. He couldn't see anyone in any of them. He had no feeling of being watched. Perhaps the phony flight plan had thrown the

hounds off the trail. He went to the driver's
door and climbed in the Chevy, where Tina was
fiddling with the heater.

'My blood's turning to ice,' she said.

Elliot held his hand up to the vent. 'We're
getting some warm air already.'

He unzipped his coat and withdrew the pistol
he had taken off Vince and which had been tucked
uncomfortably under his belt ever since they'd
touched down on the Reno runway. He put the
gun on the seat between him and Christina, the
muzzle pointed toward the dashboard.

'You really think we should confront Bellicosti
at this hour?' she asked.

'Sure. It's not very late.'

In an airport-terminal telephone booth, Tina
had looked up the address of the Luciano Bellicosti
Funeral Home. The night supervisor at the Avis
garage, from whom they had signed out the car,
had known exactly where Bellicosti's place was,
and he had marked the shortest route for them on
the free city map that was provided by the rental
agency.

Elliot flicked on the overhead light and studied
the map for a minute, then handed it to Tina. 'I
think I can find it without any trouble. But if I get
lost, you'll be the navigator.'

'Aye, aye, Captain.'

He snapped off the overhead light and reached
for the gearshift.

With a distinct click, the light which he had just turned off suddenly turned itself on.

He switched it off.

The light came on again.

'Here we go,' Tina said.

The radio came on of its own will. The station indicator began to sweep across the lighted dial, left to right, then right to left, then left to right again; the tuning knob was spinning, even though no one was touching it. Split-second blasts of music, commercials, and disc jockeys' voices blared senselessly out of the speakers.

'It's Danny,' Tina said.

The windshield wipers started thumping back and forth at top speed, adding their metronomical beat to the chaos inside the Chevy.

The headlights began to flash on and off so rapidly that they created a stroboscopic effect, repeatedly 'freezing' the falling snow, so that it appeared as if the white flakes were descending to the ground in short, jerky steps.

The air inside the car was cold and growing colder by the second.

Elliot put his hand against the dashboard vent. Heat was pushing out of there, but it did nothing whatsoever to stabilize the plunging air temperature.

The glove compartment popped open.

The ashtray slid out of its niche.

Tina laughed, clearly delighted.

The sound of her laughter startled Elliot, but then he had to admit to himself that he did not feel menaced by the work of this poltergeist. In fact, just the opposite was true. He sensed that he was witnessing a joyous display, a warm greeting, the excited welcome of a child-ghost. He was overwhelmed by the astonishing notion that he actually could feel good will in the air, a tangible radiation of love and affection. He had never experienced anything like it before. He hoped he would never have to explain it to anyone. A not unpleasant shiver raced up his spine. Apparently, it was the same amazing awareness of being buffeted by the waves of love that caused Tina's laughter.

She said, 'We're coming, Danny. Hear me if you can, baby. We're coming to get you. We're coming.'

The radio switched off all by itself. So did the overhead light.

The windshield wipers stopped thumping.

The headlights blinked off and stayed off.

Stillness.

Silence.

Just scattered flakes of snow colliding softly with the windshield . . .

In the car the air grew warm again.

Elliot said, 'Why does it get cold every time he uses his . . . psychic abilities?'

'Who knows? Maybe he's able to move objects

by harnessing the heat energy in the air, changing it somehow. Or maybe it's something else altogether. We'll probably never know. He might not understand it himself. Anyway, that isn't important. What's important is that my Danny is *alive*. There's no doubt about that. Not now. Not any more. And I gather from your question that you've become a believer, too.'

'Yes,' Elliot said, still mildly amazed by his own change of heart and mind. 'Yes, I believe there's a damned good chance you're right.'

'I know I am.'

'Something extraordinary happened to that expedition of scouts. And something downright uncanny has happened to your son.'

'But at least he's not dead,' Tina said.

Elliot saw tears of happiness shining in her eyes.

'Hey,' he said worriedly, 'better keep a tight rein on your hopes. Okay? We've got a long, long way to go. We don't even know where Danny is or what shape he's in. We've got a gauntlet to run before we can find him and bring him back. We might both be killed before we even get close to him.'

He drove away from the airport. As far as he could tell, no one followed them.

# 26

The room was deep in the secret Sierra complex, three stories below ground-level. It was approximately forty feet long, but only half that wide. The ceiling was low, covered with a spongy, pebbly, cream-colored sound-proofing material that gave the place a curious organic look. Fluorescent tubes shed cold light over banks of computers and tables laden with journals, charts, file folders, scientific instruments, and two coffee mugs.

In the middle of the west wall – one of the two shorter walls – opposite the entrance room, there was a six-foot-long, three-foot-high window that provided a view of another room, which was only half as large as the first. The window was constructed like a sandwich: Two one-inch-thick panes of shatterproof glass surrounding an inch-wide space filled with an inert gas. Two panes of ironlike glass. Stainless-steel frames. Four airtight rubber seals – one around the edges of both faces of each pane. The window was designed to withstand everything from a gunshot to an earthquake; it was virtually inviolable.

Because it was important for the men who worked in the large room to have an unobstructed view of the small chamber at all times, several angled ceiling vents in both rooms bathed the glass in a steady flow of warm, dry air, a measure which had been taken to prevent clouding and steaming. Right now the warm air wasn't doing its job. Three-quarters of the window was filmed with frost.

At the moment two people, both dressed in lab whites, were in the larger of the two rooms. Dr. Carlton Dombey, a curly-haired man with a bushy mustache, stood at the window, peering through one of the few frost-free patches of glass. Dr. Aaron Zachariah, younger than Dombey, clean-shaven, with straight brown hair, leaned over one of the computers, reading the data that was flowing across the cathode-ray tube.

'The temperature's dropped thirty-three degrees in there during the past minute and a half,' Zachariah said worriedly. 'That can't be good for the boy.'

'Every other time it's happened, it's never seemed to bother him,' Dombey said.

'I know, but—'

'Take a look at his vital signs.'

Zachariah moved to another bank of computer screens, where Danny Evans's heartbeat, blood pressure, body temperature, and brainwave activity were constantly displayed. 'Heartbeat's normal, maybe even slightly slower than before. Blood pressure is all right. Body temperature's unchanged. But there's something unusual about the EEG reading.'

'As there always is during these damned cold snaps,' Dombey said. 'Odd brainwave activity. But no other indication he's in any discomfort.'

'If it stays cold in there for long, we'll have to suit up, go in, and move him to another chamber,' Zachariah said.

'There isn't one available,' Dombey said. 'All the others are full of test animals in the middle of one experiment or another.'

'Then we'll have to move the animals,' Zachariah said. 'The kid's a lot more important. There's more data to be gotten from him.'

'We won't have to move him. The cold spell won't last,' Dombey said, squinting into the smaller room, where the boy lay motionless on a hospital bed, under a white sheet and yellow blanket, trailing the wires that monitored his vital signs. 'At least it hasn't lasted long the other times it's happened. The temperature drops abruptly, stays down for two or three minutes, never longer than five, and then it rises to normal again.'

'What the devil is wrong with the engineers? Why can't they correct the problem?'

Dombey said, 'They insist the system checks

out perfectly. There's no malfunction. So they say.'

'Like hell there isn't!' Zachariah turned away from the computer screens, went to the window, found his own spot of clear glass. 'When this started a month or so ago, it wasn't that bad. A few degrees of change. Once a night. Never during the day. Never enough of a variation to threaten the boy's health. But the last few days it's gotten completely out of hand. Again and again, we're getting these thirty- and forty-degree plunges in the air temperature in there. No malfunction, my ass!'

'I hear they're bringing in the original design team,' Dombey said. 'Those guys'll spot the problem in a minute. Anyway, I don't see what you're so riled up about. We're supposed to be testing the boy to destruction, aren't we? Then why fret about his health?'

'Surely you can't mean that,' Zachariah said. 'When the boy finally dies, we'll want to know for sure whether it was the injections that killed him. If he's subjected to many more of these sudden temperature fluctuations, we'll never be certain they didn't contribute to his death. It won't be clean research.'

Dombey laughed sourly and looked away from the window. 'Clean? This whole thing was never clean. It was a very dirty piece of business right from the start.'

Zachariah faced him. 'I'm not talking about the morality of it.'

'I am.'

'I'm talking about clinical standards.'

'I really don't think I want to hear your opinions on either subject,' Dombey said. 'I've got a splitting headache.'

'I'm just trying to be conscientious,' Zachariah said, almost pouting. 'You can't blame me because the work is dirty. I don't have much to say about research policy around here.'

'You don't have *anything* to say about it,' Dombey told him bluntly. 'And neither do I. We're low men on the totem pole. That's why we're stuck with night-shift, baby-sitting duty like this.'

'Even if I was in charge of making policy,' Zachariah said, 'I'd probably take the same course as Dr. Tamaguchi has. He *had* to pursue this research. He didn't have any choice but to commit the installation to it once we found out the damn Russians were deeply into it. It's the Russians' nasty little project, remember; we're just playing catch-up. If you have to blame someone because you're feeling guilty about what we're doing here, then blame the Russians, not me.'

'I know. I know,' Dombey said wearily, pushing one hand through his bush of curly hair. 'They scare me all right. If there's any government on earth capable of using a weapon like this, it's the Soviet Union. We don't have any choice but to maintain the balance of power. I really believe that. But sometimes . . . I wonder . . . While we're working so hard to keep abreast of the Soviets, aren't we acquiring more and more of their authoritarian characteristics? Aren't we becoming a totalitarian state, the very thing we say we despise?'

'Maybe.'

'I think – definitely.'

'What choice do we have?'

'None, I guess.'

'Look,' Zachariah said.

'What?'

'The window's clearing up. It must be getting warm in there already.'

The two scientists turned to the glass again, peered into the isolation chamber.

The emaciated boy stirred. He turned his head toward them and stared at them through the railed sides of the hospital bed in which he lay.

Zachariah said, 'Those damned eyes.'

'Penetrating, aren't they?'

'The way he stares . . . he gives me the creeps sometimes. There's something . . . haunting about his eyes.'

'You're just feeling guilty,' Dombey said.

'No. It's more than that. His eyes are . . . strange. They aren't the same as they were when he first came in here a year ago.'

'There's pain in them now,' Dombey said sadly. 'A lot of pain and loneliness.'

'More than that,' Zachariah said. 'There's something in those eyes that . . . there isn't any word for.' He walked away from the window. He went back to the computers, with which he felt comfortable and safe.

# PART FOUR

## FRIDAY
## JANUARY 2

# 27

For the most part, Reno's streets were clean and dry in spite of a recent snowfall; but here and there, patches of black ice waited for the unwary motorist. Elliot Stryker drove cautiously and kept his eyes on the road.

'We should almost be there,' Tina said.

A quarter of a mile farther, Luciano Bellicosti's home and place of business came into sight on the left, beyond a black-bordered sign that rather grandiosely stated the nature of the service that he provided: FUNERAL DIRECTOR AND GRIEF COUNSELOR. It was an immense, pseudo-Colonial house, perched prominently on top of a hill, toward the back of a two-acre property, and conveniently next door to a large, non-denominational cemetery. The long driveway curved up and to the right like a length of black ribbon draped across the rising, snow-shrouded lawn. Stone posts and softly glowing electric lamps marked the way to the front door, and warm light radiated from several first-floor windows.

Elliot almost turned in at the entrance, but at the last moment he decided to drive by the place.

'Hey,' Tina said, 'that was it.'

'I know.'

'Why didn't you stop?'

'Discretion is the better part of valor. Didn't anyone ever tell you that?'

'You just did.'

'Storming right up to the front door, demanding answers from Bellicosti – that would be emotionally satisfying and brave and bold. And stupid.'

'They can't be waiting there for us. They don't know we're in Reno.'

'Never underestimate your enemy,' Elliot said. 'They underestimated me and you, and that was a big mistake. We're not going to make the same mistake they did and wind up back in their hands.'

Beyond the cemetery, he turned left, into a residential street. He parked at the curb, switched off the headlights, cut the engine.

'What now?' she asked.

'I'm going to walk back to the funeral home,' Elliot said. 'I'll cut through the cemetery, circle around, and approach the place from the rear.'

'*We* will approach it from the rear,' she said.

'No.'

'Yes.'

'You'll wait here.'

'Bullshit.'

Pale light from a street lamp pierced the windshield and illuminated her face. She was exquisite, beautiful beyond words, and he longed to take her in his arms.

But the light also revealed hard-edged determination in her face, steely resolution in her brilliantly blue eyes. She was not going to permit him to treat her like a dainty, precious porcelain figurine.

Although he realized he was going to lose the argument, he said, 'Be reasonable. If there's any trouble, you might get in the way of it.'

'Now really, Elliot, talk sense. Am I the kind of woman who gets in the way?'

'There's eight or ten inches of snow on the ground. You aren't wearing boots.'

'Neither are you.'

'If they've anticipated us, if they've set a trap at the funeral home—'

'Then you might need my help,' she said. 'And if they haven't set a trap, I've absolutely got to be there when you question Bellicosti.'

'Look, we're just wasting time sitting here,' he said impatiently.

'I'm glad you see it my way,' she said. She opened her door and got out of the car.

It was then he knew, beyond any shadow of a doubt, he loved her.

He stuffed the silencer-equipped pistol into one of his coat pockets and got out of the Chevy. He didn't lock the doors because it was possible that he and Tina would need to get into the car in a hurry when they returned.

In the graveyard the snow came up to the middle of Elliot's calves. It soaked his trousers, caked in his socks, and melted into his shoes.

Tina, wearing rubber-soled sneakers with canvas tops, was surely as miserable as he was, but she kept pace with him, and she didn't complain.

The raw, damp wind was stronger now than it had been only a short while ago, when they'd landed at the airport. It swept through the graveyard, fluting between the headstones and the larger monuments, whispering a promise of more snow, much more than the meager flurries it now carried with it.

A low stone wall and a line of house-high spruce separated the cemetery from Luciano Bellicosti's property. They climbed over the wall and stood in the tree shadows for a minute, while Elliot studied the rear approach to the funeral home.

Tina didn't have to be told to remain silent. She waited patiently behind him, her arms folded, hands tucked into her armpits for warmth.

Elliot was worried about her, afraid for her, but at the same time he was glad to have her company.

The rear of Bellicosti's house was a hundred yards away. There was a three-car garage. A small back porch. A few evergreen shrubs, none of sufficient size to conceal a man. And there were a lot of blank, black windows; a sentry could be standing behind any of them, invisible in the darkness.

Elliot strained his eyes, trying to catch a glimpse of movement beyond the rectangles of glass.

He saw nothing suspicious.

Nothing at all.

There really wasn't much chance that a trap had been set for them so soon. And if killers *were* waiting down there, they most likely would expect their prey to approach the funeral home boldly, confidently, naively; therefore, their attention would be focused almost exclusively on the front of the house.

In any case, he told himself, you can't just stand here all night brooding about it.

He stepped out from beneath the sheltering branches of the trees. Tina moved with him.

The bitter wind was a lash. It skimmed crystals of snow off the ground and spun the stinging cold flecks onto their reddened faces.

Elliot felt naked as they crossed the luminescent snow field. He wished they weren't wearing such dark clothes. If anyone *did* glance out of a back window, he would spot the two of them instantly.

The crunching and squeaking of the snow under their feet seemed horrendously loud to him. But he knew they actually were making almost no noise at all. He was just jumpy.

They reached the funeral home without incident.

For a few seconds they paused, touching each other briefly, gathering their courage.

Elliot took the pistol out of his coat pocket and held it in his right hand. With his left hand he fumbled for the two safety catches, found them, released them. His fingers were stiff and awkward from the cold. He wondered if he would be able to handle the weapon properly if the need arose.

They slipped around the corner of the building and moved stealthily toward the front.

At the first window that had light behind it, Elliot stopped. He motioned for Tina to stay behind him and close to the house. Cautiously, he leaned forward and peered through a narrow gap in a partially closed Venetian blind. He nearly cried out in shock and alarm at what he saw in there.

A dead man.

Naked.

Sitting in the bathtub.

One wrist slashed. Bloody water.

Elliot stared into the flat, dead gaze of the pasty-faced corpse, and he knew that he was looking at Luciano Bellicosti. He also knew that the funeral director had not killed himself. The poor man's blue-lipped mouth hung in a permanent gape, as if he were trying to deny all of the accusations of suicide that were to come.

Elliot wanted to take Tina by the arm and hustle her back to the car. But she sensed that he had seen something important, and she wouldn't go easily until she knew what it was. He understood her well enough to be certain that she would have to see the grisly thing herself. He stepped back, gently pushed her in front of him. He kept one hand on her back as she leaned toward the window, and he felt her go rigid when she saw the dead man. By the time she turned to Elliot again, she was ready to get the hell out of there, without questions, without argument, without the slightest delay.

They had taken only two steps away from the window when Elliot saw the snow move no more than twenty feet from them. It wasn't the gauzy, insubstantial stirring of wind-blown flakes. It was an unnatural, lumpy, purposeful rising up of an entire mound of white stuff. Instinctively, he whipped the pistol out in front of him and squeezed off four rounds. The silencer was so good that the shots could not be heard above the brittle, papery rustle of the wind.

Crouching low, trying to make as small a target of himself as possible, Elliot ran to where he'd seen the snow move. He found a man dressed in a white, insulated, outdoorsman's suit. The stranger had been lying in the snow, watching them, waiting; now he had a wet hole in his chest. And a chunk of his throat was gone. Even in the dim, illusory light from the surrounding snow, Elliot could see that the man's eyes were fixed in the same unseeing gaze that Bellicosti was even now directing at the bathroom window.

At least one killer in the house, baby-sitting Bellicosti's corpse. Probably more than one.

At least one man waiting out here in the snow.

How many others?

Where?

Elliot scanned the night, his heart clutching up. He expected to see the entire white-shrouded lawn begin to move and rise up in the forms of hundreds of angry, vengeance-minded assassins.

But all was still.

He stood, dazed by his own ability to strike so fast and so violently. He experienced a warm, animal satisfaction, which was not an entirely welcome feeling, for he liked to think of himself as a civilized man. At the same time he experienced a wave of revulsion. His throat tightened, and there was suddenly a sour taste in his mouth. He turned his back on the man he had killed.

Tina was there, like a lovely apparition in the snow. 'They know we're in Reno,' she whispered.

'Yes.'

'They even knew we were coming here.'

'But they expected us through the front door,' he said.

342

'Why didn't—'

He took her by the arm and hushed her. 'Let's get out of here.'

They hurriedly retraced their steps, moving away from the funeral home as fast as they could. With every step he took, Elliot expected to hear a shot fired, a cry of alarm, and the sounds of men in pursuit of quarry.

He helped Tina over the cemetery wall, and then, as he was clambering after her, he was sure that someone grabbed his coat from behind. He gasped and jerked loose, and when he was across the wall he looked back, but he couldn't see anyone.

Evidently the people in the funeral home were not aware that their man outside had been killed. They were still waiting patiently for their prey to walk into the trap.

Elliot and Tina rushed between the tombstones, kicking up lime-like clouds of snow. Twin plumes of crystallized breath trailed behind them, like ghosts.

When they were nearly halfway across the graveyard, when Elliott was positive they weren't being pursued, he stopped, leaned against a tall monument, and tried not to take such huge, deep gulps of the painfully cold air. An image of his victim's torn throat exploded in his memory, and a shock wave of nausea overwhelmed him. He turned away from Tina, stumbled a few feet across a pristine mantle of snow, and vomited.

*I killed a man.*

The fact that he had acted in self-defense did nothing to set his mind at ease.

When he regained control of himself, he cleaned out his mouth with snow. The icy slush made his teeth ache.

Tina put a hand on his shoulder. 'Are you all right?'

'I killed him.'

'If you hadn't, he would have killed us.'

'I know. Just the same . . . it makes me sick.'

'I would have thought . . . well, when you were in the army . . .'

'Yes,' he said softly. 'Yes, I've . . . killed before. But like you said, that was in the army . . . Southeast Asia . . . during wartime. I've blown away at least half a dozen men . . . before this one tonight. But that was a long time ago. Somehow, it wasn't the same in the war, not the same at all. That was soldiering; this was murder.' He shook his head to clear it. He put another handful of snow in his mouth, then spat it out when it had melted. 'I'll be okay.' He tucked the pistol into his coat pocket again. 'It was just the shock. But I can handle it. I won't go to pieces on you; don't worry about that.'

'Of course I'm not worried, you dope. You're not the type that crumbles. I'm sure of that, even if you aren't.' They embraced for a moment and then she said, 'If they knew we were flying to Reno, why didn't they follow us from the airport? Then they would have known we weren't going to walk in the front door of Bellicosti's place.'

'I don't know,' he said, still shaken by the killing, not thinking as clearly as usual. 'They probably figured I'd spot a tail and be spooked by it. And I guess they were so sure of where we were headed that they didn't think it was necessary to keep a close watch on us. They figured there wasn't anywhere else we *could* go but Bellicosti's funeral home.'

'Let's get back to the car,' she said. 'I'm freezing.'

'Yeah. Me too. And it wouldn't be a bad idea to get out of the neighborhood before they find that dead man in the snow.'

They followed their own footprints out of the cemetery, to the quiet residential street where the rented Chevrolet was parked in the wan light of the street lamp.

Elliot opened the passenger-side door for Tina, closed it after she had gotten in, and walked around the back of the car, fishing in his pocket for the keys. As he was opening the driver's door, he saw movement out of the corner of his eye, and he looked up, already sure of what he would see. A white Ford sedan had just turned the corner, moving slowly; it drifted to the curb and braked abruptly; two doors opened, and a couple of tall, rugged-looking men started to get out.

'Damn!' Elliot said, immediately recognizing them for what they were. He jumped into the Chevy, slammed the door, and jammed the key into the ignition.

'We *have* been followed,' Tina said.

'Yeah,' he said as he switched on the engine and threw the car in gear. 'A beeper. They must have just now homed in on it.'

He didn't hear a shot, but a bullet shattered the rear side window behind his head and slammed into the back of the front seat, spraying gummy bits of safety glass through the car.

'Get your head down!' Elliot shouted.

He glanced back.

The two men were coming at a run, slipping a bit on the snow-spotted pavement.

Elliot stamped on the accelerator. Tires squealing, he pulled the car away from the curb, into the street.

In quick succession two bullets ricocheted off the body of the car, each trailing away with a brief, high-pitched whine.

Elliot hunched low over the wheel, expecting a bullet through the rear window. At the corner he ignored the stop sign and swung the car hard to the left, only tapping the brakes once, severely testing the Chevy's suspension.

Tina raised her head, glanced at the empty street behind them, then looked at Elliot. 'A beeper? You mean there's some sort of transmitter attached to us?'

'Yeah.'

'We'll have to abandon the car, won't we?'

'Not until we've gotten rid of those clowns on our tail,' he said. 'If we abandon the car with them so close, they'll run us down fast. We can't get away on foot.'

'Then what?'

They came to another intersection, and he whipped the car to the right. 'After I turn the next corner, I'll stop and get out. You be ready to slide over and take the wheel.'

'Where are you going?'

'I'll fade back into the shrubbery and wait for them to come around the corner after us. You drive on down the street, but not too fast. Give them a chance to see you when they turn into the street. They'll be looking at you; they won't see me; and I'll shoot out at least one of their tires.'

'We shouldn't split up,' she said.

'It's the only way.'

'But what if they get you?'

'They won't.'

'I'd be alone then.'

'They won't get me. They won't be expecting a trap. But you have to move fast. If we stop for more than a couple of seconds, it'll show up on their receiver, and they might get suspicious.'

He swung right at the intersection and stopped in the middle of the new street.

'Elliot, don't—'

'No choice,' he said, flinging open his door and scrambling out of the car.

'But I—'

'Hurry!' he said.

He ran to a row of evergreen shrubs that bordered the front lawn of a low, brick, ranch-style house. He crouched beside one of those bushes, huddling in the shadows just beyond the circle of frosty light from a nearby street lamp, and he pulled the pistol out of his coat pocket while Tina drove away.

As the sound of the Chevy faded, he could make out the roar of another car, approaching fast. A few seconds later the white sedan raced into the intersection.

Elliot stood up, extending the pistol in both hands, and snapped off three quick shots. The first two clanged through sheet metal, but the third punctured the right front tire.

The Ford had rounded the corner too fast. Now, jolted by the blowout, the car plunged out of control. It careened across the street, jumped the curb, crashed through a four-foot-high hedge, destroyed a plaster bird bath, and came to rest in the middle of a snow-blanketed lawn.

Elliot ran. Tina stopped the Chevy a hundred yards away. It seemed like a hundred miles. His pounding footsteps were as thunderous as drumbeats in the quiet night air. At last he reached the car. She had the door open. He leaped in and pulled the door shut and said, 'Go, go!'

She tramped the accelerator into the floor-boards, and the car responded with a shudder, then a surge of power.

When they had gone two blocks, he said, 'Turn right at the next corner.' After two more turns and another three blocks, he said, 'Pull it over to the curb. I want to find the bug they planted on us.'

'But they can't follow us now,' she said.

'They've still got a receiver. They can watch our progress on that, even if they can't get their hands on us. I don't even want them to know what direction we went.'

She stopped the car, and he got out. He felt along the inner faces of the fenders, around the tire wells, where a small transmitter could be stuck in place quickly and easily. Nothing. The front bumper was clean, too. Finally he located the beeper; it was fixed magnetically to the underside of the rear bumper. He wrenched it loose and pitched it away.

In the car again, with the doors locked and the engine running and the heater turned up full-blast, neither of them was able to speak for

a moment. They sat in stunned silence, basking
in the warm air, but shivering just the same.

Eventually Tina said, 'My God, they move fast!'

'We're still one step ahead of them,' Elliot said
shakily.

'Half a step.'

'That's probably more like it,' he admitted.

'Bellicosti was supposed to be the source of the
facts we need to interest a topnotch reporter in
the case.'

'Not now.'

'So how do we get those facts?'

'Somehow,' he said vaguely.

'How do we build our case?'

'We'll think of something.'

'Who do we turn to next?'

'It isn't hopeless, Tina.'

'I didn't say it was. I'm just wondering where
we go from here.'

'We can't work it out tonight,' he said wearily.
'Not in our condition. We're both wiped out.
And decisions we make now would be based on
adrenaline-hyped perceptions. We'd be operating
on sheer desperation. That would be dangerous.
The best decision we can make is to make no
decision at all. We've got to hole up and get some
rest. In the morning we'll have clearer heads, and
the answers will all seem obvious.'

'You think you can actually sleep?' she asked.

'Hell, yes. It's been a hard day's night. I've

been forced to fight for my life in my own home.
I've almost been blown up. A couple of goons in
a black van chased me all over Vegas, and then
another group of goons in a white sedan got on
my case. And I've killed a man. Enough already.
Don't tell me that you're full of vim and vigor.'

'No,' she said. 'I'm dragging.'

'Good. I know you're a strong lady, but if you
were that strong, you'd be too much for me.'

'Where will we be safe for the night?'

'We'll try the purloined letter trick,' Elliot said.
'Instead of sneaking around to some out-of-the-
way motel, we'll march right into the best hotel
in town.'

'Harrah's?'

'Exactly. They won't expect us to be that bold.
They'll be looking for us everywhere else.'

'It's risky.'

'Can you think of anything better?'

'No.'

'*Everything* is risky.'

'All right. Let's do it.'

She drove into the heart of town, and they
abandoned the Chevrolet in a public parking lot,
four blocks from Harrah's.

'I wish we didn't have to give up the car,' Tina
said as he took their only suitcase out of the
trunk.

'They'll be looking for it.'

They walked to Harrah's Hotel along windy,

neon-splashed streets. They passed the entrances to casinos, from which came loud music and laughter and the sound of slot machines, even at 1:45 in the morning.

Although Reno didn't jump all night with quite the same energy that Las Vegas exhibited, and although many tourists had gone to bed, the casino at Harrah's was still relatively busy. A young sailor apparently had a run going at one of the craps tables, and an excited crowd of gamblers urged him to roll an eight and make his point.

Elliot and Tina rode the escalator up to the hotel lobby. In virtually every major hotel in Nevada, the lobby was adjacent to or an integral part of the casino, so that guests were enticed into the action the instant they arrived – and were lured again to the tables for one last bet even as they were checking out to go home. But Harrah's had considerably more class than most Nevada hotels; and only one example of this was the fact that the registration desk was on the second floor, in a quiet cul-de-sac, out of the hurly-burly.

It was a holiday weekend, and the hotel was officially booked to capacity; however, Elliot knew there were always accommodations available. At the request of its casino manager, every hotel held a handful of rooms off the market, just in case a few regular customers – high rollers, of course – showed up by surprise, with no advance notice, but with fat bankrolls and no place to stay. In addition, some reservations were canceled at the last minute, and there were always a few no-shows. A neatly folded twenty-dollar bill, placed without ostentation into the hand of a front-desk clerk, was almost certain to cause him to discover a forgotten vacancy.

When Elliot was informed that there existed, by chance, a room that was available for two nights, he signed the registration card as 'Clifford Montgomery,' a slight twist on the name of one of his favorite old movie stars; he entered a phony Seattle address, too. The clerk requested ID or a major credit card, and Elliot told a sad story of being victimized by a pickpocket at the airport. Unable to prove his identity, he was required to pay for both nights in advance, which he did, taking the money from a wad of cash he'd stuck in his pocket rather than from the wallet that supposedly had been stolen.

He and Tina were given a spacious, pleasantly decorated room on the ninth floor.

After the bellman left, Elliot locked the door and engaged the deadbolt as well. He hooked the security chain in place and firmly wedged the heavy straightbacked desk chair under the knob.

'It's like a prison,' Tina said.

'Except we're locked in, and the killers are running around loose on the outside.'

A short time later, in bed, they held each other

close, and neither of them had sex in mind. They just wanted to touch and be touched, to snuggle, to confirm for each other that they were still alive, to feel safe and protected and cherished. It was an animal need for affection and companionship, and it was a reaction to the death and destruction with which the day had been filled. After encountering so many people with so little respect for human life, they needed to convince themselves that they really were more than dust in the wind.

After a while, although neither of them had been seeking or expecting sex, they both felt desire welling strongly within them, a warm and delicious yearning. It was a curiously dreamlike coupling. Elliot was not even sure exactly how they came to be joined together. At first they were entwined, both lying on their sides, facing each other, kissing gently and murmuring endearments, her warm breasts squashed pleasantly against his chest, and then suddenly he was atop her, and she was soundlessly, joyously urging him on with her hands. Her silken legs and arms seemed to enfold him. There was a whispery friction of flesh against flesh. He was in her before he realized it, and then they were rocking, grinding, clinging. It was a surprisingly intense experience, consummated quickly and eagerly and powerfully, in no more than two or three minutes.

When they were finished she held him close for a while, not willing to let him move even a few inches away from her. At last they disengaged and drifted apart in the same fuzzy, dreamy way they had become joined. They stretched out, side by side, on their backs, holding hands, letting their rapid breathing subside to a more ordinary pace, staring at the ceiling, spent.

After a few minutes he said, 'You were right.'

'About what?'

'About what you said last night, in Vegas.'

'Refresh my memory.'

'You said I was enjoying the chase.'

'A part of you . . . deep down inside. Yes, I think that's really true.'

'I know it is,' he said. 'I can see it now. I didn't want to believe it at first.'

'Why not? I didn't mean it disparagingly.'

'I know you didn't. It's just that . . . well, for more than fifteen years I've led a very ordinary life, a workaday life. I was convinced I no longer needed or wanted the kind of thrills that I thrived on when I was a younger man.'

'I don't think you *do* need or want them,' Tina said. 'But now that you're in real danger again for the first time since you worked in military intelligence, now that your life is really on the line again, a part of you is responding to the challenge. Like an old athlete back on the playing field after a long absence, testing his muscles and reflexes, taking pride in the fact that his old skills are still there.'

'It's more than that,' Elliot said. 'I think . . . deep down . . . I got a sick sort of thrill when I . . . killed that man.'

'Don't be so hard on yourself,' Tina said.

'I'm not. In fact, maybe the thrill wasn't so deep down. Maybe it was really pretty near the surface.'

'You sure didn't seem to take any pleasure in the killing. Unless you customarily express pleasure by throwing up.'

'I threw up because . . . I suddenly became aware of how much it pleased me to be able to shoot a man with such speed and accuracy. It was like . . . I got a glimpse of a savage creature that had my own face. It made me sick to realize what was hiding inside me.'

'You should be glad you killed that bastard,' she said softly, squeezing his hand.

'Should I?'

'Listen, if I could get my hands on the people who're trying to keep me from finding Danny, I wouldn't have any compunctions about killing them. None at all. I might even take a certain pleasure in it. I'm a mother lion, and they've stolen my cub; maybe killing them is the most natural, admirable thing I could do.'

'So there's a bit of the beast in all of us. Is that it?'

'Yes.'

'Maybe it's not just me that has a savage trapped inside.'

'No. Not just you. Not by any means. We all do.'

'But does that make it any more acceptable?'

'What's to accept?' she asked. 'It's the way God made us. It's the way we were meant to be, so who's to say it isn't right?'

'Well . . . maybe.'

'If a man kills only for the pleasure of it, or if he kills only for an ideal like some of these crackpot revolutionaries you read about, *that's* savagery . . . or madness. But what you've done is altogether different. Self-preservation is one of the most powerful drives God gave us. We're built to survive, even if we have to kill someone in order to do it. Doesn't The Bible say, ''To everything there is a season . . . a time to be born, a time to die . . . a time to kill, a time to heal . . .'' '

They were silent for a while. Then he said, 'Thank you.'

'I didn't do anything.'

'You listened.'

'That's what my ears are for.'

'And you talked a lot of sense.'

'That's what my voice is for.'

He touched her breasts. 'What are these for?'

'You, of course.'

'And this?'

'That's for you, too.'

'It's a very nice gift.'

'You like my gift?'

'I love it.'

'Then love it.'

'I can't believe I'm up to it again.'

'You sure feel up to it.'

This time their love-making was slower and more tender than before. When Tina found release, Elliot felt her climax moving through her body; tremors of pleasure washed through her like a slow, slow tide, and she thrashed in exquisite slow motion like a feathery underwater plant responding to invisible currents. When she finally finished, Elliot let go, too, on and on, until he felt utterly empty, pleasantly hollow. A few minutes later, Tina was asleep.

Exhausted, too tired even to worry about all the dangerous people who were looking for him at that very moment, he slept too.

# 28

Kurt Hensen, George Alexander's right-hand man, dozed through most of the rough flight from Las Vegas to Reno. They were in a ten-passenger fanjet that belonged to the Network, and the small plane took a battering from the high-altitude winds that were cutting across its assigned flight corridor. Hensen, a powerfully built man with white-blond hair and cruel eyes, was afraid of flying. He could only manage to get on a plane after he had taken a couple of pills to relax. As usual he nodded off minutes after the aircraft lifted from the runway.

George Alexander was the only other passenger. He considered the requisitioning of the jet to be one of his most important accomplishments in the three years he had been chief of the Nevada bureau of the Network. Although he spent more than half his time in the Las Vegas area, working out of the office there, he often had reason to fly to far points on the spur of the moment: Reno, Elko, even out of the state to Texas, California,

Arizona, New Mexico, Utah . . . During the first year he had taken commercial flights or had rented the services of a trustworthy private pilot who could fly the conventional twin-engine craft that Alexander's predecessor had managed to pry out of the Network's budget. To Alexander, it had seemed absurd and shortsighted of the Director to force a man of Alexander's position to travel by such relatively primitive means. His time was enormously valuable to the country; his work was sensitive and often required urgent decisions based upon first-hand study of information to be found only in distant places. After long and arduous lobbying of the Director, Alexander had at last been awarded this small jet, and he had immediately put two full-time pilots, both ex-military men, on the payroll of the Nevada bureau.

Sometimes the Network pinched pennies to its disadvantage. And George Lincoln Stanhope Alexander, who was an heir to both the fortune of the Pennsylvania Alexanders and to the enormous wealth of the Delaware Stanhopes, had absolutely no patience with people who were penurious.

It was true that every dollar had to count, for every dollar of the Network's budget was difficult to come by. Because its existence must be kept secret, the organization was funded out of misdirected appropriations meant for other government agencies. For example, three billion dollars, the largest single part of the Network's yearly budget, came from the Department of Health and Welfare. The Network had a deep-cover agent named Jacklin in the highest policy-making ranks of the Health bureaucracy. It was Jacklin's job to conceive new welfare programs, convince the Secretary of Health and Welfare that those programs were needed, sell them to the congress, and then establish convincing bureaucratic shells to conceal the fact that the programs were utterly phony; and as federal funds began to flow to these false-front operations, the money was diverted to the Network's funding operations, for Health was so gigantic and, by its own admission, so wasteful that it never missed such a petty sum. During his days as Secretary, Joseph Califano had estimated waste at ten billion a year, and there were those who believed the figure was wrong by as much as a factor of three. The Department of Defense, which was less flush than Health and Welfare, was nevertheless guilty of waste, too, and it was good for at least another billion a year. Lesser amounts, ranging from only one hundred million to as much as half a billion, were painlessly extracted from the Department of Energy, the Department of Education, and other government bodies on an annual basis.

The Network was financed with some difficulty, to be sure; but it was undeniably well-funded. A small jet for the chief of the vital Nevada bureau was not an extravagance, and Alexander believed his improved performance over the past year had convinced the old man in Washington that this was money well spent.

Alexander was proud of the importance of his position. But he was also frustrated because so few people were *aware* of his great importance.

At times he envied his father and his uncles. Most of them had served their country openly, in a supremely visible fashion, where everyone could see and admire their selfless public-spiritedness. Secretary of Defense, Secretary of State, Ambassador to France . . . In positions of that nature, a man was appreciated and respected.

George, on the other hand, hadn't filled a post of genuine stature and authority until just six years ago, when he was thirty-six. During his twenties and early thirties, he had labored at a variety of jobs for the government, diplomatic and intelligence-gathering assignments that were never an insult to his family name, but always minor postings to embassies in Asia and South America, nothing for which the *New York Times* would deign to acknowledge his existence.

Then, six years ago, the Network had been formed in response to the emasculation of the FBI and the CIA, which had resulted from relentless attacks staged on those organizations by the news media and both left- and right-wing elements in

Congress. The President had given George the task of developing a reliable, clandestine South American bureau of the new intelligence agency. That had been exciting, challenging, important work. George had been directly responsible for the expenditure of tens of millions of dollars and, eventually, for the control of hundreds of agents in a dozen countries. After three years the President had declared himself delighted with the accomplishments in South America, and he had asked George to take charge of the Network's Nevada bureau, which had been terribly mismanaged. This slot was one of the half-dozen most powerful in the Network's executive hierarchy. George was encouraged by the President to believe that he eventually would be promoted to bureau chief of the entire Western Division, and then all the way to the top – if only he could get the floundering Western Division functioning as smoothly as the South American and Nevada offices. In time he would take the Director's chair in Washington and would bear full responsibility for all domestic and foreign intelligence operations. With that title, he would be one of the most powerful men in the United States, certainly more of a force to be reckoned with than any Secretary of State or Secretary of Defense could ever hope to be.

But he couldn't tell anyone about his achievements. He could never hope to receive the public acclaim and honor that had been heaped upon other men in his family. The Network was secret and must remain secret if it was to have any value. At least half of the people who worked for it did not even realize it existed; some of them thought they were employed by the FBI; others were sure they worked for the CIA; and still others believed they were in the hire of various branches of the Treasury Department and the Secret Service. None of those people could compromise the Network. Only bureau chiefs, their immediate staffs, station chiefs in major cities and senior field officers who had proven themselves and their loyalty – only those people knew the true nature of their employers and their work. The moment the news media became aware of the Network's existence, reporters would begin ardently sniffing out information, and when they got sufficient proof that such an intelligence-gathering agency was real, they would blow it wide open.

It was ironic, Alexander thought, that the news media and some Congressmen, in their excessive reactions against some very real transgressions by the FBI and the CIA, through their relentless efforts to tear the guts out of some quite necessary intelligence-gathering snoop shops, had directly (if unwittingly) contributed to the establishment of the thing they feared most: the first truly secret police force in the two-hundred-year history of the United States.

As he sat in the dimly lit cabin of the fanjet and watched the clouds racing below, Alexander wondered what his father and his uncles would say if they knew that his service to his country had often required him to issue kill orders. Worse than that, on three occasions, in South America, he had been in a position where it had been necessary for him to pull the assassin's trigger himself. He had enjoyed that act so immensely, had been so profoundly thrilled by it, that he had, by choice, performed the executioner's role on half a dozen other assignments. What would the elder Alexanders, the famous statesmen, think if they knew he'd soiled his hands with blood? As for the fact that it was sometimes his job to order men to kill, he supposed his family would understand. The Alexanders were all idealists when they were discussing what ought to be, but they were also hard-headed pragmatists when dealing with what actually was. They knew that the worlds of domestic military security and international espionage were not children's playgrounds. They might even find it in their hearts to forgive George for having pulled the trigger himself. *After all,* he thought, *I've never killed an ordinary citizen or a person of any real worth.* His targets had always been spies, traitors; more than a few of them had been cold-blooded killers themselves. *Scum. I've only killed scum,* he thought. It wasn't a pretty job, but it also wasn't without a measure of real dignity and heroism. At least that was the way George saw it; he thought of himself as heroic. He was sure his father and uncles would give him their blessings – if only he were permitted to tell them.

The jet hit an especially bad patch of turbulence. It yawed, bounced, shuddered for almost a minute.

Kurt Hensen snorted in his sleep but didn't wake up.

When the plane settled down once more, Alexander looked out the window at the milky-white, moonlit, feminine roundness of the clouds, and he thought of the Evans woman. She was quite lovely. Her file folder was on the seat beside him. He picked it up, opened it, and stared at her photograph. Quite lovely indeed. He decided he would kill her himself when the time came, and that thought gave him an instant erection.

He enjoyed killing. He didn't try to pretend otherwise with himself, no matter what face he had to present to the world. All of his life, for reasons he had never been able to fully ascertain, he had been fascinated by death, intrigued by the form and nature and possibilities of it, enthralled by the study and theory of its meaning. He considered himself a messenger of death, a divinely appointed headsman. Murder was, in many ways, more thrilling to him than sex. He knew his taste for violence would not have been tolerated for long in the FBI or in many other publicly monitored police agencies. But in this unknown organization, in this secret place, he thrived.

He closed his eyes and thought about Christina Evans.

# 29

In the dream Danny was at the far end of a long tunnel. He was in chains, sitting in the center of a small, well-lit cavern, but the passageway that led to him was shadowy, and it reeked of danger. Danny called to her again and again, begging her to save him before the roof of his underground prison caved in and buried him alive. She started walking down the tunnel toward him, determined to get him out of there, and something reached for her from a narrow cleft in the wall. She was aware of a soft, firelike glow from beyond the cleft, and of a moving figure silhouetted against the reddish backdrop. She turned, and she was looking into the grinning face of Death, as if he were peering out at her from the bowels of Hell. The crimson eyes. The shriveled flesh. The lacework of maggots on his cheek. She cried out, but then she saw that Death could not quite reach her. The hole in the wall was not wide enough for him to step through, into the passageway; he could only thrust one arm at her, and his long, bony fingers fell an inch or two short of her. Danny began calling again, and she continued down the shadowy tunnel toward him. A dozen times she passed chinks in the wall, and Death glared out at her from every one of those apertures, screamed and cursed and raged at her, but none of the holes was large enough for him to get through it. She reached Danny, and when she touched him the chains fell magically away from his arms and legs. She said, 'I was scared.' And Danny said, 'I made the holes smaller. I made sure you wouldn't get hurt.'

At eight-thirty Friday morning, Tina came awake, smiling, excited. She shook Elliot until she woke him.

Elliot blinked sleepily and sat up. 'What's wrong?'

'Danny just sent me another dream.'

Taking in her broad smile, he said, 'Obviously, it wasn't the same nightmare.'

'Not at all. Danny wants us to come to him. He wants us just to walk into the place where they're keeping him and take him out.'

'We'd be killed before we could reach him. We can't just charge in like the cavalry. We've got to use the media and the courts to free him. The two of us can't fight off the entire organization that's behind Kennebeck plus the staff of some secret military research center.'

'But Danny's going to make it safe for us,' she

said confidently. 'He's going to use his psychic power to help us get in there.'

'That isn't possible.'

'You said you believed.'

'I do,' Elliot said, yawning and stretching elaborately. 'I do believe. But . . . how can he help us? How can he guarantee our safety?'

'I don't know. But that's what he was telling me in the dream. I'm sure of it.'

She recounted the dream in detail, and he admitted that her interpretation wasn't strained.

'But even if Danny could somehow get us in,' Elliot said, 'we don't know where they're keeping him.'

'That secret military installation we theorized—'

'Could be anywhere,' Elliot said. 'And maybe it doesn't even exist. And if it does exist, they might not be holding him there anyway.'

'It exists, and that's where he is,' she said, trying to sound more certain than she actually was.

She felt she was within reach of Danny. She felt almost as if she had him in her arms again, and she didn't want anyone to tell her that he might be even a hair's breadth beyond her grasp.

'Okay,' Elliot said, sitting up straighter, wiping at the corners of his sleep-matted eyes. 'Let's say the secret installation theory is correct. Let's say such a place does exist. That doesn't help us a whole hell of a lot. It could be anywhere in those mountains.'

'No,' she said. 'It has to be within a few miles of where Jaborski intended to go with the scouts.'

'Okay. That's probably true. But that covers a hell of a lot of rugged terrain. We couldn't even begin to conduct a thorough search of it.'

Tina's confidence couldn't be shaken. She said, 'Danny will pinpoint it for us.'

'Danny's going to tell us where he is?'

'He's going to try, I think. I sensed that in the dream.'

'How's he going to do it?'

'I don't know. But I have this feeling that if we just find some way . . . some means of focusing his energy, channeling it . . .'

'Such as?'

She stared at the tangled bedclothes for a minute, looking for inspiration in the creases of the linens with much the same expression that one saw on the face of a gypsy fortune-teller staring at tea leaves. 'Maps!' she said suddenly.

'What?'

'Don't they publish terrain maps of the wilderness areas? Backpackers and other nature lovers would need them. Not minutely detailed things. But maps that show the basic lay of the land: hills, valleys, the courses of rivers and streams, footpaths, abandoned logging trails, that sort of thing. I'm sure Jaborski had maps.

I *know* he did. I saw them at the parent-son scout meeting when he explained why the trip would be perfectly safe.'

'I suppose any sporting goods store in Reno ought to have maps of at least the nearest parts of the Sierras,' Elliot said.

'Maybe if we can get a map and spread it out . . . well, maybe Danny will find a way to show us exactly where he is.'

'How?'

'I'm not sure yet.' She threw back the covers and got out of bed. 'Let's get the maps first. We'll worry about the rest of it later. Come on. Let's get showered and dressed. The stores will be open in an hour or so.'

*　*　*

Because of the foul-up at the Bellicosti place, George Alexander didn't get to bed until five thirty Friday morning. Because he was still furious with his subordinates for letting Stryker and the woman escape again, he had difficulty getting to sleep. He finally nodded off around 7:00 a.m., and he was up at ten o'clock, feeling fuzzy, washed out.

He hadn't set the alarm for ten; he'd been awakened by the phone. It was the Director calling from Washington. They used a scrambler device, so they could speak candidly, and the Director certainly minced no words. The old man was furious. As he listened meekly to the Director's accusations and demands, Alexander realized that his own future with the Network was at stake. If he failed to stop Stryker and the Evans woman, his dream of assuming the Director's chair in a few years would have absolutely no chance of becoming reality.

After the old man hung up, Alexander called the office, in no mood to be told that Elliot Stryker and Christina Evans were still free. But that was exactly what he heard. He ordered men pulled off other jobs and assigned to the manhunt.

'I want them found before another day passes,' Alexander said. 'That bastard has killed one of us now. He can't get away with that. I want him eliminated.'

And I want that bitch, too, Alexander thought. I want her dead.

# 30

There were two sporting goods stores and two gun shops within easy walking distance of the hotel. The first sporting goods dealer didn't carry the maps, and the second usually had them but was currently sold out. They found what they needed in one of the gun shops: a set of twelve wilderness maps of the Sierras, designed with backpackers and hunters in mind. The set came in a leatherette-covered case and sold for a few cents less than a hundred dollars.

Back in the hotel room, they opened one of the maps on the bed, and Elliot said, 'Now what?'

Tina considered the problem for a moment. Then she went to the desk, pulled open the center drawer, and took out a folder of Harrah's stationery. There was also a cheap plastic ballpoint pen with the hotel's name on it. She picked up the pen, returned to the bed, and sat down in front of the map.

She said, 'People who believe in the occult

have a thing they call "automatic writing." Ever hear of it?'

'Sure,' he said. 'Spirit writing. A ghost supposedly guides the hand of someone living in order to deliver a message from beyond. Always sounded like the worst sort of gobbledegook to me.'

'Well, I'm going to try something like that. Except, of course, I don't expect a ghost to guide my hand. I'm hoping Danny can do it.'

'Don't you have to be in a trance, like a medium at a seance?'

'I don't know. I'm just going to make my mind as blank as I can. I'm going to completely relax, make myself open and receptive. I'll hold the pen against the map, and maybe Danny can draw the route for us.'

Elliot pulled a chair up to the bed and sat down. 'I don't believe for a minute that it's going to work. But I'll sit here as quiet as a mouse and give it a chance.'

Tina stared at the map and tried to think of nothing else but the appealing greens and blues and yellows and pinks that the cartographers had used to indicate various types of terrain. She allowed her eyes to swim out of focus.

A minute passed.

Two minutes. Three.

She tried closing her eyes.

Another minute. Two.

Nothing.

She turned the map over and tried the other side of it.

Still nothing.

'Give me another map,' she said.

Elliot withdrew one from the leatherette case and handed it to her. He took back and refolded the first map.

Half an hour and five maps later, her hand suddenly skipped across the paper as if someone had bumped her arm.

She felt a peculiar pulling sensation that seemed to come from *within* her hand, and she stiffened in surprise.

The power went out of her.

'What was that?' Elliot asked.

'Danny. He tried.'

'You're sure?'

'Positive! But he startled me, and I guess even the little bit of resistance I offered was enough to push him away. At least we know this is the right map. Let me try again.'

She put the pen at the edge of the map once more, and she let her eyes drift out of focus.

The room began to get cool.

She tried not to think about the chilly air. She tried not to think about anything too hard.

Her right hand, the one holding the pen, grew rapidly colder than any other part of her. She felt the unpleasant, inner pulling again. Her fingers were like ice, so cold they were beginning to ache. Abruptly her hand swung across the map, then back, then described a series of circles; the pen made meaningless scrawls on the paper. After half a minute of that, she felt the power leave her hand again.

The map flew into the air, as if someone had tossed it in anger or frustration.

Elliot stood up and reached for it.

But the map spun into the air again. It flapped noisily to the other end of the room and then back again, finally falling to the floor like a dead bird at Elliot's feet.

'Jesus,' he said softly. 'The next time I read a story in the newspaper about some guy who says he was picked up in a flying saucer and taken on a tour of the universe, I won't be so quick to laugh. If I see many more inanimate objects dancing around, I'm going to start believing in *everything*, no matter how freaky.'

Tina got up from the bed, massaging her cold right hand. 'I guess I'm offering too much resistance. It's just that it feels so weird when he takes control . . . I can't help stiffening up a little. I guess you were right about needing to be in a trance.'

'I'm afraid I can't help you with that,' he said. 'I'm a damned good cook, but I'm not a hypnotist.'

She blinked. 'Hypnosis! Of course! That'll probably do the trick.'

'Maybe it will. But where do you expect to find a hypnotist? The last time I looked, they weren't setting up shops on street corners.'

'Billy Sandstone,' she said.

'Who?'

'He's a hypnotist. He lives right here in Reno. He has a stage act. The Great Sandstone. It's an absolutely brilliant act. I wanted to use him in *Magyck!*, but he was tied up in an exclusive contract with a chain of Reno-Tahoe hotels. If we can get hold of Billy, he can hypnotize me. Then maybe I'll be relaxed enough to make this automatic writing work.'

'Do you know his phone number?'

'No. And it's probably not listed. But I do know his agent's number. I can get through to him that way.'

She hurried to the telephone.

# 31

Billy Sandstone was in his thirties, an average-size man like Elliot, and his watchword seemed to be 'neatness.' His shoes gleamed with vigorously applied polish. The creases in his slacks were as sharp as blades, and his blue sport shirt looked as if it had been starched. His hair was razor-cut, and he wore a mustache that was so carefully groomed it almost looked as if it had been painted on his upper lip.

Billy's dining room was neat, too. The table, the chairs, the credenza, and the hatch all glowed warmly because of the prodigious amount of furniture polish that had been buffed into the wood with even more vigor than he had employed when shining his dazzling shoes. There were fresh roses in a cut-crystal vase in the center of the table, and sharp clean lines of light gleamed in the exquisite glass. The drapes hung in perfectly measured folds. An entire battalion of nitpickers and fussbudgets would be hard-pressed to find a speck of dust in that room.

They spread the map out on the table and sat down.

Billy said, 'Automatic writing is bunk, Christina. You must know that.'

'I do, Billy, I know that. But I want you to hypnotize me anyway.'

'You're a level-headed person, Tina,' Billy said. 'This really doesn't seem like you.'

'I know,' she said.

'If you'd just tell me *why* . . . If you'd tell me what this is all about, maybe I could help you better.'

'Billy,' she said, 'if I tried to explain, we would be here all afternoon.'

'Longer,' Elliot said.

'And we don't have much time,' Tina said. 'This is a very urgent matter. Very important.'

They hadn't told him anything about Danny. Sandstone didn't have the faintest idea what they were up to.

Elliot said, 'I'm sure this seems ridiculous to you, Billy. You're probably wondering if I'm some sort of lunatic. You're wondering if maybe I've messed up Tina's mind.'

'Which definitely isn't the case,' Tina said.

'Right,' Elliot said. 'Her mind was messed up before I ever met her.'

The joke seemed to relax Sandstone, as Elliot had hoped it would. Lunatics and just plain irrational people didn't intentionally try to amuse.

Elliot said, 'I assure you, Billy, we haven't lost our marbles. And this *is* a matter of life and death.'

'It really is,' Tina said.

'Okay,' Billy said. 'You don't have time to tell me about it now. I'll accept that. But will you tell me one day when you aren't in such a damned rush?'

'Absolutely,' Tina said. 'I'll tell you everything. Just please, please, put me in a trance.'

'All right,' Billy Sandstone said. He was wearing a gold signet ring. He turned it around, so the face of it was on the wrong side, the palm-side of his finger. He held his hand up in front of Tina's eyes. 'Keep your eyes on the ring and listen only to my voice.'

'Wait a second,' she said. She pulled the cap off the red felt-tip pen Elliot had purchased at the hotel newsstand just before they'd caught a taxi to Sandstone's house. Elliot had suggested a change in the color of ink, so they would be able to tell the difference between the meaningless scribbles that were already on the map and any new marks that might be made. She put the point of the pen to the paper and said, 'Okay, Billy. Do your stuff.'

Elliot was never sure exactly when Tina slipped under the hypnotist's spell, and he had no idea how the mesmerism was accomplished. All Sandstone did was move one hand slowly back and forth in front of Tina's face, and he spoke to her in a quiet, rhythmic voice, frequently using her name.

Elliot almost fell into a trance himself. He blinked his eyes and tuned out Sandstone's melodious voice when he realized he was succumbing to it.

Tina stared vacantly into space.

The hypnotist lowered his hand and turned his ring around the way it belonged. 'You're in a deep sleep, Tina.'

'Yes.'

'Your eyes are open, but you are in a deep, deep sleep.'

'Yes.'

'You will stay in that deep sleep until I tell you to wake up. Do you understand?'

'Yes.'

'You will remain relaxed and receptive.'

'Yes.'

'You will remain totally passive until you feel the urge to use the pen in your hand.'

'All right.'

'When you feel the urge to use the pen, you will not resist it. You will flow with it. Understood?'

'Yes.'

'You will not be bothered by anything Elliot and I say to each other. You will respond to me only when I speak directly to you. Understood?'

'Yes.'

They waited.

A minute passed, then another.

Billy Sandstone watched Tina intently for a while, but at last he shifted impatiently in his chair. He looked at Elliot and said, 'I don't think this spirit writing stuff is—'

The map rustled, drawing their attention. The corners of it curled and uncurled, curled and uncurled, again and again, like the pulse of a living thing.

The air was getting colder.

The map stopped curling; the rustling sound ceased.

Tina lowered her gaze from the empty air to the map, and her hand began to move. It didn't swoop and dart uncontrollably this time; it crept carefully, hesitantly across the paper, leaving a thin, red line of ink that looked, to Elliot, like a thread of blood.

Sandstone was rubbing his hands up and down his arms to ward off the steadily deepening chill that had seized the room. Frowning, glancing up at the heating vents, he started to get out of his chair.

Elliot said, 'Don't bother checking the air conditioning. It isn't on. And the heat hasn't failed either.'

'What?'

'The cold comes from the . . . spirit,' Elliot said, deciding to stick with the occult terminology, not

wanting to get bogged down in the real story
about Danny.

'Spirit?'

'Yes.'

'Whose spirit?'

'Could be anyone's.'

'Are you serious?'

'Pretty much.'

Sandstone stared at him as if to say, *You're
nuts, but are you dangerous?*

Elliot pointed to the map. 'See?'

As Tina's hand moved slowly over the paper,
the corners of the map began to curl and uncurl
again.

'How is she doing that?' Sandstone asked.

'She isn't.'

'The ghost, I suppose.'

'That's right.'

An expression of pain settled over Billy's face, as
if he were suffering genuine physical discomfort
because of Elliot's belief in ghosts. Apparently
Billy liked his view of the world to be as neat
and uncluttered as everything else about him;
if he started believing in ghosts, he'd have to
reconsider his opinions about a lot of other things,
too, and then life would become intolerably
messy.

Elliot sympathized with the hypnotist. Right
now, he longed for the rigidly structured life of
the law office, the neatly ordered paragraphs of

legal casebooks, and the unchanging rules of the courtroom.

Tina let the pen drop out of her fingers. She lifted her gaze from the map.

'Are you finished?' Billy asked her.

'Yes.'

'Are you sure?'

'Yes.'

With a few simple sentences and a clap of his hands, the hypnotist brought her out of the trance.

She blinked in confusion for a moment, then glanced down at the route she had marked on the map. She looked at Elliot. 'It worked. By God, it worked!'

'Apparently it did.'

She pointed to the terminus of the red line. 'That's where he is, Elliot. That's where they're keeping him.'

'It's not going to be easy getting into country like that,' Elliot said.

'We can do it. We'll need good, insulated outdoor clothes. Boots. Snowshoes in case we have to walk very far in open country. Do you know how to use snowshoes? It can't be that hard.'

'Hold on,' Elliot said. 'I'm still not convinced your dream meant what you think it did. Based on what you said happened in it, I don't see how you reach the conclusion that Danny's going to help us get into the installation. We might get to this place and find we can't slip around its defenses.'

Billy Sandstone looked from Tina to Elliot, baffled.

Tina said, 'It wasn't only what happened in the dream that led me to that conclusion. What I *felt* in it was far more important. I can't explain that part of it. The only way you could understand is if you had the dream yourself. I am *sure* that he was telling me he could help us get to him. Am I the kind of woman who jumps to conclusions?'

'No,' Elliot admitted. He pulled the map around so that he could study it more closely.

'I said he would show us where he's being kept, and he drew that route for us. So far I'm batting a thousand. I also feel he will help us get into the place, and I don't see any reason why I should strike out on that one.'

'It's just . . . we'd be walking into their arms,' Elliot said.

'Whose arms?' Billy Sandstone asked.

Tina said, 'Elliot, what happens if we stay here, hiding out until we can think of an alternative? How much time do we have? Not much. They're going to find us sooner or later, and when they get their hands on us, they'll kill us.'

'Kill?' Billy Sandstone asked.

'We've gotten this far because we've kept moving and we've been aggressive,' Tina said.

'If we change our approach, if we suddenly get too cautious, that could be our downfall instead of our salvation.'

'You two sound like you're in a war,' Billy Sandstone said.

'You're probably right,' Elliot told Tina. 'One thing I learned in the military was that you have to stop and regroup your forces once in a while, but if you stop too long, the tide will turn and wash right over you.'

'Should I maybe go listen to the news?' Billy Sandstone asked. '*Is* there a war on?'

To Tina, Elliot said, 'What else will we need besides the outdoor clothes, the boots, and the snowshoes?'

'A Jeep,' she said.

'That's a tall order.'

'What about a tank?' Billy Sandstone asked.

Now that they had decided to accept and rely on the message she read into her dream, they were getting increasingly excited about mounting the rescue operation. Neither of them was more than vaguely aware of Billy's comments.

'We'll have to have a Jeep,' Tina said. 'Or another machine with four-wheel drive. We don't want to walk any farther than necessary. We don't want to walk at all if we can help it. There must be some sort of road in and out of the place, even if it is well concealed. If we're lucky we'll have Danny when we come out, and he probably won't be in any condition to trek through the Sierras in the dead of winter.'

'I guess I could have some money transferred from my Vegas bank,' Elliot said. 'But what if they're watching my accounts down there? That would lead them to us fast. And since the banks are closed for the holiday, we couldn't do anything until next week. They might find us by then.'

'What about your American Express card?' she asked.

'You mean, *charge* a Jeep.'

'There's no limit on the card, is there?'

'No. But—'

'I read a newspaper story once about a guy who bought a Rolls-Royce with his card. You can do that sort of thing as long as they know for sure you're capable of paying the entire bill when it comes due a month later.'

'It sounds crazy,' Elliot said. 'But I guess we can try.'

'I have a Jeep,' Billy Sandstone said.

'Let's look up the address of the local dealership,' Tina said. 'We'll see if they'll accept the card.'

'*I have a Jeep!*' Billy Sandstone shouted.

They looked at him, startled.

'I take my act to Lake Tahoe a few weeks every winter,' Billy said. 'You know what it's like down there this time of year. Snow up to your ass. I hate flying in on the Tahoe-Reno shuttle; the plane's so damned small. And you know what a ticky-tacky airport they have at Tahoe. So I usually just drive down the day before I open. A Jeep's the only thing I'd want to take through the mountains on a bad day.'

'Are you going to Tahoe soon?' Tina asked.

'No. I don't open until the end of the month.'

'Will you be needing the Jeep in the next couple of days?' Elliot asked.

'No.'

'Can we borrow it?'

'Well . . . I guess so.'

Tina leaned across the corner of the table, grabbed Billy's head in her hands, pulled his face to hers, and kissed him. 'You are a life-saver, Billy. And I mean that literally.'

'I'll be damned,' Elliot said, 'but it seems to me like things are breaking right for us. Maybe we'll get Danny out of there after all.'

'We will,' Tina said. 'I know it.'

The roses in the crystal vase twirled around like a group of spinning, red-headed ballerinas.

Startled, Billy Sandstone jumped up, knocking over his chair.

The drapes drew open, slid shut, drew open, slid shut, even though no one was near the draw cords.

The copper chandelier began to swing in a lazy circle.

Billy stared, open-mouthed.

Elliot knew how disoriented Billy was feeling, and he felt sorry for the man.

After thirty or forty seconds, all of the movement stopped.

The room rapidly grew warm again.

'How did you *do* that?' Billy demanded.

'We didn't,' Tina said.

'Not a ghost,' Billy said adamantly.

'Not a ghost either,' Elliot said.

Billy said, 'You can borrow the Jeep. But first you've got to tell me what in the hell is going on. I don't care how much of a hurry you're in. You can at least tell me a little bit of it. Otherwise, I'm going to shrivel up and die of curiosity.'

Tina looked at Elliot. 'Well?'

Elliot said, 'Billy, you might be better off not knowing.'

'Impossible.'

'We're up against some damned dangerous people. If they thought you knew about them—'

'Look,' Billy said, 'I'm not just a hypnotist. I'm something of a magician. That's really what I most wanted to be, but I didn't really have the skill for it. So I worked up this act built around hypnotism. But magic – that's my one great love. I just have to know how you did that with the drapes and the roses. And the corners of the map! I just *have* to know.'

That morning, it had occurred to Elliot that he

and Tina were the only two people who knew that the official story of the Sierra accident was a lie. If they were killed the truth would die with them, and the cover-up would go on. Considering the high price they already had paid for the pathetic little bit of information they'd obtained, he couldn't tolerate the thought that all their pain and fear and anxiety might count for nothing.

Elliot said, 'Billy, do you have a tape recorder?'

'Sure. It's nothing fancy. It's a little one I carry with me. I do some comedy lines in the act, and I use the recorder to develop new material, correct problems with my timing.'

'It doesn't have to be fancy,' Elliot said. 'Just so it works. We'll give you a condensed version of the story behind all of this, and we'll record it as we go. Then I'll mail the tape to one of my law partners.' He looked at Tina. 'Not much insurance, but better than nothing.'

'I'll get the recorder,' Billy said, hurrying out of the dining room.

Tina folded the map.

'It's nice to see you smiling again,' Elliot said.

'I must be crazy,' she said. 'We still have a dangerous bit of work ahead of us. We're still up against this bunch of cutthroats. We don't know what we'll walk into in those mountains. So why do I feel terrific all of a sudden?'

'You feel good,' Elliot said, 'because we're not running any more. We're going on the offensive.

And foolhardy as that might be, it does a lot for a person's self-respect.'

'Can a couple of people like us really have a chance of winning when we're up against a big government organization like this seems to be?'

'Well,' Elliot said, 'I happen to believe that individuals are more apt to act responsibly and morally than institutions ever do, which at least puts us on the side of justice. And I also believe that individuals are always smarter and better adapted to survival, at least in the long run, than any government institutions. Let's hope that my philosophy doesn't turn out to be half-baked.'

\* \* \*

At one-thirty Kurt Hensen came into George Alexander's office in downtown Reno. He said, 'They found the car that Stryker rented from Avis. It's in a public lot about three blocks from here.'

'Used recently?' Alexander said.

'No. The engine's cold. There's frost on the windows. It's been parked there overnight.'

'He's not stupid,' Alexander said. 'He's probably abandoned the damned thing.'

'You want to put a watch on it anyway?'

'Better do that,' Alexander said. 'Sooner or later, they'll make a mistake. Coming back to the car might be it. I don't think so. But it might.'

Hensen left the room.

Alexander took a Valium out of a tin that he carried in his jacket pocket, and he washed it down with a swallow of ice water, which he poured from the silver carafe on his desk. It was his second pill since getting out of bed just three and a half hours ago, but he still felt edgy.

Stryker and the woman were proving to be worthy opponents.

Alexander never had cared for worthy opponents. He preferred them to be soft and easy.

*Where were they?*

# 32

The deciduous trees, stripped of every leaf, loomed like many-armed, dark skeletons. The evergreens – pine, spruce, fir, tamarack – were filled with snow. A brisk wind spilled over the jagged horizon under a low and menacing sky. It snapped ice-hard flurries of snow against the windshield of the Jeep station wagon.

Tina was in awe of the stately forest that crowded closer as they drove north on the narrowing country road. They had turned off Interstate 80 a quarter of an hour ago, following the route that Danny had marked, circling the edge of the wilderness. On paper they were still moving along the border of the map, with a large expanse of blues and greens on their left. Shortly, they would turn off the two-lane blacktop onto another road, which the map called 'unpaved, non-dirt,' whatever that was.

After leaving Billy Sandstone's house in his Jeep, Tina and Elliot had not returned to the hotel. Both of them had the same spooky premonition that someone decidedly unfriendly was waiting in their room.

First they had visited a sporting-goods store. They had purchased outdoor clothing, boots, snowshoes, some compact tins of backpacker's rations, a couple of cans of Sterno, and other selected pieces of survival gear. If the rescue attempt went smoothly, as Tina's dream had seemed to say it would, they wouldn't have any need for much of what they bought. But if the Jeep broke down in the mountains, or if some other hitch developed, they wanted to be prepared at least minimally for the unexpected.

Elliot also bought a hundred rounds of ammunition for the pistol. That wasn't insurance against the unforeseen; that was simply prudent planning for the trouble they could foresee all too well.

From the sporting-goods store they had driven out of town, west toward the mountains. They stopped at a roadside restaurant and changed clothes in the restrooms. His insulated suit was green with a yellow stripe down each side; hers was blue with white stripes. They looked like a couple of skiers on their way to the slopes.

Entering the mountains, they had become aware of how soon darkness would settle over the sheltered valleys and ravines, and they had discussed the wisdom of proceeding. Perhaps they would have been smarter to turn around, go back to Reno, and find another hotel room, then get a fresh start in the morning. But neither of them had wanted to do that. Perhaps the lateness of the hour and the fading light would work against them, although neither of them was sure of that. Approaching in the night could even turn out to be to their advantage. The thing was – they had momentum. They both felt as if they were on a good roll, and they didn't want to tempt fate by postponing their journey.

Now they were on a narrow county-maintained road, moving steadily up as the valley sloped toward its northern end. Plows had kept the blacktop clean, except for scattered patches of hard-packed snow that filled in the potholes, and they had piled snow five or six feet high on both sides of the right-of-way.

'Soon now,' Tina said, glancing at the map that was open on her knees.

'Lonely part of the world, isn't it?' Elliot asked.

'You get the feeling that civilization could be destroyed while you're out here, and you'd never even be aware of it.'

They hadn't seen a house or any other structure for almost two miles. They hadn't passed another car in three miles.

Twilight was descending over the winter forest, and Elliot switched on the headlights.

Ahead, on the left, a break appeared in the bank of snow that had been heaped up by the plows. As the Jeep drew near the gap, Elliot braked, swung in the turn-off, and stopped. A cramped, rather forbidding track led into the woods. It was not much more than one lane wide, and the trees formed a tunnel around it, so that after fifty or sixty feet, it disappeared into premature night. The lane had been plowed. But there were a great many more patches of snow on its surface than had been on the last few miles of county blacktop. It was unpaved, but a relatively solid-looking bed had been built up over the years by the generous, repeated application of oil and gravel.

'According to the map, we're looking for an "unpaved, non-dirt" road,' Tina told him.

'I guess this is it.'

'Some sort of logging trail?'

'Looks more like the road they always take in those old movies when they're on their way to Dracula's castle.'

'That's not exactly the sort of statement that's going to keep my spirits up,' she said.

'Sorry.'

'And it doesn't help that you're right. It *does* look like the road to Dracula's castle.'

They drove onto the track, under the roof of heavy evergreen boughs, into the heart of the forest.

# 33

In the long, rectangular room, three stories underground, the computers buzzed and clicked and
beeped and murmured softly.

Dr. Carlton Dombey, who had come on duty
just twenty minutes ago, was sitting at one of the
tables against the north wall, which was opposite
the bank of computers. He was studying the set
of X-rays. There were half a dozen computer-
drawn and interpreted enhancements of the X-
rays, and he was poring over those as well. After
a while he looked up and said, 'Did you have a
look at the pictures they took of the kid's brain
this morning?'

Dr. Aaron Zachariah turned away from the
computer display screens and said, 'I didn't know
there were any.'

'Yeah. A whole new series.'

'Anything interesting?'

'Yes,' Dombey said. 'The spot that showed
up on the boy's parietal lobe about six weeks
ago.'

'What about it?'

'Darker, larger.'

'Then it's definitely a malignant tumor?'

'That still isn't clear.'

'Benign?'

'Can't say for sure either way.'

'What's the computer's opinion?'

'It won't suggest a diagnosis either,' Dombey said. 'The spot doesn't have all the spectrographic characteristics of a tumor.'

'Could it be scar tissue?'

'Not exactly that.'

'Blood clot?'

'The computer says definitely not.'

'Does the damned machine say anything useful?'

'Maybe,' Dombey said. 'I'm not sure if it's useful or not.' He frowned. 'It's sure strange, though.'

'Don't keep me in suspense,' Zachariah said, moving over to the table to have a look at the tests.

Dombey said, 'According to the computer, the growth is consistent with the nature of normal brain tissue.'

Zachariah stared at him. 'Come again?'

'The computer says it could be a new lump of brain tissue,' Dombey told him.

'But that doesn't make sense.'

'I know.'

'The brain doesn't all of a sudden start growing new little nodes that nobody's ever seen before.'

'I know.'

'Someone better run a maintenance scan on the computer. It has to be screwed up.'

'They did that this afternoon,' Dombey said, tapping a pile of print-outs that lay on the table. 'Everything's supposed to be functioning perfectly.'

'Just like the heating system in that isolation chamber is functioning properly,' Zachariah said.

Still looking through the test results, stroking his mustache with one hand, Dombey said, 'The computer notes that the growth rate of the parietal spot is directly proportional to the number of injections the boy's been given. It appeared after his first series of shots six weeks ago. The more frequently the kid is reinfected, the faster the parietal spot grows.'

'Then it must be a tumor,' Zachariah said.

'Probably.'

Zachariah glanced at the observation window that looked into the isolation chamber. 'Damn, there it goes again!'

Dombey looked up and saw that the glass was beginning to frost over.

Zachariah hurried to the window.

Dombey stared thoughtfully at the spreading frost. He said, 'You know something? That problem with the window . . . it started at the same time the parietal spot first showed up on the X-rays.'

Zachariah turned to him. 'So?'

'Doesn't that strike you as coincidental?'

'That's exactly how it strikes me. Coincidence. I fail to see any association.'

'Well . . .'

'What are you thinking?'

'Could the parietal spot have a direct connection with the frost . . . somehow?'

'Are you saying the boy might be responsible for the changes in air temperature?'

'Could he?'

'How?'

'I don't know.'

'Well, you're the one who raised the question.'

'I don't know,' Dombey said again.

'It doesn't make any sense,' Zachariah said. 'No sense at all. If you keep coming up with weird suggestions like that, I'll have to run a maintenance check on *you*, Carl.'

# 34

The oil-and-gravel trail led far into the forest. It was remarkably free of ruts and chuckholes for most of its length, although the Jeep scraped bottom three times when the track took a sudden, sharp dip.

The trees hung low, lower, lower still, until, at last, the ice-crusted evergreen boughs frequently scraped across the roof of the Jeep with a sound rather like fingernails being drawn down a blackboard.

They passed a few signs that told them the lane they were using was kept open for the exclusive benefit of federal and state wildlife officers and researchers. Only authorized vehicles were permitted, the sign warned.

'Could the installation we're looking for be disguised as a wildlife research center?' Elliot wondered.

'No,' she said. 'According to the map, that's nine miles into the forest. Danny's instructions are to take a turn north, off this road, after what looks like about five miles.'

'We've gone almost five miles since we left the county road,' Elliot said.

Branches scraped over the roof, and powdery snow cascaded over the windshield, onto the hood.

As the windshield wipers cast the snow aside, Tina leaned forward, squinting along the headlight beams. 'Hold it! I think this is what we're looking for.'

He was driving at only ten miles an hour, but she gave him so little warning that he passed the turn-off. He stopped, put the Jeep in reverse, and backed up fifteen or twenty feet, until the headlights were shining on the trail she had spotted.

'It hasn't been plowed,' he said.

'But look at all the tire marks.'

'A lot of traffic has been through there recently,' Elliot agreed.

'This is it,' Tina said confidently. 'This is where Danny wants us to go.'

'It's a damned good thing we have a Jeep.'

He steered off the plowed lane, onto the snowy trail. The Jeep, equipped with four-wheel drive and heavy chains on its big winter-tread tires, bit into the snow and chewed its way forward without hesitation.

The new track ran a hundred yards before rising and turning sharply to the right, around the blunt face of a ridge. When they came out of the curve, the trees fell back from the verge, and open sky lay above for the first time since they'd left the county blacktop.

Twilight was gone; night was in command.

Ahead of them, there was clear driving, not a speck of snow in their way. The unplowed trail had led them to a paved road. Steam rose from it, and sections of the pavement were even dry.

'Heat coils embedded in the surface,' Elliot said.

'Here in the middle of nowhere.'

He stopped the Jeep. He picked up the pistol that was on the seat between them and he flicked off both safeties. He had loaded the depleted magazine earlier; now he jacked a bullet into the chamber. When he put the gun on the seat again, it was ready to be used fast, if the need arose.

'We can still turn back,' Tina said.

'Is that what you want to do?'

'No.'

'Neither do I.'

A hundred and fifty yards farther, they reached another sharp turn. The road descended into a gully, swung hard to the left this time, and then headed up again.

Twenty yards beyond the bend, the way was barred by a high gate. On each side of the gate, a nine-foot-high fence, angled out at the top and

strung with barbed wire, stretched out of sight
into the forest. The gate was also wrapped with
barbed wire, and there were spikes along the top
of it.

There was a large sign to the right of the
roadway:

**PRIVATE PROPERTY
ADMISSION BY KEY CARD ONLY
TRESPASSERS WILL BE PROSECUTED**

'They make it sound like someone's country
estate,' Tina said.

'Intentionally, I'm sure. Now what? You don't
happen to have a key card, do you?'

'Danny will help,' she said. 'That's what the
dream was all about.'

'How long do we wait here?'

'Not long,' she said as the gate swung inward.

'I'll be damned,' Elliot said.

The heated road stretched out of sight in the
darkness.

'We're coming, Danny,' Tina said quietly.

'What if someone else opened the gate?' Elliot
asked. 'What if Danny didn't have anything to do
with it? They might just be letting us in so they
can trap us inside.'

'It was Danny.'

'You're so sure.'

'Yes.'

408

He sighed and drove through the gate, which swung shut behind the Jeep.

The road began to climb in earnest now, hugging the slopes. It was overhung by huge rock formations at some points, and by wind-sculpted cowls of snow at other places. The single lane, which widened to two at spots, switchbacked up the ridges, through trees that seemed to get larger and larger. The Jeep moved ever higher into the mountains.

The second gate was one-and-a-half miles past the first, on a short length of straightaway, just over the brow of a hill. It was not just a gate, but a checkpoint. There was a guard's booth to the right of the road, from which the gate was controlled.

Elliot picked up the gun as he brought the Jeep to a full stop at the barrier.

They were no more than six or eight feet from the lighted booth, so close they could see the guard's face. He was scowling at them through the window.

'He's trying to figure out who the devil we are,' Elliot said. 'He's never seen us or the Jeep, and this isn't the sort of place where there's a lot of new traffic.'

Inside the hut, the guard plucked a telephone receiver from the wall. '*Damn!*' Elliot said. 'I'll have to go for him.'

As Elliot started to open his door, Tina saw

something that made her grab his arm. 'Wait! The phone doesn't work. Look, he's jiggling it.'

The guard slammed the receiver down. He took a coat from the back of his chair, slipped into it, zippered up, and came out of the booth. He was carrying a submachine gun.

The gate opened by itself.

The guard stopped between the Jeep and the hut, jerked his head around, wheeled toward the gate when he saw it moving, unable to believe his eyes.

Elliot rammed his foot down hard on the accelerator, and the Jeep shot forward.

The guard swung the submachine gun into firing position as they swept past him.

Tina threw her hands up in an involuntary and totally useless attempt to ward off the bullets.

But there were no bullets.

No torn metal. No shattered glass. No blood or pain.

There was not even the sound of gunfire.

The Jeep roared across the straightaway and careened up the slope beyond, through the tendrils of steam that rose from the black pavement.

Still no gunfire.

As they swung into another curve, Elliot wrestled with the wheel, and Tina was acutely aware that there was nothing beyond the outer edge of the road, nothing at all, just a great dark void and a long drop. Elliot held the Jeep on the road as they rounded the bend, and then they were out of the guard's line of fire; and for two hundred yards ahead, until the road curved once more, there was nothing threatening in sight.

The Jeep dropped back to a safer speed.

Elliot said, 'Did Danny do all of that?'

'He must have.'

'He jinxed the guard's phone, opened the gate, and jammed the submachine gun. What *is* this kid of yours?'

As they moved up into the night, snow began to fall hard and fast, not just flurries now, but sheets of fine, dry flakes.

After a minute of thought, Tina said, 'I don't know. I don't know what he is any more. I don't know what's happened to him, and I don't understand what he's become.'

That was an unsettling thought. She began to wonder exactly what sort of little boy they were going to find at the top of the mountain.

# 35

George Alexander's men circulated through the downtown Reno hotels with glossy photographs of Christina Evans and Elliot Stryker. They talked to desk clerks, bellmen, and other hotel employees, and at four-thirty they obtained a strong, positive identification from a maid at Harrah's.

In room 918, the Network operatives found a cheap suitcase, some dirty clothes, toothbrushes, toiletry items – and eleven maps in a leatherette case, which Elliot and Tina, in their haste and weariness, had overlooked.

Alexander was informed of the discovery at 5:05; and by 5:40, everything that Stryker and the woman had left in the hotel room was brought to Alexander's office.

When he discovered the nature of the maps, when he realized that one of them was missing, and when he discovered that the missing map was the one Stryker would need in order to find the Project Pandora labs, Alexander felt his face flush with anger and chagrin. 'The *nerve!*' he said.

Kurt Hensen was standing in front of Alexander's desk, picking through the junk that had been brought over from the hotel. He said, 'What's wrong?'

'They've gone into the mountains. They're going to try to get into the laboratory,' Alexander said. 'Someone, some damned turncoat on Project Pandora, must have told them enough about its location for them to find it with just a little help. They went out and bought *maps*, for Christ's sake!'

Alexander was enraged by the cool methodicalness that the purchase of the maps seemed to represent. Who were these two people? Why weren't they hiding in a dark corner somewhere? Why weren't they scared witless? Christina Evans was only an ordinary woman. An ex-showgirl! Alexander refused to believe that a showgirl could be very bright. And although Stryker had done some rather heavy military service, that had been a long time ago. Where were they getting their strength, their nerve, their endurance? It seemed as if they must have some advantage of which Alexander was not aware. That had to be it. They had to have some advantage he didn't know about. What could it be? What was their edge? He leaned back in his chair and tried to puzzle it out.

Hensen picked up one of the maps, turned it

over in his hands. 'I don't see any reason to get too worked up about it. Even if they locate the main gate, they can't get any farther than that. There are thousands and thousands of acres behind the fence, and the lab is right smack in the middle. They can't get close to it, let alone inside.'

Alexander suddenly realized what their edge was, what kept them going, and he sat up straight in his chair. 'They can get inside easily enough if they have a friend in there.'

'What?'

'That's it!' Alexander got up. 'Not only did someone on Project Pandora tell the Evans woman about her son. That same traitor is also up there in the labs right this minute, and he's going to open the gates and doors to Stryker and the woman. Some bastard has stabbed us in the back; he's going to help the woman get her son out of there!'

Alexander dialed the number of the military security office at the Sierra lab. It neither rang nor returned a busy signal. Just the same, unsettling hiss.

'Something's happened up there,' Alexander said as he slammed the receiver into the cradle. 'The phones are out.'

'Supposed to be a new storm moving in,' Hensen said. 'It's probably already snowing in the mountains. Maybe the lines—'

'Use your head, Kurt. The lines are underground. No storm can knock them out. Get hold of Jack Morgan and tell him to get the chopper ready. We'll meet him at the airport as soon as we can get there.'

'He'll need half an hour anyway,' Hensen said.

'Not a minute more than that.'

'He might not want to go. The weather might be too bad up there.'

'I don't care if it's hailing iron basketballs,' Alexander said sharply. 'We're going up there in the chopper. There isn't time to drive. I'm sure of that. Something's gone wrong. Something is happening at the labs right now.'

Hensen frowned. 'But trying to take the chopper in there at night . . . in the middle of the storm . . .'

'Morgan's the best. He flew choppers in Vietnam. And he was on the security patrol while they were building the Alaskan pipeline. He's got snow experience.'

'It won't be easy.'

'If Morgan wants to take it easy,' Alexander said, 'then he should be flying one of the aerial rides at Disneyland.'

'But it seems suicidal—'

'And if *you* want to take it easy,' Alexander said, 'you shouldn't have come to work for me. This job requires that you take chances all the time. You know that. You're not working for the Ladies' Aid Society, Kurt.'

Hensen's face colored. 'I'll call Morgan,' he said.

'Yes. You do that.'

# 36

Windshield wipers beating away the snow, chain-wrapped tires clanking on the heated roadbed, the Jeep crested a final hill. They came over the last rise, onto a plateau, an enormous shelf in the side of the mountain.

Elliot pumped the brakes, brought the Jeep to a full stop, and unhappily surveyed the territory ahead.

The plateau was basically the work of nature, but man's hand was more than a little in evidence. The shelf could not have been as large and regularly shaped in its natural state as it was now. It was three hundred yards wide and two hundred yards deep, almost a perfect rectangle. The ground had been rolled as flat as an airfield and then paved. There was not a single tree or any other sizeable object behind which a man could hide. Skinny light posts were scattered across the featureless plain. The lamps cast only dim, reddish light; obviously they were intended to attract as little attention as possible from aircraft that strayed out of the usual flight patterns and from anyone backpacking in another part of the mountains. Yet the weak illumination that the lamps provided was apparently just sufficient for the special security cameras to obtain good, sharp images of the entire plateau. Cameras were attached to every light pole, and not an inch of the area escaped their unblinking attention.

'The security people must be watching us on video monitors right now,' Elliot said glumly.

'Unless Danny has screwed up their cameras,' Tina said. 'And if he can jam a submachine gun, why couldn't he interfere with a closed-circuit television transmission?'

'Yeah,' Elliot said, feeling a bit better about their chances. 'You're probably right.'

Two hundred yards away, at the far side of the concrete field, there was a one-story, windowless building, about a hundred feet long.

'That must be where they're holding him,' Elliot said.

'I expected an enormous structure, a gigantic complex,' Tina said.

'It most likely *is* enormous. You're seeing just the front wall. The place is built into the next step of the mountain. God knows how far they cut back into the rock. And it probably goes down several stories, too.'

'All the way to Hell.'

'Could be.'

He took his foot off the brake and drove forward, through the sheeting snow that was stained red by the strange light.

A few Jeeps, a couple of Land Rovers, and other four-wheel-drive vehicles, eight in all, were lined up in front of the low building, side-by-side in the falling snow.

'It doesn't look like there's a lot of people inside,' Tina said, 'I thought there'd be a large staff.'

'Oh, there is. I'm sure you're right about that, too,' Elliot said. 'The government wouldn't go to all the trouble of hiding this joint out here in the wilderness just to house a handful of researchers or whatever. I suspect most of them live in the installation for weeks or months at a time. They wouldn't want a lot of daily traffic coming in and out of here on a forest road that's supposed to be used only by state wildlife officers. That would draw attention to this place for sure. I suppose a few of the top people come and go regularly by helicopter. But if this is a military operation, then most of the staff is probably assigned here under the same conditions submariners have to live with; they're allowed to go into Reno for shore leave between cruises, but for long stretches of time, they're confined to this "ship".'

He parked beside another Jeep, switched off the lights, cut the engine.

The plateau was ethereally silent.

No one had come out of the building yet to challenge them, which meant Danny had almost certainly jinxed the video security system.

The fact that they had gotten this far unhurt did not make Elliot feel any better about what lay ahead of them. How long could Danny continue to pave the way? The boy appeared to have some incredible psychic powers, but he wasn't God. Sooner or later he would overlook something. He would make a mistake. Just one mistake. And they would be dead.

'Well,' Tina said, unsuccessfully trying to conceal her own fear, 'we didn't need the snowshoes after all.'

'But we might find a use for that coil of rope,' Elliot said. He twisted around, leaned over the back of the seat, and quickly fetched the rope from the pile of outdoor gear in the station wagon's cargo hold. 'We're bound to encounter at least a couple of security men, no matter how clever Danny is. We have to be prepared either to kill them or put them out of action some other way.'

'If we have a choice,' Tina said, 'I'd rather use rope than bullets.'

'My sentiments exactly.' He picked up the pistol. 'Let's see if we can get inside.'

They climbed out of the Jeep.

The wind was an animal presence. It growled softly. It had teeth, and it nipped their exposed faces. The snow on its cold breath was like icy spittle.

The only feature in the hundred-foot-long, one-story concrete facade was a steel door. There was no place to fit a key, no slot in which to put a lock-deactivating ID card. The door could be opened only from within after those who were seeking entrance had been scrutinized by means of the camera that hung over the portal.

The heavy, steel barrier rolled aside.

Was it Danny who opened it? Elliot wondered. Or was it a grinning guard waiting to put the arm on them?

A steel-walled chamber lay beyond the door. It was about the size of a large elevator cab, brightly lit, and uninhabited.

Tina and Elliot crossed the threshold. The outer door slid shut behind them, making a whooshing sound that indicated an air-tight seal.

A camera and two-way video communications monitor were mounted in the left-hand wall of the vestibule. The television screen was filled with crazily wiggling lines. Beside it, there was a lighted glass plate against which you were supposed to place your right hand, palm-down, within the outline of a hand, in order for the installation's computer to scan your prints and verify your authorization to enter.

Elliot and Tina did not put their hands on the plate, but the inner door of the vestibule opened with another puff of compressed air. They went into the next room.

Two uniformed men were fiddling with the control consoles beneath a series of twenty wall-mounted television screens. All of the screens were filled with wiggling lines. The younger of the guards heard the door opening, and he turned, shocked.

Elliot pointed the gun at him. 'Don't move.'

But the young guard was the heroic type. He was wearing a sidearm – a monstrous revolver – and he was fast with it. He drew, aimed from the hip, and squeezed the trigger with a speed and fluidity that would have been admired in the Old West.

Fortunately, Danny came through like a prince. The big revolver refused to fire.

Elliot didn't want to shoot the men. 'Your guns are useless,' he said, sweating, praying that Danny wouldn't let him down. 'Let's make this as easy as we can.'

When he discovered that his revolver wouldn't work, the young guard threw it.

Elliot ducked, but not quite fast enough. The gun struck him alongside the head, and he stumbled back against the steel door.

Tina screamed.

Through sudden tears of pain, Elliot saw the young guard rushing him, and he squeezed off one shot.

The bullet tore through the man's left shoulder and spun him around. He crashed into a desk, sending a pile of white and pink papers onto the floor, and then he fell on top of the mess he had made.

Blinking away tears, Elliot pointed the pistol at the older guard, who had drawn his revolver by now and had found that it didn't work either. 'Put the gun aside, sit down, and don't make any trouble.'

'How'd you get in here?' the guard asked, dropping his weapon as he'd been told to do. 'Who are you?'

'Never mind that,' Elliot said. 'Just sit down.'

But the guard was insistent. 'Who *are* you people?'

'Justice,' Tina said.

\* \* \*

Five minutes west of Reno, the chopper encountered snow. The flakes were hard, dry, and granular; they hissed like driven sand across the Perspex windscreen.

Jack Morgan, the pilot, glanced at George Alexander and said, 'This will be hairy.' He was wearing night-vision goggles, and his eyes were invisible.

'Just a little snow,' Alexander said.

'A storm,' Morgan corrected.

'You've flown in storms before.'

'In those mountains the down-drafts and cross-currents will be murderous.'

'We'll make it,' Alexander said grimly.

'Maybe, maybe not,' Morgan said. He grinned. 'But we're sure going to have fun trying!'

'You're crazy,' Hensen said from his seat behind the pilot.

'In Vietnam,' Morgan said, 'they called me "Bats," meaning I had bats in the belfry. They had their reasons for thinking I was nuts. Did they ever!' He laughed.

Hensen was holding a submachine gun across his lap. He moved his hands over it slowly, as if he were caressing a woman. He closed his eyes, and in his mind he disassembled and then reassembled the weapon. He had a queasy stomach. He was trying hard not to think about the chopper, the bad weather, and the likelihood that they would take a long, swift, hard fall into a remote mountain ravine.

# 37

The wounded guard was in pain, but as far as Tina could see, he was not in any danger of dying. The bullet had partially cauterized the wound as it passed through. The hole in the man's shoulder was reassuringly clean and it wasn't bleeding very much.

'You'll live,' Elliot told the guard.

'I'm dying. Jesus!'

'No,' Elliot said. 'It hurts like hell, but it isn't serious. The bullet didn't sever any major blood vessels.'

'How the hell would you know?' the wounded man asked, straining his words through gritted teeth.

'I saw wounds like it all the time when I was in Nam,' Elliot said. 'If you lie still, you'll be all right. But if you agitate the wound, you might tear a bruised vessel, and then you'll bleed to death.'

'Shit,' the guard said shakily.

'Understand?' Elliot asked.

The man nodded. His face was pale, and he was sweating.

Elliot tied the older guard securely to a chair. He didn't want to tie the wounded man's hands, so they carefully moved him into a supply closet and locked him there.

'How's your head?' Tina asked Elliot, gently putting her fingertips on the ugly knot that had raised up on his temple, where the guard's gun had struck him.

Elliot winced. 'Stings.'

'It's going to bruise.'

'I'll be all right,' he said.

'Dizzy?'

'No.'

'Seeing double?'

'No,' he said. 'I'm fine. I wasn't hit that hard. There's no concussion. Just a headache.'

'You know what?'

'What?'

'I love you.'

'I love you, too,' he said.

She kissed him quickly.

'Come on,' he said. 'Let's find Danny and get him out of this place.'

They crossed the room, passing the guard who was bound and gagged in his chair. Tina carried the remaining rope, and Elliot kept the gun.

Opposite the sliding door through which she and Elliot had entered the security room, there was another door of more ordinary dimensions and construction. It opened onto a junction of two hallways, which Tina had discovered a few minutes ago, just after Elliot had shot the guard, when she had looked through the door to see if reinforcements were on the way. The corridors had been deserted then, and they were deserted now. Silent. White tile floors. White walls. Cold fluorescent lighting. One passageway extended fifty feet to the left and fifty feet to the right; on both sides there were more doors, all shut, plus a bank of four elevators on the right. The intersecting hall began in front of them, across from the guardroom, and it bored at least four hundred feet into the mountainside; there was a long row of doors on each side of it, and other corridors opened off it, too.

They whispered:

'You think Danny is on this floor?'

'I don't know.'

'Where do we start looking?'

'We can't just go around jerking open doors.'

'People are going to be behind some of them.'

'Exactly. And the fewer people we en-counter—'

'—the better chance we have of getting out alive.'

For a moment they stood, indecisive, looking left, then right, then straight ahead.

Ten feet away, a set of elevator doors opened.

Tina cringed back against the corridor wall.

Elliot pointed the pistol at the lift.

No one got out.

The cab was at such an angle from them that they couldn't see who was in it.

The doors closed.

Tina had the sickening feeling that someone had been about to step out and had sensed their presence and had gone away to get help.

Even before Elliot had lowered the pistol, the same set of elevator doors slid open again. Then they slid shut. Open. Shut. Open. Shut. Open.

The air grew cold.

With a sigh of relief, Tina said, 'It's Danny. He's showing us the way.'

Nevertheless, they crept to the lift cautiously, looked inside apprehensively. It was empty, and they boarded it, and the doors glided together.

An indicator board was fixed above the doors, and according to it they were on the fourth of four levels, the first floor being the deepest underground. The lift controls would not operate unless one first inserted an acceptable ID card into a slot above them. But Tina and Elliot didn't need the computer's authorization to use the elevator; not with Danny on their side. The light on the indicator board changed from four to three to two, and the air inside the lift became so frigid that Tina could see her breath. The doors opened three floors below the surface, on the next to the last level.

They stepped into a hallway exactly like the one they had left upstairs.

The elevator doors closed behind them, and the air grew warm again.

Five feet away, a door was two inches ajar, and animated conversation drifted out of the room beyond. Both men's and women's voices. Half a dozen or more, judging by the sound of them. Indistinct words. Laughter.

Tina knew that she and Elliot were finished if someone came out of the room and saw them. Danny seemed able to work miracles with inanimate objects, but he could not control people. Like the guard upstairs whom Elliot had been forced to shoot. If they were discovered and confronted by a couple of dozen angry security men, Elliot's one pistol might not be enough to discourage an assault. Then, even with Danny jamming the enemy's weapons, she and Elliot would be able to escape only if they slaughtered their way out, and she knew that neither of them had the stomach for mass murder, perhaps not even in self-defense.

Laughter pealed from the nearby room again, and Elliot said softly, 'Where now?'

'I don't know.'

This level was the same size as the one on which they had entered the complex: more than four hundred feet on one side, and more than one hundred feet on the other. Forty thousand, maybe fifty thousand square feet to search. How many rooms? Forty? Fifty? Sixty? A hundred, counting closets?

Just as she was beginning to despair, the air began to turn cold again. She looked around, waiting for some sign from the child, and both she and Elliot jumped in surprise when the overhead fluorescent tube winked off, then came on again. The tube to the left of the first one also flickered. Then a third tube sputtered, still farther to the left.

They followed the blinking lights to the end of the short wing in which the elevators were situated. The corridor terminated in an airtight steel door like those found on submarines; the burnished metal glowed softly, and light gleamed off the big round-headed rivets.

As Tina and Elliot reached that barrier, the wheel-like handle in the center of it spun around. The door cycled open. Because he had the pistol, Elliot went through first, but Tina was close behind him.

They were in an oblong room that was approximately forty feet by twenty. At the far end, a window filled the center of the other short wall and apparently offered a view of a cold-storage vault; it was white with frost. To the right of the window, there was another airtight door like the one through which they'd just entered. On the left, computer hardware ran the length of the chamber. There were more cathode-ray tubes than Tina could count at a glance; most of them were switched on, and data flowed across them. Tables were arranged along the other wall, and they were covered with books, file folders, and a number of instruments that Tina could not identify.

A curly-haired man with a bushy mustache sat at one of the tables. He was tall, broad-shouldered, in his fifties, and he was wearing medical whites. He was paging through a book when they burst in. Another man, younger than the first, clean-shaven, also dressed in white, was sitting at a computer terminal, reading the information that flashed onto the display screen. Both men looked up, speechless with amazement.

Covering the strangers with the menacing, silencer-equipped pistol, Elliot said, 'Tina, close the door behind us. Lock it if you can. If security discovers we're here, at least they won't be able to get their hands on us for a while.'

She swung the steel door shut. In spite of its tremendous weight, it moved more smoothly and easily than the average door in the average house. She spun the wheel and located a pin that, when pushed, prevented anyone from turning the handle back to the unlocked position.

'Done,' she said.

The man at the computer suddenly turned to the programmer's keyboard and started typing.

'Stop that!' Elliot said.

But he wasn't going to stop until he had instructed the computer to set off the alarms.

Elliot fired once, and the display screen dissolved into thousands of splinters of glass.

The man at the keyboard cried out and pushed his wheeled office chair away from the terminal.

Elliot put a second bullet into the programmer's board.

The computer purred for a moment, made a clattering sound not unlike a man gagging, and was silent.

The man who had been trying to send an alarm jumped up from his chair. 'Who the hell do you think you are?'

'I'm the one who has the gun,' Elliot said sharply. 'That's who I think I am. And if that's not good enough for you, I can shut you down the same way I did that damned machine. Now park your ass in that chair before I blow your fuckin' head off!'

Tina had never heard Elliot speak in that tone of voice, and his furious expression was sufficient to chill even her. He looked hard and utterly vicious.

The young man in white was impressed, too. He sat down, pale.

'All right,' Elliot said, addressing the two men. 'If you cooperate, you won't get hurt.' He waved the barrel of the gun at the older man. 'What's your name?'

'Carl Dombey.'

'What're you doing here?'

'I work here,' Dombey said, puzzled by the question.

'I mean, what's your job?'

'I'm a research scientist.'

'What area?'

'My degrees are in biology and biochemistry.'

Elliot looked at the younger man. 'What about you?'

'What about me?' the man said sullenly.

Elliot extended his arm, lining up the muzzle of the pistol with the bridge of the man's nose.

'I'm Dr. Zachariah,' the younger man said.

'Biology?'

'Yes. Specializing in bacteriology and virology.'

Elliot lowered the gun but still kept it pointed in their general direction. 'We have some questions, and I suspect you two gentlemen have the answers.'

Dombey, who clearly did not share his associate's compulsion to play hero, remained very still in his chair and said, 'Questions about what?'

Tina moved to Elliot's side. To Dombey, she said, 'We want to know about my boy. My son. Danny Evans. We want to know what you've done to him. We want to know where he is.'

She saw that she could not have said anything else that would have had even a fraction as much impact on them as the words she had spoken. Dombey's eyes bulged. Zachariah looked at her as he might have done if she had been dead on the floor and then had miraculously risen.

'My God,' Dombey said.

'How can you be here?' Zachariah asked. 'You can't! You can't possibly be here!'

'It seems possible to me,' Dombey said. 'Now that I think about it, it seems inevitable. I knew this whole business was too dirty to end any way but in disaster.' He sighed, as if a great weight had been lifted from him. 'I'll answer all of your questions, Mrs. Evans.'

Zachariah swung on him. 'You can't do that!'

'Oh no?' Dombey said. 'Well, if you don't think I can, just sit back and listen. You're in for a surprise.'

'You took a loyalty oath,' Zachariah said. 'And a secrecy oath. If you tell them anything about this . . . the scandal . . . the public outrage . . . the release of military secrets . . . you'll be a traitor to your country.'

'No,' Dombey said. 'I'll be a traitor to this installation. I'll be a traitor to my colleagues, maybe. But not to my country. My country's far from perfect, but what's been done to Danny Evans isn't something that *my* country would approve of. The whole Danny Evans project is the work of a few megalomaniacs.'

'Dr. Tamaguchi isn't a megalomaniac!' Dr. Zachariah said, genuinely offended.

'Of course he is,' Dombey said. 'He thinks he's a great man of science, destined for immortality, a man of great works. And a lot of people around him, a lot of people protecting him, people in research and people in charge of project security – they're also megalomaniacs. The things done to Danny Evans do not constitute "great work." They won't earn anyone immortality. It's sick, and I'm washing my hands of it.' He looked at Tina again. 'Ask your questions.'

'No!' Zachariah said. 'You damn fool.'

Elliot took some more rope from Tina, and he gave her the pistol. 'It looks as if I'll have to tie and gag Dr. Zachariah, so we can listen to Dr. Dombey's story in peace. If either one of them makes a wrong move, blow him away.'

'Don't worry,' she said. 'I won't hesitate.'

'You're not going to tie me,' Zachariah said.

Smiling, Elliot advanced on him with the rope.

\* \* \*

A wall of frigid air fell on the chopper and drove

it down. Jack Morgan fought the wind, stabilized the aircraft, and pulled it up only a few feet short of the treetops.

'Whooooooooeeeee!' the pilot said. 'It's like breaking in a wild horse.'

In the brilliant spotlights that beamed out from the helicopter there was little to see but driving snow. Morgan had removed his night-vision goggles.

'This is crazy,' Hensen said. 'We're not flying into an ordinary storm. It's a blizzard.'

Ignoring Hensen, Alexander said, 'Morgan, goddamn you, I know you can do it.'

'Maybe,' Morgan said. 'I wish I was as sure as you. But I think maybe I can. What I'm going to do is make an indirect approach to the plateau, moving with the wind instead of across it. I'm going to cut up this next valley and then swing back around toward the installation and try to avoid some of these cross-currents. They're murder. It'll take us a little longer that way, but at least we'll have a fighting chance.'

A particularly fierce blast of wind drove snow into the windscreen with such force that, to Kurt Hensen, it sounded like shotgun pellets.

# 38

Zachariah was on the floor, bound and gagged, looking up at them. Hate and rage pushed each other back and forth through his eyes.

'You'll want to see your boy first,' Dombey said. 'Then I can tell you how he came to be here.'

'Where is he?' Tina asked shakily.

'In the isolation chamber,' Dombey said. He indicated the window in the back wall of the room. 'Come on.' He walked to the big pane of glass, where only a few small spots of frost remained.

For a moment Tina was afraid to move. She was afraid to see what they had done to Danny. Fear spread its tendrils through her and seemed to root her feet to the floor.

Elliot touched her shoulder. 'Don't keep Danny waiting. He's been waiting for a long time. He's been calling you for a long time.'

She took a step, then another, and before she knew it, she was at the window, beside Dombey.

A hospital bed stood in the center of the isolation chamber. It was ringed by electronic medical equipment.

Danny was in the bed, on his back. Most of him was covered, but his head, raised on a pillow, was turned toward the window. He stared at her through the side rails of the bed.

'Danny,' she said softly. She had the irrational fear that, if she said his name loudly, the spell would be broken and he would vanish forever.

His face was thin. Thin and drawn. He looked older than twelve. He looked like a little old man.

Dombey, sensing her shock, said, 'He's emaciated. For the past six or seven weeks, he hasn't been able to keep anything but liquids in his stomach. And not a lot of those.'

Danny's eyes were strange. Dark, as always. Big and round, as always. They were sunken, ringed by unhealthy, dark skin, and that was not as always. But that was not what made them appear so strange to her. She could not pinpoint what it was about them that made them so different from any eyes she had ever seen. But as she met Danny's gaze, a shiver passed through her, and she felt a powerful, burgeoning pity for him.

The boy blinked, and with what appeared to be a great effort, at the cost of more than a little pain, he withdrew one arm from under the covers and reached out toward her. His arm was skin and bones, a pathetic stick. He thrust it between two of the side rails, and he opened his small, weak hand beseechingly, reaching for love, trying desperately to touch her.

Her voice quavering, she said to Dombey, 'I want to be with my little boy. I want to hold him.'

As the three of them moved to the airtight steel door that led into the room beyond the window, Elliot said, 'Why is he in an isolation chamber? Is he ill?'

'Not now,' Dombey said, stopping at the door, turning to them, evidently disturbed by what he had to tell them. 'Right now he's on the verge of starving to death because it's been so long since he's been able to keep any food in his stomach. But he's not infectious. He *has* been very, very infectious, off and on, but not at the moment. He's had a unique disease, a man-made disease created in the laboratory. He's the only person who's ever survived it. He has a natural antibody in his blood that helps him fight off this particular virus, even though it's an artificial bug. That fascinated Dr. Tamaguchi. He's the head of this installation. Dr. Tamaguchi drove us very hard until we isolated the antibody and figured out why it worked against the disease. Of course, when that was accomplished, Danny was of no more scientific value. And to Tamaguchi, that meant he was of no value at all. Except in the crudest way . . . Tamaguchi decided to test Danny to destruction. For almost two months they've been reinfecting the boy over and over again, letting the virus wear him down, trying to discover how many times he can lick it before it finally licks him. You see, there's no permanent immunity to this disease. It's like strep throat or the common cold . . . or like cancer . . . because you can get it again and again, if you're lucky – or unfortunate – enough to beat it the first time. Today, he just beat it for the fourteenth time. Although he gets weaker every day, for some reason he wins out over the virus faster every time. However each victory drains him. The disease *is* killing him, no matter how indirectly. It's killing him by sapping his strength. Right now he's clean, uninfected. Tomorrow they intend to stick another dirty needle in him.'

'My God,' Elliot said. 'Oh, my God.'

Gripped by horror, Tina stared at Dombey. 'I can't believe what I just heard.'

'Brace yourself,' Dombey said grimly. 'You haven't heard half of it yet.'

He turned away from them, spun the wheel on the steel door, and swung the door inward.

A couple of minutes ago, when she had first looked through the observation window, when she had seen the frighteningly thin child, she had told herself that she would not cry. Danny didn't need to see her cry. He needed love and attention and protection. Her tears might upset him. And judging from the way he looked, she was concerned that any serious emotional disturbance would literally destroy him.

Now, as she approached his bed, she bit her lower lip so hard she tasted a hint of blood. She struggled to contain her tears, but she needed every bit of her willpower to keep her eyes dry.

Danny became excited when he saw her drawing near, and in spite of his terrible condition, he managed to thrust himself into a sitting position, clutching at the bed rails with one frail, trembling hand, eagerly extending his other hand toward her.

She took the last few steps haltingly, her heart pounding, her throat constricted, overwhelmed by a combination of joy at seeing him again and fear at seeing how horribly wasted he was. She reached for him, too, and their hands touched, and his small fingers curled tightly around hers. He held on with a fierce, desperate strength.

'Danny,' she said wonderingly. 'Danny, Danny.'

From somewhere deep inside of him, from far down beneath all the pain and fear and anguish, he found a smile for her. It was not much of a smile; it quivered on his lips as if the mildest breeze would blow it away. It was such a tentative smile, such a vague ghost of all the broad warm smiles she remembered, that it broke her heart.

'Mom,' he said in a washed-out, cracking voice that she hardly recognized.

'It's all right,' she said.

He began to shudder.

'It's all over, Danny. It's all right now.'

'Mom . . . Mom . . .' His face seemed to shiver, and his brave smile dissolved, and an agonized groan escaped him. 'Oooohhhhh, *Mommy* . . .'

She pushed down the railing and sat on the edge of the bed and she took him in her arms. He was a rag doll with only meager scraps of stuffing. A fragile, timorous creature, nothing whatsoever like the happy, vibrant, active boy he had been. At first she was afraid to hug him, for fear he would shatter in her embrace. But he hugged her very hard, and again, she was surprised how much strength he still could summon from his devastated body. Shaking violently, snuffling, he put his face against her neck, and she felt his tears on her skin. She couldn't control herself any longer, so she let her own tears come, rivers of tears, a flood. When she put one hand on the boy's back to press him against her, she discovered just how shockingly spindly he was, each rib and vertebra so prominent that she almost felt as if she were holding a skeleton, and that made her cry harder. She pulled him into her lap, and he trailed wires that led from electrodes on his skin to the monitoring machines around the bed; he looked like an abandoned marionette. When his legs came out from under the covers, when the hospital gown slipped off them, she saw that his poor limbs were too bony and fleshless to safely support him, and she cradled him, rocked him, crooned to him, told him she loved him. She wept.

*Danny was alive.*

# 39

Jack Morgan's strategy of flying with the land instead of over it was a smashing success. Alexander was increasingly confident that they would reach the installation unscathed, and he was aware that even Kurt Hensen, who hated flying with Morgan, was calmer now than he had been ten minutes ago.

The chopper hugged the valley floor, streaking northward, ten feet above an ice-coated river, still forced to make its way through a disturbingly heavy snowfall, but sheltered from the worst of the storm's turbulence by the walls of mammoth evergreens that flanked the river. Silvery, almost luminous, the river was an easy trail to follow. Occasionally, wind found the aircraft and pummeled it, but the chopper bobbed and weaved like a good boxer, and it no longer seemed in danger of being dealt a knock-out punch.

'How long?' Alexander asked.

'Ten minutes. Maybe fifteen,' Morgan said. 'Unless.'

'Unless what?'

'Unless the blades cake up with ice. Unless the drive shaft and the rotor joints freeze.'

'Is that likely?' Alexander asked.

'It's certainly something to think about,' Morgan said. 'And there's always the possibility I'll misjudge the terrain in the dark and ram us right into the side of a hill.'

'You won't,' Alexander said. 'You're too good.'

'Well,' Morgan said, 'there's always the chance I'll screw up. That's what keeps it from getting boring.'

* * *

Tina prepared Danny for the journey out of the underground laboratory. She started by removing the electrodes that were fixed to his head and body at eight places. When she gingerly pulled off the adhesive tape, he whimpered, and she winced when she saw how raw his skin was underneath. No effort had been made to keep him from chafing.

While Tina worked on Danny, Elliot questioned Carl Dombey. 'What goes on in this place? Military research?'

'Yes,' Dombey said.

'Strictly biological weapons?'

'Biological and chemical. Recombinant DNA

448

experiments. At any one time, there are about thirty projects underway.'

'I thought the United States got out of the chemical and biological weapons race a long time ago.'

'For the public record, we did,' Dombey said. 'Nixon was the first President to declare that the United States would never stoop to this kind of dirty warfare, and every chief executive since Nixon has restated that pledge. But in reality, it goes on. It has to. This is the only facility of its kind that we have. The Russians have three like it. They believe in chemical and biological warfare. They don't see anything immoral about it. They used bio and chem weapons in Afghanistan a while back, killed around eighty thousand people with what we like to call "unconventional weapons." If they felt they had some terrific new bug that we didn't know about, something against which we couldn't retaliate in kind, they'd use it on us.'

Elliot said, 'But if racing to keep up with the Soviets can create situations like the one we've got here, situations in which an innocent child gets ground up in the machine, then aren't we just becoming the same kind of monsters the Soviet leaders are? Aren't we letting our fears of the enemy turn us into them? And isn't that just another way of losing the war?'

Dombey nodded. As he spoke he smoothed the spikes of his mustache. 'That's the same question

I've been wrestling with ever since Danny got caught in the gears. The problem is that some flaky people are attracted to this kind of work because of the secrecy and because you really do get a sense of power from designing weapons that can kill hundreds of thousands of people. So megalomaniacs like Tamaguchi get involved. Men like Aaron Zachariah. They abuse their power, pervert their duties. There's no way to screen them out ahead of time. But if we closed up shop, if we stopped doing this sort of research just because we were afraid of men like Tamaguchi winding up in charge of it, we'd be conceding so much ground to our enemies that we wouldn't survive for long. I suppose we have to accept and learn to live with the lesser of the evils.'

Tina removed an electrode from Danny's neck, carefully peeling the tape off his skin.

The child still clung to her, but his sunken eyes were on Dombey.

'I'm not interested in the philosophy or the morality of biological warfare,' Tina said. 'Not at the moment, anyway. Right now I just want to know how the hell Danny wound up in this place.'

'To understand that,' Dombey said, 'you have to go back twenty months. It was around then that a Russian scientist named Ilya Poparopov defected to the United States, carrying a microfilm file of the Soviets' most important, dangerous new biological weapon in a decade. The Russians called the stuff ''Gorki-400'' because it was developed at their RDNA labs outside of Gorki, and it was the four-hundredth viable strain of man-made microorganism created at that research center.

'Gorki-400 is a perfect weapon. It afflicts only human beings. No other living creature can carry it. And like syphilis, Gorki-400 can't survive outside a living human body for more than a minute, which means it can't permanently contaminate objects or entire places the way anthrax and other virulent bacteria can. And when the host expires, the Gorki-400 within him perishes a short while later, as soon as the temperature of the corpse drops below eighty-six degrees. Do you see the advantage of all this?'

Tina was too busy with Danny to really think about what Carl Dombey had said, but Elliot knew what the scientist meant. 'If I understand you, the Russians could use Gorki-400 to wipe out a city or a country, and there wouldn't be any need for them to conduct a tricky and expensive decontamination before they moved in and took over the conquered territory.'

'Exactly,' Dombey said. 'And Gorki-400 has other, equally important advantages over most biological agents. For one thing, you can become an infectious carrier only four hours after coming into contact with the virus. That's an incredibly short gestation period. Once infected, no one lives more than twenty-four hours. Most die in twelve. Gorki-400's kill-rate is one hundred percent. No one is supposed to survive. The Russians tested it on God knows how many political prisoners. They were never able to find an antibody or an antibiotic that was effective against it. The virus migrates to the brain stem, and there it begins secreting a toxin that literally eats away the brain tissue like battery acid dissolving cheesecloth. It destroys the part of the brain that controls all of the body's autonomic functions. The victim simply ceases to have a pulse, functioning organs, or any urge to breathe.'

'And that's the disease Danny survived,' Elliot said.

'Yes,' Dombey said. 'As far as we know, he's the only one who ever has.'

Tina had pulled the blanket off the bed and had folded it in half, so that she could wrap Danny in it for the trip out to the Jeep. Now she looked up from the task of bundling the child, and she said to Dombey, 'But why was he infected in the first place?'

'It was an accident,' Dombey said.

'I've heard that one before.'

'This time it's true,' Dombey said. 'After Ilya Poparopov defected with all the data on Gorki-400, he was brought here, and we immediately began working with him, trying to engineer an exact duplicate of the Russian virus. In relatively short order, we accomplished that. Then we began to study the bug, searching for a handle on it that the Russians had overlooked.'

'And someone got careless,' Elliot said.

'Yes,' Dombey said. 'And worse. Someone got careless and *stupid*. Almost thirteen months ago, when Danny and the other boys were on their winter survival outing, one of our scientists, a sort of quirky fellow named Larry Bollinger, accidentally contaminated himself while he was working alone one morning in this lab.'

Danny's hand tightened on Christina's and she stroked his head, soothing him. To Dombey, she said, 'Surely you have safeguards, procedures to follow when and if—'

'Of course,' Dombey said. 'You're trained what to do from the day you start to work here. In the event of accidental contamination, you immediately set off an alarm. Then you seal the room you're working in, and if there's an adjoining isolation chamber, you're expected to go into that and lock the door after yourself. A decontamination crew moves in swiftly to clean up whatever mess you've made in the lab. And if you've infected yourself with something curable, you'll be treated. If it's not curable . . . you'll be attended to in isolation until you die. That's one reason our pay scale is so high. Hazardous duty pay. The risk is just part of the job.'

'Except this Larry Bollinger didn't see it that

way,' Tina said bitterly. She was having trouble wrapping Danny securely in the blanket because he didn't want to let go of her. With smiles, murmured assurances, and kisses planted on both of his frail hands, she finally managed to persuade him to tuck both of his arms close to his body.

'Bollinger snapped. He just went right off the rails,' Dombey said, sounding a bit embarrassed that one of his colleagues would lose control of himself under those circumstances. Dombey began to pace as he talked. 'Bollinger knew how fast Gorki-400 claims its victims, and he panicked. Apparently, he convinced himself he could run away from the infection. God knows, that's exactly what he tried to do. He didn't turn in an alarm. He just walked out of the lab, went to his quarters, dressed in outdoor clothes, and left the complex. He wasn't scheduled for R&R, and on the spur of the moment he couldn't think of a good excuse to sign out one of the Jeeps, so he had to escape on foot. He told the guards he was going snowshoeing for a couple of hours. That's something a lot of us do during the winter. It's good exercise, and it gets you out of this hole in the ground for a while. Anyway, Bollinger wasn't interested in exercise. He tucked the snowshoes under his arm and took off down the mountain road, the same one I presume you came in on. Before he got to the guard's hut at the upper gate, he climbed onto the ridge above, finally used the snowshoes to circle the guard, returned to the road, and threw the snowshoes away. Security eventually found them. Bollinger was probably at the bottom gate two and a half hours after he walked out of the door here, three hours after he was infected. That was just about the time that another researcher walked into his lab, saw cultures of Gorki-400 broken open on the floor, and set off the alarm. Meanwhile, in spite of the barbed wire, Bollinger climbed over the fence. Then he made his way to the road that serves the wildlife research center. He started out of the forest, toward the county lane, which is about five miles away from the turn-off to the labs, and after only three miles—'

'He ran into Mr. Jaborski and the scouts,' Elliot said.

'And by then he was able to pass the disease on to them,' Tina said as she finished bundling Danny into the blanket.

'Yeah,' Dombey said. 'He must have reached the scouts five or five-and-a-half hours after he was infected. By then he was worn out. He'd used up most of his physical reserves getting out of the lab reservation, and he was also beginning to feel some of the early symptoms of Gorki-400. Dizziness. Mild nausea. The scoutmaster had parked the expedition minibus on a lay-by about a mile and a half into the woods, and he and his assistant and the kids had walked in another half-mile before they encountered Larry Bollinger. They were just about to move off the road, into the trees, so they would be away from any sign of civilization when they set up camp for their first night in the wilderness. When Bollinger discovered they had a vehicle, he tried to persuade them to drive him all the way into Reno. When they were reluctant, he made up a story about a friend being stranded in the mountains with a broken leg. Jaborski didn't believe Bollinger's story for a minute, but he finally offered to take him to the wildlife center where a rescue effort could be mounted. That wasn't good enough for Bollinger, and he got hysterical. Both Jaborski and the other scout leader decided they might have a dangerous character on their hands. That was when the security team arrived. Bollinger tried to run from them. Then he tried to tear open one of the security men's decontamination suits. They were forced to shoot him.'

'The spacemen,' Danny said.

They all looked at him.

He huddled in his yellow blanket, on the bed, and the memory made him shiver. 'The spacemen came and took us away.'

'Yeah,' Dombey said. 'They probably did look a little bit like spacemen in their decontamination suits. They brought everyone here and put them in isolation. One day later, all of them were dead except Danny.' Dombey sighed. 'Well . . . you know most of the rest of it.'

# 40

The helicopter continued to follow the frozen river north, through the valley.

The ghostly, slightly luminous winter landscape made George Alexander think of graveyards. He had an affinity for cemeteries. He liked to take long, leisurely walks among tombstones. For as long as he could remember, he had been fascinated with death, with the mechanics and the meaning of it, and he had longed to know what it was like on the other side – without, of course, wanting to commit himself to a one-way journey there. He didn't want to die; he only wanted to *know*. Each time that he personally killed someone, he felt as if he were establishing another link to the world beyond this one; and he hoped, once he had made enough of those links, that he would be rewarded with a vision from the other side. One day, maybe he would be standing in a graveyard, before the tombstone of one of his victims, and the person he had killed would reach out to him from beyond and let him see, in some vivid clairvoyant fashion, exactly what death was like. And then he would know.

'Not long now,' Jack Morgan said.

Alexander peered anxiously through the sheeting snow into which the chopper moved rather like a blind man running full-steam into endless darkness. He touched the gun that he carried in a shoulder holster, and he thought of Christina Evans.

To Kurt Hensen, Alexander said, 'Kill Stryker on sight. We don't need him for anything. But don't hurt the woman. I want to question her. She's going to tell me who the traitor is. She's going to tell me who helped her get into the labs even if I have to break her fingers one at a time to make her open up.'

\* \* \*

In the isolation chamber, when Dombey finished speaking, Tina said, 'Danny looks so awful. Even though he doesn't have the disease any more, will he be all right?'

'I think so,' Dombey said. 'He just needs to be fattened up. He couldn't keep anything in his stomach because recently they've been reinfecting him, testing him to destruction. But once he's out of here, he should put weight on fast. There is one thing . . .'

460

Tina stiffened at the note of worry in Dombey's voice. 'What? What one thing?'

'Since all these reinfections, he's developed a spot on the parietal lobe of the brain.'

Tina felt sick. 'No.'

'But apparently it isn't life-threatening,' Dombey said quickly. 'As far as we can determine, it's not a tumor. Neither a malignant nor a benign tumor. At least it doesn't test out to have any of the characteristics of a tumor. It isn't scar tissue, either. And it's not a blood clot.'

'Then what is it?' Elliot asked.

Dombey pushed one hand through his thick, curly hair. 'The computer says the new growth is consistent with the structure of normal brain tissue. Which doesn't make sense. But we've checked our data a hundred times, and we can't find anything wrong with that diagnosis. Except it's impossible. What we're seeing on the X-rays isn't within our experience. So when you get him out of here, take him to a brain specialist. Take him to a dozen specialists until someone can tell you what's wrong with him. There doesn't appear to be anything life-threatening about the parietal spot, but you sure should keep a watch on it.'

Tina looked at Elliot, and she knew that the same thought was running through both their minds: Could this spot on Danny's brain have anything to do with the boy's psychic power?

Were his latent psychic abilities brought to the surface as a direct result of the man-made virus with which he had been repeatedly infected? That didn't seem any more unlikely than the fact that he had fallen victim to Project Pandora in the first place, and as far as Tina could see, it was the only thing that could explain Danny's phenomenal new powers.

Elliot, apparently afraid that she would voice her thoughts and alert Dombey to the incredible truth of the situation, looked at his wristwatch and said, 'We ought to get out of here.'

'When you leave,' Dombey said, 'you should take some files on Danny's case. They're on the table closest the outer door. They'll help support your story when you go to the press with it. And for God's sake, splash it all over the newspapers as fast as you can. As long as you're the only ones outside of here who know what happened, you're marked people.'

'We're painfully aware of that,' Elliot said.

Tina said, 'Elliot, you'll have to carry Danny. He can't walk. He's not too heavy for me, worn down as he is, but he's still an awkward bundle.'

Elliot gave her the pistol and started toward the bed.

'Could you do me a favor first?' Dombey asked.

'What's that?'

'Let's move Dr. Zachariah in here and take the gag out of his mouth. Then you tie me up

462

and gag me, leave me in the outer room. I'm going to make them believe he was the one who cooperated with you. In fact, when you tell your story to the press, maybe you could slant it that way.'

Tina shook her head, puzzled. 'But after everything you said to Zachariah about this place being run by megalomaniacs, and after you've made it so clear that you don't agree with everything that goes on here, why do you want to stay?'

'The hermit's life agrees with me, and the pay is good,' Dombey said. 'And if I don't stay here, if I walk away and get a job at a civilian research center, that'll be just one less rational voice in this place. There are a lot of people here who have some sense of social responsibility about this work. If they all left, they'd just be turning the place over to men like Tamaguchi and Zachariah and there wouldn't be anyone around to balance things. What sort of research do you think they might do *then*?'

'But once our story breaks in the papers,' Tina said, 'they'll probably just shut this place down.'

'No way,' Dombey said. 'Because the work has to be done. The balance of power with the Soviet Union has to be maintained. They might pretend to close us down, but they won't. Tamaguchi and some of his closest aides will be fired. There'll be a big shake-up, and that'll be good. If I can make them think that Zachariah was the one who spilled the secrets, if I can protect my position here, maybe I'll be promoted to a position with more influence.' He smiled. 'At the very least, I'll get more pay.'

'All right,' Elliot said. 'We'll do what you want. But we've got to be fast about it.'

They moved Zachariah into the isolation chamber and took the gag out of his mouth. He strained at his ropes, and he cursed Elliot. Then he cursed Tina and Danny and Dombey. When they took Danny out of the small room, they couldn't hear Zachariah's shouted invectives through the airtight steel door.

As Elliot used the last of the rope to tie Dombey, the scientist said, 'Satisfy my curiosity.'

'About what?'

'Who told you your son was here? Who let you into the labs?'

Tina blinked. She couldn't think what to say.

'Okay, okay,' Dombey said. 'I can understand that you wouldn't want to rat on whoever it was. But just tell me one thing. Was it one of the security people, or was it someone on the medical staff? I'd like to think it was a doctor, one of my own, who finally did the right thing.'

Tina looked at Elliot.

Elliot shook his head: *no*.

She agreed that it might not be wise to let anyone know what powers Danny had acquired.

464

The world would see him as a freak, and everyone would want to gawk at him, put him on display. And for sure, if the people in this installation got the idea that Danny's newfound psychic abilities were a result of the parietal spot caused by his repeated exposure to Gorki-400, they would want to test him, poke and probe at him. No, she wouldn't tell anyone what Danny could do. Not yet. Not until she and Eliot figured out what effect that revelation would have on the boy's life.

'It was someone on the medical staff,' Elliot lied. 'It was a doctor who let us in here.'

'Good,' Dombey said. 'I'm glad to hear it. I wish I'd had enough guts to do it a long time ago.'

Elliot worked a wadded handkerchief into Dombey's mouth.

Tina opened the outer airtight door.

Elliot picked up Danny. 'You hardly weigh a thing, kid. We'll have to take you straight to McDonald's and pack you full of burgers and fries.'

Danny smiled at him.

Holding the pistol, Tina led the way into the hall. In the room near the elevators, people were still talking and laughing, but no one stepped into the corridor.

Danny opened the high-security elevator and made the lift move up once they were in it. His forehead was furrowed, as if he were concentrating, but that was the only sign that he had anything to do with the elevator's movement.

The hallways were deserted on the top floor.

In the guardroom the security man was still bound and gagged in his chair. He watched them with a look of anger and fear.

Tina, Elliot, and Danny went through the vestibule and stepped into the cold night. Snow lashed them.

There was another sound besides the howling of the wind, and Tina needed a few seconds to identify it.

A helicopter.

She looked up and saw it coming over the rise at the west end of the plateau. What madmen would have a chopper out in this weather?

'The Jeep!' Elliot shouted. 'Hurry!'

They ran to the Jeep wagon. Tina took Danny out of Elliot's arms, slid him into the back seat, and got in after him.

Elliot got behind the wheel and fumbled with the keys. The engine wouldn't turn over immediately.

The chopper swooped toward them.

'Who's in the helicopter?' Danny asked, staring at it through the side window of the station wagon.

'I don't know,' Tina said. 'But they're not good people, baby. They're like the monster in the comic book. The one you sent me pictures of in my dream. They don't want us to get you out of this place.'

Danny stared at the oncoming chopper, and lines appeared in his forehead again.

The Jeep's engine suddenly turned over.

'Thank God!' Elliot said.

But the lines didn't fade from Danny's forehead.

Tina realized what the boy was going to do, and she said, 'Danny, wait!'

\* \* \*

Leaning forward to look at the Jeep through the bubble window of the chopper, George Alexander said, 'Put us down right in front of them, Jack.'

'Will do,' Morgan said.

To Hensen, who had the submachine gun, Alexander said, 'Like I told you, waste Stryker right away, but not the woman.'

Abruptly the chopper soared. It had been only fifteen or twenty feet above the pavement, but it climbed rapidly to forty, fifty, sixty feet.

Alexander said, 'What's happening?'

'The stick,' Morgan said. There was an edge of fear in his voice that had not been there throughout the entire, nightmarish trip to the mountain. 'I can't control the damned thing. It's frozen up.'

467

Eighty, ninety, a hundred feet. They soared straight up into the night.

Then the engine cut out.

'What the hell?' Morgan said.

Hensen screamed.

Alexander watched death rushing up at him and knew his curiosity about the other side would shortly be satisfied.

\* \* \*

As they drove off the plateau, around the burning wreckage of the helicopter, Danny said, 'They were bad people. It's all right, Mom. They were real bad people.'

*To everything there is a season*, Tina reminded herself. *A time to kill, a time to heal.*

She held Danny close, and she looked into his dark eyes, and she wasn't able to comfort herself with those words from the Bible, at least not to the extent that she had been able to comfort Elliot with them. In Danny's eyes there was too much pain, too much knowledge. She thought about the future. She wondered what lay ahead for them.

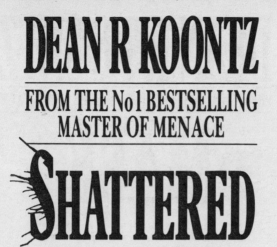